EMPEROR
THE GODS OF WAR

Conn Iggulden is one of the most successful authors of historical fiction writing today. His two number one best-selling series, on Julius Caesar and on the Mongol Khans of Central Asia, describe the founding of the greatest empires of their day. Conn Iggulden lives in Hertfordshire with his wife and their children.

www.conniggulden.com

EMPEROR
THE GODS OF WAR

CONN IGGULDEN

HARPER

HARPER

An imprint of HarperCollins*Publishers*
77–85 Fulham Palace Road
Hammersmith, London W6 8JB

www.harpercollins.co.uk

This paperback edition 2011

First published in Great Britain by HarperCollins*Publishers* 2006
3

A catalogue record for this book is available from the British Library

ISBN 978 0 00 743715 3

This novel is entirely a work of fiction.
The names, characters and incidents portrayed in it,
while in some cases based on historical figures, are
the work of the author's imagination.

Typeset in Minion with Trajan Display by Palimpsest Book Production Limited,
Falkirk, Stirlingshire

Printed and bound in Great Britain by
Clays Ltd, St Ives plc

MIX
Paper from
responsible sources
FSC
www.fsc.org   FSC® C007454

FSC is a non-profit international organisation established
to promote the responsible management of the world's forests.
Products carrying the FSC label are independently certified
to assure consumers that they come from forests that are managed
to meet the social, economic and ecological needs
of present and future generations.

Find out more about HarperCollins and the environment at
www.harpercollins.co.uk/green

To my wife

ACKNOWLEDGEMENTS

A number of people have devoted their time and energy to these books. I cannot name them all, but I must thank Fiona and Ingrid in particular for their extraordinary hard work. Thank you as well, to all those who have written to me. I have been touched by the responses to these books. Finally, I must mention the Inner Circle and Janis in Glasgow, who kept me smiling through a long afternoon.

'Great men are necessary for our life, in order that the movement of world history can free itself sporadically, by fits and starts, from obsolete ways of living and inconsequential talk.'

Jacob Burckhardt

THE ROMAN WORLD
IN THE TIME
OF JULIUS CAESAR

Mutina

Ariminum

Corsica

Corfinium

Rome
Ostia

MACEDONIA

Dyrrhachium
Apolloniae
Thessalonice
Oricum

Brundisium
Tarentum

Sardinia

Pharsalus

Athenae
Corinthus

SICILIA

Carthago

Thapsus

MARE INTERNUM

Cyrene

SYRTIS   Leptis Magna

CYRENAICA

0   100   200   300 miles

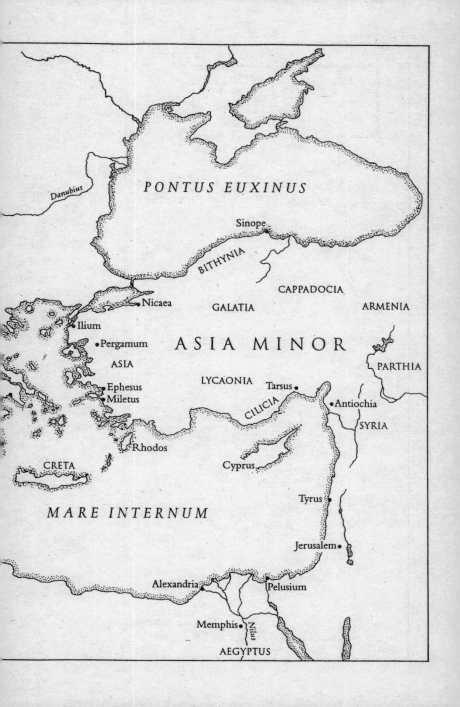

PART ONE

CHAPTER ONE

Pompey pronounced each word as a hammer blow. 'Therefore, by his actions, Caesar is today declared Enemy of Rome. His titles and honours are revoked. His right to command legions is struck from the records. His life is forfeit. It will be war.'

The senate chamber was finally still after the storms of debate, the tension showing in every face. The messengers who had killed horses to reach them had no way of knowing the pace of those who followed. The Rubicon line had been crossed and the legions of Gaul were racing south.

Pompey had aged visibly over two days of strain, yet he stood before them with a straight back, his experience giving him the strength to dominate the room. He watched as the senators slowly lost their frozen expressions and saw dozens of them meet each other's eyes in private communication. There were many there who still blamed Pompey for the chaos in the city three years before. It had been his legion that failed to maintain order then and his dictatorship that had arisen from that conflict. He knew there were more than a few voices muttering for him to put aside the position and elect consuls once again. The very building in which they sat was a constant reminder, with its smell of fresh lime and wood. The ashes of the old site had been cleared, but the foundations remained as a mute testament to the destruction and rioting in the city.

In the silence, Pompey wondered whom he could trust in the struggle. Who amongst them had the strength he needed? He had no illusions. Julius was coming south with four veteran legions and there was nothing in Rome to stand against them. In just a few days, the commander of Gaul would be hammering at the gates of the city and some of the men before Pompey would clamour to let him in.

'There are hard choices to be made, gentlemen,' he said.

They watched him closely, judging his strength, his weaknesses. One slip, he knew, and they would tear him apart. He would not give them the chance.

'I have legions in Greece who have not been infected by the enthusiasms of the mob in Rome. Though there may be traitors in this city, the rule of law has not lost its voice in our dominions.'

How closely he watched them then to see who looked away, but every eye was on him.

'Gentlemen, there is no other option but to leave Rome for Greece and gather our armies there. At present, the bulk of Caesar's forces remain in Gaul. Once they join him, the whole country could fall before we have a sufficient presence in the field. I do not wish to lose a race to reinforce. Better to be certain and go to our armies. There are ten legions in Greece waiting for the call to defend against this traitor. We must not disappoint them.

'If he remains in our city, we will return to tear him out, exactly as Cornelius Sulla did to his uncle. The battle must be joined with him. He has made that clear by ignoring the lawful orders of this Senate. There can be no agreements, no peace while he lives. Rome cannot have two masters and I will *not* allow a rogue general to destroy what we have all built here.'

Pompey's voice softened slightly and he leaned forward on the rostrum, the smell of wax and oil strong in his nostrils.

'If, through our weakness, he is allowed to live, to triumph, then every general we send out from Rome will wonder if he cannot do the same. If Caesar is not crushed, this city will never know peace again. What we have built will be worn down by constant war over generations until there is *nothing* left to show that we were once here under the eyes of the gods, and that we stood for order. I defy the man who would steal it from us. I defy him and I will see him dead.'

Many of them were on their feet, their eyes bright. Pompey barely looked at those he despised, men filled more with air than courage. The Senate had never been short of speakers, but the rostrum was his.

'My legion is not up to strength and only a fool would deny the value of the battles in Gaul to his men. Even with the guards from the road forts, we do not have sufficient force to guarantee a victory. Do not think I enter into this lightly. I greet the news with pain and anger, but I will not scorn him from our gates and then lose my city under me.'

He paused and waved his hand lightly at those who had risen. Confused, they sat down, frowning.

'When he comes, he will find this senate house empty, with the doors broken from their hinges.'

He waited through the uproar as they understood at last that he did not intend to leave alone.

'With his legions raping your wives and daughters, how many of you will stand against him if you are left behind? He will come in looking for blood and will find nothing! We are the government, the heart of the city. Where we are, is Rome. He will be nothing more than a ruthless invader without you to put the seal of law on his words and actions. We must deny him our legitimacy.'

'The people will think . . .' someone began from the back.

Pompey shouted over the voice, 'The people will endure him as they have endured all their history! Do you think it would be better to leave you here while I gather an army on my own? How long would you last under torture, Marcellus? Or any of you? This Senate would be his and the final barrier would be overcome.'

Out of the corner of his eye, Pompey saw the orator Cicero rise and suppressed his irritation. The senators looked at the small figure and then at Pompey, seeing him hesitate. Cicero spoke before he too could be waved down.

'You have said little of the communications we sent to Caesar. Why have we not discussed his offer to halt?'

Pompey frowned at the nodding heads around him. He sensed they would not stand for a blustering answer.

'His terms were unacceptable, Cicero, as he knew they would be. He seeks to drive a wedge between us with his promises. Do you really believe he will end his drive south simply because I have left the city? You do not know him.'

Cicero folded his arms across his narrow chest, raising one hand until he could stroke the skin of his throat.

'Perhaps, though this is the place to debate the issue. Better to have it out in the open than leave it to be discussed in private. Have you responded to his offer, Pompey? I recall you said you would answer him.'

The two men locked gazes and Pompey gripped the rostrum more tightly as he struggled not to lose patience. Cicero was a subtle man, but Pompey had hoped he could depend on him.

'I have done everything I said I would. I wrote under senate seal to demand he return to Gaul. I will not negotiate while his legions are within striking distance of my city and he knows it. His words are simply to confuse us and cause delay. They mean nothing.'

Cicero raised his head. 'I agree, Pompey, though I believe all information should be made available to us here.' Choosing not to see Pompey's surprise, Cicero turned his head to address the senators on the benches around him. 'I do wonder if we are discussing a Roman general or another Hannibal who will

6

be satisfied with nothing less than power torn from our hands. What right does Caesar have to demand that Pompey leave the city? Do we now negotiate with invaders? We are the government of Rome and we are threatened by a mad dog, leading armies we trained and created. Do not underestimate the danger in this. I concur with Pompey. Though it will hurt worse than anything we have suffered before, we must retreat to gather loyal forces in Greece. The rule of law must not bend for the whims of our generals, or we are no more than another tribe of savages.'

Cicero sat down, after meeting Pompey's eyes with a brief flicker of amusement. His support would sway a number of the weaker ones in the chamber and Pompey inclined his head in silent thanks.

'There is no time for lengthy debate, gentlemen,' Pompey said. 'Another day will change nothing except to bring Caesar closer. I move we vote now and plan accordingly.'

Under Pompey's stern eye, there was little chance of rebellion, as he had intended. One by one, the senators rose to show their support, and no one dared abstain. At last, Pompey nodded, satisfied.

'Alert your households and plan for a journey. I have recalled all the soldiers in Caesar's path to the city. They will be here to help man the fleet and arrange our departure.'

The sun shone on the back of Julius' neck as he sat on a fallen tree in the middle of a wheatfield. Wherever he looked, he could see dark patches of his men as they rested amongst the golden crops and ate cold meat and vegetables. Cooking fires had been forbidden as they crossed into the lowlands of Etruria. The wheat was dry and rough to the touch and a single spark could send sheets of flame racing across the fields. Julius almost smiled at the peaceful scene. Fifteen thousand of the most experienced soldiers in the world and he could hear them laughing and singing like children. It was a strange thing to be there, out in the open. He could hear the calls of birds he had known as a boy and when he reached down and took a little of the leaf mulch in his hand, he was home.

'It is a fine thing to be here,' he said to Octavian. 'Can you feel it? I'd almost forgotten what it is like to be on my own land, surrounded by my people. Can you hear them sing? You should learn the words, lad. They'd be honoured to teach them to you.'

Slowly, Julius rubbed the damp leaves together in his hand and let them fall. The soldiers of the Tenth reached a chorus, their voices soaring over the fields.

'I heard that song from the men who followed Marius, years ago,' he said. 'These things seem to survive somehow.'

Octavian looked at his general, tilting his head as he assessed his mood. 'I feel it. This is home,' he said.

Julius smiled. 'I haven't been this close to the city in ten years. But I can sense her on the horizon. I swear I can.' He raised his hand and pointed over the low hills, heavy with wheat. 'Over there, waiting for us. Fearing us perhaps, while Pompey threatens and blusters.'

His eyes grew cold as the last words were spoken. He would have continued, but Brutus rode up through the crops, leaving a snaking path behind him. Julius rose to his feet and they clasped hands.

'The scouts report eleven cohorts, maybe twelve,' Brutus said.

Julius' mouth twisted irritably. Every legion post and road fort had been cleared before them as they moved south. His march had shaken them free like ripe fruit and now they were within reach. Whatever their quality, six thousand men were too many to leave at his back.

'They've gathered in Corfinium,' Brutus continued. 'The town looks like someone kicked a wasp nest. Either they know we're close, or they're getting ready to move back to Rome.'

Julius glanced around him, noticing how many in earshot were sitting up and listening, anticipating his order. The thought of unleashing them on Roman soldiers was almost a blasphemy.

Pompey had done well to recall the guards. They would do more good on the walls of Rome than wasted against the Gaul veterans. Julius knew he should strike fast to blood the campaign and seal the decision made on the banks of the Rubicon. Brutus shifted at the delay, but Julius still did not speak, staring into nothing. The men in Corfinium were inexperienced. It would be a slaughter.

'The numbers are accurate?' Julius said, softly.

Brutus shrugged. 'As far as they can be. I didn't let the scouts risk being seen, but it's clear ground. There's no ambush. I'd say these are the only soldiers between us and Rome. And we can take these. The gods know we have enough experience breaking into towns.'

Julius looked up as Domitius and Ciro came out of the wheat with Regulus. Mark Antony was only a short way behind them and he felt the pressure to give the orders to spill Roman blood on Roman land. Once those first lives were taken, every loyal hand would be raised against him. Every legion would swear vengeance unto death against his name. The civil war would be a test of strength and numbers that he could very well lose. His mind searched feverishly and he wiped sweat from his forehead.

'If we kill them, we will destroy any hope of peace in the future,' he said, slowly. Domitius and Brutus exchanged a quick glance as Julius went on, testing the thoughts aloud. 'We need . . . guile, as well as a strong arm, against our people. We need to win their loyalty, and that cannot be accomplished by killing men who love Rome as I do.'

'They won't let us through, Julius,' Brutus said, colouring with irritation. 'Would you, if an army wanted a path to your city? They'll fight just to slow us down; you know they will.'

9

Julius frowned with the anger that was always close to the surface. 'These are our own, Brutus. It is no small thing to be talking of killing them. Not for me.'

'That decision was made when we crossed the river and came south,' Brutus replied, refusing to back down. 'You knew the price then. Or will you go alone and give yourself up to Pompey?'

Some of those who listened winced at his tone. Ciro shifted his massive shoulders, his anger showing. Brutus ignored them all, his gaze fixed on his general.

'If you stop now, Julius, we are *all* dead men. Pompey won't forget we threatened the city. You know it. He'd follow us back to Britain if he had to.' He looked into Julius' eyes and, for a moment, his voice shook. 'Now don't you let me down. I've come this far with you. We have to see it through.'

Julius returned the pleading gaze in silence before placing his hand on Brutus' shoulder. 'I am *home*, Brutus. If it sticks in my throat to kill men of my own city, would you begrudge me my doubts?'

'What choice do you have?' Brutus replied.

Julius began to pace up and down amongst the crushed wheat. 'If I take power . . .' He froze for a moment as the idea formed, and spoke faster. 'What if I declare Pompey's dictatorship to be illegal? I could enter Rome to restore the Republic then. *That* is how they must see me. Adàn! Where are you?' he called across the field. His Spanish scribe came at the run. 'Here is your answer, Brutus,' Julius said, his eyes gleaming. 'Adàn? I want a letter sent to every Roman commander. It is ten years since I was consul; there is no bar against me standing once more. Tell them . . . I reject the dictatorship that Pompey will not end.'

Julius watched impatiently as Adàn fussed with his writing tablets.

'Let them know I will respect the courts and the senate building, that Pompey alone is my enemy. Tell them that I will welcome any man who wishes to join me as we bring back the Republic of Marius and the security of the past. I carry the gold of Gaul with me and Rome will be reborn with what I have won for her.

'Tell them all that, Adàn. Let them know that I will not take Roman lives unless I am forced, that I will honour the traditions as Pompey has not. He is the one who had the senate house burnt on his watch. The gods have already shown their dislike of *him*.'

The men around him watched bemused as Julius laughed aloud. He shook his head at their expressions.

'They will want to believe in me, gentlemen. They will hesitate and wonder if I am a champion of the old liberties.'

'And will it be true?' Adàn asked softly.

Julius glanced sharply at him. 'If I make it so. My first act will be in Corfinium. If they will surrender to me, I will spare them all, if only to have them spread the word.'

His humour was infectious and Adàn smiled as he scribbled in the soft wax, ignoring the inner voice that mocked how easily he fell under the man's charm.

'They won't surrender,' Domitius said. 'Pompey would have them killed as traitors. You saw what he did to the Tenth for turning.'

Julius frowned. 'He may, though if he does, he will be helping me. Who would you follow, Domi? A man who stands for law and consul, who frees good Romans, or one who has them killed? Who is the better man to lead Rome?'

Domitius nodded slowly and Julius smiled.

'You see? It will be hard for them to condemn me if I am merciful. It will confound them, Domi. Pompey will not know how to react.'

Julius turned to Brutus, his face alight with the old energy.

'But first we must take the road guards and do it without bloodshed. They must be reduced to a level of panic so total that they will not have the chance to fight. Who leads them?'

Brutus frowned, still reeling from the sudden change in Julius' mood. The march south had been overshadowed by doubt and gloom, but in a moment Julius was as he had been in Gaul. It was frightening.

'The scouts saw no legion flags,' he said stiffly. 'Whoever it is will be a ranking officer.'

'Let us hope he is still ambitious,' Julius replied. 'It will be easier if we can tempt his guards from the town. I'll draw him out with the Tenth and see if he comes. If we can catch them in the fields, they're ours.'

All around them, those who could hear were getting to their feet, gathering their kit and readying themselves to move. An air of long-familiar tension stole over them all as they prepared themselves to go back to danger and hardship.

'I will take the Tenth closer to the town, Brutus. You have overall command of the others. We will spin these lads until they're blind and useless. Send your scouts out and this time let them be seen.'

'I'd rather be the bait,' Brutus said.

Julius blinked for a moment, then shook his head. 'Not this time. The extraordinarii will be the links between us. I'll need you back here fast enough if we are attacked.'

'What if they sit tight?' Domitius asked, glancing at Brutus' strained expression.

Julius shrugged. 'Then we surround them and offer terms. One way or another, I am beginning my run for consul and Rome. Spread the word amongst the men. These are our people, gentlemen. They will be treated with respect.'

CHAPTER TWO

Ahenobarbus read his orders again. No matter how often he went over the few words from Pompey, nothing appeared that might allow him to attack the rogue legions from Gaul. Yet the reports from his scouts gave him a chance to finally make his name and he was cruelly caught between obedience and a rush of excitement he hadn't felt for years. Pompey would surely forgive him anything if he was able to bring the traitor back to the city in chains.

The men who had been taken from every road post, toll-house and fort were gathered under the shadow of Corfinium's walls, waiting for the order to march home. There was no tension amongst their ranks. The scouts had not yet managed to leak their news to the rest of them, though it could not be much longer before they all knew the enemy was closer than anyone had guessed.

Ahenobarbus rubbed his fingers along his bony jaw, easing his thumbs into the creases at the corners of his eyes to relieve the pressure. His guards outnumbered those his scouts had spotted, but the reports had mentioned four legions coming south and the others must surely be close by. At the very worst, it could be an ambush for his men.

Watching them as they formed up did not give him confidence. Many had never seen a more challenging contest than a few drunken farmers. Years of peace while Caesar conquered Gaul had not created the sort of force Ahenobarbus would have chosen for his chance at glory, but sometimes you had to work with what the gods gave you.

For a moment, he was tempted to forget what he had been told and tread the safe path as he had for most of his twenty years as a soldier. He could march out and be in Rome in only three days, leaving his last chance behind him. It was hard to imagine the sneers of younger officers when they heard he had walked away from a force half his size. The other Gaul legions could be miles away and he had sworn an oath to protect his city. Running back to the gates at the first sign of an enemy was not what he had imagined when he joined the army.

'Six thousand men,' he whispered to himself, looking back at the lines of soldiers waiting to march. 'My legion, at last.'

He had not mentioned the thought to anyone else, but as the arrivals came in he had counted them and now walked a little taller with his private pride. In his entire career, he had never had more than a century under his orders, but for a few wonderful days he would be the equal of any one of the generals of Rome.

Ahenobarbus recognised real fear undermining his pride. If he marched into a trap, he would lose everything. Yet if he gave up a perfect opportunity to destroy the man Pompey feared, word would leak out and he'd be followed by whispers for the rest of his life. He couldn't bear the indecision and now, many of the men were watching him, puzzled by the lack of orders.

'Sir? Shall I have the gates opened?' his second in command said at his shoulder.

Ahenobarbus looked into the man's face and felt fresh irritation at the youth and confidence he saw there. The rumours were that Seneca was connected in Rome and Ahenobarbus could not help but notice the richness of his clothes. He felt old when he looked at Seneca and the comparison seemed to make his joints ache. It was really too much to be faced with his amused condescension at that moment. No doubt the younger man thought he hid his arrogance, but Ahenobarbus had seen a dozen like him over the years. There was always a glint in the eyes when they were at their most fawning and you knew you couldn't trust them if their self-interest crossed your own.

Ahenobarbus took a deep breath. He knew he shouldn't be enjoying himself, but making the decision was a real pleasure.

'Have you ever fought, Seneca?' He watched as the young man's face went carefully blank, before the smooth smile returned.

'Not yet, sir, though of course I hope to serve.'

Ahenobarbus showed his teeth then. 'I thought you would say that, I really did. Today, you get your chance.'

Pompey stood alone in the senate building, listening to nothing but his own memories. At his order, blacksmiths had broken the doors from their hinges to hang awry across the opening. The old light of Rome spilled across motes of fresh-raised dust and he grunted softly as he lowered himself onto a bench.

'Fifty-six years old,' he murmured to the empty chamber. 'Too old to be going to war again.'

There had been moments of weakness and despair, moments when the years sat heavily and his private self ached to be allowed to rest. Perhaps it was time to leave Rome to young wolves like Caesar. After all, the bastard had shown he possessed the most important quality of a Roman leader – the ability to survive. When his thoughts were not coloured by anger, Pompey could admire the younger man's career. There had been times when he would not have bet a bronze coin on Julius coming through unscathed.

The crowds loved to hear of his exploits and Pompey hated him for that. It seemed that Julius could not buy a new horse without sending a triumphant letter to be read across the city. The common citizens gathered to hear fresh news, no matter how trivial. They were insatiable and only men like Pompey shook their heads at the lack of dignity. Even the subtlety of Cicero was lost against the excitement of Gaul's battles. What appeal could the Senate offer, when Caesar wrote of storming forts and visiting white cliffs at the edge of the world?

Pompey blew air through his lips in irritation, wishing Crassus was there to share this final indignation. Between them, they had done more to nurture Caesar's ambition than anyone and the irony was bitter. Had Pompey not accepted the triumvirate? At the time, it seemed that they all benefited, but with the Gaul legions on their way to Rome, Pompey could only wish he had been wiser when it mattered.

He had sent Julius to Spain and the man had returned to be consul. He had sent him to subdue the savages of Gaul, but could they do the decent thing and send him back in pieces? No, they could not. Instead, he came home as a lion, and the citizens respected nothing so much as success.

Black anger darkened his face as Pompey thought of the members of the Senate who had betrayed him. Only two-thirds of them had answered his call to leave for Greece, for all their public vows and promises. The rest had vanished from sight, preferring to wait for an invading army rather than follow their government into exile. It had been a cruel blow on top of everything else. They knew he would not have the luxury of time to root them out of their hiding places and it grated that they were right. He had already left it dangerously late and only the need for the road guards held him in the city. If Ahenobarbus did not bring them in quickly, Pompey knew he would have to leave without them. All his planning would come to nothing if he were still in the city when Caesar came up to the gates.

Pompey hawked and would have swallowed the bitter phlegm back into his throat if he had not been leaving. Instead, he spat a dark mass onto the marble tiles at his feet and felt a little better for the symbolic act. No doubt the citizens would cheer in their mindless way as the Gaul legions marched into the forum. It never failed to astonish him what little gratitude they showed. For almost four years, he had ensured they could feed their families and earn their livings without fear of murder, rape or robbery. The riots of Clodius and Milo were memories and the city had thrived in the aftermath, perhaps in part because they had seen what true chaos was like. But they would still cheer Caesar as he won his battles and brought them excitement. Bread and safety were easily forgotten in comparison.

Pompey reached out to the wooden armrest and pulled himself to his feet. His stomach ached, and he thought he might be developing an ulcer. He felt tired, without a reason. It was hard to tell himself that he had made the right decision when he would be leaving his city behind. Every general knew there were times when the only option was to retreat, regroup and attack on your own terms. It was still hard.

He hoped Julius would follow to Greece. They had not forgotten who ruled Rome, at least. There, he would have the armies he needed and the most able and experienced commanders in the world. Julius would learn the difference between filthy tribesmen and soldiers of Rome and he would learn it in the only way that mattered.

It was strange to think Julius was no longer the young man he remembered. Pompey wondered if he too felt the cold of winter more keenly, or the doubts that came with age. Stranger still to think that he knew his enemy better than almost anyone in Rome. He had broken bread with him, schemed and fought on the same side against enemies, for the same ideals. It was a vicious betrayal to have the man turn on him, the husband of Julius' daughter. Pompey chuckled aloud at that thought. He suspected Julia did not love him, exactly, but she knew her duty far better than her errant father. She had produced a son who might one day inherit the world.

17

Pompey wondered if some part of her would welcome her father's return to the city. It had not occurred to him to ask when he sent her to the ships. Though she may have come from Caesar, she was his no longer. Her young flesh could still rouse Pompey and though she bore his touches in silence, he thought she was not unsatisfied with her life. If he brought her father's head to her, would she be appalled? It lifted his spirits to imagine it.

He walked out of the empty senate house to where his soldiers waited, noting the perfection of their lines, and taking comfort from it. Caesar made him feel as if there were no rules left, that anything could occur, any tradition be overturned just by willing it. It was comforting to see the forum crowds give his men a respectful berth.

'Is there news of Ahenobarbus?' Pompey asked his scribe.

'Not yet, master,' the man replied.

Pompey frowned. He hoped the fool had not been tempted to engage the Gaul legions. His orders had been clear.

The road was wide and open for the marching column. With a grunt of approval, Ahenobarbus noted how Seneca had laid out the men. For all his lack of actual experience, the young member of the nobilitas had been trained for a life in the legions. He had approached the problem with all the easy confidence of his birth. Centuries had been doubled into maniples and the most experienced officers set in a chain of command. Old signal horns had been procured and three simple sequences repeated until the least of them could be expected to halt, withdraw or attack. Anything more complex would give them difficulty, Seneca acknowledged, but he looked satisfied as he marched. They were well-armed, well-fed and from the greatest fighting nation the world had ever known. Every legion began with nothing more than the culture and a few good officers. For road guards who had felt forgotten by the city they served, this was their chance. It helped that they stood against traitors with the city behind them. Most had family in Rome and would fight far better for them than for some lofty ideal of the Senate.

Ahenobarbus felt the eyes of the men around him and his spirits soared at the responsibility he had prayed for all his life. Just marching with them was a joy that was difficult to mask. He could not have asked for more from the gods and swore he would make an offering of a sixth of his wealth if they gave Caesar into his hands.

The scouts had marked the enemy forces ten miles north of Corfinium and that was a distance they could cover in less than three hours. Ahenobarbus had been tempted to ride, but sense had overruled his vanity. The men would see he walked with them, and when the time came he would draw his sword and hurl his spears with the rest.

Seneca had drawn up a plan of attack and, despite himself, Ahenobarbus had been impressed at his knowledge. It was one thing to give the order, quite another to create the formations and the tactics. It helped that they were facing Roman-trained soldiers, Seneca said. Only the lie of the land was unknown. Everything else would be by the military manuals and Seneca had read all of them.

Even Ahenobarbus' initial impression of the recruits had altered as the ranks took shape. It took hard men to run isolated road posts and more than a few had fought in Greece and Spain before ending their careers on the forts. They marched in a perfect column and Ahenobarbus was only sorry they did not have drummers to sound the beat for them.

It was difficult not to imagine the honours Pompey would bestow for capturing a man who threatened the city. At the very least, it would mean a tribune's rank, or a position as a magistrate. At his age, Ahenobarbus knew he would not be allowed another command, but it did not matter. He would have this day as a memory no matter what came after. In truth, leading a legion in some lonely mountains far from home did not appeal. It was far better to picture the soft life of attending court and accepting bribes from the sons of senators.

The countryside was filled with small farms, with every piece of flat ground taken up with waving wheat and barley to feed the maw of the city to the south. Only the road remained clear and Ahenobarbus did not look at those merchants who had dragged their carts off the stones to let his legion pass. His legion.

As soon as his scouts reported that Ahenobarbus had left Corfinium, Julius gave the order to march. If the commander of the guards declined the chance to attack, Julius trusted his veterans to catch them on the road before they could reach the safety of Rome. He had no fear of the untested troops. His Tenth had faced overwhelming numbers, ambush, night attacks, even the chariots of the Britons. He would trust them against any force in the world, if it were a matter of killing. Taking the guards alive would be a harder challenge and the extraordinarii riders had been racing back and forth between Brutus and the Tenth all morning with orders. The idea of forcing a surrender was a new one in Julius' experience, especially against Roman legionaries. Without an absolutely overwhelming advantage, he knew his people would fight to the last man rather than leave Rome open. From the first contact, he had to terrify them into obedience.

The veteran Tenth breasted through the wheat, trampling it in a great swathe. Even in a wide formation, Julius could see the lines in the fields behind them stretching for miles, as if metal tines had been drawn across the earth. It was a straight path, despite the rise and fall of the landscape. The extraordinarii rode ahead, searching for the first sight of the Roman enemy. The Tenth loosened their swords in their scabbards as they marched, waiting for the horns that would send them into a battle line.

Ahenobarbus saw the dark stain of the enemy across the land and his heart began to race in anticipation. Seneca had the horns sound a warning note and the blare stiffened the backs of his soldiers, tightening their nerves. Almost unconsciously, the pace of the march increased.

'Form square!' Seneca roared along the ranks and the column dissolved as the centuries moved apart.

It was not a parade manoeuvre, but the formation appeared out of the lines like the head of a hammer, with the handle trailing behind along the wide road. Gradually, the tail dwindled in length until they were going forward in one solid mass. Their spears were gripped in sweating palms as they readied themselves for battle and Ahenobarbus could hear the muttered prayers of the men around him as they gave up their souls and pressed on. He thanked his gods to have been given such a moment as they crossed into the wheat and trampled it before them. He could not turn his head away from the shining metal of the Gaul legion. These men threatened his city and he watched them approach in fascination and swelling fear. He heard their own horns whine across the fields and saw the swift response as the lines blurred into smaller units, sliding inexorably towards him.

'Be ready,' he called across the heads of his countrymen, blinking sweat from his eyes. Then the stillness of the day snapped as the Tenth legion roared and broke into a run.

Julius advanced with the others, keeping a tight rein so as not to go beyond his loping men. He watched the distance shrink as both sides accelerated and tasted the dust of the fields in his mouth.

The Tenth had not unwrapped their spears and he hoped they understood the plans he had made. They raced across the open ground towards the road guards in their formations and after their first shout they were grim and terrifyingly silent.

Julius counted the paces between the two armies, gauging the range. He doubted Ahenobarbus could launch spears in full waves from such a motley gang, but he would have to risk the lives of his Tenth to get close enough.

At the last moment, he called the halt and the Tenth crashed to a stop. Julius ignored the enemy as they lumbered towards him. There were fifty paces to go before they were in range for spears, but he searched beyond them in the distance, looking for the rising dust that would show him his veteran legions marching around. With the tramp of the road guards in his ears, Julius rose up in the saddle, balancing on one knee.

'There they are!' he called, exulting.

Hidden by the hills, Brutus, Domitius and Mark Antony had circled and Ahenobarbus was caught between two forces. Julius knew he could have destroyed them, but his aim was more subtle and more difficult. As Ahenobarbus came into spear range, Julius raised his hand and wound it in a circle above his head. The Tenth wheeled right and marched, keeping their distance all the time. It was as if they were attached by a long rope to the enemy, and the move forced the road guards to turn with them or leave their flanks open.

Julius grinned to himself as he saw the chaos that ensued. It took more than a few simple horn signals to turn a square on the spot. He saw the lines compress and widen as those in front tried to match the Tenth and those behind became confused and angry.

The Tenth moved around the rim of the wheel and when they had made a full quarter turn, Brutus had the Third bellow out a challenge and approach. Julius nodded in fierce excitement as he saw the veterans move apart into an arc as if they were on parade.

They closed off the retreat and added to the confusion and terror in those they surrounded.

The men with Ahenobarbus were caught. Some of them tried to face the new threats, but all four legions turned about them, causing chaos in the milling centre. No spears could be launched from within that confused mass.

The revolving armies raised a plume of dust from the wheat-fields, thickening the air and making men cough and sneeze. Ahenobarbus did not see the extraordinarii until they had ridden up to close the gaps in the circle. Through his panic he could not frame orders to meet the threat. There were too many of the enemy and he knew he was going to die. The Gaul legions halted with spears resting on their shoulders and the thought of the killing to come made the road guards shrink back into the centre.

Ahenobarbus bellowed at his recruits to stand still. The ranks and files had twisted beyond recognition until they were just a crowd of angry, bewildered men. Seneca had given up shouting and looked as lost as any of them. There was nothing in the manuals to answer this. Panting, Ahenobarbus grimaced, waiting for the attack. Though it was hopeless, many of those around him raised their swords in defiance and he was proud of their courage in the face of defeat.

Ahenobarbus watched as riders approached. Part of him raged at the thought of having to meet such men. He did not want to look them in the eye and be humiliated, but anything that delayed the killing was welcome. Every moment had become precious.

He saw that two of them held shields ready for the Third and knew he was looking at the man who had beaten Gaul and now threatened their own city. The rider wore no helmet and simple armour with a dark red cloak that was crumpled under him, spilling down his mount's flank. In a crowd, Ahenobarbus might not have noticed him, but after the manoeuvres that had broken his guards without a single spear or sword thrust, the man seemed like some creature from the dark river, come to taunt him. It was easy enough to imagine the Roman blood that would stain his cloak.

Ahenobarbus stood straighter. 'When he comes close, lads, we rush him on my order. Pass the word. We might not be able to beat these bastards, but if we can kill the general, we haven't been wasted.'

Seneca stared at him and Ahenobarbus held his eyes long enough to force him to look away. The young man still thought this was some elaborate tactical game, with Rome open behind them. Some of them knew better and Ahenobarbus saw nods of assent spread out from him. Sometimes, a man could forget that his life was not the most important thing in the world, that there really were things worth dying for. In the chaos and fear, Ahenobarbus had been almost resigned to surrender, before the truth came back to him. This was an enemy, Roman or not.

Seneca came close, so as not to be overheard by the men. 'Sir, we cannot attack now. We *must* surrender,' the young man said into his ear.

Ahenobarbus glanced at him and noted the fear. 'Go back, lad, and let them see you stand. When he comes close enough, we'll cut him down.'

Seneca opened his mouth, unable to understand the dark ferocity he saw in his commander. It had never been there before and it shocked him into silence as he moved away.

Ahenobarbus chuckled to himself. He looked at the grim legions facing him. They too had halted after their display and, grudgingly, he admitted their superiority. It had been impressive enough to see the way they dismantled his rough formations. The horsemen looked eager to be sent in and the sight of those cold killers sent a shiver through his frame. On the backs of their mounts, the riders seemed enormous and Ahenobarbus knew their reputation as well as anyone else who had read the reports from Gaul. It gave the enemy a glamour he could not deny and it was hard to think of those veterans charging in amongst his inexperienced soldiers.

'Who has led you here? Let that man step forward!' a voice carried over the field.

Faces turned to Ahenobarbus and he smiled mirthlessly as he made his way through the ranks to the front. The sun shone and his vision seemed unnaturally clear, as if the edges of things had sharpened.

Ahenobarbus stepped out from his men, alone. He felt the eyes of thousands on him as the three horsemen rode closer. Gently, he drew his sword and took a deep breath. Let them come in and get his answer, he thought to himself. His heart hammered, but he felt calm and strangely detached as Julius Caesar glared down at him.

'What do you think you're doing?' Julius roared, red-faced in anger. 'What is your name?'

Ahenobarbus almost took a step back in surprise. 'Ahenobarbus,' he replied, stifling the urge to add 'sir'. He felt the men behind jostle and readied himself to give the order to attack.

'How dare you bare your sword to me, Ahenobarbus? How *dare* you! You have abused the trust placed in you. Be thankful none of your men or mine have been killed or I would see you hanged before sunset.'

Ahenobarbus blinked in confusion. 'I have orders to . . .'

'Orders from whom? Pompey? By what right is he still Dictator in my city? I stand before you as a loyal Roman and you mutter about your orders. Do you *want* to be killed? Who do you think you are to be throwing away so many lives, Ahenobarbus? Are you a lawmaker, a senator? No, you've been let down, General. You should not be here.' Julius removed his gaze from Ahenobarbus in disgust, raising his head to address the guards who watched him. 'I am returning to my city to stand as consul once more. I break no laws in doing so. I have no quarrel with you and I will not shed the blood of my people unless I am forced to.'

Ignoring Ahenobarbus, Julius walked his mount along the line, his accompanying riders moving in formation with him. For a split second, Ahenobarbus considered shouting for an attack, but then he caught the eye of one of the riders and saw him grin and shake his head as if he had heard the thought. Ahenobarbus remembered that Caesar had called him 'general' and the words died in his throat.

Julius' voice echoed across them. 'I am within my rights to have you disarmed and sold into slavery for what you have done today. I see bared swords and spears in your ranks even now! Do *not* force my hand, gentlemen. I am a loyal general of Rome. I am the commander of Gaul and in my person I am the Senate and the law. Do not *think* to raise your weapons against me.'

Every man in the guards stood appalled as his words washed over them. Ahenobarbus saw them lower swords and spears as Julius wheeled his mount and came back along the line.

'I have not come back from ten years of war to struggle against my own people here. I tell you that you have been misled. I give you my word that not one of you will be killed if you put away your weapons now.' He swept his gaze over the men. 'You have a choice, gentlemen. I will treat you with honour if you make good your mistake. Look around you. I do not *need* to be merciful. After this, I will consider you traitors to Rome.'

He had reached Ahenobarbus once more and the guard was forced to look up into the sun to meet his eyes. Julius was dark against the light as he waited for a response.

'Well? Your idiocy has brought them here,' Julius said softly. 'Will you see them all killed for nothing?' Mutely, Ahenobarbus shook his head. 'Then stand them down and bring the officers to me, Ahenobarbus. We must discuss the terms of the surrender.'

'You did break a law when you crossed the Rubicon, sir,' Ahenobarbus said stubbornly.

Julius' eyes flashed. 'And Dictatorships are meant to be temporary.

Sometimes, a man must act according to his conscience, General,' he replied.

Ahenobarbus looked away at his men for a moment. 'I have your word that there will be no punishment?' he said.

Julius did not hesitate. 'I will not shed Roman blood, General. Not unless I must. You have my word.'

Being addressed as an equal was such a small thing, but the urge to throw away his life had faded like a memory. Ahenobarbus nodded. 'Very well, sir. I will stand down.'

'Give me your sword,' Julius said.

The two men locked eyes for a moment before Ahenobarbus held it up and Julius' hand closed over the scabbard. The symbolic gesture was seen by all the guards.

'The right choice, at last,' Julius said, quietly, before cantering back to his own lines.

CHAPTER THREE

Pompey stood on the docks at Ostia and looked back in the direction of Rome. The port town was quiet and he wondered if the inhabitants understood what they were seeing. It was possible, but over his time in the Senate he had come to realise that there were thousands of citizens who barely noticed the work of their masters. Their lives went on just the same. After all, no matter who was consul, the bread had to be baked and the fish brought in.

The last of the merchant ships crackled into flame behind him, making him turn and look out to sea. *There* were lives who would be affected, he thought. The owners would be beggared at a stroke, to make sure that Caesar would not have a fleet to follow before Pompey was ready. Even at a distance, the roar of flames was impressive and Pompey watched as they reached the sail and engulfed the tarry cloth in an instant. The small ship began to settle and he hoped his men had the sense to get well clear on the boats before she sank.

Three sturdy triremes waited for the final members of the Senate and Pompey himself. They rocked in the swell as the great oars were greased in their locks and checked for fouling. The wind was running out to sea. It was fitting that Pompey should be the last to leave and he knew it was time, but he couldn't break the mood that held him on shore.

Had there ever been a choice? He had thought himself clever

when he sent the order for Julius to return. Any other general would have come with just a few guards and Pompey would have made a quick, neat end to it. Even now, he could not be sure why Julius had gambled everything on his rush south. Regulus had obviously failed and Pompey assumed he had died trying to fulfil his last orders. Perhaps the man's clumsy attempt had given Julius the truth of his master. He could not imagine Regulus breaking under torture, but perhaps that was foolishness. Experience had taught him that any man could be broken in enough time. It was just necessary to find the levers into his soul. Even so, he would not have thought there was a lever made to open Regulus.

Pompey saw the last boat from his ship bump against the quayside and Suetonius jump onto the docks. He watched as the younger man marched up the hill, stiff with self-importance. Pompey turned back towards the city he could feel in the distance. Ahenobarbus had not come and Pompey doubted he still lived. It had been a blow to lose the men he had with him, but if he had slowed Julius at all, it would have been worth it. Pompey could not believe how difficult it had been to uproot the senators from their homes. He had been tempted to abandon the endless crates of their possessions on the quayside for the merchant sailors to pick through. Their wives and children had been bad enough, but he had drawn a line at more than three slaves to each family and hundreds had been sent back to the city. Every ship and trireme for a hundred miles up and down the coast had been called in and only a few were left empty and burnt.

Pompey smiled tightly to himself. Even Julius could not conjure a fleet out of nothing. Pompey's army would have nearly a year to prepare for the invasion and then, well, let them come after that.

As Suetonius approached, Pompey noted the high polish on his armour and approved. The senator had made himself indispensable over the previous weeks. In addition, Pompey knew his hatred of Caesar was absolute. It was good to have a man who could be trusted and Pompey knew that Suetonius would never be one of those who questioned his orders.

'Your boat is ready, sir,' Suetonius said.

Pompey nodded stiffly. 'I was having a last look at my country,' he replied. 'It will be a while until I stand here again.'

'It will come though, sir. Greece is like a second home to many of the men. We'll end Caesar's betrayal there.'

'We will indeed,' Pompey said.

A waft of smoke from the burning merchant ship passed over both of them and he shivered slightly. There had been times when he thought he would never get out of the city before Caesar's legions appeared on the horizon. He had not even made the offerings in the temples that he should have, convinced that every minute counted. Now though, even if he saw his enemy riding towards him, he could stroll down into the boat and go to the ships, leaving them all behind. It was his first unhurried moment in the best part of two weeks and he felt himself relax.

'I wonder if he is already in the city, Suetonius,' Pompey said softly.

'Perhaps, sir. He will not be there for long if he is.'

Both men stood staring east, as if they could see the place that had birthed them. Pompey grimaced as he remembered the silent crowds that had lined the streets as his legion marched to the coast. Thousands and thousands of his people had come to watch the exodus. They had not dared to call out, even from the deepest sections of the crowd. They knew him too well for that. He had seen their expressions though and resented them. What right did they have to stare so, as Pompey passed by? He had given them his best years. He had been senator, consul and Dictator. He had destroyed the rebellion of Spartacus and more small kings and rebels than he could remember. Even Romans like Titus Milo had fallen to him when they threatened his people. He had been father to the city all his life and like the children they were, they stood in sullen silence, as if they owed him nothing.

Black cinders floated in the air around the two men, borne aloft by unseen currents. Pompey shivered in the breeze, feeling old. He was not ready to retire from public life, if Caesar would even have let him. He had been forced to this place by a man who cared nothing for the city. Caesar would find out there was a price to pay for ruling Rome. She had claws, and the people who cheered you and threw flowers at your feet could forget it all in just a season.

'I would not change a single year of my life, Suetonius. If I had them again, I would spend them as fast, even if they left me here, with a ship waiting to take me away.'

He saw Suetonius' confusion and chuckled.

'But it is not over yet. Come, we must be at sea before the tide changes.'

Servilia looked at her reflection in a mirror of polished bronze. Three slaves fussed around her, working on her hair and eyes as they had been for three hours before dawn. Today would be special, she knew. Everyone who entered the city said Caesar was coming and she wanted him to see her at her best.

She rose to stand naked before the mirror, raising her arms for the slave girl to add a subtle dust of rouge to her nipples. The light tickle of the brush made them stiffen and she smiled, before sighing. The mirror could not be fooled. Lightly, she touched her stomach with the palm of a hand. She had escaped the sagging belly of the Roman matron with a host of births, but age had loosened the skin, so that she could press it and see it wrinkle like thin cloth, as if nothing held it to her. Soft dresses that had once been used to reveal, now covered what she did not want seen. She knew she was still elegant and riding kept her fit, but there was

31

only one youth to be had and hers was a memory. Without dye, her hair was an iron grey and each year she tortured herself with the thought that it was time to let her age show before her paints and oils were nothing but a tawdry covering, a humiliation.

She had seen women who would not admit they had grown old and hated the thought of joining those pathetic, wigged creatures. Better to have dignity than to be ridiculed, but today Caesar was coming, and she would use all her art.

When she stood still, her skin shone with oil from the massage table and she could believe she retained a trace of her old beauty. Then she would move and the fine web would appear in her reflection, mocking her efforts. It was a tragedy that there were so few years when the skin glowed, before pigments and oils had to do the job in their place.

'Will he ride into the city, mistress?' one of the slaves asked.

Servilia glanced at her, understanding the flush she saw on the girl's skin. 'He will, I'm sure, Talia. He will come at the head of an army and ride into the forum to address the citizens. It will be like a Triumph.'

'I have never seen one,' Talia responded, her eyes downcast.

Servilia smiled coldly, hating her for her youth. 'And you will not today, my dear. You will stay here and prepare my house for him.'

The girl's disappointment was palpable, but Servilia ignored it. With Pompey's legion away, the city was holding its breath as they waited for Caesar. Those who had supported the Dictator were simply terrified that they would be singled out and punished. The streets, never safe at the best of times, were far too restless to allow a pretty young slave to go and watch the entry of the Gaul veterans into Rome. Whether age brought wisdom, Servilia was never sure, but it did bring experience and that was usually enough.

Servilia tilted her head back and held still as another of her slaves dipped a slender ivory needle into a pot and held it over her eyes. She could see the drop of dark liquid forming there, before it shivered and fell. She closed her eye against the sting and the slave waited patiently until it had faded and she could administer the drop of belladonna to the other. The poison could be fatal in any serious dose, but the diluted fluid made her pupils as large and dark as any young woman's at dusk. The discomfort in bright sunshine was a small price to pay. She sighed as she blinked away tears along her eyelashes. Even those were quickly removed with pads of soft cloth before they could touch her cheeks and ruin the work of the morning.

The youngest of the slave girls waited patiently with her pot of dark kohl, watching as Servilia checked the results in the mirror. The whole room seemed brighter as a result of the belladonna and Servilia felt her spirits rise. Caesar was coming home.

As Caesar had ordered, Ahenobarbus marched into the old barracks of Primigenia, outside the walls of Rome. They had fallen into disuse over the previous decade and he had Seneca set up work details to restore them to cleanliness and order while he was still shaking the dust of the road from his sandals.

Alone for a few precious moments, he entered the main building and sat at the table in the officers' hall, resting a wineskin in the dust. He could hear his men chatter and argue outside, still discussing what had happened to them. He shook his head, hardly able to believe it himself. With a sigh, he opened the bronze mouth on the wine and tipped it back, sending a line of harsh liquid into his throat.

It would not be long, he thought, before someone came to ask questions. The city had scouts out for miles and he knew his movements had been seen and reported. He wondered to whom they would report, now that Pompey had gone. Rome was without a government for the first time in centuries and memories of the chaos under Clodius and Milo would still be fresh in many minds. Fear would keep them in their houses, he suspected, while they waited for the new master to come in.

A clatter of iron-shod sandals made him look up and grunt at Seneca as the young man put his head around the doorway.

'Come in and have a drink, lad. It's been a strange day.'

'I have to find . . .' Seneca began.

'Sit down and have a drink, Sen. They'll get by without you for a little while.'

'Yes, sir, of course.'

Ahenobarbus sighed. He'd thought some of the reserve between them had been broken down, but with the city walls in sight Seneca had once again begun to think of his future, like every other young Roman of the times. It was the disease of the age.

'Have you sent runners out? We'd better be sure Pompey isn't still waiting at the coast for us.'

'No! I didn't think of it,' Seneca replied, beginning to rise.

Ahenobarbus waved him back to his seat. 'That will wait as well. I'm not even sure we could join him now.'

Seneca suddenly looked wary and Ahenobarbus watched as the young man pretended to be confused.

'You gave the oath to Caesar, just as I did, lad. You won't be telling me you didn't understand what it meant.'

He thought the young man might lie, but Seneca raised his head and returned his gaze.

'No. I understood it. But I swore another oath to fight for Rome. If Pompey has taken the Senate to Greece, I must follow him.'

Ahenobarbus gulped at the wine before passing it over.

'Your life belongs to Caesar, lad. He told you enough times. If you take the field against him after what happened, there'll be no mercy from him, not again.'

'My *duty* is with Pompey,' Seneca replied.

Ahenobarbus looked at him and blew air out in a long sigh.

'Your honour is your own, though. Will you break the oath to Caesar?'

'An oath to an enemy does not bind me, sir.'

'Well it binds me, lad, because I say it does. You want to think whose side you would rather be on. If you go to Pompey, Caesar will cut your balls off.'

Seneca stood, flushed with anger. 'As he did yours?' he said.

Ahenobarbus slammed his fist onto the table, making the dust rise in a cloud. 'Would you rather he had killed all of us? That's what Pompey would have done! He said he was coming to restore order and law and then he proved it, Seneca, by letting us go and trusting our oath. He impressed me, lad, and if you weren't so busy looking for your next promotion, you'd see why.'

'I can see he *did* impress you. Enough to forget the loyalty you owe the Senate and the Dictator.'

'Don't *lecture* me, boy!' Ahenobarbus snapped. 'Look up from your precious books and see what's happening. The wolves are out, do you understand? Ever since Caesar came south. Do you think Pompey's interested in your loyalty? Your noble Senate would crush you for a jug of wine, if they were thirsty.'

For a moment of strained silence, both men faced each other, breathing heavily.

'I used to wonder why a man of your years was given no more than a road fort to command,' Seneca said stiffly. 'I understand it now. I *will* lecture any Roman soldier who does not give his life into the hands of his superiors. I would expect no less from those who follow me. I won't sit this out, Ahenobarbus. I would call that cowardice.'

His contempt was written in every line of his young face and Ahenobarbus suddenly felt too tired to go on.

'Then I will pour a little wine into your grave when I find it. That's the best I can offer you.'

Seneca turned his back without saluting and left the room, his footprints visible in the dust behind him. Ahenobarbus snorted in anger and lifted the wineskin, pressing his fingers in deeply.

A stranger entered only a few minutes later, finding him drawing idly in the dust on the table, lost in thought.

'Sir? I have been sent by my master to hear if you have any news,' the man said without preamble.

Ahenobarbus looked up at him. 'Who is left to be sending anyone anywhere? I thought the Senate had all gone with Pompey.'

The man looked uncomfortable and Ahenobarbus realised he had not given his master's name.

'Some of the Senate did not see the need to travel, sir. My master was one of those.'

Ahenobarbus grinned. 'Then you'd better run back and tell him Caesar is coming. He's two, maybe three hours behind me. He's bringing back the Republic, lad, and I wouldn't stand in his way.'

CHAPTER FOUR

The extraordinarii stood by their mounts, heaving at the great doors of the Quirinal gate in the north of the city. It had been left unbarred and the walls were empty of soldiers to challenge them. Now that the moment had come, there was a hush over the city and the streets by the gate were deserted. The Gaul riders exchanged glances, sensing eyes on them.

The tramp of the four legions was a muted thunder. The extraordinarii could feel the vibration under their feet and dust shimmered in the cracks between the stones. Fifteen thousand men marched towards the city that had declared them traitor. They came in ranks of six abreast and the tail of the column stretched back further than the eye could see.

At the head came Julius on a prancing dark gelding of the best bloodlines in Spain. Mark Antony and Brutus rode a pace to the rear, with shields ready in their hands. Domitius, Ciro and Octavian made up the spearhead and all of them felt the tension of the moment with something like awe. They had known the city as a home and a distant mother and as a dream. To see the gates open and the walls unguarded was a strange and frightening thing. They did not talk or joke as they rode in and the marching men of the column kept the same silence. The city waited for them.

Julius rode under the arch of the gate and smiled as its shadow crossed his face in a dark bar. He had seen cities in Greece and

Spain and Gaul, but they could only ever be reflections of this place. The simple order of the houses and the neat lines of paving spoke to something in him and made him sit straighter in the saddle. He used the reins to turn his Spanish mount to the right, where the forum waited for him. Despite the solemnity of the moment, he was hard-pressed to keep his dignity. He wanted to grin, to shout a greeting to his people and his home, lost to him for so many years.

The streets were no longer empty, he saw. Curiosity had opened the doors of homes and businesses to reveal dark interiors. The people of Rome peered out at the Gaul legions, drawn by the glamour of the stories they had heard. There was not a man or woman in Rome who had not listened to the reports from Gaul. To see those soldiers in the flesh was irresistible.

'Throw the coins, Ciro. Bring them out,' Julius called over his shoulder and he did grin then at the big man's tension.

Like Octavian beside him, Ciro carried a deep bag tied to his saddle and he reached into it to grasp a handful of silver coins, each bearing the face of the man they followed. The coins rang on the stones of the city and Julius saw children run from their hiding places to snatch them before they could come to rest. He remembered standing at Marius' side in a Triumph long ago and seeing the crowd dip in waves to receive the offerings. It was more than the silver that they wanted and only the poorest would spend the coins. Many more would be kept for a blessing, or made into a pendant for a wife or lover. They carried the face of a man who had become famous through his battles in Gaul and yet was still a stranger to all but a very few.

The shrill excitement of the children brought out their parents. More and more of them came to reach for the coins and laugh with relief. The column had not come to destroy or loot the city, not after such a start.

Ciro and Octavian emptied the bags quickly and two more

were passed forward to them. The crowd had begun to thicken, as if half of Rome had been waiting for some unseen signal. They did not all smile at the sight of so many armed men on the streets. Many of the faces were angry and dark, but as the column wound its way through the city, they grew fewer, lost amongst the rest.

Julius passed the old house of Marius, glancing through the gates to the courtyard he had seen first as a boy. He looked behind him for Brutus and knew that he shared the same memories. The old place was shuttered and bare, but it would be opened again and given life. Julius enjoyed the metaphor and tried to frame it into something appropriate for the speech he would make, choosing and discarding words as he rode. He preferred to be seen as a spontaneous speaker, but every phrase had been written in the wheatfields, with Adàn.

It was eerie to retrace the steps he had marched with the old Primigenia, before they had been scattered by the enemies of his family. His uncle had walked right up to the steps of the senate house and demanded the Triumph they owed him. Julius shook his head in amused memory as he recalled the bull of a man Marius had been. The laws had meant nothing to him and the city had worshipped his irreverence, electing him consul more times than any man in the city's history. They were different, wilder days then and the world had been smaller.

A child scrambled onto the street after a rolling coin and Julius pulled on the reins to avoid knocking him down. He saw the boy hold his treasure aloft in a moment of pure happiness before his mother yanked him out of harm's way. Julius dug in his heels before the lines behind could close up and wondered how it would be interpreted by the readers of omens. No doubt the priests were up to their elbows in entrails in every temple, looking for guidance. Julius thought of Cabera and wished he had lived to come back with them. He had buried the old man in Gaul, in sight of the sea.

The crowd was swelling and somehow those that came later added to the mood of celebration, as if the word had already gone round the streets. The Gaul legions were not to be feared. They came in dignity, with offerings of silver and their weapons sheathed. The noise was growing in proportion to the numbers. Julius could already hear the cries of vendors selling their wares. He wondered how many of his coins would be exchanged for a cool drink in the sun or a slice of cold meat pie.

When he glanced behind him, Julius was pleased to see his men respond to the people lining the road. Those who had relatives looked for them, their faces holding that peculiarly intent expression of one who waits to smile.

The road eased downhill towards the forum and Julius could see the light of the open space long before he entered it. At the centre of the city, it was the single image he had remembered most clearly in all his years away. It was hard to hold his mount back. The road ended in wealthy houses and temples, but Julius did not see them, his gaze fixed ahead. The sun seemed to increase its heat as he rode through to the heart of Rome and he felt a rush of excitement that he could hardly believe.

There were people there, already in their thousands. Some of them were cheering, but though their mood was light, Julius knew they would demand to be entertained, to be given precious memories with which to impress their children.

They had left him a path through their midst to the new senate house and Julius glanced at the site of the old one before forgetting it. Rome was more than buildings, more than her history. She was made clean with the innocence of each new generation and he was part of this rebirth.

He looked straight ahead and smiled as the citizens raised their voices around him. He knew the legions marched at his back, but for a few moments in the sunlight it was almost as if he were coming in alone.

He could not resist the excitement any longer then, and kicked his heels in, his horse's hooves clattering over the stones. The steps of the senate house rose before him and he sent his mount lunging up them in three great strides, turning to look back over the sea of faces. It had been more than ten years and he had known fear and pain and loss. But Rome was his, and he was home.

The legions continued to flow into the forum, forming great glittering squares like islands in the colours of the crowd. Slaves and citizens mingled and pressed closer to the senate house, eager to hear, to be part of it. The poorest of Rome were there in numbers and they were raucous, pushing and shoving to reach the senate house steps. Julius saw the column halt at last, as his officers decided against bringing them all into one space. It was chaotic and dangerous and Julius laughed with pleasure.

'I have come *home*!' he roared over their heads.

They cheered him and he sat back in his saddle, raising his hands for quiet. He looked down at Brutus and Mark Antony as they brought their horses to the bottom of the steps. Both were smiling and relaxed. Brutus leaned over to murmur a few words to Mark Antony and they chuckled together.

Gradually, the noisy crowd quieted and stood waiting.

'My people, in this place,' Julius said wonderingly. 'I have waited ten *years* to stand here before you.' His voice echoed from the temples. 'I have shown the strength we have in Gaul, have I not? I have toppled kings and brought their gold back to be spent here.'

They bayed their enthusiasm for that idea and he knew he had judged the tone to please them. The more complex arguments would come later, when he had finished with this day.

'I have built our roads on new lands and marked out farms for our citizens. If you have ever dreamed of owning land, I have it ready for you and for your children. I have crossed seas for you and made new maps.' He paused, letting the noise swell. 'I carried Rome with me through the years and I did *not* forget my city.'

41

Their voices crashed against him and he held up his hands again.

'Yet even this moment is tainted. As I stand before you and breathe the air I love, I know there are some calling against me.' His expression became stern and the silence was perfect.

'I am here to answer any charges against my name. But where are those who accuse Caesar? Will they not stand forward when I call for them? Let them come; I have nothing to hide.'

Someone shouted a reply that Julius did not hear, though those around the speaker laughed and chattered.

'Can it be true that Pompey has left my city? That the Senate you trusted to protect you has abandoned Rome? I tell you to judge them by their deeds. Rome deserves better men than they. You deserve better than men who slip away in the night when their lies are challenged! I am here to stand for consul, not to threaten or bluster. Who denies me my right? Which one of you will argue the law with me?'

He swept his gaze over the crowd as they shifted and swirled like water in the forum. He loved them in all their vulgar, corrupt, violent glory. He loved them for their refusal to bow their heads and be docile, and he loved the exhilaration that came from riding their emotions. It had broken men before him, but there was no other risk worth taking.

'For those of you who fear the future, I will say this. I have seen enough of war. I will try for peace with Pompey and the Senate and if I am refused, I will try harder. I will not take a Roman life unless I am forced. That is my vow.'

A scream sounded from somewhere in the crowd and Julius saw a dozen of the Tenth detach with Regulus to see to the disturbance. The forum was packed so fully as to make any movement difficult, and Julius wondered at those who would take even this day as an opportunity for theft or rape. He hoped Regulus would break the heads of those responsible.

'If I must end Pompey's Dictatorship on the field of battle, then I will do it far from here. While there is life in me, I will protect Rome. That is my oath and I swear it before all the gods in this place. I will stand for lawful election and if you make me consul, I will follow Pompey to the end of the earth to bring him down. He will not come here while I live.'

In one swift movement, Julius swung his leg over the saddle and knelt on the white marble, letting the reins fall from his hand. The crowd craned and shuffled to see him bow and kiss the stone. His armour shone in the sunlight as he rose to his feet.

'I am loyal. My life is yours.'

Perhaps his legions began the roar of appreciation, but he could not be sure. For all the joys he had known, there was nothing to approach the unalloyed pleasure of his own people calling his name.

He took up the reins once more, quieting the horse with a gentle hand.

'I have given you Gaul. The earth is black and rich there for your farms. Its gold will build a new Rome, greater than anything we have seen before. A new forum, courts, amphitheatres, race-tracks, theatres and baths. All this is my gift to you. In return, I ask that you raise your heads and know you walk the streets of the centre of the world. All roads lead here, to us. All courts have their authority from us. Weigh every act with that in mind and be sure you act nobly, for we are the nobility of all cities. We hold the torch for Greece, Spain, Gaul and Britain to follow. To the least of you, to the poorest, I tell you to work and there will be food for your table. Struggle for justice and it will be there for you.'

He was aware that the soldiers under Regulus had caught whoever was responsible for the unseen crime. Three men were swiftly trussed and Julius swore privately that they would regret interrupting his speech. He glanced to where the heavy bronze doors of the senate house hung at angles. Despite himself, his mood was souring and he took a deep breath before speaking again.

'You will elect a new Senate with the courage to stand and face the results of their actions. Those who have run are worthless men and I will tell them so, when I catch them.' He nodded as laughter spread over the forum.

'If Pompey refuses to accept the peace I offer, I will not desert you, or leave you without protection. I will leaven you with the best of my soldiers, so that there will be order and law behind me. My city is *not* to be abandoned. It is not to be risked.'

They hung on the words that came from him and he felt his spirits lift again.

'That is far in the future. Tonight, and tomorrow, my men will want good wine and the company of beautiful women. I will buy every amphora in Rome and we will celebrate. Gaul is ours and I am home.'

Ciro and Octavian threw silver coins over the people as they cheered themselves hoarse as Julius turned away, gesturing to his officers to follow him inside the empty senate chamber.

Brutus turned at the doorway and looked back at the crowd. 'What if Pompey had stayed?' he said.

Julius shrugged, his smile vanishing. 'I would have killed him. Rome is mine and always has been.' He walked into the cool interior, leaving Brutus alone on the steps.

The echoing senate house was subtly different to the one Julius remembered. The sheath of creamy marble on the walls showed the attempt to recreate the old Curia, but it was not the chamber where he had seen Marius and Sulla argue, or heard Cato's voice dominate the discussion. Though he had not thought the loss could touch him, there was a dull pain somewhere deep. All the foundations of his life were being removed and part of him would always want to go back.

He tried to stifle his thoughts as the men with him took seats on the benches. Marius would have berated him for that sort of weakness. The past was comforting because it was safe. It was also dead and gone; there were no mysteries to be found there. Facing the future, with all its uncertainty, took courage and strength. He inhaled deeply of the air in the chamber, smelling the oiled wood and clean plaster.

'Fetch Adàn for me, Ciro. I will need a record of my orders,' he said.

Ciro rose quickly and disappeared out into the sun. Julius looked at the others, and smiled. Octavian, Mark Antony, Brutus and Domitius. They were men he could trust. Men with whom he could begin an empire. Though the future had its fears, it was the place for dreams. He hardly dared think where his path could take him by the end.

'So, gentlemen, it was worth crossing the Rubicon, at least so far. It is a good place to start.'

Adàn came in and took a seat as he gathered his writing materials. He could not resist glancing around the chamber. For him, it was a place of legend, having never known the other. His eyes shone.

'We must find barracks and homes for our men inside the city before tonight,' Julius continued, once Adàn was settled. 'Ciro, that is your task. Domitius, I want every drop of wine the city has to offer to be distributed freely. Get the best price you can, but I want the whole of Rome drunk by midnight. Spread the first taste of our gold into their pouches and tell them I want parties in every street and great house, open to all. Torches on the walls and crossroads. We'll light the city from one end to the other – buy oil and use the Tenth to keep order for tonight, the Third for tomorrow. We must have some sober soldiers to keep the peace.

'Octavian, you will send a century of the extraordinarii to Ostia, to make certain Pompey has left. We've no reason to doubt our informants, but the old fox has been cunning before.'

He paused to think and Mark Antony cleared his throat. 'What about the senators who did not go to Greece?'

Julius nodded. 'They must be courted. They will be the core that gives stability after the elections. Spread the word that they are brave men to have resisted Pompey. Make them all heroes. We will ask for their help in the new administration and give my word they will be safe. We need them.'

'And the elections?' Mark Antony continued. 'I would want to hold them as soon as possible.'

'Then you have the task. Consuls, magistrates, senators, quaestors and praetors for the new regions of Gaul – we must have them all. Begin the notices the day after tomorrow, when the hangovers start wearing off. I will leave the details to you, but I want the posts filled quickly. We will have two consuls to head the Senate, once I have seen who is left among the nobilitas. If they are the men I think they are, they should already be considering the benefits of staying behind.'

A frown crossed his face for an instant. 'Not Bibilus, though. If he is still in the city, I do not want him. The man is not fit for authority of any kind.'

Mark Antony nodded and Adàn scratched on his tablets until Julius noticed.

'Wipe that part clear, Adàn. I do not want every private opinion recorded. It is enough to have it said between us.'

He watched as the young Spaniard ran a callused thumb over the wax square and was satisfied.

'This is a new start, gentlemen. It will take months to build a fleet and I intend to use that time to revise the laws of Rome from the very beginning. When we leave, the city will be peaceful and more secure than we found her – and the laws will apply to all.

They will see that I have kept my word to them. I will begin with a reform of the courts. There will be no more bribery and favours. This is a chance to make the city work as it was meant to. As it did for our fathers.'

He stopped, looking around the echoing chamber and imagining it full once again of the lawmakers and rulers of Rome.

'We have the whole of Gaul to administer. The roads and enclosures there must continue. Taxes must be paid and revenues collected for the public buildings. It will be hard work. I should think our legions in Gaul will be pleased to get the call home when we are ready.' He grinned as he considered the enormity of the task before them.

'When I have a fleet, I will call all but one legion south. Gaul will not rise again this generation, not after us.'

'Will we have enough men to beat Pompey?' Mark Antony said quietly.

Julius glanced at him. 'If every legion in Greece goes over to him, we could be overwhelmed, but we pardoned the men of Corfinium, did we not? The word will spread, even to Greece. Pompey's own men will take that piece of gossip to the legions there. Our people will wonder if they are on the right side in this. I expect many to come to me before the end.' He paused to look around at the men who had come so far with him.

'There can be only one ending between us after we meet in the field. Pompey will never be second to me. I will let it be known that any man who surrenders to my forces will be pardoned and honoured for his loyalty. I will be the symbol of the old Rome against the new and I will have my private letters copied and distributed, begging Pompey to choose exile over the death of Roman citizens.' He grinned suddenly. 'It will drive him mad.'

'Who will rule Rome while you are away?' Mark Antony asked.

Brutus glanced up and his hand gripped the wooden rest tightly. Julius did not look his way.

'You have proved yourself, Mark Antony. I can think of none better to administer Italy while I fight the war in Greece. Stand for the second consul's seat with me. I can trust you to remain loyal for my return.'

Mark Antony stood on shaking legs and embraced his general.

'The gates will be open to you,' he said.

Brutus too rose, his face pale with strong emotion. For a moment, it seemed as if he would speak and Julius turned to him, questioningly. Brutus shook his head and his mouth tightened.

'I must check the men,' he said at last, his voice choked. He walked into the sun and was gone.

Mark Antony looked troubled, decency forcing him to voice his thoughts. 'Did you consider Brutus, sir? He deserves it as much, if not more.'

Julius smiled wryly. 'You will keep Rome in order, Mark Antony. You will respect the law and take satisfaction from the thousand problems each day will bring. However, do not be offended when I say you are not the general I need to beat Pompey in the field. You have different strengths and I'll need Brutus in the battles to come. He has a talent for death.'

Mark Antony flushed, unsure if he was receiving a compliment. 'I think you should tell him that, sir.'

'I will, of course,' Julius replied. 'Now, to business, gentlemen. I want the city to sing tonight. By all the gods, we are home at last.'

Outside, the light of day seemed to claw at Brutus as he came onto the steps. He found himself breathing heavily as he looked over the drifting crowd. If they saw him, they did not respond and he was struck by the image of being invisible to them all, like a ghost. He was almost tempted to call out, just to hear his own voice and break the spell. He felt strangely cold, as if he stood beneath a shadowed arch on stones always hidden from the sun.

'I am owed a little more than this,' he said, his voice a breath. He opened his right hand to find it cramped and yellow with tension. He had not felt the grip tighten as Julius gave Mark Antony everything that mattered in the world. If Brutus had known how the man would become a rival, he would have taken him aside one dark night in Gaul and cut his throat. The picture was a sweet thing in his mind and it brought a righteous anger to the fore. On the Rubicon, he had believed he was needed, that the generals would risk it all together. Julius had spoken to the crowd as if he had come south on his own.

Brutus watched the people of Rome and found their ignorance of his presence was a sort of freedom. He felt bonds fall away and almost staggered in relief and pain. He looked for the boy holding his horse and walked down the white steps, dazed. The crowd melted around him like smoke and in a few moments, he was lost amongst them.

CHAPTER FIVE

Regulus frowned as he saw Brutus appear once more. The silver-armoured figure stood like a statue by the white columns and Regulus shivered, surprising himself. There was something eerie in the general's stillness as he looked over the milling crowd. Even from a distance, Brutus looked pale and Regulus broke suddenly into a fast walk towards him, convinced something was wrong. The path was dense with citizens, but Regulus ignored the shouts of those he sent sprawling, his eyes never leaving Brutus. He saw the general take his horse and swing himself into the saddle without a glance or word for those around him. Fear touched Regulus then. He called out as Brutus dug in his heels, knocking down a young boy who had clustered too close to his hooves.

Brutus did not stop or even turn at the cry. He rode stiffly and his face was bloodless and grim. They passed within feet of each other and Brutus didn't feel the hand grasp desperately for his reins, nor hear his name.

Regulus swore under his breath as the horse clattered by out of reach. He looked up at the senate building and was caught between ordering his men to stop Brutus and finding out what had happened. He had nothing solid to support the feeling of dread that had stolen his peaceful mood. The moment of indecision passed with torturous slowness and Regulus found himself marching up the steps.

He heard their calm voices before he saw the generals of Gaul and Regulus shook his head in confusion. His mind had filled with violent images, but there was Adàn with his tablets and Ciro rising slowly with a questioning gaze.

'What is it?' Julius said.

Regulus hesitated, unwilling to voice what seemed like childish fears. What had he been thinking to allow such flights of fancy? 'I . . . saw Brutus leave, sir. I thought there might be further orders.'

A subtle tension went out of the men as he spoke and Regulus saw Mark Antony too showed strain on his patrician features.

'Join us, Regulus,' Julius said. 'Have one of your men keep order in the forum. You know Pompey as well as anyone and I want you to be part of the planning.'

Regulus felt a weight lift. He had been mistaken and chose not to mention his moment of superstitious fear. Yet as he seated himself he recalled the wildness in Brutus' eyes and decided to seek him out before the day was over. Regulus did not enjoy mysteries, and he had never been a trusting man. With the decision made, he was able to turn to the business of the meeting and the incident slipped from his conscious thought.

Servilia's house had hardly changed in the time Brutus had been away from the city. The three-storey building was clean and well-kept, with a single torch burning over the doorway at all hours of the day and night.

He paid a boy to look after his horse and walked into the main hall, removing his helmet and running a hand through sweat-soaked hair. He stood awkwardly as he announced himself, detached from the empty faces around him. He felt like a spectator in a play, hearing his own breath more loudly than the words of the servants.

She came out in a rush when she heard his name and he

embraced her awkwardly, feeling her stiffen on the instant she came into contact. Her smile vanished.

'What is it? Is there fighting?' she said.

He shook his head and, without warning, tears threatened to humiliate him. 'No. The city is cheering him in the forum. Julius is in the senate building.'

'Then what is it? You're so pale! Come inside, Brutus, and tell me.'

He followed past the stares of clients into the private suite of rooms and sank onto a couch, gazing at nothing. Servilia sat next to him and took his hands in hers. He saw how she had painted and prepared herself, and knowing it was for Julius was almost enough to make him walk out, if his legs would have borne him.

'Tell me,' she said softly.

He was surprised to see a rim of tears on her lashes. He reached up to touch them gently with his thumb and let his hand fall as she flinched from anything that would spoil her perfection. 'I'm leaving, Servilia,' he said. 'I'm free of him.'

Servilia shook her head in confusion, gripping his hand. 'What are you saying?' she demanded.

He grimaced. 'Exactly what you heard me say, Mother. I am done with Julius and he is done with me.'

'Will you tell me what happened?'

'I saw him make Mark Antony first in Rome and it all became painfully clear. Julius was never the man I thought he was. Never. He's played with my loyalty as cleverly as any other of those senate bastards, until we are all working for them, giving our lives for nothing more than their promises and prestige.'

'What does it matter if he honours Mark Antony? The man is no more than competent. There are dozens like him working for Rome. Julius *needs* you. I have heard him say it.'

Brutus shook his head in disgust. 'He doesn't *need* anyone. Just followers. I've done that for too many years and I've been his dog for most of my life. That can end too, like anything else.' He closed his eyes for a moment, overcome by memory and pain.

She reached a hand to his cheek and he flinched away, wounding her.

'Have you thought what you will do, at all?' she said, her voice hardening. 'Have you planned how you will live? Or must a son of mine be reduced to mercenary work and petty theft? How will you eat?'

'I'm a little old to be looking for another life, Mother, don't you think? I'm a Roman general and I know how to train soldiers. There will always be a place for men like me. I'll go as far as I can until I have to work and there I'll stay. I'll build armies for someone else and never see Rome until Julius has gone from her. You may prefer me to stay and wash his feet for the rest of my life, but I will not.'

'You *must* talk to Julius,' she said, her eyes pleading. 'No, let *me* talk to him. You stay here for an hour and I will see him. He loves you, Brutus, as much as I do.'

He rose and she stood with him, not willing to let him go.

'He will hurt you too in the end,' Brutus said softly. 'And he won't even know.'

He tilted his head, watching as tears flowed down her cheeks and spoiled the powder. As he began to step away from her, she reached out with surprising strength and drew him into an embrace. For a long time, she held him in silence and he could feel the wetness of her tears on his throat.

'You are my only son,' she said, at last. 'Did I tell you how proud I was when you stood on the tourney sand and the crowd rose to cheer you? Did I tell you that?'

'You did, and I knew it anyway,' he murmured into her hair. 'You were shining with it, in front of them all.'

'Is there nothing I can say to you? Will you not even give me an hour? It is not such a great thing.'

'Let it go, Mother,' he said, his expression hardening. 'Let me go.'

'Never,' she said. 'You are too precious to me.'

'What a pair of fools we are,' he said. He raised his hand to her face and this time she did not draw back as he smoothed the tears from her. 'In my letters, did I ever say there was a battle where I wore his helmet and cloak?'

She shook her head and he shrugged, looking back into the past.

'They thought they were following him. The legions were tired and starving and in pain, but they followed because they thought he was calling them out for one last charge. He was helpless with his shaking sickness and he could not do it. I led them because I love him more than any other man I have known. He has been with me all my life and we have seen places I would not have believed. We have conquered countries together, and by the gods you should have seen the armies we broke. Enough to fill little Rome twice over, and we went through them.'

'Then why?'

'Because I cannot give my whole life to a man who does not even know what he has been given. He showed how much he valued me with his gift to Mark Antony.'

He clenched his fists at that memory.

'I could have been more, do you understand? If he had died in Gaul, I would have mourned him, but I would have taken his place and cut my own path. I could have done it, Servilia. He and I have something running in our blood that no one else in this feeble city has, not any more. Either one of us could have risen over all of them and accepted no equals – no masters, Servilia. Yet with him, I am a servant. He sends me, I go. He tells me to stay, I stay. Can you imagine how that feels, for me?'

He stroked her hair gently as he spoke, but his eyes were distant and cold.

'I am the *best* of my generation, Mother. I could have ruled. But I had the misfortune to be born to a Rome with Julius in it. I have suffered it for *years*. I have pledged my life to him and he cannot see it.'

She pulled back from him at last and shook her head. 'You're too proud, Brutus. Even for a son of mine you are too proud. You're still young. You could be great and still be loyal to him.'

Temper flushed his cheeks. 'I was born for more than that! In any other city, I could have ruled, don't you understand? The tragedy is that I was born into *his* generation.' He sighed in misery. 'You couldn't know. I have won battles when Julius had already given them up. I have led men when they would have run under any other general. I have *trained* generals for him, Servilia. There are places in Gaul where my silver armour is part of legends. Don't tell me I'm too proud. You were not there.'

His eyes glinted with banked fire.

'Why should I throw my years away for him like so many others? Renius died to save him, and Cabera gave his health because it was Julius asking. Tubruk died to save his wife. They were good men, but I won't go with them across the river, not for him. I have won Gaul for Julius; let that be the end of it. He has had enough from me.' He gave a bitter laugh, which chilled his mother. 'Perhaps I should cross to Pompey and offer him my allegiance. I doubt he would scorn what I could bring.'

'You won't betray Julius,' Servilia said, her eyes dark with horror. 'Even your arrogance wouldn't stretch that far.' For an instant, she thought he might strike her.

'My *arrogance*? Is that what you call it? Well, why not, Mother? Where else in the world is crying out for good Roman generals? Perhaps when Julius comes asking for me, you should tell him he will find me in Greece, on the other side of a battle. Perhaps he would understand then what he has lost in me.'

He detached her clinging hands and smiled at the ravages her crying had made in her face. Her age was no longer concealed and he wondered if he would ever see her again.

'I *am* your son, Servilia, and I do have too much pride to follow him any longer.'

She looked up into his eyes and saw his furious determination. 'He will kill you, Brutus.'

'Such little faith in me, Servilia. Perhaps I shall kill him.' He nodded as if they had come to an end and kissed her hand before walking out.

Alone, Servilia sank slowly onto the couch. Her hands were shaking and she clasped them together, before reaching for a tiny silver bell at her side. A slave girl entered and stood appalled at the destruction of the morning's work.

'Fetch your paints and oils, Talia. We must repair the damage before he comes.'

Brutus guided his Spanish horse through the streets, taking a path that would leave the forum far to the east. He had no wish to meet any of the men he was leaving and the thought of having to speak to them gave him an urgency that cut through his stunned misery.

He rode without care for the citizens and slaves who scurried out of his way. He wanted to leave it all behind and get to the coast where he could buy his way onto a fishing boat or anything else that would take him. The familiarity of the city seemed to mock his decision and every turning brought fresh memories. He had thought he had few ties with the people, but instead of faces he found he knew the calls of vendors, the colours, even the smells of the alleys that led away from the main roads.

Even though he was mounted, hurrying citizens kept pace with him as he rode through their midst, rushing endlessly from place to place in the city. He flowed with them and felt the stares of stall-keepers as he rode stiffly through the arteries of trade. It was all familiar, but still he was surprised when he found he had taken the road that led to Alexandria's shop.

There were ugly memories waiting for him there. He thought of the riots that had left him wounded. Yet he was proud of saving those who could not protect themselves and he sat a little straighter in the saddle as he approached.

He saw her in the distance as he gathered the reins to dismount. Though she was facing away from him, he would have known her anywhere. His hands froze on the high pommel as a man at her side reached around her waist with casual affection. Brutus' mouth pursed in thought and he nodded to himself. It didn't touch him except as a distant pain that something else in his life had ended. He was too numb with a greater loss. Her letters had stopped a long time ago, but somehow he had thought she might have waited, as if her life could only go on while he was there. He shook his head and saw a grubby child watching him from an alley between the shops.

'Come here, boy,' he called, holding up a silver coin.

The urchin came out with a swagger like a dockworker and Brutus winced at the lack of meat on the young bones.

'Do you know the lady who works in this shop?' Brutus asked.

The boy flickered a glance after the couple further along the road, an answer in itself. Brutus did not follow the look, but simply held out the coin.

'Is she doing well?' he asked.

The boy looked cynically at him, eyeing the silver and clearly caught between fear and need. 'Everyone knows her. She won't let me in the shop, though.'

'You'd steal the brooches, I should think,' Brutus said, with a wink.

The boy shrugged. 'Maybe. What do you want for the coin?'

'I want to know if she wears a ring on her hand,' Brutus replied.

The boy thought for a moment, rubbing his nose and leaving a silvery trail on his skin. 'A slave ring?'

Brutus chuckled. 'No, lad, a gold marriage band on the fourth finger.'

The boy still looked suspicious, but his eyes never left the promised reward. At last, he came to a decision and reached for it. 'I've seen a ring. She has a baby at home, they say. Tabbic is the one who owns the shop. He hit me once,' he said in a rush.

Brutus chuckled and let him take the coin. On impulse, he reached into his pouch and brought out a gold aureus. The boy's expression changed the instant he saw it, going from confidence to frightened anger.

'Do you want it?' Brutus said.

The child scrambled away at high speed, leaving Brutus bemused behind him. No doubt the boy had never seen gold before and thought it would mean his death to own such a thing. Brutus sighed. If the local wolves found out he had such a treasure, it probably would. Shaking his head, he put the coin back in the pouch.

'I thought it was you, General,' a voice came.

Brutus looked down at Tabbic as the jeweller strolled onto the road and patted his horse's neck. His bald head gleamed from the forges and white chest hairs tufted over the apron he wore, but he was still the same steady figure Brutus remembered.

'Who else?' Brutus replied, forcing a smile.

Tabbic squinted upwards as he rubbed the horse's muzzle, seeing eyes still red with tears and anger. 'Will you come in and try a drink with me?' Tabbic said. 'I'll have a boy stable this fine mount of yours.' When he saw Brutus hesitate, he went on. 'There's spiced wine on the forge, too much for me.'

He looked away as he asked, making it easy to refuse. Perhaps that was why Brutus nodded and swung a leg over the saddle.

58

'Just the one then, if you can make it strong. I'm going far tonight,' he said.

The interior of the shop was subtly different to how Brutus remembered it. The great forges still stood solidly, a banked fire gleaming red under the grates. The benches and tool racks were new-looking, though the smell of oil and metal was like stepping back into old memories. Brutus breathed in, smiling to himself and relaxing a fraction.

Tabbic noticed the change as he crossed to the heavy iron kettle on the edge of the forge. 'Are you thinking of the riots? Those were black days. We were lucky to get out with our lives. I'm not sure I ever thanked you for helping us.'

'You did,' Brutus replied.

'Draw up a seat, lad, while you taste this. Used to be, it was my winter brew, but it warms a summer evening just as well.' Tabbic ladled steaming red liquid into a metal cup, wrapping it in cloth before handing it over.

Brutus took it gingerly, breathing in the fumes. 'What's in it?' he asked.

Tabbic shrugged. 'A few things from the markets. To be honest, it depends on what I have to hand. It tastes different every year, Alexandria says.'

Brutus nodded, accepting the old man's lead. 'I saw her,' he said.

'You would have done. Her husband came to bring her home just before I saw you,' Tabbic replied. 'She's found a good man, there.'

Brutus almost smiled at the old jeweller's transparent worry. 'I'm not back to pick at old scabs. All I want is to get as far away as I can. I'll not trouble her.'

He hadn't noticed the tension in Tabbic's shoulders until the old man relaxed. They sat in peaceful silence then and Brutus sipped at the mug, wincing slightly. 'This is sour,' he grumbled.

Tabbic shrugged. 'I wouldn't waste good wine on a hot cup. You'll find it has a bite, though.'

It was true that the bitter warmth was easing some of the tightness in his chest. For a moment, Brutus resisted, unwilling to let go of even a part of his anger. Rage was something he had always enjoyed as it flooded him. It brought a kind of freedom from responsibility and to feel it ebb was to face the return of regret. Then he sighed and offered his cup for Tabbic to refill.

'You don't have the face of a man who came home this morning,' Tabbic observed, almost to himself.

Brutus looked at him, feeling weary. 'Maybe I have,' he said.

Tabbic slurped the dregs of his own cup, belching softly into a fist as he considered the response. 'You weren't the sort to wrap yourself in knots the last time I saw you. What's changed?'

'Has it occurred to you that I might not want to talk about it?' Brutus growled.

Tabbic shrugged. 'You can finish your drink and leave, if you like. It won't change anything. You'll still be welcome here.'

He turned his back on Brutus to lift the heavy kettle off the forge and fill the cups once again. Brutus could hear the dark liquid slosh.

'I think it's grown stronger,' Tabbic said, peering into the pot. 'This was a good batch.'

'Have you any regrets, old man?' Brutus asked him.

Tabbic grunted. 'I thought you had something troubling you. I'd go back and change a few things if I could – be a better husband, maybe. If you ever left your mother's tit, there'll be things you wish you hadn't done, but it's not all bad, I've found. A little guilt has made more than a few men live better than they would have done – trying to even the scales before they cross the river.'

Brutus looked away as Tabbic drew up an old bench, wincing as his knees flexed.

'I always wanted a little more than that,' Brutus said at last.

60

Tabbic sipped at his drink, the steam rising into his nostrils. After a time, he chuckled. 'You know, I always thought that was the secret of happiness, right there. There are some people who know the value of a kind wife and children who don't shame you. Maybe they're the ones who had a cruel time of it when they were young; I don't know. I've seen men who had to choose whether to feed the children or themselves each day, but they were content, even then.'

He looked up at Brutus and the man in silver armour felt the gaze and frowned to himself.

'Then there are those who are born with a hole in them,' Tabbic continued softly. 'They want and *want* until they tear themselves to pieces. I don't know what starts the need in a man, or how it's stopped, except for killing.'

Brutus looked quizzically at him. 'You're going to tell me how to find a good woman after this, aren't you?'

Tabbic shook his head. 'You don't come in here and ask me if I have any regrets without a few of your own. Whatever you've done, I hope you can mend it. If you can't, it will be with you a long time.'

'Another refill,' Brutus said, holding out his cup. He knew his senses were being dulled, but he welcomed the feeling. 'The trouble with your rustic philosophy,' Brutus began, tasting the new cup. 'The trouble is that there have to be some of us who want and want, or where would we be?' He frowned then as he considered his own words.

'Happier,' Tabbic replied. 'It's not a small thing to raise a family and provide for them. It might not seem much to armoured generals of Rome, but it earns *my* respect. No poems about us.'

The mulled wine was more powerful than Brutus had expected on an empty stomach. He knew there was a flaw in Tabbic's vision, but he couldn't find the words to make him see it.

61

'You need both,' he said at last. 'You have to have dreaming, or what's the point? Cows raise families, Tabbic. Cows.'

Tabbic looked scornful. 'I've never seen a worse head for drink, I swear it. "Cows", by the gods.'

'One chance you get,' Brutus went on, holding up a finger. 'One chance, birth to death, to do whatever you can. To be remembered. One chance.' He slumped, staring at the red glow of the forge in the growing darkness.

They emptied the kettle down to bitter pulp at the bottom. Brutus had long ceased to move or speak when Tabbic eventually heaved him onto a cot in a back room, still in his armour. At the doorway, the jeweller paused, looking down at the sprawled figure, already beginning to snore.

'My daughters remember me every day,' he said softly. 'I hope you make the right choices, lad. I really do.'

Julius picked a piece of fennel sausage out of his teeth and smiled as he watched the drunken guests become ever wilder as the moon sank towards the horizon. The music too became more frenzied as the wine flowed into the players. The drums and pipes beat out counterpoint rhythms, while the cithara players made their strings jump with blurring fingers. Julius had not heard a single dirge or ballad from them all the time he had been there, and their excesses suited his mood perfectly. The food too was magnificent after soldiers' rations.

The invitation was one of dozens that had been delivered before sunset, but the host, Cassius, was a senator who had remained behind and Julius wanted to cultivate the man. Only the first hour had been spent in conversation, as Julius became reacquainted with the social class of his city. The free wine had been delivered all over Rome and they seemed determined to obey his command to celebrate, becoming increasingly wild as the moon set over the hills.

Julius barely listened to a drunken merchant who seemed to have fully recovered from his initial awe. The man wandered through topics without needing more than the occasional nod to keep him going. While he beamed and talked, Julius eyed the young ladies who had come to the party, not unaware that most of them had appeared only after his own presence became known. Some of them were shameless in their competition for his glance and he had already considered more than one of those to share his bed that night. Their faces were flushed with sexual excitement as the red wine lit them up and Julius found the spectacle mesmerising. He had been a long time in the field and the opportunities for female companionship had been few. Brutus had called it 'scratching his itch' and it had been no more satisfying, on the whole.

In comparison with the camp whores, the beauties of Rome were like a flock of painted birds arrayed for his enjoyment. Julius could smell the mingling perfumes in the air, even over the fennel.

He sensed his companion had stumbled at last to a halt and Julius looked at him, wondering if a question had been asked. He was a little drunk himself, though his wine was cut with water. Since passing through the Quirinal gate, he had felt the intoxication of challenge and sheer pleasure at being back with his people. The wine bore but a little responsibility for his good spirits.

'My brothers in particular will be pleased to see a steady hand on the city after Pompey,' the merchant continued.

Julius let his voice become a background noise as he watched the people around him. Apart from the simple arousal at the thought of bedding one of the Roman women, he wondered if he should be looking for something more than a night. He had once laughed at the suggestion that he needed heirs, but he had been younger then and many of those he called friends had still been alive. The thought sharpened his appraisal of the young women in the crowd, looking for more than a simple turn of leg and thigh,

63

or the quality of the breasts. Given the option, he knew he would prefer a beauty, but perhaps it was also time to think of the connections and alliances of a union. Marriage was one of the powerful counters in the politics of Rome and the right choice could benefit him as much as the wrong one could be wasted.

With a slight gesture, Julius summoned Domitius from another knot of conversation. Senator Cassius saw the movement and came bustling over first, determined that Julius' slightest whim should be met. He had been honoured by the arrival of the general and Julius found the constant attention flattering, as it was intended to be. The man was as slender as a youth and bore himself well amongst the guests. Julius had encouraged him with subtle compliments and felt sure the senator would be one of those returning to the new government. If the others who had stayed were as amenable, Julius thought the elections would go very smoothly indeed. The senate house could well be filled with his supporters.

He had intended to discuss the women with Domitius, but with Cassius there, Julius addressed him instead, choosing his words carefully. 'I have been away for too long to know which of your guests are unmarried, Cassius.' Julius hid his smile by sipping his wine as he saw the senator's interest sharpen.

'Are you considering an alliance, General?' Cassius asked, watching him closely.

Julius hesitated only for a moment. Perhaps it was the excitement he had felt since his return, or part of his sexual interest that night, but he was suddenly certain. 'A man cannot live alone, and the company of soldiers does not meet every requirement,' he said, grinning.

Cassius smiled. 'It will be a pleasure for me to arrange introductions for you. There is only a small selection here, though many are unpromised.'

'A good family, of course, and fertile,' Julius said.

Cassius blinked at the bluntness, and then nodded enthusiastically. He practically shook with the desire to spread the information and Julius watched as he searched for a way to take his leave without being rude.

Cassius found his solution in the slave messenger who entered the main room, moving quickly through the revellers towards Julius. The man was simply dressed and wore his iron ring to show his status, but to Julius' eye he looked more like a bodyguard than a simple messenger. He had been around enough soldiers to know the manner and he felt Domitius prickle at the man's approach, always wary as he had been trained to be.

As if sensing the discomfort his entrance had caused, the slave held up his hands to show he bore no weapons. 'General, I have come from my mistress. She waits for you outside.'

'No name? Who is your mistress?' Julius asked.

The omission was interesting enough to halt even Cassius in the act of slipping back to the other guests. The slave blushed slightly. 'She said you would remember the pearl, even if you had forgotten her. I am sorry, sir. Those are the words she gave me to say, if you asked.'

Julius inclined his head in thanks, quite happy to leave Cassius mystified. He felt a stab of guilt that he had not taken the time to see Servilia before the sun had fallen on his first day.

'I will not need you, Domitius,' he said, and 'Lead the way,' to the slave, following him outside and down the main stairs of the house. The doors were opened for him and he was able to step straight into the carriage waiting outside.

'You did not come to me,' Servilia said coldly as he smiled at her. She had always looked beautiful in moonlight and for a moment he was content just to drink her in.

'Enough of that, Julius,' she snapped. 'You should have come as you promised. There is a great deal to discuss.'

Outside the snug confines of the carriage, her driver snapped his whip over the horse and the carriage trundled away over the stone streets, leaving the painted women of Rome to discuss the general's interest without him.

CHAPTER SIX

The summer dawn came early, though it was grey and cold as Brutus shoved his head into a water barrel in the public stables. He came up gasping and rubbed his face and neck vigorously until the skin reddened and he began to feel a little more useful. He had taken a risk by staying a night in the city. Julius would have used the time to strengthen his grip on Rome. His men would be guarding the gates and Brutus knew he might have to bluff his way through. He had considered hiding the armour, but the horse bore a legion brand and legionaries would be far more interested in a horse thief than a general out for a morning ride.

He used the mounting block to jump into the saddle, the horse skittering sideways as his weight came on. Brutus took up the reins with unusually tight hands. Tabbic's company had been like balm on an open wound, but he should have ridden straight for the coast.

Grim-faced, he threw a coin to one of the stable boys and clattered out onto the street. The closest gate was the Quirinal, but he headed instead for the Esquiline in the east. It was a traders' gate and would be busy even at the early hour with countless merchants and labourers. With a little of the gods' luck, the guards there would pass him with just a glance and a wave.

As he trotted stiff-backed through the city, Brutus felt himself sweating out the poisons of the night before. It was hard to imagine the optimism he had felt on coming into the city with the others. Even the thought of it brought his anger sliding back to the surface. His glare sharpened unconsciously and those who saw his expression kept their eyes downcast until he had gone.

There was one place in the world where he would be welcome, though he had said it half in bitter jest to his mother. Why should he weigh an old friendship in the balance of his life? It mattered nothing to Julius, after all. That had at last become clear. There would be no day when Julius turned to him and said, 'You have been my right hand since the beginning,' and gave him a country, or a throne, or anything approaching his worth.

He passed through the Esquiline gate with an ease that mocked his earlier worry. Julius had not thought to warn the guards and Brutus returned their salutes without a sign of tension. He would go to Greece. He would go to Pompey and show Julius what he had lost in passing him over.

With Rome behind, Brutus rode fast and recklessly, losing himself in the sweat and risk of hard ground. The exertion felt like tearing free, an antidote to the lingering effects of the mulled wine. The familiarity helped to keep his mind numb at first as he fell into the rhythms of a cavalry scout. He did not want to begin the endless self-examination he knew would follow his decision to leave Julius. Though it loomed over him like winter, he leaned forward in the saddle, concentrating on the ground and the sun on his face.

The sight of a marching column interrupted his reverie, snapping him back to a world where decisions had to be made. He yanked the reins to bring the horse to a skidding stop, both front hooves flailing for a moment in the air. Was it possible that Julius had sent men ahead to cut him off? He watched the snake of legionaries in the distance. They carried no flags and Brutus hesitated, turning his mount in a tight circle. There were no armed forces in the south that had not been dragged into the threatening war. Pompey's legion had gone with him and he thought the Gaul veterans were safe in the city. Yet he had delayed a night in Tabbic's shop. Julius could well have sent them out to hunt him down.

The thought brought back his anger and pride. He ignored his first impulse to circle around the column and approached warily, ready to kick his mount to a gallop. Julius would not have sent infantry, he was almost certain, and he saw that the column had no horses with them, not even for officers. Brutus felt a deep relief at that. He had trained the extraordinarii to hunt a single rider and he knew they would show no mercy to a traitor, even the man who had led them in Gaul.

The train of thought made him flinch unconsciously. He had not had time to consider what those left behind would think when they heard. They would not understand his reasons. Friends who had known him for years would be appalled. Domitius would not believe it at first, Brutus thought bitterly. Octavian would be crushed.

He wondered if Regulus would understand. The man had betrayed his own master, after all. Brutus doubted he would find sympathy there. The rabid loyalty that Regulus had shown to Pompey had been transferred in one violent jolt to his new master. Regulus was a zealot. There could be no half measures for him and he would hunt Brutus tirelessly if Julius gave the order.

Oddly, it was most painful to imagine Julius' face as he heard the news. He would assume there had been a mistake until Servilia spoke to him. Even then, Brutus knew he would be hurt and the thought made his knuckles whiten on the reins. Perhaps Julius would grieve for him in his sanctimonious way. He would shake his balding head and understand that he had lost the best of them through his own blindness. Then he would send the wolves after him. Brutus knew better than to expect forgiveness for his betrayal. Julius could not afford to let him reach Pompey.

Brutus glanced behind him, suddenly afraid he would see the extraordinarii galloping in his wake. The fields were quiet and he took a better grip on his emotions. The column was a more immediate threat, and as he came closer he saw the pale ovals of faces glancing in his direction and the distant din of a sounding horn. He dropped his hand to his sword and grinned into the wind. Let the bastards try to take him, whoever they were. He was the best of a generation and a general of Rome.

The column came to a halt and Brutus knew who they were the moment he saw their lack of perfect order. The road guards had been sent to the old Primigenia barracks, but Brutus guessed these were the stubborn ones, finding their own way to reach a general who cared nothing for them. Whether they realised it or not, they were natural allies and a plan sprang full-grown into his head as he rode up to them. An inner voice was amused at how his thoughts seemed to come faster and with more force the further away he was from Julius. He could become the man he should have been without that other's shadow.

Seneca turned in panic as the cornicen sounded a warning note. He felt a cold thumping in his chest as he expected to see the ranks of Caesar's horsemen riding down to punish him.

The relief of seeing only a single rider was something like ecstasy and he could almost smile at how afraid he had been. Ahenobarbus' talk of oaths had troubled him and he knew the men shared something of the same guilt.

Seneca narrowed his eyes in suspicion as the rider approached the head of the column, looking neither right nor left as he passed the standing ranks. Seneca recognised the silver armour of one of Caesar's generals and on the heels of that came a fear that they were being surrounded once again. Anything was possible from those who had spun a wheel around them and made them look like children.

He was not the only one to have the thought. Half the men in the column jerked their heads nervously, looking for the tell-tale dust that would reveal the presence of a larger force. The ground was dry in the summer's heat and even a few riders should have given themselves away. They saw nothing, but dared not cease their searching after the harsh lesson they had been taught outside Corfinium.

'Ahenobarbus! Where are you?' Brutus called as he reined in, his dark eyes examining Seneca for a moment and moving on, dismissing him from notice.

Seneca coloured and cleared his throat. He did remember this one, from the negotiations in Caesar's tent. The mocking smile was always his first expression and the eyes had seen more war and death than Seneca could imagine. On the high-stepping Spanish gelding, he was a forbidding figure and Seneca found his mouth was dry from fear.

'Ahenobarbus! Show yourself,' Brutus shouted, his impatience growing.

'He is not here,' Seneca replied.

The general's head snapped round at his words and he wheeled his horse with obvious skill. Seneca felt a little more of his confidence drain away under the man's stare. He felt as if he was being judged and found wanting, but the initiative seemed to have been lost from the moment they sighted the rider.

'I do not remember your face,' Brutus told him, loud enough for them all to hear. 'Who are you?'

'Livinius Seneca. I do not . . .'

'What rank do you hold to lead these men?'

Seneca glared. Out of the corner of his eye, he could see a few of the guards turn their heads to hear his answer. Against his will, he flushed again. 'Pompey will decide how to reward my loyalty,' he began. 'At the moment . . .'

'At the moment, you may be a few hours ahead of Caesar's legions once he discovers you have left the barracks,' Brutus snapped. 'I assume command of these cohorts by right of my rank as general of Rome. Now, where are you heading?'

Seneca lost his temper at last. 'You have no right to give orders here!' he shouted. 'We know our duty, sir. We will not return to Rome. Ride back to the city, General. I don't have time to stand here and bicker with you.'

Brutus raised his eyebrows in interest, leaning forward to take a better look. 'But I'm not going back to Rome,' he said softly. 'I'm taking you to Greece to fight for Pompey.'

'I won't be tricked by you, General. Not twice. I saw you in Caesar's tent with Ahenobarbus. Are you telling me you have turned traitor in a day? That's a lie.'

To Seneca's horror, the silver-armoured general swung a leg over his saddle and vaulted lightly to the ground. He took three paces to stand close enough to feel the sun's heat off his armour and his eyes were terrible.

'You call me a liar and a traitor and expect to live, Seneca? I am no man's servant but Rome's. My sword has killed more men than stand here for the Senate and you dare to use those words to *me*?'

His hand caressed the hilt of his gladius and Seneca took a step back from his rage.

'I have told you where I'm going,' Brutus continued relentlessly. 'I have told you I will fight for Pompey. Don't question me again, boy. Be *warned*.' The last words were a harsh whisper, before the light of madness fell from his gaze and his voice changed to a more normal tone. 'Tell me where you are heading.'

'The coast,' Seneca said. He could feel a fat line of sweat run down his cheek and did not dare to scratch the itching trail.

Brutus shook his head. 'Not with two cohorts. There aren't fishing boats enough for all of us. We'll need to head for a port and hope there is a merchant vessel Pompey didn't manage to burn. Brundisium is two hundred miles south and east from here. It's large enough.'

'It's too far,' Seneca said instantly. 'If they send the extraordinarii . . .'

'You think you'll be safer with your back to the sea? Then you're a fool. We need a ship and there must be some trader still working.'

'But if they send the riders?' Seneca said desperately.

Brutus shrugged. 'I trained those men. If Caesar sends the extraordinarii out against us, we'll gut them.'

As Seneca stared at him, Brutus walked calmly back to his horse and leapt into the saddle. From that lofty position, he looked down at Seneca and waited for further opposition. When none came, he nodded to himself, satisfied.

'Brundisium it is. I hope your lads are fit, Seneca. I want to be in Brundisium in ten days or less.'

He turned his horse to face the south and waved on the first rank of guards. To Seneca's private fury, they turned to follow him and the column began to move once more. As he matched his pace to the ranks around him, Seneca realised that he would spend the next week staring at the rear of the horse.

In the soft light of morning, Julius paced the length of Marius' old entrance hall, watched by the generals he had summoned. He looked exhausted and pale, a man made older by the news.

'It's not just that the betrayal will hurt our standing with the remaining senators,' he said. 'We could keep that quiet if we say he was sent away on some private task. But he has with him the knowledge of our strengths, our weaknesses, even our methods of attack! Brutus knows the details of every battle we fought in

Gaul. He practically invented the extraordinarii as we use them. He has the Spanish secret of hard iron. Gods, if he gives all that to Pompey we will be beaten before we begin. Tell me how I can win against that sort of knowledge.'

'Kill him before he can reach Pompey,' Regulus said into the silence.

Julius glanced up, but did not reply. Domitius frowned in bemusement, wiping clammy sweat from his face. His thoughts were still heavy from a wild party in a house off the forum. The sweet smell of drink was on all of them, but they were steady. Domitius shook his head to clear it. They could not be discussing Brutus as an enemy, he told himself. It was not possible. They had taken salt and pay together, shed blood and bound each other's wounds. They had become generals in hard years and Domitius could not shake the thought that Brutus would return with an explanation and a joke, with a woman on his arm, perhaps. The man was practically a father to Octavian. How could he have thrown that away for his stupid temper?

Domitius rubbed his callused hands over his face, looking at the floor as the angry conversation continued around him. They had come into the city only the morning before and already one of them was an enemy.

Mark Antony spoke as Julius resumed his pacing. 'We could spread the word that Brutus is a spy for us. That would undermine his value to the forces in Greece. Pompey won't be willing to trust him as it is. With just a little push, he might reject Brutus altogether.'

'How? How do we do that?' Julius demanded.

Mark Antony shrugged. 'Send a man to be captured on the Greek coast. Give him your ring or something, to show he spies for us. Pompey will torture it out of him and then Brutus will lose his value.'

Julius considered this in angry silence. 'And who shall I send to be tortured, Mark Antony? We are not discussing a beating. Pompey would take hours over him to be certain he has the truth. I've seen him work on traitors before. Our spy would lose his eyes to hot irons and with them the hope of surviving the ordeal. Pompey will be thorough with him. Do you understand? There'll be nothing left but meat.'

Mark Antony did not reply and Julius snorted in disgust, his sandals clicking as he walked the marble floor. At the furthest point from them, he paused and turned. He couldn't remember when he'd last slept and his mind was numb.

'You are right. We must lessen the coup of having Brutus go over to them. Pompey will trumpet it far and wide if he has any sense, but if we can sow distrust, Pompey could well waste our *precious* general. Do the men know yet that he has left?'

'Some will, though they may not guess he has gone to Pompey,' Mark Antony replied. 'It is beyond belief for any of us. They would not think of it.'

'Then a loyal man will suffer the worst agonies to undo this betrayal,' Julius said grimly. 'It is the first of what he will owe us. Whoever we send cannot know the truth. It would be burnt out of him. He must be told that Brutus is still one of us, but playing a subtle game. Perhaps we can have him overhear the secret, so he does not become too suspicious. Who can you send?'

The generals looked at each other reluctantly. It was one thing to order men into a battle line, but this was a dirty business and Brutus was hated in that room.

Mark Antony cleared his throat at last. 'I have one who has worked for me in the past. He is clumsy enough to get himself caught if we send him alone. His name is Caecilius.'

'Does he have family, children?' Julius asked, clenching his jaw.

'I don't know,' Mark Antony said.

'If he has, I will send a blood-price to them when he is clear of the city,' Julius said. It did not seem enough.

'I will summon Caecilius here, with your permission?' Mark Antony asked.

As always, the final order and the final responsibility rested with Julius. He felt annoyed that Mark Antony would not take the burden with a few easy words, but Brutus would have and Brutus had turned traitor. It was better to be surrounded by weaker men, perhaps.

'Yes. Have him come here. I will give the orders myself,' Julius confirmed.

'We should send an assassin with him, to be certain,' Octavian said suddenly. All eyes turned to him and he faced them without apology. 'Well? Regulus has said what we are all thinking. Am I the only other one who will say it? Brutus was as much my friend as any of you, but you think he should live? Even if he tells Pompey nothing, or this spy weakens his position, he must be killed.'

Julius took Octavian by the shoulders and the younger man could not look him in the eyes. 'No. There will be no assassins sent by me. No one else has the right to make that decision, Octavian. I will not order the death of my friend.'

At the last word, Octavian's eyes blazed with fury and Julius gripped him harder.

'Perhaps I share the blame for Brutus, lad. I did not see the signs in him until he had gone, though they trouble me now. I have been a fool, but what he has done changes nothing, in the end. Whether Pompey appoints him general or not, we must still go to Greece and fight those legions.' He paused until Octavian looked up. 'When we do, if Brutus is there, I shall order that he is kept alive. If the Gods kill him with a spear or an arrow, then my hands are clean. But if he lives through the war to come, I will not take his life until I have spoken to him, perhaps not even then. There is too much between us to think otherwise. Do you understand?'

'No,' Octavian said. 'Not at all.'

Julius ignored the anger, feeling it himself. 'I hope you will in time. Brutus and I have shared blood and life and more years than I can remember. I will not see him dead at my order. Not today, for this, nor at any other time. We are brothers, he and I, whether he chooses to remember it or not.'

CHAPTER SEVEN

Seeing Brundisium without the usual bustle of merchant and legion galleys was strange for such a key port in the south. When Brutus crested the last hill with the exhausted guard cohorts, he was disappointed not to find anything larger than a lobster boat tied to the quays. He tried to remember if he knew the quaestor of the port and then shrugged to himself. Whatever small contingent of Roman soldiers was stationed there would not be able to interfere. Outside of Rome herself, there was nothing in the south to trouble them.

The guards followed him down to the port, ignoring the stares and pointing fingers of the workers there. It was a strange feeling for most of them, but Brutus was familiar with hostile territory and fell back into the attitudes of Gaul without really thinking about it. The sight of soldiers would have brought a sense of peace and order only a short time before, but with a looming civil war they would be feared as much as any other band of scavengers. It was unpleasant to see the faces of those who stepped aside for the two cohorts of guards. Even with all his experience, Brutus could not ignore a subtle discomfort and found himself growing increasingly irritable as he led the column through to the import buildings on the docks. He left them there in the sun as he dismounted and strode inside.

The quaestor's clerk was on his feet, arguing with two burly men.

All three turned to face him as he entered and Brutus saluted lazily, knowing his arrival had been the subject of their debate.

'I need food and water for my men,' he said abruptly. 'See to that first. We will not trouble you for long, gentlemen, so put yourselves at ease. I want to find a ship to take me to Greece.'

As he mentioned his destination, he noticed the clerk's eyes flicker to a piece of parchment on his desk and then back up, guiltily. Brutus smiled, crossing the room. The dockworkers moved to block him and he dropped a casual hand onto his sword.

'You are unarmed, gentlemen. Are you certain you'd like to try me?' he asked.

One of the men licked his bottom lip nervously and would have spoken, but his companion tapped him on the arm and they both edged away.

'Very good,' Brutus said to them, letting his hand fall. 'Now then; food, water and . . . a ship.'

He reached down to the desk and gripped the clerk's bony hand, moving it firmly off the papers. Brutus took the sheaf and scanned them quickly, letting each fall until he came to one midway through the pile. It was a record of a legion galley that had landed at the port just the day before to replenish its fresh-water barrels. There was little detail to be gleaned from it. The captain had returned from the north according to the record and set sail after only a few hours in Brundisium.

'Where was he heading?' Brutus demanded.

The clerk opened his mouth and closed it, shaking his head.

Brutus sighed. 'I have a thousand men standing on your docks. All we want is to leave here without trouble, but I am not patient today. I can give the word to set fire to this building and anything else you value. Or you can just tell me. Where is this galley?'

The clerk bolted for a back room and Brutus heard the clatter of his sandals as he rushed up a flight of stairs. He waited in uncomfortable silence with the two dockworkers, ignoring them.

A man wearing a toga that had seen better days came down the steps behind the clerk. Brutus sighed at the quaestor's appearance.

'Provincials,' he murmured under his breath.

The man heard him and glared. 'Where are your letters of authority?' the quaestor demanded.

Brutus stared at him, focusing on a food stain on the man's robe until he flushed.

'You have no right to threaten us here,' the quaestor blustered. 'We are loyal.'

'Really? To whom?' Brutus asked. The man hesitated and Brutus enjoyed his discomfort before he went on. 'I have two cohorts going to join Pompey and the Senate in Greece. That is my authority. Your clerk was good enough to show me the records and a galley passed through here yesterday. Tell me where they were heading.'

The quaestor fired a poisonous glance at his hapless servant before coming to a decision. 'I spoke to the captain myself,' he said reluctantly. 'He was on patrol off Ariminum when the message reached him to come in. He was going to land at Ostia.' He hesitated.

'But you told him that Pompey had already left,' Brutus said. 'I imagine he would want to join the fleet by sailing around the south coast, meeting them halfway. Does that sound like the conversation you remember?'

The quaestor stiffened at the tone. 'I had no new orders for him. I believe he may have put to sea to deny the value of his ship to . . . rebel forces.'

'A sensible man,' Brutus said. 'But *we* are loyal to Pompey, sir. We need that galley. I expect such a thoughtful captain would have told you his next port in case the right person came asking. Somewhere further south, yes?'

As he spoke, he watched the clerk's eyes and saw them shift

guiltily. The quaestor was a far better gambler than his servant, but he caught the glance and the muscles stood out on his jaw as he considered what to do.

'How do I know you are not with Caesar?' he asked.

The question had a far greater effect than the quaestor could have intended. Brutus seemed to grow slightly, making the little office feel smaller and oppressively hot. The fingers of his right hand drummed for a moment on the silver breastplate, the noise startlingly loud in the silence.

'Do you think I have a secret password for you?' he snapped. 'A special sign to show I am loyal? These are complicated days. There is nothing more I can say to you, except this. If you do not tell me, I will burn this port to the ground and you in it. I will have my men bar the doors and listen to you scratching at them. That is all I offer.' He stared the quaestor down, knowing there would be no hint of a bluff in his eyes.

'Tarentum. He said he would make a landing at Tarentum,' the clerk said, breaking the tension.

The quaestor was visibly relieved to have had the decision taken from him, but he still raised his fist in reaction, making the clerk flinch. Brutus looked for some hint that they were lying, but he was satisfied and then ignored the pair, calculating quickly. Tarentum was a port he could reach in just a few hours of hard riding across an isthmus the galley would have to sail around.

'Thank you, gentlemen, your loyalty will be rewarded,' he said, watching their fear and confusion as they digested his words. He supposed it would be much the same all over Roman lands very soon, as the question of allegiance became more and more important. Civil war engendered a distrust that had already begun to eat at the foundations of their world.

Outside in the sun, Brutus watched the cohorts fill their water-skins from a well in reasonable order. He was tempted for a moment of wildness to have them burn the port as he had threatened. After all, it could well be one of those Julius would use to send a fleet to Greece. He did not give the order, preferring not to send a column of smoke to show their position. There was also a little pride in wanting Julius to make the crossing as soon as he could. Brutus needed just a few months to establish himself in Pompey's forces and after that Julius could come and be welcome.

'Seneca, there's a legion galley heading for Tarentum. I shall ride there. Follow me when you have found provisions.'

Seneca looked at his men and his mouth became a firm line.

'We have no silver to pay for food,' he said.

Brutus snorted. 'This is a port without ships. I'd say the warehouses are full of whatever you need. Take what you want and come after me as fast as you are able. Understood?'

'Yes, I suppose . . .'

'Yes, *sir*,' Brutus snapped. 'Then you salute as if you know what you're doing, understood?'

'Yes, sir,' Seneca replied, saluting stiffly.

Brutus led his mount over to the well and Seneca watched irritably as he moved amongst the guards with an ease Seneca could only envy. He saw Brutus make some comment and heard their laughter. The general was a hero to men who had done nothing more than keep road forts safe for Rome. Seneca felt a touch of the same admiration himself and wished he could find a way to start again.

As he watched Brutus mount and trot out onto the southern road, Seneca felt the men look to him for orders once more. He realised that few others of his generation had the chance to learn their trade from a veteran of Gaul. He approached the group around the well, as he had seen Brutus do. It had not been his practice to mix with them and they glanced at each other, but then one of them handed him a waterskin and Seneca drank.

'Do you think he'll find us a galley, sir?' one of the men asked.

Seneca wiped his mouth. 'If he can't, he'll probably swim across, towing us behind him,' he replied, smiling to see them relax. It was such a small thing, but he felt more satisfaction in that moment than he could remember from all his tactical drills.

Brutus galloped across the scrub grass of the southern hills, his eyes steady on the horizon for his first glimpse of the sea. He was hungry, tired and itching under his armour, but if the galley was making only a brief stop at Tarentum, he had to push himself on. He did not dwell on what he would do if the captain had gone. The longer Brutus was on land, the more the danger increased, but there was no point worrying. In his years in Gaul, he had learned the mental trick that allowed him to ignore what he could not control and bring his full weight onto levers he could move. He cleared his mind of the problem, concentrating on making the best speed over rough ground.

It surprised him that he felt responsible for the guards. He knew better than Seneca what would happen if Julius caught them. They had all taken solemn vows not to fight for Pompey and Julius would be forced to make an example. No doubt he would shake his head at the horror of it all before giving the order, but Brutus knew Julius was a general first and a man only rarely, when it profited him. The guards were inexperienced and out of their depth in the power struggle. They could very well be ground into bloody ash between the two sides, casualties of the civil war before it had properly begun. The ship had to be there, waiting for them.

It was easy to dream of the future as Brutus rode, taking the most direct route through rocky fields and valleys. If he arrived at Pompey's camp with two cohorts, he would have influence from the first moment. Alone, he would have to rely on Pompey's whim as to whether he was given a command. It was not a pleasant thought. Pompey would not dare to trust him at first and Brutus knew there was a chance he would find himself in the front line as a foot soldier. The silver armour would draw Julius' Tenth like moths and he would never survive the first battle. He needed Seneca's men even more than they needed him, perhaps.

The countryside to the south of Rome was a far cry from the lush plains of the north. Small farms survived by growing olives and thick-skinned lemons on twisted wooden skeletons, all wilting in the heat. Thin dogs yapped around his horse whenever he slowed and the dust seemed to coat his throat in a thick layer. The sound of hooves brought people out from the isolated farmhouses to watch suspiciously until he was off their land. They were as dark and hard as the ground they worked. By blood, they were more Greek than Roman, the remnants of an older empire. No one called to him and he wondered if they ever thought of the great city to the north. Somehow, he doubted it. Rome was another world to them.

He stopped at a small well and tied the reins to a stunted tree. He looked for some way of reaching the water, his gaze resting on a tiny house of white stone nearby. There was a man there, watching him from the comfort of a rough bench by his door. A small dog sat and panted at his feet, too hot to bark at the stranger.

Brutus glanced impatiently at the sun. 'Water?' he called, holding cupped hands to his mouth and miming drinking.

The man regarded him steadily, his eyes taking in every detail of the armour and uniform. 'You can pay?' he said. The accent was hard, but Brutus understood him.

'Where I am from, we do not ask payment for a few cups of water,' he snapped.

The man shrugged and, rising, began to move towards his door.

Brutus glared at his back. 'How much?' he demanded, reaching for his purse.

The farmer cracked his knuckles slowly as he considered. 'Sesterce,' he said at last.

It was too much, but Brutus only nodded and dug savagely amongst his coins. He passed one over and the man examined it as if he had all the time in the world. Then he disappeared into the house and returned with a stitched leather bucket and a length of rope.

Brutus reached for it and the man jerked away with surprising speed. 'I'll do it,' he said, walking past him towards the dusty well.

His dog struggled to its feet and wandered after him, pausing only to bare yellow teeth in Brutus' direction. Brutus wondered if the civil war would touch these people. He doubted it. They would go on scratching a living out of the thin soil and if once in a while they saw a soldier riding past, what did that matter to them?

He watched the farmer bring up the bucket and hold it for the horse to drink, all at the same infuriatingly slow speed. At last, it was passed to Brutus and he gulped greedily. The cool liquid spilled down his chest in lines as he gasped and wiped his mouth. The man watched him without curiosity as he took his waterskin from the saddle.

'Fill this,' he said.

'A sesterce,' the man replied, holding out his hand.

Brutus was appalled. So much for honest country farmers. 'Fill the skin or your dog goes down the well,' Brutus said, gesturing with the sagging bag.

The animal responded to his tone by pulling its lips back in another miserable show of teeth. Brutus was tempted to draw his sword but knew how ridiculous it would look. There wasn't a trace of fear in the farmer or his mongrel and Brutus had the unpleasant suspicion that the man would laugh at the threat. Under the pressure of the open hand, Brutus swore and dug out another coin. The skin was filled with the same slow care and Brutus tied it to his saddle, not trusting himself to speak.

When he was mounted, he looked down, ready to end the conversation with some biting comment. To his fury, the farmer was already walking away, winding the rope around his arm in neat loops. Brutus considered calling to him, but before he could think of anything, the man had disappeared into his house and the small yard was as still as he had found it. Brutus dug in his heels and rode for Tarentum, the water sloshing and gurgling behind him.

As he headed out of the valley, he caught his first scent of a salt breeze, though it was gone as soon as he had recognised it. It was only another hour of hard riding before the great blue expanse came into sight. As it always had, it lifted his spirits, though he searched in vain for a speck that would mean the galley was out. Seneca and his men would be marching behind him and he did not want to have to dash their hopes when they finally arrived at the port.

The land grew harsher before the coast, with steep tracks where he was forced to lead his horse or risk falling. In such an empty place, he thought it safe enough to remove his armour and the breeze cooled his sweat deliciously as he strode panting up the last slope and looked at the little town below.

The galley was there, at the end of a thin pier that looked as rickety as the rest of the place. Brutus thanked all the gods he could think of and patted his mount's neck excitedly before taking a long drink from the skin. The land seemed to suck the moisture out of him and the sun was fierce, but he didn't care. He mounted again with a whoop and began to trot down the hill. Pompey would understand his value, he thought. Letters would be sent to all the legions mentioning the Gaul general who had chosen honour and the Senate over Caesar. They knew nothing of his past except what he would tell them and he would be careful not to boast or to reveal his old mistakes. It would be a new start, a new life and, eventually, he would go to war against his oldest friend. The sun seemed darker at that thought, but he shrugged it off. The choice was made.

The sun was going down by the time Seneca arrived with his two cohorts. The bustle aboard the galley had increased as the soldiers and crew made ready to sail. It was a relief to see Brutus talking to an officer on the wooden pier and Seneca realised how much he had been depending on the man.

He halted the cohorts, painfully aware of the scrutiny of the galley crew as they coiled ropes and heaved the last of the fresh-water barrels up the planking and into the hold. This time, his salute was as perfect as he could make it and both men turned to him.

'Reporting, sir,' Seneca said.

Brutus nodded. He seemed angry and a glance at the galley captain told Seneca he had interrupted an argument.

'Captain Gaditicus, this is Livinius Seneca, my second in command,' Brutus said, formally.

The captain didn't bother to look his way and Seneca felt a surge of dislike amidst the pleasure at his new title.

'There is no conflict here, Captain,' Brutus continued. 'You were heading for Ostia to pick up men such as these. What does it matter if you cross to Greece from here?'

The captain scratched his chin and Seneca saw the man was unshaven and looked exhausted.

'I was not aware that Caesar had come back to Rome. I should wait for orders from the city before . . .'

'The Senate and Pompey gave you orders to join them, sir,' Brutus interrupted. 'I should not have to tell you your duty. Pompey ordered these men to Ostia. We would be with him now if we had not been forced to cut across country. Pompey will not be pleased if you delay my arrival.'

The captain glared at him.

'Don't flaunt your connections, General. I have served Rome for thirty years and I knew Caesar when he was just a young officer. I have friends in power I can call on.'

'I don't recall him mentioning your name when I served with him in Gaul,' Brutus snapped.

Gaditicus blinked. He had lost that particular contest. 'I should have known from the armour,' he said slowly, looking at Brutus in a new light. 'But you're going to fight for Pompey?'

'I am doing my duty. Do yours,' Brutus said, his temper fraying visibly. He had had about enough of the opposition that seemed to spring up at every stage of this endless day. He looked at the galley rocking gently in the waves and ached to be leaving the land behind.

Gaditicus swept his eyes over the column of men waiting to board. All his life he had followed orders and though it smelled wrong, he knew he had no choice.

'It will be tight, with so many. One storm and we'll go down,' he said, with the last of his resistance.

Brutus forced a smile. 'We'll manage,' he said, turning to Seneca. 'Take them on board.'

Seneca saluted again and went back to his men. The pier shivered underfoot as the column approached and the first ranks began to clamber up the gangplank onto the wide deck.

'So why will you be fighting against Caesar? You did not say,' Gaditicus murmured.

Brutus glanced at him. 'There is bad blood between us,' he replied, with more honesty than he had intended.

Gaditicus nodded. 'I wouldn't like to face him myself. I don't think he has ever lost a battle,' he said thoughtfully.

Brutus responded with a flash of anger, as Gaditicus had hoped he would. 'The stories are exaggerated,' he replied.

'I hope so, for your sake,' Gaditicus said.

It was a little revenge for having been forced to back down, but he did enjoy Brutus' expression as he looked away. Gaditicus remembered the last time he had been in Greece, when a young Caesar had organised attacks on the camp of Mithridates. If Brutus had seen that, he might have thought twice before choosing Pompey as his master. Gaditicus hoped the arrogant general in his silver armour would be taught a harsh lesson when the time came.

When the last of the guards were on board, Gaditicus followed them, leaving Brutus alone on the dock. The sun was setting in the west and he could not look in the direction of Rome. He took a deep breath as he straightened and stepped onto the deck, gently moving on the swell. He had left them all, and for a while he could not speak for the memories that overwhelmed him.

The ropes were coiled and hung as the galley moved out onto the waters, the chant of the slaves at their oars like a lullaby beneath his feet.

CHAPTER EIGHT

The city was closed while the voting went on, the gates sealed. The crowd on the Campus Martius were raucous and cheerful, as if electing consuls was a public holiday rather than a rejection of Pompey and his Senate. The sun beat on them all and there were many enterprising young families charging a bronze coin to enjoy the shade of an awning they had carried out to the great field. The smell of sizzling meat, the conversations, the laughter and the shouts of vendors all mingled into a sensual cacophony that felt very much like life and home.

Julius and Mark Antony climbed the steps up to the platform the legion carpenters had made for them. They stood together in white togas trimmed with purple. Julius wore the laurel wreath of a successful general, the dark leaves fresh-bound in gold wire. He was rarely seen in public without it, and there were some who suspected the attachment was in part to conceal the balding head beneath.

The Tenth were polished and shining as they stood guard on the new consuls. They held their spears and shields ready to signal for silence, but Julius was content simply to stand there, gazing over the heads of the vast crowd.

'The last time I was made consul in this place, I had Gaul ahead of me,' he said to Mark Antony. 'Pompey, Crassus and I were allies. It seems more than a lifetime ago, now.'

'You did not waste the time,' Mark Antony replied and they shared a smile as they remembered those years. As always, Mark Antony had a polished look, as if he were carved from the best Roman stone. It sometimes irked Julius that of all the men he had known, Mark Antony looked most like a consul should look. He had a strong face and a powerful frame, coupled with a natural dignity. Julius had heard that the women of Rome fluttered and blushed in his wake.

Julius looked up at the taller man, knowing he had made the right choice in having him stand to lead the Senate. He was loyal, but not as Regulus was loyal, where a careless word might send death on quick wings to an enemy. Mark Antony cared deeply for the old Republic and would make it live while Julius went to Greece. He had shown a disdain for wealth that only those born to it could assume. He could be trusted and it was a relief for Julius not to have to worry that his precious city would suffer while he was away. Of all men, he knew the fragility of apparent peace, and the lessons of Milo and Clodius had not been lost on him, even as far away as Gaul. Rome needed a steady hand and peace to grow. Pompey could never have given that to her.

Julius smiled wryly, knowing he too was not the man to run a peaceful city. He had loved the conquest of Gaul and Britain too much to consider spending his latter years in sleepy debates. He cared enough for the law when he could change it to match his vision, but the tedious administration that followed would be a slow death. Like Pompey, he preferred to tear through the skin of comfort and find new places, new struggles. It was somehow fitting that the last lions of Rome should be facing each other at last. If Pompey had not been there to try him, Julius thought he would still have found himself handing power to Mark Antony, at least for a while. He would have gone to conquer Africa, perhaps, or to follow the footsteps of Alexander to the strange lands he had described in the east.

'Shall we address our people, Consul?' he said, signalling a centurion of the Tenth.

The soldiers around the platform crashed their spears into their shields three times and then there was silence and they could hear a breeze whisper across the field of Mars. The crowd stood respectfully, before some of them started cheering and the rest joined in before Julius could speak. The sound was carried upwards by thousands of throats as the sun beat down.

Julius looked at Mark Antony and was surprised to see there were tears in his eyes. He did not feel it so strongly himself, perhaps because his mind was already on the campaign to come, or because he had been a consul once before. He envied his companion, understanding without sharing the emotion.

'Will you speak first?' he asked softly.

Mark Antony inclined his head in thanks for the offer. 'After you, General. They are yours.'

Julius rested his hands on the wooden rail his men had made for him, exactly at the height he wanted. He took a deep breath and flung out his voice.

'The centuries have voted today and their mark has been made in the soil of our fathers. Mark Antony and I stand before you as consuls and Pompey will hear your voices even in Greece. He will know his absent Senate has been replaced. That is our message to him. No man is more than Rome, no single man more than those I see before me today.'

They cheered and stamped to show their pleasure at his words.

'We have shown that Rome can survive the loss of those who care nothing for her. We have shown that there can be law without corruption. Have I fulfilled my promises to you?'

They roared incoherently in what may have been agreement.

'I have,' Julius told them, firmly. 'The courts have been cleansed and bribery punished openly. There will be no secret deals in my city by those who rule. The workings of the Senate will be published each day at sunset. Your votes are a loan of power, but only to work in your interests, not to press you down. I have not forgotten this, as some have. Your voices sound with me each day and I will take their echoes to Greece to pass them to the armies there.'

The crowd had grown denser at his feet as those behind pressed forward. He wondered how many had come to the Campus to vote in the new posts. They had been standing since dawn and would be hungry and thirsty, their few coins gone to the vendors long before. He resolved to be brief.

'The legions in Greece will have heard us here, today. They will wonder how they support a man who has lost the faith of the people who matter most. There can be no authority without your voice. You have made some of your number into magistrates and quaestors, yes, and even into consuls!' He waited through the response, smiling down at them. 'We have accomplished much in these last few months. Enough that when I leave I know that my city will be safe and at peace. I will take your votes to Pompey and I will tell him that he has been rejected by the citizens who raised him. I will serve my city faithfully and Mark Antony will be your hands, your eyes, your *will* in the Senate.'

As they cheered, he brought Mark Antony forward with a hand on his arm.

'And now they are yours,' he murmured.

Without a glance back at the massed citizens, he walked down the steps to the ground and left Mark Antony alone to face them. It was important that the new consul be seen to act on his own and Julius walked away to where his horse was held ready. He took the reins from a legionary of the Tenth and threw a leg over the saddle, sitting straight and taking a deep breath of the cool air.

As Mark Antony began to speak, Julius shook his head in gentle amusement. Even the man's voice was perfect. It rang over the crowd and if Julius knew the words had been hammered out in late-night sessions, it did not show.

'To stand here, my brothers, with the city behind us, is the reason I was born . . .' Julius heard, before the voice was lost on the breeze. The extraordinarii formed up around him and they cantered towards the gates of Rome.

Julius watched in silence as two of the strongest men dismounted and walked towards the plates of bronze and wax that sealed the city. They carried heavy hammers and as they raised them Julius heard the noise of the citizens swell like the sound of distant waves. With a crack, the plates fell away and the gates swung open for him to ride back to his work. The elections had given him legitimacy, but he would still have to take his legions over a hostile sea to Greece. For a moment, the thought that he would face Brutus there made him falter. It was a pain he crushed ruthlessly whenever it surfaced. The gods would grant him another meeting with his oldest friend, or they would not. He would lead his army to triumph, or he would be killed and his path would end. He could not allow himself to weaken, having come so far.

'It is just a step,' he said to himself as he crossed the line of the walls.

Servilia was there at the old house of Marius when Julius arrived, sweating and dusty from his ride through the sweltering city. She looked fresh in comparison, but in the bright light of day, her age was ever more visible. She had always been a woman for the evening. He busied himself with the saddle for a moment while he collected his thoughts, unwilling to launch straight into another difficult discussion. The crowds of Rome were far easier to handle than Servilia, he thought.

A slave brought him a cup of iced apple juice and Julius emptied it as he walked into the rooms where she waited. Water could be heard from the fountain in the courtyard and the inner rooms were arranged as squares around an open centre so that the scent of plants and flowers was always in the air. It was a beautiful home and it was rare now that he imagined the voice of Marius echoing through it.

'Consul once again,' he said to her.

Her eyes softened for an instant, touched by his pride. There had been precious little softness from her since the night Brutus had left. At first, Julius had thought she felt guilt for her son's betrayal, but he should have known better.

'Your wife will be pleased, Caesar,' Servilia said.

Julius sighed and saw her eyes flash with anger. He went to her and took her in his arms. 'But I came here to you, Servilia, as I said I would. Pompeia is at the estate to give me an heir. Nothing more than that. We have discussed this enough, don't you think? The granddaughter of Cornelius Sulla is the best match I could have found to give me a son. He will have the blood of two noble families running through him. One day, the boy will lead Rome after me.'

Servilia shrugged and he knew the hasty marriage still festered within her.

'You were the one who warned me first that I would want a son, Servilia,' he reminded.

She snorted. 'I know that, but I also know the part men think with. You are not a breeding bull, Julius, for all your boasting. Oh yes, I've heard your drunken soldiers talk about your stamina. What a joy it was to hear how many times you ploughed her in a single night.'

Julius whooped with laughter. 'You cannot hold me responsible for my soldiers!' he said. 'You should know better than to listen to such things.' He took her by the shoulders, his amusement obvious. 'I am here; does that tell you nothing? Pompeia will be mother to my children, that is all. I will not tell you there is no pleasure in fathering them. The girl is *extremely* well-proportioned . . .'

Servilia pushed him away.

'I have seen her,' she said. 'Pompeia is beautiful. She is also witless, which I suspect you missed while you were gazing at her breasts.'

'I wanted health and strength, Servilia. As the breeding bull, I will provide the wit for my children.'

'You are a goat, at least,' she said and he laughed again.

'A goat who is consul for the second time, Servilia. A goat who will rule.'

His humour was infectious and she could not resist him. Gently, she slapped his face to interrupt his mood.

'All men are fools around women, Julius. If you leave her out in that estate for too long without you, there will be trouble.'

'Nonsense, she will pine for me. After a touch of Caesar in the night, all women . . .'

She slapped him again, with a little more force. 'You chose for beauty and children, but keep a close eye on that one. She is far too pretty to be left alone.'

'I will keep her away from the young men of Rome, of course. Now, enough of this, Servilia. As consul, I demand food and the best wine from the cellar. I have to go to Ostia later to see the new keels and I'm up at dawn tomorrow to take the auspices with Mark Antony. It will be a good year for Rome, I can feel it. There will be lightning tomorrow as the earnest priests look for signs.'

Servilia sighed. 'And if there isn't?'

'Domitius will come and report he has seen some. That has always worked in the past. The priests won't argue. We will have a year of good fortune, regardless.'

He stepped away from her and she ached to be held as strongly again. For all his laughing dismissal of his new wife, he had not shared Servilia's bed for some weeks and the last time was almost a requiem for the closeness she remembered. There had been little hunger in him then; not for her. She swallowed her pride in his presence, but the marriage had hurt.

Yet he was with her, as he said, and his wife was out of the city with no one but slaves for company. Servilia had seen passion become friendship before. She knew she should be easing into that state, as she had once done with Crassus. But the slightest touch from Julius or a kiss would make her remember riding together in Spain and sitting at the feet of Alexander's statue in the first glow of new love. It was too painful.

A slave entered and bowed to Julius before speaking. 'Master, there are visitors at the gate,' he said.

'Excellent,' Julius replied, turning to Servilia. 'I asked Domitius, Octavian and Ciro to bring their promotion lists to me.' He seemed uncomfortable for a moment and the amusement faded from his face. 'We have had to make changes since Brutus left for Greece. Will you sit in on the discussion?'

'No, you don't need me here,' Servilia replied, raising her chin. Had she been summoned only to be ignored? Even for a leader of Rome, Julius was capable of the most appalling breaches of courtesy. It was more than possible that he thought the brief exchange was enough to fulfil his obligations to her. She folded her arms with slow care, and he looked at her then, seeing the irritation. His eyes lost their distracted blankness and she could almost feel the full force of his attention.

'I should have kept the afternoon for you,' he said, taking her hands. 'Shall I send them away, Servilia? We could take horses out to the racetrack, or sit by the Tiber and enjoy the sun. I could teach you to swim.'

It was an effort not to fall under the charm of the man. Despite all that had happened between them, Servilia could still feel the glamour he cast.

'I can already swim, Julius. No, you see your men and go to Ostia. Perhaps you will still have a chance to visit your young wife tonight.'

He winced at that, but they could both hear the clatter of his

97

officers as they came into the main house. His time for her was coming to an end.

'If there were two of me, it would not be enough for all I have to do,' he said.

'If there were two of you, you would kill each other,' she retorted, as Domitius came into the room. He beamed at seeing Servilia and she acknowledged him with a smile before excusing herself. In a moment, only her fragrance remained in the air and Julius was busy welcoming the others and calling impatiently for food and drink.

In her own house, Servilia relaxed, the soft footsteps of her slaves hardly interrupting her thoughts.

'Mistress? The man you wanted is here,' her slave announced.

Servilia rose from her couch, her gold bracelets chiming gently in the silence. The slave retired quickly and Servilia regarded the man she had summoned with careful interest. He was not richly dressed, though she knew he could mimic any one of the classes of Rome if he chose to.

'I have another task for you, Belas,' she said.

He bowed his head in response and she saw that he had grown bald on the crown. She remembered when he had worn his hair down to his shoulders in heavy blond locks and she grimaced at the unfairness of it. Age touched them all.

'I am playing Dionysus for three more days,' he said without preamble. 'The performance has been described as sublime by those who know the theatre. After that, my time is yours.'

She smiled at him and saw to her pleasure that he was still a little in love with her. It may have been that he saw her through a gauze of memory, but he had always been faithful in his adoration.

'It will not be difficult work, Belas, though it will take you out of the city for a while.'

'Out? I do not like the towns, Servilia. The peasants would not know a fine play by Euripides if it ran around them shouting vulgar obscenity. I haven't left the city for almost twenty years and why would I? The world is here and there are some who come to every performance that has a part played by Belas, no matter how small.'

Servilia did not laugh at his vanity. Though he claimed a genius as yet unrecognised, he could be a hard and cunning man and he had been reliable in the past.

'Not even the towns, Belas. I want you to watch an estate outside the city for me, a woman there.'

Belas took in a sharp breath. 'Is there a tavern near this place? Surely I am not required to lie in stinking ditches for you? Dionysus should not be reduced to such a level.'

'There is no tavern, my fox, and I suspect you have already guessed the place I will send you. As I remember the play, Dionysus would lie anywhere for a few good pieces of gold as well.'

Belas shrugged and his face changed subtly, his features a mask for the man within. 'It can only be this new wife of Caesar's. The whole city is talking of the girl. No courtship, I noticed, or poems bought from the writers of such lines, not for him. He must have spent her weight in gold, judging by the estate her father is suddenly looking at buying.'

He watched her closely as he spoke and could not resist smiling smugly as her face showed the accuracy of his chatter.

'It has been a month since the hasty ceremony and still no announcement of a swelling belly,' he went on. 'Did he not sample her before the wedding? Pompeia comes from a fertile family and I have been waiting for the happy news and more free wine to drown our envy. He may be bald under those leaves, but he has had a daughter before, so perhaps she is barren?'

'You are a malicious little gossip, Belas, did I ever tell you?' Servilia replied. 'He is not bald yet and not every marriage is blessed with children from the first night.'

'I have heard he tries valiantly, though. Stallions have done less with mares in heat, from what I . . .'

'Enough, Belas,' she said, her expression growing cold. 'An aureus a week, until the army leaves for Greece. Will you tell me you can do better in a playhouse somewhere?'

'Not better than the payment, but my public will forget me. I may not get work as easily afterwards. They are fickle, you know, in their affection and prices have risen with all the gold Caesar brought from Gaul. Two gold pieces a week would keep me alive long enough to find work, when you are finished with old Belas.'

'Two it is, but I will want your eyes on that house at all times. I do not want excuses from you, or one of your wild stories about gambling games that dragged you in against your will.'

'My word is good, Servilia. You have always known that.' His tone was serious and she accepted it.

'You have not said what I am looking for,' he went on.

'She is very young, Belas, and the young can be fools almost as much as the old. Watch she does not stray or be tempted by some fine boy in the city.'

'And your interest in this, my beautiful queen? Could it be that you are hoping she will be tempted? Perhaps I should put temptation in her path for her to stumble over. Such things could easily be arranged.'

Servilia bit her lip as she thought, before shaking her head. 'No. If she is a fool, it will not come through me.'

'I am curious to know why you would spend gold on another man's wife,' Belas said, tilting his head as he watched her reactions. To his astonishment, spots of colour appeared on her cheeks.

'I . . . will help him, Belas. If to be useful is all I can be to him, then I will be useful.'

At her words, his face softened and he approached her, taking her in his arms. 'I have been as hopeless, once or twice. Love makes fools of great hearts.'

Servilia pulled free of the embrace, touching at her eyes.

'Will you do it then?'

'Of course, my queen. It is done, as soon as I put the mask of beloved Dionysus back in the box and the crowds have sighed their last at my lines. Would you like to hear the climax? It is a rare piece.'

She glanced in gratitude at him for the chatter that smoothed over the moment of sadness. 'Let me summon the girls, Belas. You are always better when there are pretty women listening to you,' she said, relaxing now that their business was over.

'It is my curse to have them inspire me,' he said. 'May I choose a favourite when I am done? An actor of my quality must be rewarded.'

'Just one, Belas,' she said.

'Two? I thirst for love, Servilia.'

'One,' she said, 'and a cup of wine for the thirst.'

Caecilius shivered as the cold sea spattered over the bows of the tiny boat in the darkness. He could hear the hiss and slap of waves, but on the moonless night it was as if he were floating through absolute darkness. The two rowers never spoke as they guided the craft and only the stars glimpsed through drifting cloud kept them on course for the Greek shore. The sail had been brought down some time before and though Caecilius was no sailor, he guessed the act had some significance.

'In my favour, two knives and an assortment of Greek coinage, value as yet unestablished at current prices,' Caecilius murmured to himself. One of the rowers shushed him between strokes and Caecilius went on in silence with his mental list. In times of discomfort, he had found that it helped him to see his way more clearly if he could take the most formless of situations and add a little structure.

'A gold ring of Caesar's tied into a pocket of a good leather belt. A pair of stout sandals with wool to pad the feet against blisters. A little food in case I have to hide for a few days. Salt and oil to add taste to the food. A waterskin that appears to have a small leak.'

These were the things he had brought to spy on Pompey's army, he thought miserably. It didn't seem like a great deal in the circumstances. As another spray of cold water crossed his seat, Caecilius took a better grip on his plummeting morale.

'A fine mind, a good knowledge of Greek that can pass as a peasant, at least. Sharp eyes. Experience and some wisdom picked up along the way.'

He sat a little straighter in the boat as he listed those accomplishments, feeling better. After all, he had been recommended for the task and Caesar would not have sent a fool. All he had to do was gauge the strength of the legions and the numbers of galleys Pompey had assembled. With his Greek, he thought he would probably get work in one of the camps until it came time each month to head back for the coast and deliver his reports. Eventually, whoever came to meet him would tell him the task was finished and he could jump in and be carried back home.

'Will it be you coming for me?' he whispered to the closest oarsman.

The man hissed an angry reply before he had even finished his question. 'Keep your mouth shut. There are galleys in the water around here and voices carry.'

It was not much of a conversation and Caecilius tried to settle back and ignore the water that seemed to delight in leaping over the bows and greeting him like an old friend. No matter how he tried to shelter himself, another splash would find him and work its way into his most intimate crevices.

'On the other side,' he thought to himself, 'I have a right knee that hurts whenever I put weight on it. Two fingers that ache when it rains. A strong desire not to be here. I do not know what I will be facing and there is a chance that I will be captured, tortured and killed. And surly companions who care nothing for my troubles.'

As he finished his list, both rowers paused at some instinct and sat absolutely motionless in the boat. Caecilius opened his mouth to whisper a question, but the nearest pressed a hand over his face. Caecilius froze and he too looked around into the darkness, his ears straining.

Somewhere in the distance he could hear the soft hiss of waves on a pebble beach and he thought that was what had stopped their progress. Then, from the dark, he heard creaking and a noise like fish leaping from the water. He squinted into the blackness and saw nothing at first, until a moving shadow loomed up on them, a white flower of foam at the bow.

Caecilius swallowed painfully as the little craft began to rock in the swell from the galley. As it closed on them, he could see the huge oars that dipped into the water and hear the muffled thumping of a drum somewhere close. The galley was going to smash them into splinters, he was sure of it. It seemed to be heading right at them and he knew he did not have the courage to sit and let the keel slice through the boat, taking him down along the slick green spine to be thrown out nicely bloody for the sharks. He began to stand in panic and the oarsman gripped his arm with the casual strength of his profession. A brief, silent struggle ensued before Caecilius subsided. The galley was a towering black mountain over them and he could see the dim light of lanterns on the deck above.

His companions lowered their blades into the water with infinite care, using the noise of the galley's passage to hide their own. With a few strong pulls, they were out of range of the crushing keel and Caecilius swore the galley oars had passed over his head on the upsweep. It was a moment of pure terror to imagine them coming down on the boat, but the oarsmen knew their business and the galley moved on without an alarm being sounded.

Caecilius realised he had been holding his breath and panted in the bow as the two men resumed their steady stroke without a word. He could imagine their scornful glances and once again went through his lists to calm himself.

It seemed forever before they brought in the oars once again and one of the men leapt out into the surf to hold the bobbing craft steady. Caecilius looked down at the black water and clambered out with enormous care, causing the man in the water to swear softly with impatience.

Finally, he was clear of the boat, with gentle waves up to his waist and cold sand pressing between his unseen toes.

'Good luck,' one of the men whispered, giving him a gentle push to start him on his way.

Caecilius turned and his companions seemed already to have vanished. For an instant, he thought he heard the sound of their oars and then they were gone and he was alone.

CHAPTER NINE

Pompey enjoyed the warmth of the sun on his armour as he waited, his horse whinnying softly to itself. The parade ground at Dyrrhachium had been built after his arrival in Greece and the walls and buildings enclosed a vast yard of hard red clay. The breeze lifted bloody swirls of the dust and overhead, seabirds called mournfully to each other. Three shining legions stood to attention in his honour, their ranks stretching into the distance. Pompey had completed his inspection and wished Caesar could see the quality of the men who would end his pretension to rule Rome.

The morning had passed with pleasurable swiftness as Pompey watched their formal manoeuvres. The cavalry units were particularly impressive and he knew Caesar could not match more than a quarter of their number. Pompey had thrilled to see them gallop the length of the great yard in perfect formation, wheeling at a signal and sending stinging swarms of spears to destroy the practice targets. These were the men who would win Rome back from the usurper. Caesar was just the name of a traitor to them and Pompey had been warmed by the earnest support of their commanders as they gave their oaths of loyalty.

Ten legions had marched across Greece to join the evacuated Senate on the west coast and he had found them well-led, disciplined men with high morale. He basked in their indignation at his having been forced from their home city. There was no political weakness to be found in the legions of Greece: he had given the order and they had come. They were hungry to meet the enemy and Pompey had been amused to find that the reports from Gaul had rankled with these professional soldiers. They relished the chance to destroy the vanity of Caesar's veterans, feeling it to be unjustified arrogance. They were good men with whom to go to war.

The quality of the Greek forces helped to diminish the constant irritation Pompey faced from the senators and their families. More than once he regretted bringing them at all, despite the weight of law they gave his position. They complained about the water, claiming it loosened their bowels; about the heat, about their accommodation in Dyrrhachium and a thousand other small gripes. Few of them appreciated how little use they were to Pompey now that he was in the field. Instead of giving him a free rein, they sought to influence his decisions and remain a force in an area for which they were poorly suited. Pompey had been tempted to ship them to one of the Greek islands for the duration. Only the fact that such a decision might undermine his authority prevented him giving the order.

Every eye was on him as he kicked his Spanish charger into a gallop and raced towards the target. He felt the warm Greek air whistle past his ears, and the thunder of hooves merged into a drumming vibration that heightened his concentration. The bag of straw sewn into the likeness of a man seemed to grow, and he thought he could see every stitch of the thread that held it together.

With the lines of soldiers watching, it had to be perfect, but he did not make a mistake. As the spear left his hand, he knew it would strike. The eyes of professional men followed the path of the spear and there were many who knew it was good before the straw figure jerked, twisting around with the impact. They cheered and Pompey raised his hand in salute, breathing hard. His face was pouring with sweat and his right shoulder ached terribly, answered by a blooming spot of pain in his gut. He had felt muscles tear as he released, but that did not matter. Romans respected strength and the demonstration would give them pride in their commander.

Pompey turned and rode along the line of men, noting their fierce faces and discipline. Only their commanding officer, Labienus, met his eyes and saluted as Pompey reined in.

'I am pleased with them, Labienus,' Pompey said, loud enough for the legionaries to hear. 'Dismiss them to eat, but not too much on each plate. I want them lean and hungry.' His voice dropped to a more conversational tone. 'Accompany me to the temple, General. There is much still to discuss.'

'Yes, sir,' Labienus replied. His sharp eyes noted how Pompey favoured his right arm, but it would be disrespectful to mention it if Pompey chose not to. Labienus was pleased to see no sign of discomfort on Pompey's flushed face. The Dictator was a hard, proud man and he cut a fine figure on a horse, even at his age. 'They are always hungry, sir,' Labienus added. 'They will not disappoint you.'

'No they will not,' Pompey told him grimly. 'They will scatter Caesar's raptores like seeds on the wind.'

Labienus bowed his head in response, his eyes cast down. It was no hardship to show honour to such a man. What he had seen of Pompey had impressed him since his arrival. The Dictator carried his authority with an ease and dignity the men respected. Labienus knew the legionaries were confident and in truth many would welcome the chance to fight against a traitor. Greece had been peaceful too long for some, especially those who hoped for a bright career. As the lowest spear-carrier knew well, war brought promotion far faster than peace. The very least of them would be hoping to make his name against Caesar, to become a centurion and a respected member of the officer class.

Pompey waited while Labienus mounted his own gelding and

was pleased to find nothing to fault in the man or his manner. The general was physically unremarkable, with hair shaved close to his head and dark eyes in a face of hard planes. His record was excellent and Pompey had felt no qualms about including him in his councils. There was a solidity to Labienus that he appreciated, almost an antidote to the poisonous intrigues of the Senate. Officers such as he could be found in every port and city that bowed its head to Roman law. They took no bribes, nor wavered in their loyalty. Their iron discipline kept posts for years, and when they went to war, they knew no equals in the field. They were the hard bones of Rome. Pompey nodded to Labienus, showing his pleasure.

Under that benign eye, Labienus gave the order and the lines of men dissolved as they fell out to head for the barracks. The smell of hot food was already wafting through the air and Pompey remembered Labienus would be as hungry as they were after such a long morning. He would have the best meats brought for the general. Labienus would understand the compliment without more having to be said.

As they rode towards the temple Pompey had taken as his base, Labienus cleared his throat. From experience, Pompey knew the man would not speak without permission. He was a fine example to his men.

'Speak, General. Tell me what is on your mind,' Pompey said.

'I would like to send a galley to watch Ostia, with your permission. If we know when they sail, we will be prepared to receive them. Our fleet could very well sink the enemy ships before they are even in sight of Greece.'

'You would regret that, Labienus, I imagine? It would deprive us both of the chance to beat him here,' Pompey replied.

Labienus lifted his shoulders slightly. 'A little, sir, but I would not ignore a chance to end it, even so.'

'Very well, use my seal on the orders, but tell the captain to stay well clear of the coast. I have a spy in the port there to tell me when Caesar assembles his legions. We will not be surprised by them.'

'I expected as much, sir,' Labienus said. The two men glanced at each other and both smiled.

The temple of Jupiter in Dyrrhachium had nothing like the opulence of the one in the forum in Rome. It had been built for Greek gods before its current role and Pompey had chosen it for its space and central location rather than any religious significance. Nonetheless, it seemed fitting to have the head of the pantheon watch his preparations and Pompey had noticed his servants and soldiers were subtly awed by their surroundings. There was no coarse language heard within its walls and it was rare that their voices were raised above murmurs. Pompey had made a large donation to the temple priests and it came as no surprise that they approved his choice. Jupiter Victor was a military god, after all.

Leaving their horses in the hands of legion grooms, both men strode inside through the high white columns. Pompey paused for a moment on the threshold, his eyes watching for signs that the men within were not busy at their work.

The air of quiet bustle was exactly as he had left it that morning. More than two hundred officers, clerks and slaves were there to administer his new legions and the clacking sound of hurrying sandals echoed in the space. Pompey had brought in heavy tables for his maps and at each of those were senior officers, their heads bent as they made marks and discussed the positions. Silence spread as they stood stiffly to salute. Pompey returned the gesture and the work resumed without ceremony.

Labienus gave his helmet and sword to a waiting slave and Pompey ordered food brought for them as they walked down the central aisle together. The main map had been hung on the wall and Pompey went straight for it, already considering the problems of the campaign. As tall and wide as a man, it was painted onto squares of soft calfskin, smoothed to velvet with pumice stones. The whole of Italy and Greece lay there, rendered in perfect colour and detail.

Pompey checked his hands were free of dirt and touched the key ports of the western coast of Greece.

'I would appreciate your views, Labienus. If the fleet does not stop Caesar, he will have hundreds of miles of coast to choose for his landing, north and south. If I gather our army in any one place, he can avoid the area we control and establish his camps in perfect safety. Yet even with fifty thousand men, I cannot guard every single mile of Greece.'

Labienus looked up at the map, his hard face resembling a man at prayer.

'We must assume all seven of his legions survive the gauntlet of our ships,' Labienus said. 'It is not likely, but we must plan for it. They will need a huge amount of supplies each day and he will not be able to wait for us to come to him, unless he lets them starve. I have found that food and water win battles as readily as strength of arms.'

'I have prepared,' Pompey replied. 'Dyrrhachium will be our main store. The city is bursting with grain.' He expected a compliment and was surprised when Labienus frowned.

'Perhaps it would be better not to leave such a resource in one single town. I do not say it can be done, but if he were able to cut us off from Dyrrhachium, where would we be? Eleven legions need even more meat than seven.'

Pompey called a clerk and dictated an order. In the months since their first meeting, he had come to realise that Labienus had a mind for such details and a quick grasp of the problems of a long campaign. Simply gathering eleven legions in one place caused immense difficulties of supply. Labienus had first come to his attention as he had created lines from the farms and cities of

110

Greece into the west. As far as Pompey knew, not a single man had been short of rations from the first month. It was an awesome achievement.

'If he avoids our fleet and lands in the east,' Labienus continued thoughtfully, 'he will have been at sea for more than a month and be running low on fresh water. His men would have to march hundreds of miles just to reach us. If he were not given to the sort of innovation you have described, I would ignore the east completely. Far better for him to make for one of the main ports in the west, though our galleys are swarming here. Dyrrhachium in the north, Apollonia or Oricum would be my estimate. I would bet on those three, or some stretch of the coast in between. He will not want to be at sea longer than he has to, with our galleys ready to attack.'

'Of those, which would be your choice?' Pompey asked.

Labienus laughed, a sound like chopping wood that disappeared as quickly as it came. 'I can only guess at his choice, sir. If I were running his campaign, I would choose Oricum, knowing your legions will be spread around the cluster of ports further north. At least then I would not have to fight on two fronts.'

The sound of loud footsteps interrupted them and Pompey looked down the length of the temple, his good humour evaporating. Brutus.

Having one of Caesar's most trusted men come over to him should have been a cause for rejoicing, Pompey knew. When Brutus had stepped ashore with his cohorts, the Greek legions had buzzed with the news and excitement. He had even saved the loyal members of the road guards from Caesar's anger and the younger soldiers walked in awe of the Gaul veteran. Brutus had given up a great deal to risk his life with Pompey and he deserved to be honoured. If it were only so simple.

Pompey watched coldly as Brutus strode up the central aisle towards him. The silver armour had been burnished till it glowed.

111

He saw Brutus had removed his sword as ordered and took a deep breath as the general came close. He could feel Labienus' eyes on him, noting his reaction even as he tried to mask it.

Brutus saluted. 'I am at your orders, sir,' he said.

Pompey frowned at him, unable to remember if he had arranged a meeting, but unwilling to admit such a thing in front of either man. There had been a time when his mind was as sharp as anyone's in Rome, but age had taken the edge off his memory as much as his physical strength. His shoulder seemed to ache more fiercely as a reminder. Some of this irritation could be heard in his tone as he replied.

'I have decided not to confirm your command of the Fifth legion, Brutus. Your cohorts will make up the numbers there and you will accept the orders of the Legate Selatis. I will watch you closely and if you do well . . . if I find you loyal, you will be quickly rewarded. You are dismissed.'

Not a trace of disappointment showed on Brutus' face. It was almost as if he had expected the answer.

'Thank you, sir,' he said, saluting and spinning on his heel.

Pompey saw that every eye in the temple followed the silver general as he left and he sighed to himself. The man was a thorn in his side, but he was also a legend. 'What would you do with that one, Labienus?' he said. 'Would you trust him?'

Labienus hesitated. He was far less comfortable speaking of other officers than he was of the sweep of tactics or the difficulties of supply. As Pompey turned to him, he spoke. 'No more than you have, sir, though I would be ready to give him a legion as soon as I was sure of him. He is . . . a most interesting officer. I have never seen a better swordsman. The legionaries seem to revere him and his experience suggests he is capable of leading well under your command. If he has fallen out with Caesar, as he claims, he will strive to prove your trust.'

'That is the heart of the problem, Labienus. If he has been

thrust upon me by some stratagem of Caesar's, he could do as much damage as another legion on their side in the right place. A key charge withheld, a deliberate withdrawal at a crucial point, a sudden move to block my reserves. Any of those things could lose me the war.

'If I could only be *certain* of his loyalty, I would honour and parade him in that flashy silver armour. I could not have hoped to command one of Caesar's own generals. I could use him, Labienus. As it is, I dare not even trust the information he brings. I'd rather be ignorant than misled into a disaster.'

'It is better to be cautious at this point, sir. When he kills the first of Caesar's soldiers, we will know he is loyal. Or I will have him taken.'

The two men met each other's eyes and Pompey nodded, accepting the suggestion.

The food arrived on silver plates and Pompey made sure Labienus took the best of what was offered. They ate standing by the map, continuing to discuss the problems of the campaign. Long after the plates were empty, they were still talking and the sun was sinking towards the horizon before it was time for Pompey to visit the angry old men of his Senate once more.

Brutus buckled on his gladius as he walked outside into the sun, leaving Labienus and the old fool to cook up their plans on their own. The pair of them suited each other, he thought. If there had ever been a spark of life in Labienus, it had been dried out on the stove of his years in Greece, and Pompey had lost his courage with his youth.

He glanced behind him and grunted as he caught sight of the two men Labienus had assigned to watch his movements. At first, he had accepted their presence, telling himself that he would have done the same. How could they trust a general of Gaul who had been Caesar's right hand for so many years? As the months passed and Pompey had remained aloof, the injustice of his situation had begun to fester more and more. Brutus had a greater knowledge of Pompey's enemy than any man alive and he knew he could be the key to destroying him. Instead, his suggestions were received almost with insolence by Pompey's clerks. Brutus had begun to doubt they even passed on the majority of his messages. It was a bitter irony and the constant shadow of Labienus' men irritated him more than usual that afternoon.

He grimaced as he walked, knowing they would be trotting behind him. Perhaps it was time to make them breathe a little harder than usual for their pay. He knew Dyrrhachium well enough after spending three months stationed in the barracks there and for once he was willing to ignore the inner voice that told him to bide his time until he was trusted. On that day, he was suddenly sick of it and as he turned a corner he burst into a run, accelerating across the street under the surprised gaze of a cart driver and his oxen.

Brutus dodged down an alleyway and raced to its end without looking back. That was one thing Renius had taught him the last time he had been in Greece. In the first moments of flight, looking back can only slow you down. You *know* they are there, following you.

He took two more corners at high speed and his legs were warming nicely. He was as fit as any of the soldiers in the barracks with the constant training and he felt as if he could run all day. An open door beckoned and Brutus charged straight through a strange house, coming out into a street he did not know. He didn't stop to see if they were still following him, but pounded on for half a mile of twisting roads until he was sure he had lost them.

They would report it to the cold-hearted Labienus, he was certain, though it would earn them a flogging. The general was not cruel, but he enforced his orders to the letter and Brutus did not envy the pair. Pompey would certainly be told and his suspicions aroused. Perhaps a patrol would be sent out to comb the streets. Brutus panted lightly as he considered his position. At best, he had an hour before he was captured. Labienus was nothing if not efficient and it would not take much longer to close the net. Brutus grinned, knowing there was only one place worth visiting in such a short period of freedom. He took his bearings quickly and loped off, his sandals beating the red dust of the city in a rhythm he could keep up for miles.

Once, he thought he saw running legionaries in the distance, but Brutus kept a street between them and they never came closer. Sweat drenched his hair, but his lungs were still drawing well by the time he made his way to the centre of the city and the garden courtyard where he knew he would find the daughter of Caesar; a pretty bird in a cage.

Like the Senate themselves, Julia had no real role to play in the months of waiting for Caesar to build a fleet and cross. Brutus had seen her on the arm of her husband in the first few weeks after his arrival, but as the work had increased for Pompey, she had been left to her own devices. It had been a strange thing to be introduced to her in Pompey's offices, so far from Julius' estate. On that first meeting, Brutus had only managed a few polite words, but he thought he had caught a sparkle beneath her formality. Pompey's slaves had painted and clothed her in jewels exactly as she had once predicted. For Brutus, the mixture of cold reserve and heavy perfume was deeply exciting, a warning and a challenge.

When he had first seen the garden where she sheltered from the heat of the afternoon, he had noted the entrances almost idly. He knew Pompey remained at the temple until evening and then went on to one of his dull meetings with the senators. Apart from a few personal slaves, his wife was often left practically alone.

Brutus guessed Pompey would have soldiers somewhere near her, but as he looked through the gate to the cool inner courtyard, no one else was visible. His heart beat faster at the danger of it. Pompey knew he had met Julia before through her father. It would not take a great deal for him to become suspicious of something more than a casual acquaintance.

Perhaps it was the fact that he had been denied his orders to lead a legion, or simply the irritation at the constant mistrust and distance that Pompey imposed. Either way, Brutus felt a thrill of pleasure despite the appalling risk.

'Are you well, Julia?' he called softly through the ornate bars.

He saw her stiffen and she looked round, the image of Julius' first wife, Cornelia. She was a beautiful woman and the sight of her brought back memories of their single night together with surprising force. There had been little blood, he remembered, though enough perhaps to bind her to him.

She stood and came to the gate, her face flushed. 'What are you doing here?' she demanded. 'My husband . . .'

'Is discussing his dreary plans with Labienus, as always, Julia, as I'm sure you know. Why he leaves a woman like you alone on such a beautiful day, I cannot understand.'

He heard the high voice of a child sing tunelessly in the background.

'Your son? Who else is with you here?'

'You must not talk to me, Brutus!' she said, looking around nervously. 'He has guards within call and there are always slaves here. This is not private.'

A little boy tottered out of the house and Brutus winked at him. The child beamed.

'He is very handsome, that one. Look at the size of his hands. He will be a great swordsman.'

Julia's fear softened at the compliment and she turned to her son. 'Go inside. I will play with you in a moment,' she said. They both watched as the boy nodded gravely and made his way back across the garden.

'Are you going to let me in?' Brutus asked.

Julia shook her head firmly. 'Definitely not. I cannot be seen with you and I don't think I could trust you.'

'I *was* remembering a night in a stable,' he admitted, enjoying the way she blushed. 'You can't tell me you prefer Pompey now?'

'He is my husband,' she said, but the firmness was gone from her voice.

Unconsciously, she had crept closer to the bars. If they had not been there, he could have taken her into his arms and kissed her, but he thought she was ready to leap away if he made such an attempt.

'Why did you leave my father?' she asked, suddenly. 'I never expected that from you. It was not to be with me, I know that.'

His reply came so quickly that she didn't notice him look away for a flickering instant. The lies came easily to him in that mood.

'Your father is the best man I have ever known, Julia. Pompey will have to be very lucky to beat him, for all his confidence.'

'Then why did you *desert* him?' she said, her eyes flashing.

He wondered at the conflict in her to have her husband planning a war with her father. As she looked at him, he had an idea as exciting as it was simple. By the gods it was a risk, though. How far could he trust what he saw in her eyes? Would she betray him?

'Do I have your oath not to tell Pompey?' he whispered.

'On the life of my son,' she replied, leaning even closer.

'I have not left Julius,' he said. 'I am here to help him win.'

Her red lips opened as she took in what he was saying. He wanted to kiss them hungrily and his hand moved of its own accord to stroke her hair. She pulled back out of range on the instant.

'No one else knows,' he said. 'I have told you only because I could not bear to have you think of me as a traitor.'

117

He could see she wanted to believe him and it was all he could do not to burst into laughter.

'Your husband does not trust me, though,' he continued. 'He will not let me command enough men to make a difference. I think he intends to put me in the front ranks, to be killed in the first skirmish.' Was he being too obvious? He had intended a subtle barb to have her fear for him, but it was difficult to find exactly the right tone.

Still she did not reply and he could see the agony in her expression as she found herself caught between conflicting loyalties. She loved her father, he knew. He had gambled that she would not tell Pompey and see him executed. If affection had grown for the Dictator, Brutus knew his life could be measured in hours. Already he was appalled at the risk he had taken, and as she remained silent he would have given anything to take back the words.

'Does my father want you to lead a legion?' she asked faintly.

He smothered a grin then, knowing she was his and he had won. 'He does, Julia,' he said.

'Then I will persuade my husband to give you a command.'

He forced surprise onto his face, as if he had never considered the idea.

'Can you do it? He will not like to be pushed,' he said. He saw she had grown pale and now that the idea had been planted, he had a sense of time running away from him. He could not be found at her gate, especially now.

'I know him well,' she said. 'I will find a way.' On impulse, she pressed her face against the bars and kissed him hard on the lips. 'Let my father know I have not forgotten him,' she said.

'I will, girl, but I must go now,' he replied.

He could have sworn he heard the clatter of iron-shod sandals in the distance. He would have to be far away when they found him, preferably in a tavern with a girl on his arm. It would be difficult to talk his way out of it, but not, he hoped, impossible.

118

'When will I see you again?' she asked.

'Dismiss the slaves two days from now at the same time. If I can, I will be here,' he said, rejoicing inwardly. It was far more than he had hoped for at the beginning. Instead of the private pleasure of rolling Pompey's wife once in a while, the stakes had become frighteningly large.

'Go quickly!' she said, catching his nervousness.

He nodded and ran at last, taking the first corner at a sprint. She watched him go and jumped as her husband's soldiers clattered by a few moments later. He would lead them a merry dance, she thought, and for the first time since her arrival in Greece, her heart beat wildly with excitement.

CHAPTER TEN

The festival of Bona Dea was in full cry and Rome was filled with women. On this one day each year, the men closed their doors and went to sleep early while the free women of the city drank and sang and danced. Some went bare-breasted, revelling in the festival's freedoms while their families were safely at home.

Many male citizens climbed to the roofs of their houses to watch the proceedings, but if they were seen, a barrage of stones would send them back out of sight. It would have been even less pleasant to be caught alone in the streets. Every year there were stories of young men who had been cornered after curiosity kept them out too long. Some of them were found trussed and naked the following morning, still too shocked to talk about what had happened.

Belas watched the old house of Marius from a high window opposite, wondering how to get closer. He had seen Caesar bid his wife a laughing farewell before heading off for an all-night meeting with his officers. The consul had left it late to make a dignified passage and his men were hooted as they marched down the Quirinal hill towards the forum. The normal rules were suspended for the Bona Dea and Belas had enjoyed the consul's evident discomfort. There was no dignity in trying to resist the women's festival, even for members of the Senate.

From his vantage point, Belas watched with interest as a group of Vestal virgins came whooping up the hill, accompanied by the sensual beat of drums and flutes. The two leaders were naked to the waist and their breasts bounced most attractively, in Belas' opinion, their long oiled legs gleaming in the light of torches. He did not dare to lean out where they might glance up and see him. The Vestals in particular could be wicked when they caught sight of a man on that night. It was death even to touch one of them and the sentence was always enforced. Belas reassured himself nervously that he had locked the door of the house below, after renting his room for the evening.

Marius' house was growing busy with the guests Pompeia had invited. As the wife of a consul, she had gained an instant social prestige and was clearly enjoying her new status. Belas watched the women of the great families arrive from all over the city and tapped his fingers on the windowsill in frustration at not being able to see what went on inside. Most men in Rome were prepared to add to the rumours of the festival, but Belas knew the gossip was based on very little. The secrets of the Bona Dea were well kept.

He strained to see through the open gate when it was not blocked with new arrivals. Large though the house was, Belas thought the grounds must be bursting with noble daughters. Their voices were raucous as they sang and laughed and chanted, knowing full well that men would hear and wonder what debauchery they were attempting.

Belas did not want to be there and he had told Servilia as much, saying that Pompeia could hardly shame Caesar on that night, above all others. She had been firm and he had taken his place in the high room that overlooked the street, with nothing but a little cheese and bread for companionship. It would be a long night on such a lonely vigil.

As the moon rose, there were tantalising glimpses of flesh in the street below, as all inhibitions were shed. Belas fidgeted as he waited through the hours, tormented by his own imagination. He could hear a woman snoring somewhere nearby, perhaps in the very doorway to his refuge. Sweat clung to his skin as he squinted through the glow of torches and tried not to picture the wine they would be pouring down each other's skins, dark red on gold.

Lost in his reverie, he did not at first notice anything unusual about the swaying figure that came up the hill. Her hair was long and bound tightly in a club on her neck. She wore a cloak that fluttered in the breeze, revealing a stola as black as night underneath. Belas heard her footsteps patter on the stones below, pausing as they reached the house he watched.

He could not help but look again, his heart hammering as he edged closer to the window and peered down. His hands gripped the sill with sudden tension, his mouth opening to whisper a curse. What he saw was surely impossible.

The figure carried a limp wineskin like the scrotum of an old man. Belas watched as she tilted up her head so that the light from the torches caught the line of her throat. It was not a woman. The painted face was skilfully done and even the gait was female, despite the apparent drunkenness. But Belas had played women in the great theatres and he was certain. In the shadows, he applauded the man's daring and wondered how long it would be before he was discovered. They would not be gentle. Midnight had come and gone and no man had the right to walk the city in those hours. If the Vestals caught the interloper, he would be lucky not to be held down and castrated. Belas shuddered at the thought and considered offering the stranger sanctuary until dawn. He was taking a breath to do so when he saw the man's movements become subtly sharper as he looked into the garden.

The drunkenness too was feigned, Belas realised. The stranger was no young fool on a dare for his friends then, but someone more dangerous. Could he be an assassin? Belas cursed to himself that he had no way to contact Servilia during the Bona Dea.

No matter what happened, he did not dare leave the sanctuary of his little room.

He watched as the man took in the sights and sounds that were denied to Belas and then staggered inside the gates to the scented gardens beyond. Belas was left alone, consumed with curiosity. Even in his wildest youth, he would not have risked being out on that festival.

Belas waited impatiently, expecting a sudden eruption of indignant screams as the man's fraud was discovered. When it didn't come immediately, he found himself shifting from foot to foot with the tension.

It took a long time to realise the man wasn't going to come out, forcibly or otherwise. So concerned had he been with the danger that when the suspicion first struck him, Belas froze, almost in indignation. He did not believe the stranger could fool so many women for long, if at all, so had he been expected? In the darkness, Belas considered the possibilities. The man could have been a prostitute, perhaps, hired for the evening. That was infinitely preferable to a cold-blooded adventurer who might at that very moment be lowering Pompeia onto a silken couch. Belas began to hum to himself, as he sometimes did in moments of worry. He knew he had to look into the house.

He crept down two flights of stairs in pitch darkness until he could feel the polished wood of the door to the street. Gingerly, he opened it and glanced out. The snoring woman fell in as he removed her support and Belas froze as she slumped at his feet. She did not wake as he took her under the armpits and moved her to one side. He could feel his pulses throbbing as he watched her for movement. He deserved better pay for such a night.

Belas offered up a prayer to all the most masculine of Roman gods to keep him safe and darted across the street, leaving the door slightly ajar behind him. With exaggerated caution, he peeped around the gatepost of the old Marius house, his imagination running riot.

A naked woman lay sprawled just inside the gate, with an empty wineskin at her side. Even through his fear, Belas realised she was a beauty, but not Pompeia. Sudden laughter from the house made him shrink back and Belas glanced up and down the street outside, terrified that he would be discovered by someone coming up behind. He shuddered as he imagined their glee. He crept further into the gardens and hid as a pair of women came past, only inches from discovering him. The fear was too much and he could smell his own acrid sweat.

He was almost ready to leave when he saw his stranger once more. The disguise was spoilt by the casual strength of the man as he walked into the open with a naked woman in his arms. She had her legs curled up like a kitten and was murmuring as he carried her towards some private place. Belas could only shake his head at the stranger's brazenness. He still wore the dress, but his arms were too heavily muscled to be female. The woman seemed to be trying to sing through a spate of hiccoughs. As her head lolled, Belas caught a glimpse of Pompeia's features and watched in amazement as she wrapped an arm about the man's neck and pulled his head down to her lips. She had rarely looked finer, Belas could see, her dark hair spilling over her shoulders and swaying as she kissed the stranger. Her cheeks were flushed with wine and passion and Belas rather envied the man who had risked everything to be there in that garden.

It occurred to him that if he left and said nothing, there would be little damage done to anyone. Part of him wanted to do just that, but he had accepted Servilia's gold and everything that entailed.

'Is she worth your life?' he said suddenly, pitching his voice to carry.

The stranger almost dropped Pompeia at the sound and turned

quickly towards the source. Belas ducked out of sight and scurried away. He was back across the street before any alarm could be given.

He had done his work and the young man knew he had been seen. Belas sighed as he watched the chaos that ensued from his high window. The stranger had disappeared, perhaps through the gardens to climb a wall to safety. The rest of the women in the house were roused by their mistress and they searched the area with oaths and threats. One of them even thumped on the door opposite, but Belas had barred it securely and could smile. He wondered if the stranger had been returning from a bed rather than going to one. The man deserved something for his efforts, after all. By the time morning came, there was going to be trouble.

Julius yawned as he ate the cold lamb and roasted onions that had survived the night. With the first grey light of dawn showing in the forum, the plans and discussions had begun to blur into one another until he knew it was time to call an end to it. Adàn too was yawning hugely, having spent the entire session with two other scribes taking down orders and keeping the records in perfect detail.

It was strange to be in the Curia without a single senator on the benches. Filling the seats with the officers of his legions had given an air of a military court and Julius wished the real Senate could see the efficiency of these men. There had been no wasted, pompous speeches throughout the long hours of darkness: there was too much real work to do.

Despite the freedoms of the festival, they had heard little to disturb the long watches of the night. In a breach of tradition, Julius had posted soldiers on the senate house steps to prevent any of the more foolhardy women coming close enough to inter-fere. It seemed to have worked, but the dawn light still brought a few smiles to the chamber as it signalled an end to the Bona Dea and the chance to get to bed at last.

Julius looked proudly round at the men who had assembled at his order. As well as the seven generals, he had called his most senior centurions and military tribunes to hear the final arrangements for leaving Rome behind them. More than three hundred men were packed into the seats and at times the discussion had been as noisy and jocular as a full Senate debate.

Though he was weary, Julius was content with the preparations for war. The fleet was waiting to sail at Ostia and he had the men to fill them, now that three more of his legions had come south and set up tents in the Campus Martius. Mark Antony was steady in his role as consul and every soldier in the room knew the main plans for the first landings in Greece, if not the final date.

'One more month,' Julius murmured to Domitius at his side, 'then we will be free to go to war again.'

'One more throw for the whole game,' Domitius replied, echoing a conversation on the Rubicon months before.

Julius laughed at the reference. 'It seems that whenever I think I have mastered a game, I find I have been playing blind on a greater board. I send Caecilius to Greece to be captured, but instead we receive detailed reports every month that are more valuable than gold. The man is a fox, it seems, and the gods have a strange sense of humour.'

Domitius nodded, feeling the same sense of satisfaction that showed in Julius' face. The reports from Caecilius were a vital part of their preparations, and those who knew he had been sent simply to sow mistrust of Brutus were privately pleased that stratagem had failed, at least so far. Even then, the war to come was only half the task that faced them. Julius was obsessed with leaving the city safe and they had worked for months to prepare Rome to be handed over to Mark Antony.

The new magistrates had taken to heart the single instruction

Julius had given them: 'Work faster and take no bribes.' Backed by their awe of the man, it had been enough to tackle some of the backlog of cases that had grown in the months preceding Pompey's departure. Few of the officials had fallen back into corruption and those who did were at the mercy of their victims, now that complaints were taken seriously.

The city was working again, despite the upheavals. The people had been asked for their trust and had given it, at least for the present. Mark Antony would inherit a great deal of good will when the legions left. Julius had kept the promise he had made in the forum and provided ten full cohorts to keep the peace while he was gone. Leavened with more experienced officers, the road guards from Corfinium had been perfect for that task and Julius had been happy to confirm Ahenobarbus as their general.

At that thought, Julius raised his cup to Ahenobarbus in a private salute. He did not regret sparing him and the man's stolid lack of imagination was well suited to the duties of keeping peace in Rome. Julius could see his pride as he returned the toast.

A soldier entered the chamber, one of those Julius had left guarding the bronze doors outside. Julius rose stiffly to his feet as he saw Servilia walked with him. With a clatter, the rest of his officers followed his example and in the silence they all heard the metallic whine of a plate as it spun on the marble floor before someone put his foot on it.

Servilia did not smile as she greeted him and it was with a sinking feeling that Julius regarded her.

'What brings you here?' he said.

Her glance took in the solid ranks of his officers and he understood she was reluctant to speak in public.

'Come to my house, on the Quirinal,' he said. 'I will dismiss the men.'

'Not there, Consul,' she said, hesitating.

Julius lost his patience and took her by the arm, walking outside to the steps that led down to the forum. They could both see right across it and the clean air helped to settle his mind after the long hours of breathing the oil fumes of torches.

'I take no pleasure in this,' she began, 'but I had a man watch your house last night.'

Julius glared at her, his thoughts jumping immediately to suspicion. 'We will discuss your right to do so another time. Tell me what he saw,' he said.

She passed on the details that Belas had witnessed and watched him grow colder and angrier as she spoke. For a long time, he was silent, gazing out over the expanse of the forum. A few moments before he had wanted nothing more than sleep, but his light mood had been torn away by her words.

He clenched a fist unconsciously, before he forced himself to speak again. 'I will have the truth of this from her.'

Pompeia's eyes were red with weeping as Julius came storming in. He had left his soldiers in the street rather than have them witness this most private of meetings. One glance at her guilty expression and his humiliation was complete.

'I am sorry,' she said as she saw him, and before he could speak she began to sob like a child.

The question simmered in him like stomach acid, but the words had to be spoken aloud. 'It's true then?'

She could not look at him as she nodded, burying her face in a tear-stained cloth. He stood in front of her, his hands opening and closing as he struggled to find a response.

'He came last night? Was it rape?' he said at last, knowing it was impossible. Attempting a rape on the Bona Dea would be tantamount to suicide. His thoughts had wrapped themselves so tightly that he could barely think at all. Shock was making him foolish, some small part of him noted, and he knew that when the anger finally came it would be terrible.

'No, not that. I can't . . . I was drunk . . .'

Her snivelling began to grind at his stunned calm. Visions of the brutal punishments he could exact flashed into his mind, tempting him. His men would not dare to come into the house, even if he strangled her. His hands clutched convulsively, but he did not move closer.

Raised voices in the street made him turn, almost with relief at the distraction. He heard a strange voice shouting and when he glanced back at Pompeia he saw she had gone as pale as milk.

'Oh no . . .' she whispered. 'Please don't hurt him. He's a fool.' She stood and reached for Julius.

He stepped back as if from a snake, his face twisting in rage. 'He's here?' he demanded. 'He's come back to my house?'

Julius strode to the front gate where his soldiers had pinned a bawling figure to the cobbled street. His mouth was bloody, but he struggled like a madman. Pompeia gave a cry of sheer horror as she saw him. Julius shook his head in amazement. The stranger Belas had seen was a youth, no more than eighteen years old. He had long hair to his shoulders, Julius noted sourly. Looking at him made Julius feel old and his bitterness increased.

The soldiers held the intruder in grim silence as they realised their general was with them. One of them had taken a cut to his lip in the struggle and was red-faced with exertion.

'Let him up,' Julius said, his hand dropping automatically to his gladius.

Pompeia cried out in panic and Julius turned to slap her hard across the face. The shock silenced her and her eyes filled with tears as the young man rose to his feet and stood to face his tormentors. He was breathing heavily as he wiped the blood from his mouth with the back of his hand.

'Take me,' he said clearly. 'Let her go.'

'Get him *inside*,' Julius snapped. 'I won't have the whole of Rome watching this.'

His men laid heavy hands on the youth, dragging him into the garden and locking the gate behind them. Pompeia followed, her eyes dark with terror and misery as they moved out of the sun into the cool halls beyond.

The soldiers threw the young man down on the marble with a hard slapping sound. He groaned in pain before staggering upright. He looked at Julius with reproof.

'Well?' Julius said. 'What's your name, boy? I am curious to find out what exactly you thought would happen here.'

'My name is Publius and I thought you might kill her,' the young man replied.

He held his head proudly and Julius lost his temper for an instant, rapping him hard across the mouth with his knuckles. Blood drooled slowly down Publius' face, but the eyes remained defiant.

'We are talking about my wife, boy. You have no right to an opinion,' Julius said slowly.

'I love her. I loved her before you married her,' Publius said.

It was all Julius could do not to kill him. The rage he had expected was banishing the weariness from his mind at last, fuelling a restless energy that made him want to cut the arrogant fool down.

'Please don't tell me you expected to save her, puppy? Should I give her to you and wish you both luck? What do you think?'

As Publius began to reply, Julius hit him again, knocking him down. Publius panted hard as he struggled up and his hands were shaking.

Julius saw that blood had spattered across the marble of the entrance hall and fought for control of his emotions. Pompeia was sobbing again, but he could not look at her for fear his anger would become uncontrollable.

'I am leaving Rome in less than a month to fight an army twice as large as the one I have. Perhaps you are hoping that I will leave you two together while I am gone? Or that I may not return, even?' He swore, disgustedly. 'It's a long time since I was as young as you, Publius, but I was never such a fool. Never. You've staked your life on a romantic gesture and the trouble with the great poems and plays is that they rarely understand what it means to stake your *life*. It means I have my men take you somewhere quiet and beat you until your face caves in. Do you understand? How romantic will you look then, do you think?'

'Please don't,' Pompeia said. 'Please let him go away from Rome. You'll never have to see him again. I will do anything you want.'

Julius turned his cold eyes on her. 'Are you offering to be a faithful little wife now? It's too late for that. My heir must carry my blood, girl, without rumour, without gossip. That's all you had to do for me.' He grimaced, unable to bear the sight of her any longer. 'In front of these witnesses, girl. Three times I say this to you: I divorce you. I divorce you. I *divorce* you. Now get out of my house.'

She took a step away, unable to reply. Dark circles made her eyes looked bruised. She looked at Publius and they shared a glance of despair.

'I doubt that dry womb of yours will ever be filled, but if it shows life while I am gone, the child will be a bastard,' Julius told her. He wanted to hurt and was pleased as she flinched.

When Julius faced Publius again, he snorted at the look of hope on the young man's face. 'Please tell me you're not expecting to get through this, boy? You've lived long enough to know what must happen, surely? No one can be that young and stupid.'

'If you are letting Pompeia go free, it's enough,' Publius said.

His eyes were bright with righteousness and Julius was tempted to hit him again. Instead, he nodded to two of his men. 'Take her out and leave her in the street. Nothing in this house is hers.'

Pompeia began to scream then, as the soldiers grabbed her and dragged her outside. The sound continued in the background as Publius and Julius looked at each other.

'Will you kill me now?' Publius asked, holding his head up.

Julius was ready to give the order, but the boy's courage was extraordinary. Even in the absolute certainty of death, he remained calm and almost aloof from what was going on around him.

'If it hadn't been you, the whore would have had someone else in her bed,' Julius said softly.

Publius lurched at him and the soldiers beat him to the ground with a rain of heavy blows.

'No, I'm not going to kill you,' Julius told him, leaning down. 'A brave lad like you will do well in my legions. I'll see you get a posting to the front line. You will learn my trade quickly there, one way or the other. You're going to Greece, boy.'

CHAPTER ELEVEN

In the darkness, Julius could see the stern lamp of a galley like a distant firefly, twitching with the motion of the sea.

'Tell the captain to take us a little closer,' he said to Adàn. He heard the young Spaniard's feet as he took the message forward, but the gloom swallowed him as if they were all blind. Julius smiled to himself. He had chosen the moonless night for exactly that quality and the gods had given him cloud to mask even the dim glow of the winter stars.

Huddled on the deck and in every space on the galley, the soldiers of the Tenth either dozed or applied one last coat of oil to protect their armour against the sea air. Only utter exhaustion could have dulled their tension into light sleep. They had launched knowing that there was just one chance to surprise the Greek ports. If that failed and the rising sun found them still far from the enemy coast, Pompey's sleek galleys would descend on them and destroy them all.

'No sign of dawn?' Octavian said suddenly, betraying his nerves.

Julius smiled unseen in the darkness. 'Not yet, General. The night will keep us safe a little longer.'

Even as he spoke, he shivered in the icy breeze and drew his cloak more tightly around his shoulders. The wind was strong, but changed without warning and Julius had seen the oars reach out for the dark waves three times since leaving Brundisium. At such a pace, the slaves below would be approaching their limits, but there was no help for that. They too would be drowned if they were caught by the coming day.

With only the shuttered lamp from the galley ahead to give them direction, it was easy to think they were alone on the sea. Around them were thirty galleys built in Ostia by the best Roman shipwrights. They carried Julius' fortune: his men and his life. With some bitterness, he acknowledged the fact that there would be no son and heir if he died in Greece. His disastrously short marriage had been the gossip of the city and he still smarted under the humiliation. In the aftermath, he had found a young woman named Calpurnia and married her with unseemly haste. His name had been the subject of comic songs as his enemies mocked his desperation to father a son.

Calpurnia had nothing of the beauty that marked Pompeia. Her father had accepted the suit without a moment of hesitation, as if he were relieved to be rid of her. Julius considered her somewhat bovine features with little affection, even with the gloss of memory. She stirred little passion in him, but she came from a noble house fallen on difficult times. No one in Rome could question her line and Julius doubted she would have the temptations that had undone his second wife.

He grimaced at the thought of their last meeting and the tears Calpurnia had shed on his neck. She wept more than any woman he had ever known, considering the short time they had been together. She wept for happiness, for adoration and then at the slightest thought of him leaving. Her month's blood had started the day before he took ship and she had cried at that as well. If he failed against Pompey, there would be no other chance to leave more than a memory of his name. This was his path, his final throw of the dice. This was the real game.

He took a deep breath, letting the cold air slide into the deepest recesses of his chest. Even then, he felt weary and knew he should sleep. Somewhere nearby, a man was snoring softly to himself and Julius chuckled. His Tenth were not the sort to be frightened by a little journey of seventy miles in the dark.

The last three days had been hard on all of them. When Julius finally gave the order, all seven legions had marched from Rome to Brundisium, covering the miles at a brutal pace. He'd sent out two fast galleys to chase Pompey's spy ship clear of the coast and the fleet had launched, moving swiftly to pick up the legions on the other side of the mainland. Even at that late point, Julius had been tempted to hold back the strike until he had a fleet to match the one that Pompey controlled. Yet every day delayed was another for Pompey to entrench himself. Every hour. With the gods' luck, the former consul would not be expecting Julius to arrive until spring.

Julius offered up a silent prayer that he was right. If Pompey's spies had reached the Greek shore first, dawn would bring the last hours of sunlight they would ever see. The stakes of the gamble both appalled and excited him, but there was no calling it back. The moment his galleys had glided free of Brundisium, new-laden with his legions, the course was set for all of them.

The snoring soldier made a sound like a honking goose and one of his companions jerked him awake with a muffled curse. Julius had given orders for silence, but the night seemed alive with the hiss of waves and the creaking of ropes and beams. His spirits rose as he recalled other voyages, some so distant as to seem like another life. In a sense, he envied the freedoms of the young man he had been. His choices had seemed simpler and he could only shake his head at how innocent he must have seemed to men like Marius or Sulla.

Adàn returned to his side, staggering slightly as the galley pitched through a wave.

'The watch glass has been turned three times, sir. Dawn cannot be far away now,' he said.

135

'Then we will know at last if they are waiting for us,' Julius replied.

The night had seemed endless at the beginning and yet somehow it had flown. The generals of seven legions were aboard ships around him, waiting impatiently for the light. Each galley had a man at the highest point to call out the first grey gleam of dawn and scan the sea for the enemy. He felt an odd freedom as he realised there was nothing left for him to order or correct. It was a lull in the tension that he could almost enjoy and in the darkness he thought back to Renius, wishing he were there to see them. The old man would have enjoyed the gamble he had taken and seen the sense in it. Julius looked ahead, as if he could sight the coast of Greece by force of imagination. There were so many ghosts behind him, and somewhere ahead there was Brutus.

After the success of Caecilius reaching Pompey's legions, Julius had sent another five men to infiltrate the Greek towns. Caecilius had reported their executions month by month until he was again the only voice reporting Pompey's movements. It was galling to place so much trust in a single spy, and Julius worried constantly that the man had been turned against him.

In the dark, he shrugged off that weight with the rest. That too was beyond his power to change. If the reports were accurate, Pompey was in the north, around Dyrrhachium. His legions had been placed to defend the west coast, but they could not know exactly where Julius would land until it was too late. Unless they were ready for him. He smiled to himself, knowing the moment of peace had been an illusion. He could not stop his endless examination of the plans any more than he could stop the wind that froze his men where they lay.

A thump of hard bare feet on the wooden deck made him turn.

'Sir? Dawn's coming,' the sailor said, pointing into the east.

Julius stared into unchanged darkness. Just as he was about to speak, a patch of grey became visible and with it the black line that separated the world from the heavens. He had seen the sun rise at sea before and still it caught his breath as the first line of gold wormed into existence and the underbelly of the clouds lit in bruised shades.

'Enemy sail!' another lookout called, shattering the vision.

Julius gripped the wooden rail, willing the light to come faster. Somewhere close, one of Pompey's captains would be roaring panicky orders as the fleet materialised. Julius would not alter course. He imagined he could smell land in the sea air and knew it was desperation.

Dim shapes appeared around him as his thirty galleys were lit by the dawn. The decks were busy with activity as they prepared and Julius could feel his heart beat more strongly, almost painfully, as he waited for the word that Greece could be seen.

Three of Pompey's galleys were visible now, the nearest close enough to see the flecks of white at its sides as the oarsmen churned the water.

'Land!' came the cry and Julius let out a roar of excitement, raising his fist to the sky.

His soldiers released the tension in a great cheer that echoed over the water as they saw the brown stain across their path that meant they would not be caught alone in the ocean.

The drums that had been silent all night came suddenly to life, setting an even faster, man-killing pace. Hearts would burst as they crossed the last length to land, but the drums pounded on at the charge and the galleys soared in together.

Julius could see the houses of a waking town and like the buzzing of an insect he heard alarm horns summon the soldiers of Greece to defend the inhabitants. Was it Oricum? He thought it was, though it had been almost twenty years since he last took ship from that port.

The sound of the drums fired his blood even higher as he watched the port come closer. Three galleys were in the dock there and even as Julius watched, they came alive with running, shouting men. He grinned at the thought of their fear. Let him just touch land and he would show them that Rome could still produce a general.

Brutus rose from the hard sleeping mat in his quarters and began the series of exercises with which he greeted every new dawn. Renius had set the original form, but Cabera's influence had altered the routine, so that now there were as many moves to increase suppleness as to maintain strength. After half an hour, his body was gleaming with sweat and the sun had risen above the distant city of Dyrrhachium. He took a sword and began the routines he had learned with Julius decades before, the simpler forms growing into more complex strikes, almost as a dance. The routine was so much a part of him as to leave his mind completely free and he used the time to consider his position in Pompey's forces.

It had become a dangerous game with Labienus after the first evasion of his guards. The Greek general was still suspicious and Brutus knew he was spied upon at all times. He thought he could have slipped away from their sight with enough effort, but that would only have added to Labienus' mistrust. Instead, Brutus had confounded the man by complaining directly, dragging one of the watchers into Labienus' presence.

Brutus had enjoyed seeming as indignant as any other loyal general would be. Labienus had been forced to apologise and claim a mistake had been made. The spies who watched Brutus had been replaced with new faces the following day.

Brutus smiled to himself as he lowered slowly into a lunge that ended with his outstretched gladius held straight for five heart-beats. To see Julia was an intoxicating challenge and simply vanishing from sight would begin another hunt for him. It was far better to act as an innocent man. On the two other occasions that he had stolen time with Julia since their first meeting in the garden, Brutus had gleefully ordered Seneca's men to arrest the watchers. It changed nothing. Brutus knew Labienus would never be truly sure of him until he fought Julius in the field and proved his loyalty beyond all doubt.

Brutus spun lightly in a move he had learned years before from a tribe that fought with bronze weapons. Renius would have disapproved of anything that broke contact with the ground, but the leap was spectacular and hid the movement of the sword for instants that had saved his life on two separate occasions. As Brutus landed, he gripped the wooden floor of the barracks with his bare feet, feeling his own strength. He had been first sword in Rome and a general in Gaul. To have Labienus sniffing around him for disloyalty was an affront he would one day repay in full. Not one of Pompey's men would ever appreciate what it had cost him to betray Julius. He knew they weighed his contribution to tactical discussion with a jaundiced eye. Part of him understood the necessity for their doubts, but still it was infuriating.

As he came to rest at last and brought his sword up to the legionary's first position, he considered the irony of his new role. He had only ever fought under Julius' command and he found Pompey merely competent in comparison. The man was a solid general, but he lacked the fire of innovation that Julius could bring to the direst situation. Brutus had seen Julius standing with arrows thumping into the ground around him as he turned a battle lost into a triumph. Though it did not sit easily with his pride, there were times when Brutus could admit he had learned more from Julius than he ever would from Pompey.

The silence of the night was broken as the soldiers around him woke and began to wash and dress. The temporary barracks had been sited near a stream that had its beginning above the snowline of distant mountains and Brutus could hear the men swear at the cold as they bathed. He reached under the cloth at his groin and scratched himself idly. There was a bathing room nearby, with a fire to heat buckets of water, but it had become a point of pride for the men that their officers dared the icy river with them. He smiled at the thought of the transformation he had wrought in the road guards. Even Labienus had complimented him in his stiff way. Seneca's cohorts would hardly recognise the untrained soldiers they had been, after the months of drill and manoeuvres. Brutus had undertaken their instruction with deliberate thoroughness, knowing that only their skill would keep him alive when Julius came to Greece.

He left his set of silver armour in the room, preferring a simple set of leather and iron with long woollen bracae to protect his legs from the cold. A call brought a slave to carry them and Brutus went out into the pale morning sun.

The city of Dyrrhachium was wreathed in mist in the distance, with the grey sea shining at its westernmost point. Brutus tilted his head in ironic appreciation of Labienus, somewhere within that place. He did not doubt that his orders to train away from the city came from the subtlety of the general, solving his problem by removing the man who caused them.

As he strolled to the river's edge, Brutus saw Seneca had risen before him and was standing naked on the bank, rubbing himself vigorously to revive his frozen flesh. The young officer grinned at Brutus, but then both men became still as they sighted movement near the city and peered into the distance.

'Now who could be joining us out here?' Brutus said to himself. The smudge of moving men was too far away to see details and Brutus resigned himself to a quick plunge and scrub so as to be ready to receive them.

Seneca was already pulling on his clothing and tying laces and straps that gleamed with oil. As Brutus waded gasping into the water, the alarm was being given around the camp and the wooden buildings clattered with the noise of men gathering weapons.

Brutus bore the cold in tense silence as he ducked under the surface, though it numbed him in moments. He panted sharply as he came out and accepted a blanket to towel himself dry.

'I'm not due to report for another three days,' he told Seneca as he pulled on his bracae and the wool sheaths that protected his feet from the worst cold. He did not voice his fear that Pompey had discovered his meetings with Julia. He was certain she would not have betrayed him, but Labienus could have had spies watching her as well, men he had not seen. He shook his head. Why send a column out to take him when he could be ambushed during his report?

Brutus and Seneca watched the soldiers from Dyrrhachium approach and both of them searched their consciences for some transgression, exchanging only a single baffled glance. The cohorts they commanded lined up in perfect order and Brutus took pride in their bearing. The days were gone when they could answer only a few horn calls in a battle line. They were as disciplined and hard as he could make them.

At the head of the approaching men, Brutus recognised Labienus himself, riding a black horse. He could not escape a chill at the sight of the second in command under Pompey coming out to see him personally. It did not bode well and he wished he had brought the silver armour from the barracks.

Labienus reined in only a few feet from the rigid figures that waited for him. Centurions cried the halt and the column stood facing them. Labienus dismounted with his usual care and Brutus noted again the quiet calm of the man that was so different from his own style. Battles won by Labienus were triumphs of discipline and economy. He never wasted men on pointless actions, but still had one of the finest records in Greece. Brutus detested his dry reserve on a personal level, though he could not deny the man understood tactics.

'General Brutus,' Labienus said, inclining his head in greeting.

Though the title was still officially used, Labienus' eyes flickered over the tiny force Brutus commanded, apparently aware of the irony. Brutus let the silence stretch until Labienus grew uncomfortable. At last, he greeted Labienus by his own title and the tension receded.

'Pompey has given these men to your command, General,' Labienus continued.

Brutus hid his pleasure as he replied, 'Your recommendation is valuable, then. You have my thanks,' he said.

Labienus flushed slightly. He spoke carefully, as he had always done, knowing that to voice his distrust openly would invite a duel of honour he could not possibly win. 'It was not my recommendation, as I am sure you realise. Pompey has other advisers. It seems he has been reminded of your success with extraordinarii in Gaul. After the first battle, you will command these men as a mobile force to shore up weaknesses in the lines as you see fit.'

'*After* the first battle?' Brutus queried, guessing what was coming.

Labienus produced a bound scroll from beneath his cloak, marked clearly with Pompey's seal. As he placed it in Brutus' hands, he spoke again with a glimmer of enjoyment. 'For the first meeting of forces, your men will stand in the front rank against the enemy. That is Pompey's direct order.'

He hesitated, choosing his words with extreme care.

'I am to say that Pompey hopes you will survive that first attack, that he may use your abilities to the full in the latter stages of the war.'

'I'm sure he said exactly that,' Brutus replied coldly.

He wondered if the advice to use his abilities came from within Pompey's own house. Julia had promised her influence and he had no other voice to speak on his behalf. Pompey was caught between a desire to use an extremely able general and the constant fear that Brutus was a spy for the enemy. Julia's influence could have been the whisper he needed to gain this small concession.

Labienus watched his reaction with mixed feelings. He found the Gaul general unsettling. In training with the Greek legions, he had shown an understanding of terrain and men that was second to none. At the same time, he was arrogant and occasionally disrespectful to the point of outright insolence. Like Pompey, Labienus was loath to waste a man who had more years of actual battle experience than any other three generals in Pompey's forces. Such a man could be vital in blunting Caesar's eventual attack. If only they could trust him.

'I will not take refreshment,' Labienus said, as if any had been offered. 'The fortifications are far from complete.'

Brutus raised his eyes at the mention of an area of policy he had not been able to influence. At Pompey's order, vast stretches of walls and hill forts had been begun, stretching for miles around Dyrrhachium. They may have made the old man feel secure, but Brutus had scorned the very idea. As nothing else could, it showed that Pompey held Julius in too much respect as a commander, and preparing defensive positions before the enemy had even arrived did not inspire the men. Worse, Brutus thought it sapped at their courage to know that there were safe positions if they retreated.

'Let us hope it does not come to that, Labienus,' he said, more curtly than he had intended. 'When Caesar comes, we may be able to break his forces without hiding from them.'

Labienus' cold eyes went hard at the implication, unsure whether he should react to the perceived insult or not. In the end, he shrugged. 'As you say,' he replied. He signalled to a personal guard of a century to fall out and escort him back to the city. The rest stood impassively by the river, shivering in the wind.

Brutus was pleased enough not to play his games any longer and he saluted Labienus, noting the man's relief as he returned the gesture.

'Tell Pompey I will obey his orders and that I thank him for the men,' Brutus said.

Labienus nodded as he mounted his horse once more and their eyes locked as if Labienus thought he could discern loyalty by the intensity of his gaze. At last, he wheeled his mount and rode stiffly back to the city.

As the galleys reached the docks, the spiked corvus bridges came crashing down, followed immediately by the soldiers of Julius' legions. The galleys in the port were wedged in place before they could escape and many of the men who jumped onto Greek soil did so from their decks. They flooded ashore, killing the crews with merciless efficiency and moving on.

Oricum became jammed as they forced their way inland. The port town was manned by a thousand legionaries in billets and those were the first to be overwhelmed. Some of them managed to light signal fires of green wood and the plumes of smoke soared upwards to alert the country. Julius did not allow his men to show mercy before they were well established and that first thousand were cut to pieces in the streets of Oricum.

The three galleys that had sighted their fleet had not attempted to land, but turned north to take word of the invasion. Julius knew he had to use the surprise attack to its utmost advantage. If he had had more men waiting to come across, he might have secured a safe area around the port. As it was, Julius had thrown his entire force at the coast. He needed to be mobile and chafed at every moment of delay as the heavy equipment began to be winched out of the galleys. He was safe from the sea for the present. No other force could land easily behind him, with his galleys blocking the port. When the last ballistae and scorpion bows had been lifted out, he ordered them sunk, choking it completely.

Before the sun had reached its noon zenith, the veterans were ready to march inland. Spires of smoke rose from the port town around them, smudging the clear air as they waited in perfect rows and columns. Julius looked at them with pride and dropped his arm to signal the horns to sound.

The streets had given way to scrub fields by the time they saw the first of Pompey's legions in full array in the distance. The veterans of Gaul roared their challenge and there was no reluctance in them. Who could have guessed how they would feel when they sighted a Roman legion as an enemy? Julius saw the feral interest as the legionaries watched the moving force in the distance. Wolf brothers could tear each other to pieces, regardless of shared blood.

Whoever commanded the five thousand men clearly rejected the opportunity to have them destroyed by such an overwhelming force. Even as Julius watched, the heavy column changed direction and headed north. Julius laughed aloud at the thought of the consternation in those ranks. They had not expected him and now it was too late. He slapped his horse's neck in excitement, looking around at a country he had not seen for decades.

The land was bare in winter, with twisted trees bereft of their foliage and thin grass clinging to the soil. The stony earth was a dry dust that he remembered from fighting Mithridates many years before. Even the air smelled subtly different to Rome or Gaul. This was a hard land, where life had to be brought carefully into being. It was a good place to go to war. As he cast his eyes along the colourful lines of his legions, Julius thought of Alexander before him and straightened in the saddle.

His gelding was skittish as he rode along the silent ranks. One by one, he greeted his generals. Some, like Octavian, Domitius, Ciro and Regulus, he had known for years. Others had proved themselves in Gaul and been promoted after Brutus' betrayal. They were good men and he felt his confidence soar. It seemed a dream to be actually on Greek soil, with the land opening up before them. He was back in his most natural element and all the stifling subterfuge of political Rome could be left behind. Flags snapped and fluttered in a winter breeze that could not cool the pleasure he felt to be at last in reach of his enemy. Pompey had almost twice as many men under his command, with the advantage of fighting on land they knew and had prepared. Let them come, Julius thought. Let them try us.

CHAPTER TWELVE

Pompey paced the central length of the temple he had made his headquarters, his hands clasped tightly at his back. All other sound had ceased and his iron-shod sandals threw back a perfect single echo from the walls, as if his footsteps were stalked by an unseen enemy.

'So he is among us,' he said. 'Despite the vaunted promises of my captains, he slips through them and takes Oricum from my control. He strikes at the heart of the coast and meets nothing more than a token resistance! Tell me again how this is possible!'

His last steps brought him face to face with Labienus, who stood at the entrance to the temple. His expression was as hard to read as ever, but he sought to soothe his commander's anger.

'There were good reasons not to expect him to cross in winter, sir. He gained the length of darkness he needed to avoid the fleet, but the ground is barren.'

Pompey gestured for him to continue, a spark of interest showing in his eyes.

Labienus cleared his throat. 'He has risked a great deal to make a secure landing, sir. Until the spring crops have ripened, his men, his pack animals must survive on nothing more than they brought with them. At best, they can have two weeks' rations in dried meal and meat. After that, they will grow weak. The decision could only have been made in desperation, sir. He *will* regret it.'

Pompey's eyes seemed to darken as fury overtook him once

more. 'How many times have I heard that he has overreached himself? Yet still he seems to go on, while my advisers tell me he should be long dead. His luck is uncanny, Labienus.'

'Sir, we *have* his measure. I have ordered our fleet to block the coast behind him. He cannot be supplied by sea. No matter how lucky he is, he cannot put grain that doesn't exist into the stomachs of seven legions. Perhaps if he were left unchallenged he could raid the cities to steal food, but when we are there to harry his flank he will command slowly starving men.'

'Oh I shall be there, Labienus. Gather our legions ready to move against him. I will not let him roam Greece as if he owns it!'

'Yes, sir,' Labienus replied swiftly, pleased to have been given the order after an hour of enduring Pompey's temper. He saluted and turned to leave, but Pompey's voice interrupted once again.

'Be sure that Brutus is there to be seen by all of Caesar's followers,' Pompey said, his voice strained. 'He will prove loyal or be cut down.'

Labienus nodded. 'My own legion will never be far from him, sir. There are men I trust to contain him if he is false.' He would have left then, but could not help but voice the concern that nagged at him. 'It would be easier, sir, if he had only the cohorts he arrived with. The extra thousand you gave him will be an obstacle if he turns against your authority.'

Pompey looked away from his general's coolly assessing eyes. 'If he honours his oath to me, they will play a key part in the conflict to come. I would be a fool to hamstring the man who knows Caesar's tactics best of all with only two cohorts. The decision is final, Labienus.'

Labienus left, still wondering who could have been influencing Pompey. Perhaps it was a voice in the exiled Senate that claimed so much of his time. Though it was uncomfortable even to think such disloyal thoughts, Labienus had found little to respect in the bickering old men Pompey had brought from Rome. He comforted himself with the knowledge that he could honour the senators for their position, no matter how much he disliked them personally.

Seven of the eleven legions Pompey commanded were encamped around Dyrrhachium. The main force would meet and absorb the others as they moved south to counter the invasion. Labienus found the sight of the host pleasing and was certain he had given Pompey the right advice. Fifty thousand men were the largest army he had ever seen in one place. The best reports of Caesar's legions gave him no more than twenty-two. Labienus was of the opinion that Pompey had far too much respect for the upstart who had usurped the Senate of Rome. That the Gaul legions were veterans was beyond dispute, but veterans could be holed by spears as well as any other man.

In the near distance, Labienus heard the bellowing of a white bull, slaughtered by the takers of auspices. He would see their report before Pompey and alter it, if necessary. Standing in the sun, he rubbed his thumb over the tip of his sword hilt, polishing it in a nervous habit. He could not have imagined seeing Pompey so shaken by Caesar's landing at Oricum. There would be no more bad news to jar his confidence.

Labienus watched as messengers approached to take his word out to the waiting legions.

'We march,' he told them, bluntly, his mind already on the campaign to come. 'Give the order to break camp. General Brutus will form the vanguard, with my Fourth legion behind him.'

The messengers scattered down the roads out of the city, competing to be first on the field with the news. Labienus took a deep breath and wondered if he would have the chance to see the face of the enemy who could shake the confidence of Pompey. He shrugged to himself. Caesar would regret coming to Greece with his ambition. They had not forgotten the rule of law.

Julia was sitting in Pompey's townhouse playing with her son on her lap when her husband came home. The peace of the day was shattered as he bellowed for servants to attend him. She winced at the strident tone and the child on her knee giggled at her expression, trying to copy it. The boy carried the promise of his father's heavy features and she wondered if he would inherit the same brooding disposition. A clatter of dropped dishes nearby told her that Pompey had made his way through the main rooms and was coming out to see her. She could hear every word as he called for his best armour and sword to be brought. She knew then that Julius had come to Greece at last and her heart thumped as she rose.

'There you are!' Pompey said, as he came into the garden. He stooped to kiss her on the forehead and she bore it with a tight smile. Their little son held out his arms and was ignored.

'It is time, Julia. I will be leaving and I want you moved to a place of greater safety.'

'He has landed?' she asked.

Pompey frowned and searched her eyes. 'Yes. Your father made it through my fleet.'

'You will destroy him,' she said and without warning kissed her husband hard on the mouth. He flushed in pleased surprise.

'I will,' he said, smiling. The heart of a woman was ever a mystery to him, he thought, but his wife had accepted her new loyalty without pain or argument. She was a fitting mother to his son.

'And Brutus? You will use him?'

'As soon as I am certain, I will set him free to wreak havoc where he can. You were right about his extraordinarii, Julia. The man works best when he is not too tightly tied into the chain of command. I gave him two more cohorts.'

Gently, Julia placed her son on the ground and pushed him away. She stepped closer to her husband and enfolded him in a passionate embrace. She allowed her hand to slip down towards his groin and he jumped, laughing.

'Gods, I haven't the time!' he said, raising her hand to his lips.

'You have grown more beautiful in Greece, wife. The air suits you well.'

'You suit me,' she said.

Despite his worries, he looked pleased. 'Now have your slaves gather whatever you'll need.'

Her smile faltered. 'Surely I am safe here?' she said. 'I would not like to be moved to a strange place at this time.'

Pompey blinked in confusion. 'What are you talking about?' he demanded, suddenly impatient.

She forced herself to reach out to him again, taking his hand in hers. 'You will be a father once more, Pompey. I would not risk the child.'

Her husband's face changed slowly as he took this in and considered. He eyed her figure. 'It does not show.'

'Not yet, but you could be in the field for months. It will.'

He nodded, coming to a quick decision. 'Very well. This city is far from any fighting, after all. I just wish I could persuade the Senate to stay here with you, but they insist on accompanying the legions.'

The thought of having the Senate to question every order was enough to smother even the happiness of her news, Julia saw.

'You must have their support, at least for the moment,' she said.

He raised his eyes in exasperation. 'It is a high price, Julia, believe me. Yet your father has been elected consul once again and I am forced to bend to the will of those fools. They know I need them now, that is the problem.' He sighed. 'You will have the company of their families, at least. I will leave another century to keep you safe. Now, promise me you'll not stay if there is any danger. You are too precious to me to risk in this.'

She kissed him again. 'I promise.'

Pompey ruffled the hair of his son affectionately. His voice rose to its previous volume as he went back inside the house, calling fresh orders to the guards and staff. After a while, he was gone and the house began to settle back to its usual sleepy quiet.

'Are you going to have a baby?' her son asked in his high voice, holding out his hands to be picked up.

Julia smiled, thinking how Brutus would react when she told him. 'I am, darling.'

Her eyes were cold in the weak sunlight. She had made her choice. Knowing Brutus was ready to betray Pompey had proved a heavy burden since he had confided in her. Part of her felt pain at her own betrayal, but between her father and her lover, there was no loyalty left for Pompey.

'Sir, there really is very little time,' Suetonius said.

Cicero followed his gaze over the balcony of the meeting hall and his lips tightened. 'Unless you would have me drag the great and good of Rome by the scruff of their necks, there's little else to do but wait,' he said.

The previous hour had seen Suetonius' manner change from breezy confidence to indignation at the lack of progress. He watched as yet another group of slaves came in to add to the general confusion. It astonished him how many crates and packages were involved in moving the Senate and he could imagine Pompey's growing impatience.

Below the pair, another argument erupted.

'I should go down there,' Suetonius said, reluctantly.

Cicero considered letting him try. It would be amusing at the very least and he had little liking for the senator. Maturity had not brought him wisdom, Cicero decided, looking him over. Yet he was a link to the military machine under Pompey and must be cultivated if the Senate were to maintain any influence during the campaign. The gods knew they needed every advantage they could gather.

'They are in no mood to take orders, Suetonius, even if Pompey himself were here. Better to wait it out.'

They peered over the balcony again, looking for some sign that the chaos was lessening. Hundreds of slaves bore papers and materials in a snake of men that seemed to have no end. Suetonius tightened his grip on the railing, unable to hide his irritation.

'Perhaps you could explain the urgency to them, sir,' he said at last.

Cicero laughed aloud. 'Urgency? Pompey has made it plain enough that we are nothing but baggage ourselves. What does he care if baggage take baggage with them?'

In his frustration, Suetonius spoke with less than his usual care. 'Perhaps it *would* be better to have them stay. What use would they be on a battlefield?'

Cicero's silence made him glance round. The orator was coldly angry, his words clipped. 'We were to be government in exile, young man, not held at a distance from every decision. Without us, Pompey has no right to wage war in the name of Rome. No more legitimacy than Caesar and perhaps even less.'

He leaned forward and glared from under bushy eyebrows.

'We have endured a year in this place, Suetonius, far from comfort and respect. Our families clamour to be taken home, but we tell them to endure until the lawful order is re-established. Did you think we would not be a part of the campaign?' He nodded to the bustle in the hall. 'You will find men here who understand the most rarefied subtleties of civilisation, those ideals most easily broken under a soldier's sandals. Amongst them are writers of law and mathematics, the very ablest of the great families. Minds to have working *for* you when you face an opponent like Caesar, don't you think?'

Suetonius did not want to be drawn, but he knew if the choice had been his, he would have left the Senate behind without a backward glance. He took a deep breath, unable to meet Cicero's sharp anger.

'Perhaps the decisions would be better left to Pompey now, sir. He is an able general.'

Cicero barked a laugh that made Suetonius jump. 'There is more to this than sending in the flank! Caesar commands *Roman* legions. He has assumed authority over a new Senate. You may think of nothing more than the flags and horns, but there will be political decisions to be made before the end, you may count on it. Pompey will need advisers, whether he knows it or not.'

'Maybe, maybe,' Suetonius said, nodding, trying to placate him.

Cicero was not so easily put off. 'Is your contempt so strong that you will not even trouble to argue?' he demanded. 'What do you think will happen if Caesar wins? Who will govern then, do you suppose?'

Suetonius stiffened and shook his head. 'He cannot win, sir. We have . . .' He broke off as Cicero snorted.

'My daughters have sharper minds, I swear it. *Nothing* is certain in battle. The stakes are too high to simply throw armies at each other until there is one man left standing. Rome would be defence-less and our enemies would have nothing to stop them walking into the forum as they pleased. Do you understand that much? There must be a surviving army when all the posturing and bluster is finished.' He sighed at Suetonius' blank expression. 'What will next year hold for us, or the year after? If the victory is decisive, there is no one else to limit the authority of Pompey when Caesar has fallen. If he chooses to make himself a king, or an emperor, even, to abandon the Republic of his fathers, to launch an invasion of Africa – there will be no one who could dare to refuse. If Caesar is triumphant, the same applies and the world will change regard-less. This is a new order, boy, no matter what happens here. When one general falls, there must be stability. That is when we will be needed.'

Suetonius remained silent. He thought he could hear fear in Cicero's warnings and he scorned the old man's worries. If Pompey triumphed, Suetonius would know only joy, even if it led to an empire begun on the fields of Greece. Caesar was outnumbered and would soon be hungry. Even to suggest that Pompey might not win was an insult. He could not resist a final barb.

'Perhaps your new order will need younger blood, Senator.'

The old man's gaze didn't waver.

'If the time for wisdom and debate has passed, then the gods help us all,' he said.

Brutus and Seneca rode together at the head of a host of legions that blackened the countryside of Greece for miles. For once, Seneca was silent and Brutus suspected he was thinking of the orders from Labienus and what they would mean. Though in theory it was an honour to lead the vast army, both men knew the test of loyalty was likely to leave them dead on the field after the first charge.

'At least we don't have to tread through dung like the rest of them,' Brutus said, glancing over his shoulder.

Seneca forced a tense smile. The legions were separated from each other by thousands of pack animals and carts and it was true that those further back would march a path made deeply unpleasant by their passing.

Somewhere ahead of them were the legions that had landed at Oricum, led by a general whose name was almost a byword for victory in the army. Every man there had followed the reports from Gaul and, even with the advantage of numbers, there were few who thought the battles to come would be anything but brutal.

'I think Pompey is going to waste us,' Seneca said, almost too quietly for Brutus to hear. As he felt his general's eyes on him, he shrugged in the saddle. 'When I think of how far I've come since Corfinium, I would rather we were not slaughtered in the first moments of battle just to test your loyalty.'

Brutus looked away. He had been thinking the same thing and was still struggling to find a solution. Labienus' fourth legion marched close behind his cohorts and the orders had been painfully clear. Any creative interpretation would invite a swift destruction from their own rear. Though it would throw Pompey's initial attack into confusion, Brutus knew Labienus was quite capable of such a ruthless act and it was all he could do not to look behind to see if the general was watching him. He felt the scrutiny as much as he had in Dyrrhachium and it was beginning to grate on his nerves.

'I doubt our beloved leader will order a straight thrust against the enemy,' he said, at last. 'He knows Julius will be planning and scheming for advantage and Pompey has too much respect to go in at the charge when we meet. Julius . . .' He caught himself and shook his head angrily. 'Caesar will likely have trapped and spiked the ground, dug pits and hidden flanking forces wherever there is cover. Pompey won't let him have that advantage. Wherever we find them will be a trap, I guarantee it.'

'Then we will be the men who die discovering it,' Seneca said grimly.

Brutus snorted. 'There are times when I forget your lack of experience, which is a compliment, by the way. Pompey will take up a position nearby and send out scouts to test the ground. With Labienus to advise him, we won't be sent in until there's a sweet wide path for us all to thunder through. I'd stake my life on it, if Labienus hadn't done so already.' He laughed as Seneca's spirits visibly improved. 'Our legions haven't charged in like madmen since Hannibal and his bastard elephants, Seneca. We *learn* from mistakes, while every new enemy is facing us for the first time.'

Seneca's smile faltered. 'Not Caesar, though. He knows Pompey as well as anyone. He knows us.'

'He doesn't know me,' Brutus said sharply. 'He *never* knew me. And we'll break him, Seneca.'

He saw Seneca's grip on the reins was tight enough to make his knuckles white and wondered if the man was a coward. If Renius had been there, he would have snapped something to stiffen the young officer's courage, but Brutus could not find the words he needed.

He sighed. 'If you want, I can send you back before the first charge. There'll be no shame in it. I can order you to take a message to Pompey.' The idea amused him and he went on. 'Something like, "Now look what you've done, you old fool." What do you think?'

Seneca didn't laugh, instead looking at the man who rode so confidently beside him. 'No. These are my men. I'll go where they go.'

Brutus reached over between the horses and clapped him on the shoulder. 'It has been a pleasure to serve with you, Seneca. Now stop worrying. We're going to win.'

CHAPTER THIRTEEN

Despite the heavy winter cloak that protected him from the worst of the cold, Pompey felt frozen into his armour. The only heat seemed to be in the bitter liquid that roiled and surged in his throat and bowels, making him weak. The fallow fields were littered with ice-split clods and progress was painfully slow. As a young man, he remembered being able to shrug off the worst extremes of campaigning, but now it was all he could do to clench his jaw and prevent his teeth from chattering audibly. Twin plumes of vapour came from his horse's nostrils and Pompey reached down absentmindedly to pat its neck. His mind was on the army he could see in the distance.

He could not have asked for a better vantage point. Caesar's legions had stationed themselves forty miles east of Oricum, at the end of a plain surrounded by forests. Pompey's scouts had reached a crest of rising ground and immediately reported back to the main force, passing Brutus and Seneca without a sideways glance. Pompey had come forward to confirm their sighting and now he watched in suspicious silence.

The biting air was at least clear of mist. Though Caesar's forces must have been two miles away, they stood out against the scrub grass of the plain. From so far, they looked a pitiful threat, like tiny metallic brooches pinned to the hard ground. They were as still as the patchy forest that covered the hillsides and Pompey frowned.

'What is he *doing*?' he muttered from between clenched teeth.

There was a part of him that had felt joy at finding the enemy within reach, but his more natural caution had reasserted itself. Julius would never stake his survival on a simple clash of arms. The plain where he had gathered his army was good land for a charge and Pompey knew his cavalry could smash through the smaller number of extraordinarii Julius had brought to Greece. It was far too tempting and Pompey shook his head.

'How many legions can you count, Labienus?' he said.

'Only six, sir,' Labienus replied immediately. From his sour expression, Pompey could see he shared the same doubts.

'Then where is the seventh? What are they busy doing while we stand here watching the rest? Send the scouts wide. I want them found before we move on.'

Labienus gave the order and the fastest of their cavalry horses galloped out in all directions.

'Have we been seen?' Pompey asked.

In answer, Labienus pointed to where a distant horseman was trotting along the rocky tree line that bordered the plain. As the two men watched, the man raised a flag and signalled to Julius' forces,

'I don't like it,' Pompey said. 'Those woods could hide anything. Yet it looks so much like a trap, I wonder if that is the conclusion he wants us to draw.'

'You have men to spare, sir. With your permission, I will send a single legion out to test them – perhaps the cohorts with General Brutus, sir.'

'No. Too few would not spring the trap, if it is one. He would let them close and then destroy them. We would lose men for nothing. I am reluctant to send more until I am better informed. Tell the men to stand down until the scouts return. Get a hot meal inside them and tell them to be ready for anything.'

The wind was increasing in force as the day waned. Dyrrhachium was a long way behind them and Pompey knew his men were tired. Perhaps it was better to set up hostile camps for the night and move on at dawn. He suspected Labienus was not impressed by his caution, but Pompey could still remember Julius gathering the old Primigenia legion around him and making them the core of his famous Tenth. Even those who hated Caesar admitted his ability to seize success against the odds. His skill could be read in the reports, and Pompey knew Julius was one of those rare ones who kept a sense of a battle even as it raged around him. Gaul had not fallen on its own, nor the shores of Britain. His men gave him their first loyalty, above the Senate and Rome. When he asked them to die, they went because he was the one asking. Perhaps because of that faith, they had become used to victory. Labienus had never even met the man, and Pompey was determined not to be another name on the list of those Julius had broken. His stomach twisted with a pang and he shifted uncomfortably in the saddle.

'Sir! They are moving east!' one of the scouts called out, just as Pompey became aware of it himself. Ten heartbeats after the enemy legions began to shift, the distant whisper of their horns reached them, almost lost on the wind.

'Your opinion, General?' Pompey murmured.

'They could be trying to draw us in,' Labienus said doubtfully.

'That is my feeling,' Pompey replied. 'Have the scouts keep the widest chains back to us as we move around it. I want them in sight of each other at all times.'

Labienus cast a concerned glance at the thick woodland that gripped the earth in patches all around them. Even in winter, the branches formed an impenetrable mass and it would be difficult to stay in contact on that terrain.

'It will be dark in only a few hours, sir,' he said.

'Do the best you can with the daylight left to us,' Pompey snapped. 'I want them to feel us breathing down their necks as night comes. Let them fear what we will do when they can no longer see us. Tomorrow will be long enough to kill them all.'

Labienus saluted and rode clear to give the orders. The legionaries who had already begun to huddle together in expectation of a meal were called to their feet by centurions. Labienus chose not to hear the muttered complaints of the rank and file as he rode through to pass the word to the officers. Soldiers loved to criticise the hardship of their lives, he knew, but these were experienced men and it was almost out of habit rather than any real feeling. From the beginning, they had known a winter campaign would be a test of their fitness and endurance. He did not expect them to fail.

As the great column began to move, Brutus rode back past the lines of scouts, his silver armour drawing the eye of Pompey's officers. He was flushed with some emotion and rode with effortless skill. Pompey saw him approach and his expression became subtly tauter, his mouth a pale line in the tanned skin.

Brutus drew up beside Pompey's horse, saluting quickly. 'Sir, my men are ready to attack. With your order, I will let them loose.'

'Return to your position, General,' Pompey replied, wincing as his stomach spasmed. 'I will not send a charge over ground he has had time to prepare.'

Brutus showed no reaction to the dismissal. 'He's moving now, sir, and that is a mistake. He hasn't had time to trap the whole area.' Pompey's expression did not change and Brutus spoke more urgently. 'He knows us both, sir. He will expect us to wait and judge his plans before we strike. If we go in now we can wound them before it gets dark. By the time we must withdraw we will have raised morale with a victory and damaged his confidence.'

When Brutus finished, Pompey made a small gesture with his hand on the reins. Labienus took the cue, riding up to Brutus' right side.

'You have your orders, General,' he said.

161

Brutus glanced at him and for an instant Labienus stiffened at what he saw there. Then Brutus saluted once more and rode back to the front ranks.

Pompey drummed his fingers on the high pommel of his saddle, a sign of the tension Brutus had created. Labienus did not break the silence of the march, allowing Pompey the privacy of his own thoughts.

The scouts reported every hour to keep them on course when line of sight became impossible for the main force. The winter night was coming quickly and Pompey waited with growing impatience for the enemy legions to call a halt.

'If they don't stop soon, they will be spending the night in the open,' Pompey said irritably. 'Half of them will freeze to death.'

He squinted through the shadows of trees into the distance, though there was nothing visible. The enemy had vanished in the gloom, but the most distant of the scouting riders still reported their progress back down the line. Pompey clenched his jaw against the cold and wondered if this too was a test. Perhaps Julius was hoping to lose them, or simply march them to death over the Greek plains.

'They may have already prepared a camp, sir,' Labienus said.

His lips were numb and he knew Pompey would have to let the men rest or start seeing them drop. He smothered any sign of his irritation as Pompey rode on as if unaware of the suffering of those around him. He did not want to prompt his commander, but if they did not make camp soon they risked losing the edge they had worked so hard to gain.

The sound of galloping hooves distracted both men from their thoughts and the cold. 'They have halted, sir!' the scout reported. 'A small party are riding towards us.'

Pompey raised his head like a dog with a scent. 'How many?' he demanded.

Even in the last grey light, Labienus could see the scout was frozen to the point of barely staying in the saddle. He moved his own horse closer and took the reins from the younger man's stiff fingers. 'Your general asked you how many were coming,' he said.

The scout blinked, summoning his wits. 'Three sir, under a flag of truce,' he replied.

'Order a hostile camp, Labienus,' Pompey said, at last. 'I want high walls around us by the time they arrive. No doubt they will report every detail to Caesar on their return. Let there be nothing out of place.' He paused and straightened his back to conceal his discomfort. 'Send my physician to me. I need a little of his chalk and milk to settle my stomach.'

Labienus sent men running to fulfil the order. Weary and cold as they were, the army of fifty thousand would make short work of the walled camps. It was almost second nature to them after so long in training and he was pleased as the squares began to take shape. The sound of axes chopping into trees was as familiar as home to him and he began to relax. Pompey had left it late, Labienus acknowledged to himself. Part of the work would be finished in the dark and there would be accidents.

The three men Caesar had sent to speak to Pompey worried him far more. What was there to say at this late stage? It could not be to surrender before a single spear had been thrown in anger. Labienus grimaced in the gloom as he considered sending a few of his cavalry out to make the group disappear. He did not fear the consequences, knowing that if the bodies were well hidden, Pompey would think it was a delaying tactic. Labienus had loyal men he could trust to kill them in the dark and then it would just be another tiny mystery, quickly forgotten.

The alternative was to feed what he now saw as Pompey's fear of this enemy. The confidence that had drawn Labienus to him on their first meetings seemed to have vanished with the news of the landing at Oricum. Labienus had seen the way he pressed a hand into his stomach and he feared the sickness was affecting more than his health and temper. Pompey had aged before them all and Labienus was faced with a role as second in command that went far beyond anything he had expected.

He was on the point of calling men he knew over to him when one of the scouts reported. The three riders had reached the mile perimeter and were being escorted in. Labienus let his hand fall, irritated that his own hesitation had stolen the chance. Perhaps that was the secret of Caesar's genius, he thought, a wry smile tugging at his mouth. Those who faced him tied themselves in knots guessing what he would try next. Labienus wondered if he would prove as vulnerable as Pompey seemed to be and took heart from the city of soldiers they had brought out of the north. No matter what cleverness Caesar summoned to the field, he had never faced Roman legions in their full strength. Gaul would not have prepared him for their onslaught.

By the time the three riders appeared out of the darkness, the camps were taking shape. Thousands of legionaries had dug trenches and banked earth to the height of two men. Every tree for miles around had been cut and pegged, sawn and strapped into place. Banks of earth and grass sod buttressed the columns, proof against fire and enemy missiles. They built fortresses out of nothing in just hours, havens of order and safety in the wilderness. Torches stood on iron stands all around the camp and lit the night in flickering yellow. Labienus could smell meat cooking on the night wind and his empty stomach creaked. His own needs would have to wait a little longer and he forced down his body's weakness.

He waited for the three riders as they were passed through the scout lines into the camp, noting the insignia of the Tenth legion and their centurion's armour. Julius had sent senior men to speak to Pompey, Labienus observed. They had been forced to walk through the defensive rings with drawn blades at their backs. Labienus watched them with narrowed eyes. At his order, their horses were taken and the three soldiers quickly surrounded.

Labienus walked across the frozen ground towards them. They exchanged a glance as he approached and their leader spoke first.

'We have come at the order of Gaius Julius Caesar, consul of Rome,' he said. The centurion stood confidently as if he were not ringed with men willing to cut him down at the first sudden move.

'You seem a little blunt for diplomacy, soldier,' Labienus replied. 'Speak your message, then. I have a meal waiting.'

The centurion shook his head. 'Not to you, Labienus. The message is for Pompey.'

Labienus regarded the men, his face showing nothing of his irritation. He had not missed the fact that his name was known to them and wondered how many spies Caesar had in Greece. He really should have had them killed before they had reached his position, Labienus thought ruefully.

'You may not approach the general with weapons, gentlemen,' he said.

They nodded, and removed swords and daggers to fall at their feet. The wind howled around them and the nearest torches fluttered madly.

'Remove the rest of your clothes and I will have more brought to you.'

The three men looked angry, but they did not resist and were soon shivering and naked. Their skins showed each of them had fought for years, collecting a web of scars. The man who had spoken had a particularly fine collection and Labienus thought Caesar must have excellent healers for him to have survived. They stood without embarrassment and Labienus felt a touch of admiration at how they refused to hunch against the cold. Seeing their arrogance, he considered ordering a more intimate search, but decided against it. Pompey would be wondering about the delay as it was.

Slaves brought rough wool shifts, which the centurions draped over their skins, already turning blue.

165

Labienus examined their sandals for anything unusual and then shrugged and tossed them back.

'Escort them to camp one – to the command tent,' he said.

He watched their faces closely, but the men were as impassive as the soldiers around them. Labienus knew his meal would have to wait a little longer. He was too curious to find out why Caesar would send valuable men to such a meeting.

Camp one contained eleven thousand soldiers and the key links in the command chain. It was surrounded by four others of similar size so that from above they would look like the petals of a flower drawn by a child. Three roads crossed the heart of the camp and as Labienus walked along the Via Principalis towards Pompey's command tent, he noted how the centurions took in every detail around them. He frowned at the thought that they would carry their observations back to an enemy and once again considered having them quietly dispatched. Rather than waste another chance, he broke away from the escort and gave quick instructions to a tribune from his own fourth legion. Without hesitation, the man saluted and went to gather a dozen others for the task. Labienus hurried along the main road to catch up with Caesar's men, feeling better about their mission.

The Praetorium tent was an enormous leather construction towards the northern gate of the camp. Reinforced with beams and taut with ropes, it was as solid as a stone building and proof against rain or gale. The whole area was well lit with oil torches partially shielded by a lattice of iron. Their flames streamed out with the wind, casting odd shadows as Labienus reached his men and had them halt outside. He gave the password of the day to the outer guards and ducked inside, finding Pompey in discussion with a dozen of his officers. The tent was simply furnished, with one long table and an ornate oak chair for Pompey. Benches rested against the walls for meetings and it had a spartan air of which Labienus approved. More importantly, the tent was far warmer than the outside. Braziers glowed on the packed earth, making the air thick and sluggish with heat. Labienus felt sweat break out on his skin at the sudden change.

'You've brought them here?' Pompey asked. His hand crept towards his stomach as he spoke.

'I've stripped and searched them, sir. With your permission, I will have my men bring them in.'

Pompey gestured to the maps that lay across a heavy table and one of the officers quickly gathered them into neat scrolls. When there was nothing important visible, he seated himself carefully, twitching his toga into perfect folds over his legs.

The three centurions held themselves well as they came into Pompey's presence. Even dressed as they were, their short-cropped hair and scarred arms marked them immediately for what they were. The escort kept their weapons bared as they took positions around the walls of the tent and left the three men facing Pompey. Labienus found himself breathing more heavily as he waited, his hunger forgotten.

'So tell me what Caesar has to say that is so important as to risk your lives,' Pompey said.

In the silence, only the crackle of the braziers could be heard.

The centurion who had spoken before took a step forward and, as one, the guards in the tent went from stillness to a knife edge of danger. He glanced around at them and raised his eyes for a moment as if he was amused by their stance.

'My name is Decimus, sir. Centurion of the Tenth legion. We have met once before, in Ariminum.'

'I remember you,' Pompey said. 'At the meeting with Crassus. You were there when Caesar brought gold back from Gaul.'

'I was, sir. Consul Caesar preferred to send a man you would recognise to show his good faith.'

Despite the neutral tone, Pompey coloured with anger immediately. 'Do not use a false title in my presence, Decimus. The man you follow does not have the right to claim consul in front of me.'

'He was elected by the voting centuries, sir, in accordance with the most ancient traditions. He claims his authority and rights as given him by the citizens of Rome.'

Labienus frowned, wondering what Decimus could hope to achieve by antagonising Pompey so early in the meeting. He could not escape the worrying thought that the words were intended for the other men there, who could be counted upon to discuss them with friends and colleagues. As if he shared the suspicion, Pompey glanced around the men in the tent, his eyes narrowing.

'As Dictator, even false consuls are answerable to my orders, Decimus, but I suspect you are not here to argue that point.'

'No, sir. I have been ordered here to request that soldiers loyal to Rome leave this camp and either quit the field or join Caesar's legions against you.'

There was immediate uproar. Pompey rose from his seat and at his signal, all three men were hammered to their knees by the guards closest to them. None of them made a sound. Pompey controlled himself with difficulty.

'Your master is insolent, Decimus. There are no traitors here.'

Decimus looked a little dazed from a blow to the back of his head. He raised a hand to rub where he had been struck and then thought better of the action. The guards around him were eager to cut him down at any provocation.

'In that case, I have his authority to offer peace, sir. For the good of Rome, he asks that you listen.'

Pompey remembered his dignity with difficulty. He raised his hand in preparation for ordering the deaths of the centurions and Decimus watched its movement, his eyes glittering in the light of the torches.

'Be warned, Decimus,' Pompey said at last. 'I will not be rebuked in my own camp. Choose your words carefully or you will be killed.'

Decimus nodded. 'Caesar wishes it to be known that he serves Rome above his own safety or ambition. He does not wish to see her armies broken against each other and so leave the city poorly defended for a generation. He offers peace, if certain conditions are met.'

Pompey clenched the fist he held up and one of the men with Decimus flinched slightly, expecting to feel cold iron in his back at any moment. Decimus did not respond to the threat, and as Pompey held his gaze they all heard voices raised outside the tent.

An instant later, Cicero entered with two other senators, sweeping into the warmth with crystals of ice on their cloaks. They were pale with the cold, but Cicero took in the scene before him immediately. He bowed to Pompey.

'General, I have come to represent the Senate at this meeting.'

Pompey glowered at the old man, unable to dismiss him while the three centurions watched.

'You are welcome, Cicero. Labienus, draw up a bench for the senators, that they may witness the impertinence of Caesar.'

The senators settled themselves and Decimus raised his eyebrows in inquiry. 'Should I repeat myself, General?' he said.

His calm was unnatural for a man with sharp iron at his neck and Labienus wondered if he had chewed one of the roots that were said to dull fear. Pompey resumed his seat and his long fingers fussed with the lines of his toga while he thought.

'Caesar has offered peace,' he said to Cicero. 'I suspect it is yet another attempt to sow discord amongst our men.'

Decimus bowed his head for a moment, and took a deep breath. 'My master claims the rights granted him by the people of Rome in lawful election. With those rights, he accepts the responsibility to avoid a war if it is possible. He fears that a conflict between us would leave Greece stripped and Rome undefended. He thinks first of Rome.'

Cicero leaned forward like an old hawk. 'But there is a sting to be borne, yes? I would not expect Caesar to brave our fleet to reach Greece and then meekly give up his ambition.'

Decimus smiled. 'No, Senator. He looks for a peaceful resolution only because he would not see Rome weakened.'

'What does he offer?' Cicero said.

Pompey flushed at the old man's interruptions, but pride prevented him from showing his anger in front of his most senior officers.

As if he sensed Pompey's discomfort, Decimus turned away from Cicero and addressed Pompey directly. 'Caesar offers a truce between the two armies. No man will be punished or held responsible for his officers at this time.'

He took another deep breath and Labienus tensed, sensing the strain Decimus was under.

'He asks only that Pompey take a small honour guard and leave Greece, perhaps to peaceful allies. His army will return to their posts and no harm will come to them for taking arms against the lawfully elected consul of Rome.'

Pompey rose once again, standing over the kneeling men. His voice was choked with fury. 'Does your master think I would accept a peace under those terms? I would rather be ashes than take my life at his generosity!'

Labienus looked around at the other men in the tent. He was bitter with regret and knew he should have had the men killed before they could reach Pompey. Who could tell what damage the offer might achieve by the time it had spread to the lowest ranks?

'I will let him know your response, General,' Decimus said.

Pompey shook his head, his expression hard. 'No, you will *not*,' he said. 'Kill them.'

170

Cicero rose in horror and Decimus too stood up as he heard the order. A legionary stepped towards the centurion and with a sneer Decimus opened his arms to receive the blade.

'You are not *fit* to lead Rome,' he said to Pompey, gasping as the gladius was shoved hard into his chest.

The pain distorted his features and yet he did not fall, but reached out to the hilt with both hands. Holding Pompey's gaze, Decimus pulled it further into himself, letting loose an animal cry of rage. As the other two had their throats opened, Decimus collapsed and the sickly smell of blood filled the tent. Some of the men made the hand gesture against evil spirits and Pompey himself was shaken by the man's extraordinary courage. He seemed to have shrunk in his chair and he could not tear his gaze from the bodies at his feet.

It was left to Labienus to give orders and he had the dead men removed, the guards following them. He could not believe what he had seen Decimus do, or his complete disregard for his own death. Caesar had chosen wisely in sending such a man, he was forced to acknowledge. Before dawn, every soldier in Pompey's camp would have heard of the centurion's words and actions. Above all things, they respected courage. Labienus frowned as he thought how best to handle the spread of information. Could he blunt the force of the tale with a counter rumour? It would be difficult, with so many witnesses. He knew his soldiers. Some of them would indeed wonder if they followed the right man.

As he stepped out into the howling wind and pulled his cloak more tightly around him, he could applaud the use of three lives for such an effect. They faced a ruthless enemy, and when it came he would relish Caesar's eventual destruction all the more.

He looked away into the distance as he considered his own commander. Labienus had known men who survived for years with ulcers or hernias. He remembered an old tent-mate who delighted in showing a shiny lump that stood out from his stomach, even taking coins from those who wanted to force it back in with a finger. Labienus hoped Pompey's illness was not the source of his weakening spirits. If it was, there could only be worse to come.

CHAPTER FOURTEEN

Julius could not remember ever having been so cold. Knowing he would make the crossing to Greece in winter, he had paid for his men to be outfitted in the best cloaks and woollen layers for their hands and feet. After marching through the night with only a few mouthfuls of rubbery meat to keep up his strength, his very thoughts seemed to flow more slowly, as if his mind was sluggish with ice.

The night had passed without catastrophe as his legions took a wide berth around Pompey's camp. The gibbous moon had given them enough light to make good progress and his veterans had stuck to the task doggedly, without a word of complaint.

He had met with Domitius' legion ten miles west of Pompey's camp and delayed two hours there while the cart animals were bullied and struck into movement. They too had been sheltered with blankets from the stores and they had eaten better than the men.

As dawn came, he could only estimate how far they had come north. Pompey's army would be preparing to march against an abandoned position and it could not be long before his absence was discovered. Then they would be hunted, by men who were rested and well fed. It would not take long for Pompey to guess his destination and seven legions left a trail that could hardly be disguised. Their iron-shod sandals beat the earth into a wide road a child could find.

'I . . . I do not remember Greece being this cold,' Julius stammered to the muffled figure of Octavian at his side. The younger man's features were hidden by so much cloth that only the plume of white breath proved he was somewhere within the mass.

'You said a legionary should rise above the discomforts of the body,' Octavian replied with a slight smile.

Julius glanced at him, amused that his relative appeared to remember every conversation they had ever had.

'Renius told me that a long time ago,' he confirmed. 'He said he'd seen dying men march all day before they fell. He said the true strength was in how far we could ignore the flesh. I sometimes think the man was a Spartan at heart, except for the heavy drinking.' He looked back at the column of his legions as they marched in grim silence. 'I hope we can outrun our pursuers.'

He saw Octavian's head turn stiffly towards him and he met the eyes that were deep within the folds of the hood.

'The men understand,' Octavian said. 'We will not let you down.'

Julius felt a tightness in his throat that had nothing to do with the cold. 'I know, lad. I do know,' he said gently.

The wind battered against them like the pressure of a warning hand as they pushed on. Julius could not speak for the pride he felt. He thought he hardly deserved the simple faith his men placed in his leadership. The responsibility was his alone to see them survive their time in Greece and he knew what he had been given in their trust.

'Pompey will be in our camp by now,' Octavian said suddenly, looking at the sun as it fought clear of the eastern hills. 'He'll come fast when he sees where we're going.'

'We'll run them into the ground,' Julius said, not sure if he believed it.

He had planned and prepared as much as he could before leaving Rome, but the simple fact was that he needed to find food for his men. Caecilius had said Dyrrhachium held the main supply and Julius would have to push his legions on through exhaustion to reach it. He had other reasons for going to the city, but without food, his campaign would come to a shuddering halt and everything they had fought for would be lost.

He feared the pursuit. Though his men had been well rested as they prepared the feint to the east, they could not march for ever in such conditions. No matter what Renius had thought of the spirit of fighting men, the strength of their bodies could only take them so far. Julius glanced behind him out of primitive fear, knowing that if Pompey's army was sighted, he would have to double the pace. His men would begin to fall without rest and Dyrrhachium was still far to the north.

Every stage of the campaign seemed to have skirted the edge of disaster, he thought privately. Perhaps after seizing the supplies in Dyrrhachium, he would have time to breathe without Pompey's army nipping at his heels. The only cause for optimism was that his knowledge of Pompey seemed to be giving him an edge in the manoeuvres. He had hoped Pompey would not attack while a full legion remained out of sight. Domitius had been ready to take Dyrrhachium alone if necessary, while Julius decoyed his enemy into the east, but Pompey had behaved exactly as he had hoped.

Julius told himself over and over that he had to be cautious, though he had never expected Pompey to abandon Rome. He could not shake the suspicion that the Dictator had lost his taste for war. If that was true, Julius knew he should do everything possible to keep Pompey afraid.

He looked at the sun and gave way to the inevitable.

'Call a halt here and let the men eat and sleep. We will rest for four hours before moving on.'

The horns sounded and Julius dismounted painfully, his hips and knees aching. All around him, the legionaries sat down where they were and took what little food they had from their packs. The dried meat was like stone and Julius looked dubiously at his ration as it was brought to him. It would need a lot of chewing before it approached being edible. Shivering like an old man, he forced a piece of it between his lips and took a swig from a waterskin to begin the softening. From a pouch in his cloak, he took a wad of dried watercress that was said to reverse baldness, pushing it into his cheek in a quick, furtive motion. Visions of soft bread and fruit in Dyrrhachium filled his thoughts as he worked his jaw.

Pompey was ten hours or less behind them and would make better time in the short winter day. Julius passed his reins to a soldier on first watch and lay down on the hard ground. He was asleep moments later.

Octavian smiled with affection as he saw the still, pale features. Careful not to wake him, he took an extra blanket from his saddle and draped it over his general.

Pompey put his hand into the ashes of a watch fire, frowning as he felt the warm heart. His stomach had revolted at the thought of food and he had eaten nothing since noon the day before. He swallowed bitter acid and winced as it seared his throat.

'Are the trackers in?' he demanded, his voice harsh with anger and pain.

'They are, sir,' Labienus replied. 'The path leads south and west before curving north towards Dyrrhachium.'

He stood stiffly in the wind, ignoring the discomfort of the cold while his thoughts raged within. The men would know very well that Pompey had lost an army of twenty thousand men through his caution. It would not help morale, after coming close enough to see them the day before. They had woken from sleep with the nervous tension that was to be expected before a battle and now there was no enemy to be seen.

'I knew it,' Pompey snapped, furious. 'As soon as I heard they had gone, I knew it. We should be able to cut that curve and gain

176

an hour on them.' He clenched a fist and tapped it on his leg. 'If it is Dyrrhachium they're after, there must be spies in the camps,' he said, working his mouth.

Labienus stared at the horizon.

'How could they go round us without a single scout marking their movement, Labienus? Tell me that!' Pompey demanded.

Labienus knew as well as he that the proof that it could be done lay in the fact that it had been. By taking a wide route, Caesar had not come closer to Pompey's camp than two miles and it had clearly been enough. Pompey did not seem to require an answer.

'It seems that I must follow,' he went on, angrily. 'They have had the night to get ahead. Can we catch them?'

Labienus looked at the sun automatically, judging how many hours had been lost. His sour conclusion was that it would be near impossible, but he could not find it in himself to tell Pompey in that mood.

'At our best speed, eating on the march and without sleep, we should hit their rear before they are in the city,' he said. 'Your new walls may slow them.' He paused to choose the right words that would not worry Pompey further. 'Even if they reach the city, they will need time to replenish their supplies. We can deny them that.'

Labienus was careful to keep any hint of criticism from his voice, though he was privately appalled at the turn of events. Dyrrhachium was a key port on the coast and still the main store for the army in the field. Caesar's legions should not have been allowed to make a strike for it. He knew some of the responsibility lay on his shoulders, but it profited nothing to dwell on past mistakes. The new position was not yet lost.

Pompey glared around him. 'Then let us leave this barren place. Everything but food and water must come behind us at the best speed they can manage. The Senate too: they won't stand the pace we will set.'

As Labienus saluted, Pompey mounted, his movements stiff

with anger. He did not need to say that his family and the families of the Senate were in Dyrrhachium. Once Julius had them as hostages, his position would be immeasurably stronger. Pompey shook his head to clear it of hatred and fear. His stomach seemed to have settled as he made the decision and he hoped a dose of chalk and milk would keep it docile for the day. His legions began to move around him, but he could no longer take comfort from their numbers.

Julius calculated the distance they had come, wishing he had the map in front of him. They had marched for twelve hours and the men were dragging their feet in the dust. Though they bore it grimly, some of them were staggering along and Julius had finally given the order to close up and rest an arm on the shoulder in front. It made them resemble invalids or refugees rather than legions of Rome, but every mile was one further from the enemy behind.

'It should be in sight by now, surely?' Octavian said at his side.

Julius stared at him in silence until his younger relative swallowed and looked away. Julius squinted into the distance, searching for the first sign of the city. The sea glimmered silver to the west and that gave him hope that they were close. His eyes felt painful with weariness and he might have closed them as he rode, if the weakness would not have been seen.

Julius remembered marching in the wake of Spartacus' slave army years before, and it was strange to realise there was a huge advantage in being the hunter in such a chase. Something about being followed sapped the will to go on and Julius saw more and more of the heads turn to watch the land behind as they marched. He was on the point of snapping an order to keep their eyes to the front when he saw Domitius was there ahead of him, bellowing out commands as he rode up and down the ranks.

The ground they walked on was stained in places by dark splashes of urine. It was not an easy thing to do whilst marching, but the men were long inured to it. The ones at the back would be walking on damp ground all the way to Dyrrhachium. When they stopped to rest, there was no time to dig a latrine pit, and they had to use whatever foliage they could find to wipe themselves clean. Some of the men carried a cloth that they dampened with water, but the material became slick and foul after the first night and day. A long march was an unpleasant, stinking business for all of them and the cold ate at their strength far worse than a summer's heat.

The day seemed to have lasted for ever and although Julius had been irritated with Octavian's comment, he too thought Dyrrhachium should have been in sight by then. The sun was already dropping towards the horizon and the order to snatch another four hours of precious rest would have to come soon.

A warning note sounded from the rear of the column and Julius turned in the saddle, craning to see. In the distance, something glinted amidst a low line of dust. He shook his head in desperation. Just at the moment when he would have called a halt, Pompey had appeared on the horizon. Julius did not know whether to rage at the fact that the gap had been closed, or be thankful his aching, exhausted men had not been told to stop at this most dangerous time. He looked at the stumbling, swaying lines of men and knew they would somehow have to go on.

Two of his far-flung extraordinarii came galloping back to his position and saluted as they turned their mounts.

'What news?' Julius asked, impatient at the slightest delay.

'The city is in sight, sir. Three miles ahead.'

Automatically, Julius looked at the sun and back at his column. It would be dark before they reached the walls, but the news would keep the men going, for all that.

'There is a wall before the city, sir, about two miles away. It looks manned.'

179

Julius swore aloud. Pompey had been busy. The thought of having to break through a defensive line while Pompey came racing up behind was almost too much to bear.

'I'll ride forward with you,' he said quickly. 'I must see this for myself.' As he took a tighter grip on the reins, he looked over his shoulder at Octavian. 'Tell the men to resume the standard distance between ranks. I will not be shamed in front of the enemy. Increase the pace for the last miles.'

He saw Octavian hesitate, not daring to voice his dislike of such an order.

'They will not let me down, General. My Tenth will lead them in.'

In the gloom of the fading day, the army of Caesar sent tremors of fear into the hearts of every soldier who stood on the uncompleted wall around Dyrrhachium. At the full height of twelve feet and with a few thousand men, they might have had a chance of stopping the Gaul legions, but more than one section was just a few beams across a gap. It would not be nearly enough.

The warning shouts of Pompey's officers sent the Greek labourers haring back to the protection of the city, tools littering the ground around them. Those grim soldiers who were left took positions as they were ordered, drawing swords and exchanging a few last words. They did not consider turning away, though the wind made them shiver as they waited.

'Hold until you are relieved,' the senior centurion bellowed, making his voice carry. It was taken up further down the line and the defenders raised their shields and readied themselves. They all knew there would be no relief force, but it was strange how the words brought a little hope.

Caesar's legions came closer and closer, until faces could be seen despite the failing light. Both sides roared a challenge as the Gaul legions reached the last barrier to Dyrrhachium and forced their way through. The gaps in the wall vomited men and the defenders were cut down, their bodies tumbling. Julius' Tenth stormed through with barely a check on their speed, loping on towards the unprotected city.

CHAPTER FIFTEEN

Julius rode slowly through dark streets, struggling with exhaustion. A local man led the way with a gladius prodding his back, but it was still disconcerting to be so deep in a maze of streets that none of them had ever seen before.

Only the Tenth had been allowed into the inner city. The other six legions would see no more of it than the walls they manned. Julius was determined not to give them a loose rein in hostile territory. He still shuddered to remember a town in Gaul where he had lost control of his men. Whenever his heart was made to race by the thunder of a charge or the snap of flags in a stiff breeze, he would recall Avaricum and how the streets had looked with the coming of day. He would not allow such actions to be repeated under his command.

If any other man had led the Greek legions, Julius would have expected an assault in the night. Pompey's officers knew the city well and there could even have been entrances Julius had not seen. It was enough of a threat to keep his own men out of trouble on the walls, but he did not think Pompey would risk the lives he valued in Dyrrhachium. The days of reckless youth were behind for both of them.

His guide mumbled something in Greek and pointed to a wide gate set into a wall. A single lamp hung from a brass chain to light the entrance and Julius had the whimsical thought that it had been set there to welcome him. He gestured and two men with hammers stepped forward to break the lock. In the silent street, the sound was like a ringing bell and Julius could feel eyes on him from all the local houses. Possibilities swirled in his head and he took a deep breath of the night air, thinking of the enemy outside the walls of Dyrrhachium.

To fight a war with subtlety and propaganda was dangerously intoxicating. Julius seized on every tiny detail of Pompey's strengths and weaknesses, anything that might be used. He had sent men to undermine the Dictator in his own camp, knowing they could be killed. It was a vicious sort of war they had carried to Greece, but he had come too far and lost too much to lose it all.

His sombre thoughts were interrupted as the gate fell with a clang on the stones of the street. The noise had woken the house and lamps were being lit inside, acting as a spark for the local inhabitants as they roused and sought light to banish terror.

As he had expected, the sound of marching feet came quickly behind the hammer blows and it was only moments before the space in the wall filled with grim soldiers. Julius did not speak at first, watching with professional interest as they locked their shields to prevent a sudden rush.

'You are late, gentlemen,' he said, dismounting. 'I could have been inside by now if I hadn't waited for you.'

Five hundred of his Tenth were stretched along the street and he could feel their tension in the biting air. A single word from him and they would cut the defenders down. He looked into the eyes of the centurion guarding the gate and was intrigued to find no sign of fear there. The officer did not bother to answer and merely returned his stare. Pompey had chosen well.

'I am a consul of Rome,' Julius said, taking a step forward. 'Do not dare to block my way.'

The men in the gateway shifted uncomfortably, the words pulling at everything they had been taught from childhood.

The centurion blinked and Julius saw him reach out to one of the defenders, settling him.

'My orders are from Pompey, Consul,' the centurion said. 'This house is not to be touched.'

Julius frowned. It would not be a good beginning for his new policies if he butchered decent men doing their duty. With the restrictions he had imposed on himself, it was an impasse.

'Will you allow me entry on my own? I will come unarmed,' he said, stepping into range of the weapons held before him.

The centurion narrowed his eyes and Julius heard a hiss of breath from the soldiers of the Tenth. His legion would not like him walking into danger, but he could see no other choice.

A voice sounded from within the grounds. 'Let me through!'

Julius smiled as he recognised it. A low murmur of protest came from somewhere out of sight.

'The man you have kept waiting is my father. I don't care what your orders are, you will let me through to him!'

Once again the soldiers at the gate shifted, this time in excruciating embarrassment. Julius laughed at their predicament.

'I don't think you can stop her coming out to me, can you, gentlemen? Will you lay hands on Pompey's own wife? I think not. My daughter walks where she chooses.'

Though he spoke to all of them, his eyes held those of the centurion, knowing the decision was his. At last the man spoke a few curt words and the shields were pulled back.

Julia stood there, her son in her arms. Julius breathed in deeply and noticed the fragrance of the garden for the first time, as if she had brought the scent with her.

'Will you invite me in, Julia?' he asked, smiling.

Julia cast a scornful glance at the soldiers around the gate, still standing awkwardly. Her face was flushed and Julius thought his daughter had never looked more beautiful than in the light of the single lamp.

'You may stand down, Centurion,' she said. 'My father will be tired and hungry. Run to the kitchens and have refreshments brought.'

The centurion opened his mouth, but she spoke again before he could voice any objection.

'I want the best sausage, fresh bread, hot wine from my husband's cellar, cheese and a little fruit.'

The beleaguered soldier looked at father and daughter for a long moment before he gave up. With stiff dignity, he retreated at last.

'My home is yours, Consul,' Julia said and from the way her eyes sparkled, Julius knew she had enjoyed the clash of wills. 'Your visit is an honour.'

'You are kind, daughter,' he replied, enjoying the mock formality. 'Tell me, are the families of the Senate still in the city?'

'They are.'

Julius turned to his men, noting the nervous figure of the Greek who had guided them in from the walls. The man shook with fear as Julius considered him.

'You will lead my men to the families,' Julius said. 'They will not be harmed, I swear it.' The Greek bowed his head as Julius addressed his men. 'Gather them . . .'

He paused to look at his daughter. 'I do not know this city. Is there a senate building, a meeting hall?'

'The temple of Jupiter is well known,' Julia replied.

'That will do very well,' Julius said. 'Remember, gentlemen, that my honour protects them. I will hang you for a single bruise. Is that clear?'

'Yes, sir,' his centurion replied for all of them.

'Send men to General Domitius and tell him to begin loading the supplies onto our carts. I want to be able to leave quickly in the morning.'

The soldiers of the Tenth marched away, the noise of their steps fading slowly in the echoing street.

'So this is my grandson,' Julius said. The little boy was still half asleep and did not stir as Julius laid a hand gently on his head. 'Am I truly welcome here, Julia?' he said softly.

'How could my father not be?' she asked him.

'Because I am at war with your husband and you are caught between us.'

She reached out to touch the man who had been absent for all of her childhood and most of her life. He had escaped showing her the normal faults of fathers. She had never seen him beat a dog or fall down drunk, or show some petty spite. She knew him only as the general of Gaul, a consul of Rome. It was true that she had hated him with all the passion of a young girl when he first offered her to Pompey as a wife, but the habit of adoration was too strong for that to last. Brutus had brought her into her father's conspiracies for the first time, and it was a heady joy to be valuable to this man. It was too much to put into words and instead she decided to give the only proof of loyalty that she had.

'If your blood did not run true in me, I would have given Brutus away,' she whispered into his ear.

Time stood still for Julius as his mind raced. He struggled to remain calm.

'What did he tell you?' he said.

She blushed a little and he could not help the suspicion that came into his thoughts.

'That his betrayal is part of your planning.' She saw that he closed his eyes for a moment and misunderstood. 'I told no one. I even helped him get another two cohorts from my husband.'

She raised her chin with fragile pride that wounded him. He felt the exhaustion of the long march north as if it had been waiting for just such a moment. He swayed slightly as he looked at her and put out his hand to the wall.

'Good . . . good,' he said absently. 'I did not think he would tell you that.'

186

'He trusted me,' Julia said. 'And I trust you to let my husband live, if it falls to your hand by the end. That is the choice I made, Father. If you win, both of you will survive.' She looked at him with pleading eyes and he could not bear to tell her there was no secret agreement with Brutus. It would destroy her. 'The pardon at Corfinium was news here for months,' she went on. 'Can you do less for him?'

With infinite tenderness, Julius took her hand. 'Very well. If it is in my gift, he will live.'

The temple to Jupiter in Dyrrhachium was very nearly as cold as the streets outside. Julius' breath was a streamer of mist as he entered, his men taking places along the walls with clattering efficiency.

All noise ceased as he walked down the long central aisle towards the great white statue of the god. His sandals clicked and echoed, and at the end he saw the families of the Senate still blinking in the light. They resembled refugees after their hasty summons by armed guards. The benches were packed with them and more sat on the cold marble floor. They fluttered with renewed fear at the sight of the general their men had come to Greece to destroy.

Julius ignored their beady-eyed scrutiny. He halted before the statue of Jupiter and went down briefly onto one knee, bowing his head. It was an effort to concentrate and he had to smother the worry and fear his daughter had caused him. Brutus was a practised seducer, and it was easy to see how vulnerable she would have been. Yet to involve her in such a way was breathtakingly callous. It was no comfort to know that Julius had given her to Pompey with as little compunction. That was his right as her father. The general who knelt in the lamplight added the information to what he knew of Pompey's forces. Brutus was a little in love with risk and perhaps that could be used. The father and the man were so angry he could barely reason.

187

'So will you close the doors and have us killed?' a harsh voice came, shattering his reverie.

Julius looked up sharply as he rose, recognising Cicero's wife, Terentia. She looked like a raven swathed in black, with sharp features and sharper eyes.

Julius forced himself to smile, though the effect caused some of the younger children to start bawling, grating on his ears.

'I am a consul of Rome, madam. I do not make war on women and children,' he said coldly. 'My honour keeps you safe.'

'Are we to be hostages then?' Terentia demanded. Her voice had a particularly shrill note that made Julius wonder what Cicero saw in her.

'For tonight. My men will make you as comfortable as they can in this building.'

'What are you planning, Caesar?' Terentia said, narrowing her eyes. 'Pompey will never forget this, do you realise that? He will not rest until your armies are butchered.'

Julius felt anger surge through him. 'Be silent,' he snapped, his voice rising in volume. 'You know nothing of my business, or Pompey's. Leave your threats for your sisters. My men fight because they love Rome and because they love me. Don't *speak* of them.'

Bitter shame flooded him as he saw the fear in their faces. He was sickened by his own weakness. With a huge effort, he took control, clasping his shaking hands behind his back.

Terentia raised her head in defiance. 'So you are one of *those* men, Caesar,' she said, sneering. 'You put swords into your enemies and you think it is something wonderful. A butcher might as well sing songs about the pigs he kills each day.' One of the other women put a hand on her arm but she shook herself free. 'You are here because you chose to be, Caesar, do not forget that! You could have gone back to Gaul with those legions that "love" you. If you valued their lives, you would have saved them then.'

Fear became palpable as the rest froze. Something in Julius' own pale fury made her realise she had gone too far, and she looked away, biting her lip. After a long pause, he spoke with terrible force.

'Men *will* die, but they give their lives because they understand more than you ever could. We are here to make the future, woman, nothing less. We will not be ruled by kings. For your safety, for our citizens in Spain and Greece and Gaul, we are here to remake the Republic. It's a worthy dream. What makes us different from the tribes of Gaul, or the men of Greece? We eat, we sleep, we trade. But there is more, Terentia. More than comfort and more than gold. More even than family, which must eat at you. You sneer because you cannot see there must be a time when a man looks up from his work and says, "No. This is too much to bear."'

Terentia might even then have replied if the women around her had not whispered harshly in warning. She subsided under Julius' glare and would not look at him again.

'If you have sense,' Julius went on, 'you will tell the Senate that I have only one enemy in Greece and I have offered him exile rather than this conflict. I have shown my honour at Corfinium. Tell them to remember that I am consul by the same citizens who granted their authority. Rome is with *me*.' He looked at their hard faces and shrugged. 'Make your personal needs known to my men, within reason. I will be on the walls. I will send word to your husbands and fathers that you are safe and unharmed. That is all.'

Without another word, Julius spun on his heel and strode back towards the great doors to the temple. His eyes itched with exhaustion and the thought of collapsing into a soft bed drew him with the force of lust. He knew his battered body would carry him on for a little longer, but then he would run the risk of pushing himself into a fit on this crucial night. He still rode the knife edge and a single slip could cost him the war.

As he reached his guards, the centurion met his eyes for an instant and nodded briefly, proving he had been listening. Julius

189

returned the gesture with a tight smile as he went outside into the cold dark. Dawn was still far away and the stunned city was silent with fear. The invader walked amongst them.

Pompey looked up at the walls of the city, thankful for the darkness that hid his despair. He had dismissed Labienus with only the barest attempt at civility, furious that they had not reached Dyrrhachium before Caesar was safe to strut inside. The pain in his stomach felt like he was being eaten alive from within. The chalky gruels that had helped in the beginning now seemed almost useless. A soft moan came from his mouth as he kneaded his gut with a fist. He had wiped blood from his lips before coming out and viewed the red specks that stained the white cloth with sick dread. His own body was turning on him and he shoved hard fingers into his flesh as if he could dig the sickness out by force. He could not afford to be ill and he thought the Senate demands had become more strident with the worsening pain. It was as if they scented his weakness and were ready to tear him apart.

Only the stern resistance of his soldiers had kept Cicero and his colleagues from reaching him in his tent. What was there to be gained from another bickering discussion with them? Pompey couldn't bear the thought of having to be polite to those frightened men as they bleated about their precious wives and slaves.

He did not know what Caesar would do with the city. Of course, the stores would disappear into the ravening maw of his legions. Pompey had listened to Labienus' dispassionate appraisal of their own supplies now that Dyrrhachium was closed to them. He thanked his gods that he had found the foresight to shift tons of it before the war started. At least his own men would not starve while Julius grew fat on salt beef and black treacle.

He heard the sound of hooves in the darkness and looked up at the shadowy figure of Labienus approaching. With an effort,

Pompey stood straighter to receive him, letting his hand fall. The pain in his stomach seemed to intensify, but he would not show it to his general.

'What is it now?' he snapped as Labienus dismounted.

'A messenger from Caesar, sir. He has come under a flag of truce,' Labienus replied.

Both men thought of the three centurions Julius had used before and wondered if this man too would sow discord in the camps.

'Have him brought to me in my tent, Labienus. Inform no one if you value your commission.'

Pompey struggled to maintain his impassive expression as a spot writhed in his stomach. Without waiting for a reply, he walked past his guards and seated himself in his tent, ready to hear what Caesar wanted.

He had barely settled when Labienus brought the man into his presence. Sweat broke out on Pompey's brow despite the cold and he mopped at it with a cloth, unaware of the brown stain of old blood.

The messenger was a tall, thin soldier with close-cropped hair and dark eyes that took in every detail of the man he faced. Pompey wondered if his illness would be reported and it took all his strength to ignore the pain he suffered. No sign of it must reach Caesar.

'Well?' he demanded impatiently.

'General. My master wishes you to know that the Senate families are unharmed. He will return them to you at dawn. The city of Dyrrhachium will be yours by noon. He has forbidden looting or damage of any kind.'

Pompey saw Labienus blink in surprise. It was unheard of for an army to give up the advantage they had won so easily.

'What does he want?' Pompey said, suspiciously.

'Three days, sir. He offers you the families and the city for the

191

supplies within and three days of truce to get clear. He asks that you accept these terms.'

'Labienus,' Pompey said, 'take him away while I think.'

In the moments of precious privacy, Pompey leaned forward, wincing. By the time Labienus returned, he was upright again and his face was bright with sweat.

'Are you ill, sir?' Labienus asked immediately.

'A passing discomfort. Tell me what you think of these terms.'

Pompey's mind felt clouded and the pain made it almost impossible to plan. As if he understood, Labienus spoke quickly.

'It seems generous, though once again our men will see Caesar act the role of statesman. They will see the families released and the truce days will be another victory as we are forced to follow his lead.' Labienus paused. 'If the stakes were not so high, I would attack at dawn, as the gates are opened to release the families.'

'They could be killed in such a venture,' Pompey snapped.

Labienus nodded. 'That is a risk, though I doubt it. Caesar would have been denied the chance to show his generosity to us all. Morale is low in our camps and three more have been caught trying to desert.'

'I was not informed!' Pompey said angrily.

Labienus held his gaze for a moment. 'You were not available, sir.'

Pompey remembered his earlier dismissal and flushed.

'Make it known that any deserters will be killed in front of the rest. I will remind them of their duty with the blood of those men.'

'I thought we might question them first, sir, and . . .'

'No. Kill them at dawn as a lesson to the others.' He hesitated, anger struggling against the need to send the man away and tend his pain. 'I will grant the truce, Labienus. I have no choice if my Dictatorship is to be renewed. The Senate families must be kept from harm.'

'And the city, sir? If we let him go without resistance, he will have the supplies to keep him in the field for three months at least. We must attack when the Senate families are safe.'

'And how long do you think it would be before every common soldier knows I broke my word? You see the choice he has left me?' Pompey said.

'This is a chance to end it, sir,' Labienus said softly.

Pompey glared at him, wanting him gone. His eyes strayed to a pestle and mortar that contained a little of the gruel from an hour before. He could hardly bear to have Labienus continue a moment longer in his presence. He remembered a time when his oath had made him who he was.

'Get out, General. Caesar has offered a good price for three days of truce. After that, we will be free to take the war to him again. No more now.'

Labienus saluted stiffly. 'I will tell the messenger what you have ordered, sir,' he said.

Alone at last, Pompey called for his physician and closed his eyes against the pain that consumed him.

CHAPTER SIXTEEN

Julius sighed with pleasure as he finished his meal. Every cart with his legions groaned under the weight of the provisions they had taken from the city. For the first time since coming to Greece, the men were able to eat well. Their new confidence could be seen as they marched and even the cold did not seem to bite with such ferocity.

In the command tent, his generals were in jovial mood as they sampled good wine and tore into meat and fresh bread made from Greek grain. The fact that it had come from Pompey's supplies seemed to give it all a special flavour.

Julius looked around at the seven men he had gathered in this place, proud of them all. He knew there would be harder days to come, but why should they not laugh and joke amongst themselves? They had fooled Pompey in the field and then forced him to accept a truce in exchange for a city. That was a move they applauded more than the legionaries, who felt cheated of their usual spoils. Even then, they had such a belief in Julius that the grumbling was muted. As soldiers, they rejoiced in stratagems that humbled their enemy without a major battle.

'If I can drag you away from your trough, gentlemen,' Julius said, tapping the table for attention, 'the scouts are in and there is news.' He put a hand over his mouth to belch and smiled, remembering the long hard march to take the city. The gods were smiling on his venture and though he warned himself against overconfidence, the latest reports confirmed what he had come to believe. He had their attention.

'Pompey's army has not left Dyrrhachium. He has continued with his line of forts and walls, now that we have shown the need for them.'

Octavian slapped Domitius on the back at this and Julius smiled at their enthusiasm.

'We have only one man in the city itself and Caecilius has not been able to reach us. The scouting reports are all we have. It may be that Pompey intends to ring the city with a line of solid forts before he takes the field once more. Or perhaps he has lost his taste for war completely. He is not the man he once was. When I think of how he fought Spartacus, the change is extraordinary.'

'He's grown old,' Regulus said.

Julius exchanged a glance with him, knowing that Regulus knew Pompey as well as any of them. 'He's not yet sixty, though I cannot think of any other reason for him to play such a defensive role. He has twice the men at my command, yet they sit around Dyrrhachium and do nothing but build walls to keep us out.'

'Perhaps he's terrified of us,' Octavian said, between mouthfuls of salted beef. 'We've given him cause after leading him around Greece by the nose. The Senate have their wives and daughters back by your generosity and they must know we could have burnt Dyrrhachium.'

Julius nodded, thinking. 'I had hoped some of his legions would have joined us by now. I have done everything but ride to ask them personally, yet still there are only a few who dare to defy Pompey and the Senate. The scouts report more than eighty heads adorning his new walls, honourable men who answered our call and were caught. Fewer still have made it to our camps.'

'It will not help him,' Domitius said. 'The more he kills for desertion, the more will lose respect for him. We gave them

Dyrrhachium without hurting a hair of the citizens' heads. Killing his own men must aid our cause.'

'I hope so, though I wish more had tried to reach us,' Julius said. 'Their loyalty is proving a difficult obstacle.' He rose to his feet and began to pace the floor of the tent. 'Unless we can reduce his numbers, we have not gained more than a respite. How long will this new meat and grain last? Pompey can be supplied by sea while we have to carry everything with us.' He shook his head. 'We must not be complacent. I have tried to beat him without bloodshed, but I think it is time to risk a little more than that.'

Julius held up a written report and glanced at the words on the parchment once more.

'His legions are spread thinly to build these walls. Only six cohorts are stationed at the furthest eastern point of his lines. If I take a single legion, leaving our equipment here, we can cut them out of his control and reduce his strength. More importantly, we need a solid victory to sway more of his men into coming over to us. This could give us that.'

The mood in the tent changed as they realised the days of planning and strategy were over. Food was laid aside and they watched their pacing leader, feeling the old excitement stiffen their backs.

'I do not want to be dragged into a major confrontation, gentlemen. This is to be a fast strike, in and then out again. Ciro, you may remember how we fought Mithridates in this same land. That is what I have in mind. We will destroy these cohorts and then withdraw before Pompey can summon his main army.'

He paused, looking around at the faces of the men he trusted.

'Domitius, you will command four cohorts and hit them on one side as I attack on the other. We have the advantage of surprise and darkness and it should be over quickly.'

'Yes, sir,' Domitius said. 'Will four cohorts be enough?'

'With four more under me, it will. A small force can move quickly and silently. Any more and Pompey may have the chance to prepare a counterattack. This is all about speed. We'll march in darkness, smash them and disappear.' He rubbed a point on his forehead as he thought. 'It may sting Pompey into taking the field. If that happens, all legions are to withdraw south until we reach land best suited for a defence.'

'What if he does not move?' Ciro asked.

'Then he has lost his nerve completely. I assume the Senate will attempt to replace him with another from his Greek legions. I will then reopen negotiations. Without Pompey, any action they take will be illegal and we should have more of them desert to us.' He picked up his cup of wine and raised it in a toast to them.

'There is no moon tonight. As they will not come out, we will take the fight to them.'

The work of building Pompey's walls never ceased. Even in the winter darkness, the men laboured in shifts under flickering torches. Labienus looked over the hillside, listening to the calls and orders as his legion built an extension to the fortifications around Dyrrhachium.

'This is madness,' he murmured under his breath.

Even standing alone, he glanced around him to see if any of his men could have heard. Ever since Dyrrhachium had been handed back to Pompey, Labienus had found his personal discipline strained to the point of breaking. He was forced to watch as Pompey gave up chances to end the war, wasting his men on forts around a city that had already lost its only real value. True, more supplies were being landed in the port, but to spend time and strength on protecting one small area while Caesar roamed the rest of Greece went against all Labienus' instincts. In his most private thoughts, he had realised Pompey was terrified. Whether it was the illness he vainly sought to hide, or simply that his courage had deserted him, Labienus could not tell. He did not care what the reason was. The largest army Greece had seen in generations was either growing soft in the city or building useless defences.

It was infuriating to see loyal legions become sullen and watchful. Only that morning, Labienus had carried out the execution of another four men at Pompey's order. The record of punishment would show they were insolent, though that had come only after Pompey condemned them. It had begun with a flogging for carrying bone dice on watch. Three of them had been fools enough to let their anger show.

Labienus clenched his fist in a spasm. He had known one of them personally and suffered the misery of having to reject a private appeal. He had risked a request for mercy, but Pompey would not see him until the executions had been carried out.

It was fear, Labienus supposed, to see enemies even amongst your own men. Pompey took out his frustration on the legions of Greece and the worst of it was that they knew very well what was happening and despised him for it. Labienus could sense their restlessness and growing anger. Eventually, the most loyal of soldiers would rebel under such treatment.

In a climate of suspicion, Labienus detested the risks he was forced to take. When he tried to consult with Pompey, he was rebuffed, but the chain of command threw up its orders and requests as always. He could not allow his subordinates to see Pompey's weakness. Each morning, Labienus issued crisp instructions as if they were from Pompey, hoping all the time that the Dictator would come to his senses and resume control. It was a suicidally dangerous game, but Pompey's only interest seemed to be the defensive walls that grew like ugly bones across the landscape. With the pace he demanded, lives were lost building them and the mood of the legions was souring further each day. They knew their strength and numbers should not be wasted, even if Pompey didn't.

Only that morning, Labienus had had to send his military tribunes away as they broached the subject of Pompey's leadership. They did not understand he could not be seen to waver. His loyalty had to be public and absolute, or the chain of command would shatter. It was too dangerous even to discuss and he was still furious with their stupidity. More worrying was the fact that if senior men dared to bring it up, the rot must be deep amongst the lower ranks.

Labienus suspected he had not been sent so far from the city by accident. Perhaps Pompey already doubted his loyalty. He was certainly suspicious enough. The last time Labienus had been admitted into his presence, one of Julius' propaganda sheets had been found circulating and Pompey had raged about the traitors amongst them, promising more and more savage reprisals. Copying the letters had become punishable by death, but still they appeared. Pompey had insisted on reading Caesar's words aloud, spittle and chalk forming a paste at the corners of his mouth. In the days that followed, he had begun sudden inspections of the legions around the city, punishing the slightest error with brutal floggings.

The thought that could never be spoken aloud had become a whisper at last for Labienus. Unless Pompey recovered from whatever plagued him, he could destroy them all. Though it was almost painful to consider, Labienus knew there could come a time when he would have to take control himself.

He thought the Senate would back him, if they could bring themselves to overturn Pompey's authority. The Dictatorship they renewed each year was ending in only a few days. It would either pass without incident, or Pompey would be broken. If Pompey called on the legions without a Senate mandate, Labienus knew he would have to oppose him. It would be chaos. Some would follow Pompey, perhaps more would desert to Caesar. Labienus shuddered, telling himself it was just the cold.

Julius lay flat on the hard earth and felt the chill of it seep into him. Hidden by the darkness more than the undergrowth, he watched the building work for a full hour, noting every detail of the men who toiled on Pompey's walls and forts.

The soldiers who carried wood and bricks were never far from their weapons, he saw. Only the fact that they did not have sentries out for miles showed their feeling of safety. Julius bit his lip as he considered whether it meant a larger force was close enough to answer their horns. He had no way of being sure without going past the line of Pompey's walls, and the plan had already been set. Domitius had taken two thousand men of the Third legion in a wide circle to the north. When Julius fired flaming arrows into the air, they would hammer both sides of the camp at the same time. With the gods' luck, it would be a quick destruction.

Julius wondered suddenly if Brutus was down there amongst his enemies, perhaps anticipating just such an attack. They had mounted night missions in Gaul; would he have warned Pompey? Julius shook his head in a spasm, angry that he was allowing his thoughts to wander. He had seen it happen to others, when foresight tipped over into indecision. He clenched his jaw against the cold and concentrated on seeing only what was real.

In the deep darkness, the sentries seemed to vanish between the lamps that lined the perimeter of the camp. The wall too was lined with them, so that its glittering length stretched away towards Dyrrhachium.

He glanced up to where Venus had risen. He had waited long enough for Domitius to get into position. Slowly, Julius drew the sword at his waist and heard the sibilant whisper as the soldiers of the Third legion did the same around him. To their credit, there was not a single murmur to disturb the silence of the night. He had chosen them in part because they had been Brutus' legion. He knew they needed to be blooded against the enemy more than any other group. They had suffered jeers and humiliation after their general's betrayal and they still burned with the shame of it. This night would go some way to restoring their pride.

'Pass the word for archers,' Julius whispered, keeping so low that he could smell the dark earth. He had brought a full hundred of them to attack the camp and once the fire arrows had flown, they would wreak havoc amongst the enemy.

Julius winced as their flints sparked. Their bodies hid the flashes as they worked, but he still worried that some sharp-eyed sentry would spot the light and sound an alarm. He breathed out in relief when flames flickered at last, passed quickly along the line until a hundred arrows burned.

'Now!' Julius called and the flames shot high into the air. Domitius would see them and come in to shatter the camp.

Julius rose to his feet. 'With me,' he said, beginning to run down the slope. They followed him.

Domitius crawled through the darkness, pausing only to take a sight of the stars he needed to stay on course. The route he had chosen led him inside the unfinished wall and he was able to use their own lights to judge his progress. There were no sentries within the perimeter and his two thousand were still undiscovered. He prayed they would remain so, knowing that Julius must not attack without him.

He was proud of the trust Julius had placed in his leadership, but it added to the terrible tension he felt as he wormed his way across the dark landscape. Sweat stung his eyes from the physical effort, but he was determined to be in position by the time Julius gave the signal.

He glanced behind him at the men who had come on the attack. Their faces had been blackened with charcoal and they were almost invisible. When they rose to attack the flank of the legion camp, they would seem to come from nowhere. Domitius grunted as a sharp stone scraped along his ribs. He was thirsty, but they had not even brought water with them on this lightning raid. He was thankful not to have to drag a skin or a shield through the undergrowth. Their only encumbrances were swords and even those caught on roots and made progress harder.

Two of Domitius' forward scouts came crouching back to him. He jumped as they appeared at his shoulder without a sound.

'Sir, there's a river ahead,' the closest one whispered into his ear.

Domitius stopped moving. 'Deep?' he demanded.

'Looks like it, sir. It's right in our path.'

Domitius grimaced. He ordered his men to halt, knowing that time was running out for all of them. Venus was approaching the zenith and Julius would go in knowing Domitius would be there to support him.

Half-rising, Domitius ran forward for a hundred paces. He heard the sound of water and saw a strip of moving blackness. Sudden fear touched him.

'How wide is it?'

'I don't know, sir. I went in up to my waist, then came back to warn you,' the man replied. 'There's a vicious current. I don't know if we can get across it.'

Domitius grabbed him, almost throwing him towards the water. 'We have to! This is why you are sent ahead. Take a rope across while I bring the men up.'

As the scout clambered into the shallows, Domitius ran back to the silent cohorts. It took only moments to bring them to the river and together they waited in the darkness.

Domitius clenched his fists as the minutes stretched with no sign.

At intervals, he reached out to touch the rope that had been tied around a fallen tree. It twitched invisibly and he cursed the delay. He should have given the scout some sort of signal to tell them he had reached the other side, he realised. Such tiny details were easy to forget in the heat of the moment, but now he had to suffer the wait. The scout could have drowned, or he could just as easily be making his slow way back to them. He reached for the rope again and swore softly. It was slack and there was no movement.

The enemy camp was visible beyond the far bank. Domitius could see their lamps like gold coins in the dark. He fretted and shivered in the cold.

'Two more into the water here,' he ordered at last. 'Ten more in each direction to find a fording place. We have to cross this.'

As he spoke, he saw bright streaks of fiery arrows leap into the air from the other side of the camp.

'Oh gods, no,' he whispered.

Labienus was jerked from his thoughts by screaming. He hesitated only for an instant as he saw a line of black figures appear in the pools of lamp-light and slaughter the first of his legionaries.

'Horns!' he bellowed. 'We are attacked! Sound horns!'

He began to run towards the enemy as the strident notes sounded, knowing he had to take control quickly. Then he halted, skidding, and slowly turned towards the other side of the camp, to the peaceful darkness there. He was reacting as Caesar would hope him to, he realised.

'First Cohort – guard the west.'

He saw men reverse direction at his order and only then did he run to his horse, throwing himself into the saddle. His legion were experienced men and he saw structure in the hurrying figures around him. He heard his centurions call for a defensive line and the beginnings of one form out of the first moments of chaos. He showed his teeth.

'Defend the east!' he bellowed. 'Shield line and spears.' He dug in his heels and galloped through the camp towards the sounds of death and iron.

CHAPTER SEVENTEEN

Julius knew he was in trouble. The legion he faced had wasted very little time before a strong defensive line formed and the counterattack began. Wherever he looked, he could see soldiers rushing towards his position. Whoever commanded them clearly knew his business and Julius could feel the sudden wavering of his men as their charge staggered and slowed.

'Forward, Third!' Julius ordered.

The original plan for a fast destruction and withdrawal lay in ruins. He could not withdraw and leave the cohorts with Domitius to be slaughtered. Though surprise had been lost, Julius knew if he could hold for long enough, Domitius would send a shiver through the defenders and he could still salvage the attack. He needed to push the enemy back just to give the Third space to retreat, but there was no weakness in the lines. Julius had to watch as his men were hammered from their feet and more and more of the enemy charged in to add their strength. It was carnage.

Three ranks of men separated him from the killing and Julius could see his soldiers glance back at him as more and more were slain, willing him to call a retreat. The ground was covered with his black-faced soldiers and in the cold their wounds steamed visibly as blood pumped into the soil.

Julius waited, growing desperate. Domitius had to come soon or he would lose everything.

'Archers! Signal again!' he bellowed, though many of them were dead.

His men held firm as they heard, standing toe to toe with the enemy. Without shields, they were terribly vulnerable and Pompey's men used the advantage, ramming their own shields into faces, or down to break the small bones of sandaled feet. Julius winced at the screaming and even as the flaming arrows soared over their heads once more, he felt something shift in his men. He could not see the start of it, but where they had been holding, suddenly they were turning to run.

Julius stood in stunned disbelief as men he had trained began to pelt past him. He heard his centurions snap furious orders, but the effect whiplashed through the Third and terror broke them apart.

In the distance, Julius heard the rumble of cavalry and his heart sank. Pompey was coming and his men were routed. He saw the standard-bearer of the Third come racing past him and Julius ripped the flag from his grasp.

'Third to *me*!' he roared, brandishing the pole in great sweeps.

The crowd of rushing men did not pause in their flight as they went around him. He saw a great dark mass of riders and realised he would die when they charged. In the churning chaos of the rout, Julius felt an eerie calm settle on him. He could not rally the Third and soon he would be left alone. His arms ached and he wondered how Brutus would take the news when he heard. That was just one regret in a sea of them and he felt the ground shake as thousands of Pompey's extraordinarii galloped in from the dark.

He barely noticed that a few of the Third had responded and were forming up around him. New horn calls split the air and Julius saw the surge of cavalry halt. It did not matter. He could not outrun them. He waited for the end and wondered at his own lack of emotion. It had happened so quickly that he could hardly take in the change in fortunes. Pompey had no other opponents in Rome. Mark Antony would be brushed aside, quietly banished or killed.

Julius leaned on the flagpole, panting. He did not speak to the men around him in the dark, feeling only contempt for them. He had learned the lessons of fear too long ago to remember. Perhaps it had been Renius' example, or his own father, or Tubruk's simple brand of courage, but it had stayed with him. No matter what else a man accomplished, it was all worthless if he allowed fear to rule his actions. If it was terror of pain, it should be faced and crushed. What was pain, after all? Wounds healed and even those that did not were better than having to live in shame. Julius had seen men with crippling injuries who still held themselves proudly. They bore the scars with the same courage they had shown to receive them.

He held his head high as the enemy riders milled, waiting as he did for the order that would send them flying towards him. He would not cry out. He would not run.

Pompey rode to the head of his cavalry, every jolt from his horse sending a stab of pain that dimmed his vision. He had heard the alarm calls and interrupted his inspection to answer them, but now his eyes narrowed at the sight of Julius' legionaries running away.

He saw Labienus come galloping towards him and accepted his salute.

'What's happening?' he asked.

'A night attack, sir. We have beaten it back. A cavalry charge will finish them.'

Both men looked across the camp towards the fleeing enemy disappearing into the dark. A distant lonely figure waved a flag in the gloom and the movement attracted Pompey's eye. He saw the man plant the standard in the hard earth, where the breeze tugged at it. The man stood unnaturally still, the white speck of his face turned towards the horsemen. Pompey frowned in suspicion.

'It is a victory, sir,' Labienus said, more urgently. 'With your permission, I will take the extraordinarii and ride them down.'

'It is a trap,' Pompey replied. 'I am certain of it. When have you ever heard of Caesar's legions running in fear? He *wants* us to race out into the night for whatever he has waiting there. No. You will hold position until dawn.'

Labienus took a breath that hissed through his teeth as he struggled to control his temper. 'Sir, I do not believe that. They have lost *hundreds* against my lines.'

'And he sent three to die in my tent, just to spread lies amongst the faithful, Labienus. That should have told you the quality of the man. He is a deceiver and I will not be deceived. You have heard my orders.'

Pompey's eyes were coldly implacable and Labienus knew he either had to kill him or accept what he had been told. It was not a real choice.

'Yes, sir,' he said, bowing his head. 'I will have my men stand down.'

Pompey saw the distress even as Labienus tried to hide it. Despite the pain that spread in waves to torment him, he forced himself to speak. 'You have done well here, General. I will not forget your loyalty.'

Looking out past the camp, Pompey saw the flag-bearer turn and be swallowed by darkness. The flag was left to flutter as a smudge of dim colour against the night. With a last glance at Labienus, Pompey wheeled his mount and rode away, his cavalry turning with him.

Labienus could see the frustration in their faces, mirroring his own. It had not been a trap. Labienus had seen enough battles to know the moment when the enemy broke. It could come from a single coward throwing down his sword, or even a strange unseen communication when the courage would drain from men who could not have imagined it only an hour before. He clenched his fists in rage, looking out into the blackness. His second in command hovered at his shoulder and Labienus had no words for him that he dared speak aloud.

At last, he smothered his disappointment behind a stiff mask. 'Have the men build a hostile camp around the fortifications,' he said. 'It will slow the work, but what does that matter?'

He clamped his mouth shut rather than continue and his second saluted and went away to pass the orders on. Labienus felt the stares of his soldiers around him and wondered how much they understood of the battle.

'You have done well tonight,' he told them on impulse. 'We have wounded Caesar at last.'

They cheered at his approval and order began to return around him. The cohort he had sent to the west came in looking fresh compared to their colleagues. They had not been needed, but Labienus found a few more words for them before he returned to his tent to write the formal report. For a long time, he sat by the light of a single lamp and stared into space.

Julius marched numbly through the darkness. Tiredness made him clumsy and every bush and thorn seemed intent on impeding his progress. More of the Third legion had coalesced around him, though the gods alone knew where the rest had scattered. It was the worst defeat he had seen in years and he walked as if dazed. He could not understand what had happened. When the attack had not come, he had given up his station by the flag and turned his back on Pompey. Even then, he had expected them to ride him down.

Julius had seen the Dictator in the lamp-lights and known him even at a distance. His red cloak had swirled around him in the wind and it had been easy to picture the man's savage pleasure when he was brought Julius' body. There had even been a moment when Julius felt Pompey looking directly at him, but still he had been allowed to slip into the sheltering night and head for the safety of his own lines.

When he heard the noise of marching men nearby, Julius drew his sword, convinced it was Pompey's men come at last. When he saw Domitius he did not speak, indeed he felt unable to utter a word to any of them. The soldiers of the Third had disgraced themselves. They knew it and marched across the land with their heads bowed in private misery. Even their ranks were chaotic as each man found his own pace, like a band of marauders rather than a disciplined force. No orders were called. It was as if the failure had stripped them of any claim to be soldiers of Rome. Julius had never seen such a dejected group and he had no sympathy for any of them.

Dawn was coming by the time they neared their main camp and with the grey light, Julius believed at last that Pompey had lost his nerve. There was no other explanation that he could see. Domitius tried to speak, and was quickly silenced by a glare. The sentries let them pass without a challenge and they did not call out for news. The woeful expressions and dragging spears were clear enough.

Julius strode into his tent and threw down his helmet and sword with a clatter, before sitting at his map table. He rested his head on his hands for a moment and considered the events of the night. He had been terrified when he felt Pompey's gaze on him from across the camp, but there was no shame in being afraid, only in what followed. Men could still stand while they sweated in fear. They could resist pain and exhaustion and weakness. They could beat it all down inside and stand their line. That was Rome's strength and his men knew it as well as he did. Yet somehow the Third had run.

210

Approaching steps made him straighten in his seat and he took a deep breath as Ciro made it first into his presence. Regulus, Octavian and Domitius were close behind and Julius watched Domitius without expression as he came to stand before him. Had he too lost his courage that night?

Under the black smears, Domitius looked exhausted. He removed his sword and laid it on Julius' table.

'Sir, I ask to be relieved of command,' he said. Julius did not reply and Domitius swallowed. 'I . . . could not reach the position in time, sir. There is no excuse. I will resign my commission and return to Rome.'

'If our enemies were led by a man who knew how to win, I would be dead,' Julius said softly.

Domitius stared straight ahead in silence.

'Tell me what happened,' Julius said.

Domitius took a deep breath that shuddered out of him. 'We found a river too deep to get across, sir. I saw the arrow signal while I was still on the wrong bank. By the time we had found a fording place, Pompey's legions had answered the horns and it was too late. I could still have attacked then. It was my choice alone that I did not. We recrossed the river and made our way back here.' He did not say that to have attacked Pompey's legions would have been suicide. His orders had not allowed him to make the decision.

Julius drummed his fingers on the table. 'Did you see why Pompey halted the attack?'

'I saw him talk to his officers, but they were too far away,' Domitius replied, ashamed not even to be able to provide this small piece of information.

'I have not yet decided your fate, Domitius. Leave me and summon the Third before my tent. Have my Tenth march prisoner escort to them.'

Domitius saluted, his raised hand trembling. Julius waited until he had left before speaking again.

'I never thought I would see a legion of mine run in fear,' he said. He looked up at his generals and they could not meet his gaze. 'I held the legion standard and they ignored it. They went past me.' He shook his head, remembering. 'I left it there for Pompey. He has their honour, he might as well have their flag.'

They all heard the shouts and tramp of feet as the Tenth and Third gathered. Julius sat looking at nothing while his generals waited. The defeat seemed to have aged him and when he stood at last his eyes were blank and tired.

'Take your places, gentlemen. The day must run its course,' he said, gesturing outside. Without a word, they left the tent and he followed them into the pale sun.

The Third legion stood in silent ranks on the frozen ground. Many still bore the marks of the soot they had used on their faces, though most had taken a wet cloth and removed the worst of it. They carried their shields and swords and stood like men waiting for execution, with fear in every eye.

At their backs stood the Tenth; older and harder men. Julius remembered a time when some of them had run in the battles against Spartacus. He wondered if any of them were thinking back to that bloody day when Pompey himself had ordered the decimation of their ranks. The soldiers marked by the count had been beaten to death by the fists of their closest friends. It had been the most brutal thing Julius had ever witnessed at that time, yet out of it he had formed the Tenth and given them a name to record the deed.

The Third legion waited in silence for him to speak. A cold breeze blew through their ranks as Julius walked to his horse and mounted.

'You have fought with me in Gaul. Shall I name the tribes, the battles? The Helvetii, the Suebi, the Belgae, Nervii, more? You fought with me at Gergovia, Alesia, against Vercingetorix and in Britain. You were with me when I pardoned the men of Corfinium. You took Dyrrhachium with me here.'

He paused, closing his eyes for a moment in disgust.

'You left your honour on the field when you ran. All that you have been before was made ashes last night. You dishonoured and shamed me and I never thought I'd see that. Not from you. Only my Tenth have been longer at my side.'

From the height of his mount, he could see right across the gathered ranks. They stared ahead without daring to look at him, but he saw some of them were shaking with humiliation as if he were a father lecturing repentant sons. He shook his head and stared into nothing for a long time.

'Your lives are forfeit,' he said harshly, forcing himself on. 'There can be only one payment for cowardice.'

Octavian had mounted his own horse and trotted along the silent lines towards Julius. When he was close, he leaned forward and spoke for Julius alone. 'Sir, the Tenth are undermanned. Let them choose the best of them.'

Julius turned red-rimmed eyes on his younger relative and after a time he nodded. He raised his head to speak once more to the Third.

'I have no sons. I have never needed them while I have known you. Let it be over between us. We have come far enough.' He cleared his throat and threw his voice as far as he could. 'My Tenth are short of men. They will walk among you and some will swell their ranks. The rest of you will be decimated. The survivors will fill the places of the dead in my loyal legions. I have no use for you now.'

A low murmur of agonised fear came from the ranks of the Third. No one moved from their position. Julius could hear the pleading note in their voices and he hardened himself to it.

'Tenth legion! Stand forward and take the best of them. You will oversee what comes after.'

He watched as the centurions of his Tenth moved out amongst them. He was exhausted and despair filled him. They had lost hundreds of men the night before to death or capture. Yet there were still more than three thousand of a veteran legion remaining. He could not disband them so far from Rome. They would be forced to prey on the villages and towns of Greece just to survive. He would be releasing a plague on Roman citizens that would eventually have to be hunted down and killed. He had no choice but to mark the day in their blood. They had run.

The officers of the Tenth indicated their choices with a brief touch on the shoulder. Each man chosen seemed to crumple slightly, as if he could not believe what was happening. They left gaps in the lines as they walked back to the Tenth and humiliation and relief rode them in equal measure.

As the process continued, Julius shot a suspicious glance at Octavian and found his general already watching him. The younger man was stiff with tension and when Julius opened his mouth to interrupt the choosing, he saw Octavian shake his head minutely, his eyes begging. Julius resumed his gaze over the legions and said nothing.

The chosen men re-formed as a third group standing by the Tenth and it was soon clear that the officers had interpreted Julius' orders to suit them. Julius guessed Octavian was behind the idea and he could only watch as every single man of the Third was tapped on the shoulder and marched over to the new position. They had left no one behind and Julius saw the beginnings of hope on the faces of the Third as they understood. The pressure of Octavian's gaze was relentless.

Julius beckoned Octavian over to him. When he was close enough, Julius leaned towards him, his voice low. 'What have you done?' he murmured.

'Their lives belong to the Tenth now,' Octavian replied. 'Please. Let it stand.'

'You undermine me,' Julius said. 'Would you have them go unpunished?'

'The Third are gone, sir. These men are yours again. They will not forget the chance if you grant it to them.'

Julius stared at Octavian, seeing again how far he had come from the boy Julius had known. The warrior and general before him had outgrown his youth. Julius knew he had been manipulated, but he took an odd pride in seeing it from his own blood.

'They are yours, then, General. Domitius will lead the Tenth.'

Octavian shifted in his saddle. 'You are honouring him?' he said.

Julius nodded. 'It seems I can still surprise you. It is the only choice now. This "new" legion will fight well for you, as the man who saved them. If I let Domitius command any lesser men than my own Tenth, he will lose face and that will eat at his discipline. This will show I do not hold him to account for the failure.' He paused, thinking. 'In fact, I do not. I should have allowed for delays and arranged for a different system of signals. Too late now, but the responsibility is my own as well.'

He saw Octavian relax as he realised his scheme to save the Third would not be overturned. He had presented Julius with the choice of humiliating both Octavian and the Tenth, or making the best of it. The cleverness of it appealed to Julius as it would have to no other Roman commander.

'Have you a name for them?' Julius asked.

Had Octavian thought that far ahead? It seemed he had, as the younger man answered immediately.

'They will be the Fourth Greek legion.'

'There is already one of that name,' Julius replied coldly. 'They are the ones we fought last night. Labienus commands them.'

'I know it. When they next meet in battle, they will fight all the harder to earn the right to keep it,' Octavian said.

Despite his experience, he searched Julius' face for approval and in response Julius reached out and clapped him on the shoulder.

'Very well,' he said, 'but if they ever run again, I will crucify them to the last man. I will not save you from their punishment, Octavian. Do you still want to lead them?'

Octavian did not hesitate. 'I do, sir,' he said, saluting. He took up his reins and trotted back to the lines, leaving Julius alone.

'My Tenth have bought new honour for you,' Julius said, his voice ringing over them. 'If they can see your worth, I will not refuse them this. The Third are no more and their name will be removed from the Senate rolls in Rome on our return. I cannot give you back your history. I can only offer a new start and a new name. You will be the Fourth Greek legion. You know that name from the men we faced last night. We will take it from them, and when we meet in war we will take back our honour with it.'

The soldiers who had been freed raised their heads in relief. Many of them shook with the power of their deliverance and Julius was satisfied he had made the right choice.

'General Domitius is free of blame and will command the Tenth to show the honour I place in him. General Octavian has asked to be given the new Fourth and I have accepted. Remember that your lives have come from the honour of my Tenth and you carry that honour with you. Do not shame them.'

He swept his gaze over the thousands before him and felt that some of the shame of the previous night had indeed been washed away. He knew now that Pompey had lost his courage. He could be beaten.

Labienus stood still on the training yard at Dyrrhachium. More than two hundred of Caesar's Third legion were on their knees in the red dust, their hands bound behind them. The wind whipped across the yard, coating them in grit so that they were forced to lower their heads and blink out the stinging grains.

Labienus was still furious with the man who watched the proceedings from the back of a fine Spanish gelding. He knew his duty, however, and he would not hesitate to give the order for the execution to begin. A dozen officers were under guard in another barracks and would be tortured for information. The rest were simply an example to be made.

Labienus glanced at Pompey, waiting for his nod. He could not escape the feeling that the three legions Pompey had assembled hardly needed to see more Roman blood. They had witnessed enough of their own being shed to learn anything new from the process. This was not for them, he thought. This was for Pompey. Perhaps there was a part of the old man who knew what a fool he had been in holding back the extraordinarii the night before. Labienus had sent out his trackers at dawn and they had found no sign of any larger force. Labienus knew the information would seep out and morale would sink even lower.

As Pompey met his eyes, Labienus realised he had been staring and saluted hurriedly to cover his embarrassment. Pompey looked as if the stiff breeze could blow him down and his skin was taut and yellow across his bones. Labienus thought he was dying, but until the Senate revoked his Dictatorship, he had the power of life and death over them all.

Pompey nodded sharply and Labienus turned to the five men who had been chosen for the task. He could see they did not relish it, though he had picked the most brutal killers under his command.

'Begin,' Labienus said.

Four of them walked forward, their knives held ready, but the fifth hesitated.

'Sir, these are Roman. It's not right.'

'Stand still,' Labienus snapped at him. 'Centurion! Come to me!'

The soldier shook his head in terror as his officer approached. 'I'm sorry, sir. I only meant . . .'

Labienus ignored him. The centurion who had come at his order was pale and sweating, he saw.

'This man has refused my order. He will join the others,' Labienus said.

The soldier opened his mouth to cry out and the centurion struck him hard with his fist before he could add to the shame he had brought to his legion. Two more crashing punches forced the dazed soldier to his knees and Labienus watched dispassionately as he was disarmed and trussed at the end of the line of prisoners. They did not look at him.

Labienus expelled a slow breath, stilling his racing pulse. Pompey had witnessed the incident, but it seemed he chose to ignore it. Labienus clenched his fists behind his back, trying not to show the tension he felt. In calmer days, he might have had the man whipped for insolence, but Pompey was capable of executing the entire century for the idiocy of one man. That had been averted at least and Labienus offered up a silent prayer to see him through the day.

The four remaining men of the execution party went to work with swift efficiency. They walked behind the kneeling prisoners with knives reaching to encircle their throats. One quick jerk and then a shove to send dying men onto their faces and they moved on. The dust grew darker with blood until the ground was full and could take no more. Then lines of it moved sluggishly out in twisting branches, like a red tree drawn on the ground.

Pompey waited until the last of the prisoners fell twitching before he summoned Labienus to his side.

'The Senate have demanded a meeting with me, General. It is strange that they should ask so soon after the events of last night, is it not? I wonder if there is someone amongst your ranks who could be passing information to them?'

Labienus met his stare without daring to blink. He thought of the letter he had written and left unsigned, but no sign of guilt showed in his face. It was done and he could not regret it.

'Impossible, sir. They have been under my eye ever since we came back.'

Pompey grunted and shrugged. 'Perhaps it is just to confirm my Dictatorship then. It is due for renewal in two days, though it is just a formality. Your men must return to work on the walls, General. As soon as these bodies have been burnt.'

Labienus watched Pompey leave the parade ground and wished he could be present to hear what the Senate would say to him. He suspected the future would be shaped by it.

CHAPTER EIGHTEEN

'My health is not at issue here!' Pompey shouted, red in the face. 'You dare to suggest I am incapable?'

The sinews on his hands stood out like wires as he gripped the rostrum and faced the Senate. The meeting hall was packed and many were on their feet to speak. It was chaotic without the ordered traditions of Curia debates. Pompey had already been interrupted twice and a vein throbbed visibly in his temple as he considered stalking out and leaving them. He would have done if he had had even a month in hand before his Dictatorship was to be renewed. They knew the leverage they had and seemed determined to extract its value.

Cicero dropped his gaze to scan a parchment in his hand. Pompey would have given a great deal to know its author. As Cicero looked up again, the rest fell silent with a discipline they had not shown to Pompey.

'Your health is at issue when illness prevents you from acting in the best interests of Rome,' Cicero said, glancing infuriatingly at the parchment once more. 'You should stand down until you are well, Pompey. If it was another man, you would be among the first to say it.'

Pompey glared at him, feeling the gaze of them all batter at his defences. The pain in his gut was a wild red thing and it took every grain of his strength not to let it show.

'You were not so insolent when Rome was burning and I was granted my Dictatorship,' Pompey said. 'I kept order then, when no one else could. I broke Spartacus when his army threatened us all; do you remember that? And you dare to suggest I am not fit for my command? Why don't you read that paper in your hand, Cicero, instead of hinting at its contents? I fear no criticism from you or any man. My record speaks for me.'

There was a murmur of approval from the benches and Pompey was pleased to see Cicero did not have the complete support of the others in the hall. Many of them would be horrified at an attempt to end the Dictatorship on such grounds. If they had been in Rome, it could not have been contemplated, but Pompey knew the campaign had not been going well. There were too many in the Senate who understood nothing of war and were suffering without the comfort and respect they enjoyed in their own city. He knew he had to find words to move them.

'Your record is without equal,' Cicero said, 'but you are sweating now, Pompey, because you are in agony. Stand down for a month and we will have the best healers brought to you. When you are well, you will resume the war.'

'And if I do not? Speak your threats aloud, Cicero, so that we can all hear. Let us know what treason you are considering,' Pompey said harshly, leaning forward on the rostrum. More murmurs met his words and he saw Cicero look uncomfortable.

'Your Dictatorship ends in two days, Pompey, as you know. It is better that it lapse until you are healthy enough to continue.'

Cicero met his gaze steadily and Pompey knew he would not dare to suggest that sickness had stolen his courage. He had heard the whispers about him and he scorned them. He would have replied, but he saw Suetonius stand and gestured towards him. He could not carry the vote on his own, and as he and Cicero took their seats he was desperate with hope.

Suetonius cleared his throat. 'This question should never have been raised,' he began. Cicero rose immediately and Suetonius fixed him with a glare. 'I have the floor,' he said. 'There are setbacks in every campaign, as those with experience know well. It was at Pompey's word that the Greek legions gathered. It was he who lured Caesar from the safety of Rome to a better field for war. This is where we want him to be and that was achieved only through Pompey's skill. Which of you had the vision to see the war must take place in Greece? Pompey has taken hard decisions on our behalf. His Dictatorship was created to withstand threats too great for the common rule of law. He has fulfilled his obligations and to consider removing his authority at this stage is a dangerous gamble.'

He paused to sweep his eyes over the assembled men.

'I do not know of another general capable of beating Caesar. I *do* know that Pompey is more than capable. I will vote to continue the Dictatorship. There is no other honourable course.'

He sat down to a strong ripple of approval that gave Pompey some comfort. He felt a spasm build in his stomach and delayed standing for a moment, using a fine cloth to dab his lips. He did not dare look at it as he pushed it inside his toga.

Cicero too hesitated before standing. He knew Pompey's illness was worse than he pretended. If he were left in command, he could very well hand the victory to Caesar. Perhaps that *was* the better course, in the end. If Labienus took the field, the two armies could waste their strength against each other and where would Rome be then? He had hoped that after Pompey was removed some new accommodation could be found with Caesar, but now his thoughts were jumbled and he did not know how to bring the Senate round. It was a difficult path to walk. There were many there who wanted Pompey to wage outright war without pause or mercy. That was why they had come to Greece, after all. Cicero could only shake his head at the blindness of such men. He cared little for Pompey and less for Caesar. The future of Rome outweighed them both.

Cicero saw his delay had not gone unnoticed. He spoke quickly to cover the lapse. 'I speak for the good of Rome, Pompey, can you deny it? I have waited here for you to win this war, but you have not managed to *meet* the enemy. These are not the "setbacks" of a campaign that Suetonius mentioned. You have killed more of your own men for mutiny than Caesar has managed. Morale is low and you threw away the single chance you had to attack with Labienus.' He took a deep breath, knowing he was making a dangerous choice. 'How many more will you shrink from taking?'

'There it is, at last,' Pompey said.

He grimaced suddenly and looked down at his hands. Cicero felt a rush of hope that the pain would be revealed to the others. Let him collapse, or cry out and it would all be over.

Pompey raised his head slowly, his eyes glittering.

'You dare to suggest I have lost my courage, Cicero? Is that what has begun this personal attack? I have built walls to protect a city that was taken once by Caesar. I have sought him out in the field and, yes, he eluded me.' Pain prevented him from speaking for a moment and he waited for it to pass.

'You have twice the men and four times the cavalry,' Cicero interrupted. 'In better times you would have carried the day by now. Only your illness . . .'

'My *illness*, as you call it, is nothing more than a griping stomach controlled by draughts of chalk and milk,' Pompey snapped. 'I will not stand here and have you question me in this way.'

'Your Dictatorship . . .' Cicero tried again.

'Enough!' Pompey roared at him. 'Very well, if you want to see war, I will give it to you! I will take my army out and force an end to this. Is that what you want to hear? I will crush Caesar and bring back his head, or I will die. That is my word. Vote to continue my Dictatorship or not, as you please. By the time it passes, I will be in the field.'

Cicero paled as the bulk of the Senate cheered the announcement.

Of all things, he had not meant to sting Pompey into being so rash. The last thing he wanted was an outright confrontation.

'For the good of Rome . . .' he called, but he was ignored.

The Senate rose to their feet. Pompey accepted their approval with a last poisonous glare at Cicero and descended the rostrum, making his way out. Suetonius and the other tribunes fell in behind him and Cicero was left to sink slowly into his seat, staring at nothing.

Brutus stood with his arms outstretched, taking long, slow breaths. His body had been oiled and scraped and his skin shone with health. His mind was on the battle to come and he hardly noticed the silent slaves as they raised his tunic over his head and tugged it into place, gathering it in a knot tied at the nape of his neck. His armour hung on a wooden tree in the tent and he looked it over with a critical eye, noting where old scratches and dents had been hammered and polished out. The silver had not lost its lustre with use and though it was a softer metal than iron, he knew its white gleam could be seen across a battlefield. Julius would see it as soon as the armies met.

While he stood motionless, the slaves buckled a wide leather belt around his waist, drawing in the folds of dark linen. Before they could proceed, he flexed his shoulders and checked he was still free to move. The ritual was carried out in silence and Brutus took comfort from its familiarity. Nothing he wore was new and the woollen bracae and tunic had been part of his kit in Gaul. The colours were faded from being washed a thousand times, but they were comfortable as new, itchy material could never be. He bowed his head as the slaves tied a light scarf around his throat to protect his neck from chafing. He loosened it slightly with two fingers and stared at nothing, thinking of facing Julius.

Pompey had come back from the Senate meeting with a fire

under him at last. There would be no rest for any of them until their enemies were beaten in Greece. It was as Brutus had wanted from the beginning and he knew his four cohorts would be first in the line of battle.

That was the thought that sent a shudder of fear down his spine. For all his training, if Julius sent in the Tenth as his front line, it would be hard and bloody work. Brutus had seen them fight enough to know they would not give ground except over their dead. They were the surviving veterans of countless battles and the Greek legions had nothing like their experience.

'We have the numbers,' Brutus murmured, causing the dress slaves to pause and look at him inquiringly. 'Go on,' he said to them.

One of the men knelt at his feet to tie the laces of his sandals, checking they were taut with elaborate care as he crossed them up to Brutus' ankles. The soft woollen cloth under them bulged against the restraining net of leather and Brutus splayed his toes comfortably. He raised his arms again as a leather kilt was tied around his waist to protect his groin and felt a thrill of anticipation as both men turned towards the armour at last.

The chestplate brought back bittersweet memories as he thought of the hands that had made it. Alexandria had loved him when she worked on the design and her care showed. It was a beautiful thing, with a representation of muscle overlaid by carved figures of Mars and Jupiter, joining hands at his throat. Brutus took a deep breath as it was fastened to its mate at his back, releasing the air as the buckles were pulled tight. It would not restrict him. He moved his head from side to side and felt the beginning of excitement that wearing it always brought. The shoulder pieces were joined at his throat and made secure and again he tested it, checking for snags in movement. He brought his left leg forward to have the silver greave attached and then took the helmet and lowered it onto his head. It too was a marvel of light design and shone even in the dimness of the tent. It would draw the enemy to him, he knew.

He secured the buckle that held the cheek-guards and enclosed his head in metal.

Seneca entered the tent as Brutus stood there testing every one of the knots and buckles the slaves had tied. Seneca knew better than to interrupt the ritual, but Brutus looked at him and smiled.

'Are you ready?' he said.

'I am, but that is not why I've come here. There is a stranger from the city who has come to see you.'

'Send him away,' Brutus replied immediately. 'Whatever it is can wait. We're marching at dawn.'

'I would have, but when I told him to go back he gave me this.'

Seneca held up a ring Brutus knew very well. It was a simple gold seal and his hand shook slightly as he took it.

'Do you know what this is?' he said.

Seneca shook his head and Brutus rubbed his fingers over the crossed arrow design that had once belonged to Marius. It felt hot in his hand and he thanked his gods that Seneca had not understood its significance. If Pompey had seen it, or any of the older men, it would have meant his death.

'Bring him to me,' he said, dismissing the slaves. Seneca looked curiously at his general, but he saluted and left him alone without a word.

Brutus found himself sweating as he waited. After consideration, he walked to where his weapons lay on a table and took up the gladius he had won in the tournament for all Rome. Like his armour, it was beautiful, finely balanced and made of the best iron in the world. He would have liked to draw the blade to check for flaws as he had a thousand times before, but at that moment Seneca returned, bringing the stranger.

'Leave us alone, Seneca,' Brutus said, staring at the newcomer. He was not an inspiring sight and looked like any other Greek peasant who thronged the city. For a moment, Brutus wondered if he had found the ring and hoped to claim a reward, but why would he bring it to him, of all people?

'Where did you find this?' he asked, holding the ring up between them.

The man looked nervous and before he spoke he rubbed sweat from his forehead. 'It was given to me, sir. By his hand, it was.'

'Say his name,' Brutus whispered.

'Caesar,' Caecilius replied. 'I am his spy.'

Brutus closed his eyes for a moment, feeling danger loom over him. Was this another test from Labienus? The general was easily cunning enough to have thought of it. He could be waiting outside with a century of men to take him for questioning. Surely he would have seen some nervousness in Seneca, some signal that something was wrong?

'Why did you bring it to me?' Brutus asked him. He dropped his hand to his sword pommel, more for the comfort of its touch than any threat. Caecilius saw the motion and seemed to twitch.

'I was sent to report on Pompey's army, sir. Before I left, I found out that you were still loyal. I have seen you many times in the city, but I did not approach in case it put you in danger.'

'Why now then?' Brutus said. Games within games, he thought. If the man were truly a spy, why would Julius have lied to him? It made no sense.

'I am leaving Dyrrhachium, sir. Someone must carry a warning to Caesar and I believe I am the only one of his spies left alive. I do not expect to return here and I thought you would want me to take a word from you to him.'

'Stay there,' Brutus snapped, striding to the flap of the tent and throwing it open. He stood in the light, staring around him, but there was nothing out of the ordinary. Men scurried everywhere as they prepared to march. Orders were being shouted, but there was no sign of Labienus or Pompey, or any threat to him. He shook his head in confusion and let the flap fall.

If the little man was an assassin, Julius had made a poor choice, Brutus thought. Without warning, he grabbed hold of Caecilius and searched him roughly and thoroughly. The thought crossed his mind that Pompey would appreciate having a spy brought before him, but Brutus crushed the idea even as it formed. The man believed Brutus was playing some elaborate double role. It would not do to have that suspicion brought to Pompey just before he marched. He would be likely to leave Brutus behind.

Something of these thoughts showed in his face and Caecilius flinched before his gaze.

'Sir, if there is no message, I will leave. I have barely enough time as it is, even if I start now.'

Brutus examined him closely. The man seemed genuine, but Julius had misled him deliberately and that was a mystery. Unless Pompey was meant to discover him. Under torture, the man would have his knowledge exposed and Brutus would have been finished. He chuckled as he saw he had it at last and walked over to his weapons, picking up the silver-handled dagger and unsheathing its blade.

Caecilius watched his every movement with growing discomfort. 'Sir, I should leave. I must carry the warning.'

Brutus nodded, walking smoothly towards him. 'I understand,' he said. In a sharp movement, he grabbed Caecilius by the hair and whipped the knife across his throat, dropping him to the floor. The little spy clawed at the wound in agony.

'But I do not *want* him warned,' Brutus said, wiping the knife between two fingers. There were spots of blood on his armour and he cursed as they formed beads over the oil. It would have to be rubbed clean once more.

CHAPTER NINETEEN

Ten miles south of Dyrrhachium, Julius stood on the saddle of his horse, watching the distant column. His cloak snapped and fluttered like a live thing, tugging at the clasp that held it around his neck. Octavian stood with reins in one hand, gripping Julius' ankle with the other. Both men were gritty with dust and hungry from marching all day.

'He's coming straight at us,' Julius said. 'No word from Caecilius?'

'None. Unless he's in Pompey's camp, he's been left behind by now,' Octavian replied. He shifted from one foot to the other in impatience. 'What can you see?'

From so far away, Pompey's column was a black smear across the landscape, with tiny figures of outriders like crawling insects.

'I can't tell if he has his entire force in the field. Gods, there are a lot of them,' Julius said. 'Has our beloved Dictator lost patience with us, do you think?'

'We can lose him after dark,' Octavian said.

Julius glanced down at the general holding him in position. 'That's not why I came to Greece, lad. I won't have my legions run from Pompey, not after the shame of the men you now command. We have food enough and we are strong again. I would put our veterans against an army twice the size of this one and expect to win.'

Julius fell silent as he stared at the numbers ranged against him.

He had always known Pompey would eventually leave the safety of the walls around Dyrrhachium, but something had forced him out before they were finished and once again both armies were close enough to threaten war. Julius pretended a confidence he did not feel. It was true that he had done what he could to sap the morale of the Greek legions. Every one of them would have heard his offers to Pompey and those who had been caught deserting would have had friends and colleagues. They had seen Dyrrhachium returned whole with the Senate families and Julius knew the act would have struck to the heart of the Greek legions. They were honourable men, living and working far from the intrigues and plotting of Rome. If he could only have had an hour with them to make his case! Everything Julius had done had been to sow doubt amongst their ranks and he hoped Pompey's ruthlessness would have tested their loyalty even further.

The sight of so many bent on his destruction should have been frightening, but Julius felt a slow anger grow. Pompey was arrogant with such a following, but those who marched with him were not *his* men. They were soldiers of Rome, doing their duty as they saw it. The veteran legions from Gaul belonged to Julius alone.

Julius looked over his shoulder at the ranks he had sent marching further south. He could catch them on horseback easily enough and had stayed behind to make his own judgement of the army they faced. It still awed him to see so many legions in the field. Closer now, the ranks fluttered with flags, and bronze eagles shone in the setting sun. If they had not been enemies, he would have gloried in the sight. In all his experience, he had never seen so many of Rome's warriors and it moved him. The army of the Helvetii had been far larger, but these were legionaries, with the same blood and the same armour. The same history. It would be like fighting brothers, and he knew there could be bitterness for years when they were done. His Tenth would never forgive Romans who had stood against them.

'We can take these,' Julius said. Octavian stared upwards and saw a smile twist at the corners of his mouth. 'They've seen Pompey humbled at Dyrrhachium. They've seen him waste the chance he had with Labienus. They will not want to die for such a man, Octavian, and that will weaken them.'

He watched the column approach, knowing he would have to move soon or fall into the range of their scouts.

'Come to me,' he said, almost too softly for Octavian to understand. Both of them could hear the closest riders sound their tinny horns as they sighted them.

'We should go,' Octavian said.

Julius did not move and Octavian watched nervously as the scouts kicked their horses into a gallop and began to converge on their position.

'Sir, we should go now.'

'They have the numbers, Octavian,' Julius said. 'Just matching their front line will leave us thin on the ground, but this is why we came. This is why we crossed the Rubicon. We have nowhere else to go, General. Find me a place to stand and we'll *break* them.'

To Octavian's relief, Julius lowered himself into his saddle and took the reins once more. Octavian leapt onto the back of his own gelding and they galloped clear of the approaching scouts, racing long shadows beneath them. A few of Pompey's riders stayed on their trail for a mile before wheeling back, their horns sounding mournful regret as they faded behind.

Brutus yanked savagely on his reins as the order to halt split the air. He could see Julius' legions still marching ahead and every mile lost would be another to make up the following day. It was strange to think how well he knew the men in those ranks. He had fought with them for years and he could imagine the voices of friends and colleagues as they dressed their lines. Part of him ached for that old familiarity, but there was no going back. Julius was somewhere in the mass of men and Brutus would see him dead by the time they were done. He was hungry for the confrontation and his men walked carefully around him as he gazed over the hills.

By the time the walls were up and the trenches dug, darkness had fallen and the first lamps had been lit. Pompey had ordered a single camp to enclose his entire army. It was a city in the wilderness, and inside its safe barriers the Greek legions put a last edge to their swords and ate without talking, sitting around watch fires. Many made their wills and those who could write earned a few extra coins copying for their friends. There was no laughter and Brutus felt uneasy as he listened to them in the night. They outnumbered the enemy and they should have been raucous and loud with boasting. There were no songs sung in the camp and the sour mood seemed stifling.

Brutus strode over to where Seneca stared into the flames of a watch fire, chewing idly on a last piece of roasted sausage. The men who had crowded to the warmth moved aside at his approach and Brutus sat down with a sigh, looking around. The silence was strained and he wondered what they had been saying before he came.

'Well this is a cheerful group,' Brutus said to Seneca. 'I would have thought I'd hear a bit of singing at least.' Seneca smiled, but did not reply and Brutus raised his eyebrows. 'I've done a great deal for you, you know. I found a galley to take you to Greece, didn't I? I've given you my time and experience. Have any of you polished my armour or passed on a little of your pay out of gratitude? No. Have any of you even offered me wine?'

Seneca chuckled, looking at the man who sat in his silver armour.

'Would you like a little wine, General?' he said, reaching behind him for an amphora.

232

'No. Not a little,' Brutus replied, taking a tin cup from the man next to him as he held it out. The man blinked in surprise.

'We're going to win, you know,' Brutus said, holding out the cup to clink it against Seneca's. Seneca emptied his without a word. 'He can't stop us flanking him with our cavalry, can he? And once we're behind his lines, they'll roll up like an old carpet. You heard how they ran from Labienus? How do you think they'll do against the rest of us?'

He watched as Seneca nodded reluctantly, seeming to lose a little of his heavy mood. When Brutus had heard the news of his old legion being routed, he had been sure it was some clever plan. He had ridden out at the first light of dawn to read the ground, but there had been no print or trace of an ambushing force. He could still hardly credit it. In a way, it was a twisted comfort: the Third had never run while he commanded them. Perhaps Julius was losing his touch.

Draining his own wine, Brutus reached inside his armour to produce a bag of dice. He chose two without looking and rattled them in the cup. The sound worked like magic on the faces of the men around him, making them look up with sudden interest.

'Ah, I have your attention now,' Brutus said cheerfully. 'Shall we have a little game before we turn in? I'm thinking about buying a new horse and funds are low.'

An hour later, Labienus passed the group and saw Brutus at the centre of them. The laughter and shouting had drawn in many more to watch and other games had started on the fringes. Labienus let out a slow breath as he watched Brutus scoop up a pile of coins, cheering his own success without embarrassment. The camp stretched away into the darkness around them and Labienus smiled to himself before moving on.

At dawn, Pompey rose from his bed and summoned his healer. His stomach was hard and swollen, the skin so tight as to send spasms of pain at the slightest touch. He gritted his teeth as he probed it with stiff fingers, letting anger shield him from the pain until he gasped. Should he allow the physician to cut him? There were nights when it was bad enough for Pompey to take a knife to it himself out of sheer desperation. Each morning, he fantasised about a thin blade to let out all the wind and pus that was making it swell, but then he would force himself to dress, binding the swollen mass himself so that no one else could see.

He rubbed a rough hand across his face, seeing it come away shining with night sweat. His eyes were sticky and sore and he rubbed at them, furious with the body that had let him down.

Pompey sat on the edge of his pallet, doubled over the bulging skin. His physician entered and frowned at his sickly colour. In grim silence, the man laid down his bag of materials, crossing to him. A cool palm was pressed against Pompey's forehead and the healer shook his head.

'You are running a fever, General. Is there blood in your stools?'

'Make your mixtures and get out,' Pompey snapped without opening his eyes.

The healer knew better than to respond. He turned away and laid out his mortar and pestle with a row of stoppered bottles. Pompey cracked open an eye to watch him as he added ingredients and ground them into a white paste. The healer sensed the interest and held up his bowl to show the milky mucus that lined the sides.

'I have hopes for this preparation. It is a bark I found in Dyrrhachium, mixed with olive oil, water and milk. The man I bought it from swore it would help with any illness of the stomach.'

'It looks like semen,' Pompey said through clenched teeth.

The healer flushed and Pompey gestured irritably, already tired of the man.

'Give it to me,' he said, taking the bowl and using his fingers to scoop the mixture into his mouth. It tasted of nothing, but after a time it did seem to ease him a little.

234

'Make another batch. I can't be running to you whenever the pain worsens.'

'It's working, is it?' the healer said. 'If you would only let me release the poisons in you, I could . . .'

'Just seal another dose of it under wax so I can take it later,' Pompey interrupted. 'Two doses, and one more of your usual muck.'

He shuddered as he thought of stomach wounds he had seen in the past. When he was little more than a boy, he had killed a rabbit and slit its guts as he tried to remove the skin. Stinking black and green curds had stained his hands, tainting the good meat. He had been forced to throw the whole rabbit away and he could still remember the stench. Pompey had seen simple spear punctures bruise with filth once the stomach was open to the air. Death always followed.

'As you wish, General,' the man replied, offended. 'I have more of the bark in my own tent. I'll have it sent to you.'

Pompey only glared until he left.

When he was alone, Pompey levered himself to his feet. The legions would be ready to march, he knew. The light was already brightening at the flap of the command tent and they would be in ranks, waiting for his appearance. Still, he could not summon his dress slaves until he had bound his stomach. Only the healer had seen the expanse of angry flesh he hid with strips of clean linen and even he knew nothing of the blood Pompey spat during the night. When he was in public, he swallowed the gummy mass back each time it rose into his throat, but it grew more difficult each day.

As he stood, a wave of dizziness struck him and he swore softly to himself, waiting for it to pass. More itching sweat dripped down his face and he found his hair was wet with it.

'Give me just a few more days,' he whispered and did not know if it was a prayer to the gods or to the sick growth that consumed him.

He reached for the sweat-stained strips he had placed over the end of his pallet and began to wind them around his torso, constraining the swelling with savage jerks that left him trembling. His fingers were clumsy on the knots, but at last he was able to stand straight and took a series of deep breaths. He crossed to a water bucket and splashed it on himself before tugging a tunic over his head.

He was panting by the time he called for his slaves. They entered with downcast gazes and began to fit his armour to him. Pompey wondered if they guessed at the reason for the delay and decided he did not care. The gods would give him the time he needed to humble his last enemy. When Julius was dead he would let them cut him, but until then he would get through each day, each hour, until it was over.

The healer's paste had taken the edge off his discomfort, he thought with relief. As the slaves were dismissed, Pompey touched a hand to the pommel of his gladius and raised his head to walk out to the waiting men. He paused on the threshold and took a deep breath. Perhaps it was some calming property of the healer's paste, or perhaps because he was finally committed to his path. For the first time in months, he realised he was not afraid of his enemy.

On the third morning of the march south, the scouts came back to Julius' column, their faces flushed in the race to be first with the news. They described a vast and empty plain just a few miles ahead. Pharsalus.

There were few in the ranks who recognised the name, but those who knew Greece felt the first twinges of excitement. At last, they were coming to a place well suited for battle.

It was somehow fitting that the struggle should be settled as the old Roman generals had fought. On the flat earth of the valley floor, there could be no traps or clever use of land. Only a muddy brown river ran through the southern part of the plain, making a natural boundary. If Pharsalus were the battleground, Julius knew it would come down to speed, tactics and simple strength. The commanders would face each other across lines of men and their armies would clash and kill until just one earned the right to return to Rome. Scipio Africanus would have approved the choice. Julius made the decision quickly. He would stand at Pharsalus.

The Gaul legions entered the plain two hours later and the column did not pause as they marched across the open land. It was a barren place. Even in the protective shadow of the mountains, the winter had left a black landscape of smooth dry earth and broken boulders, shattered as if they had been thrown by vast forces. It was a relief to have firm ground under their feet, though it was so dry that curling dust shapes screamed across it, vanishing into the distance. The legionaries leaned into the wind and shielded their eyes from grit that rattled against their armour.

The city of Pharsalus lay beyond the sluggish river to the south, too far to be seen. Julius dismissed it from his thoughts. The citizens there would play no part in the battle unless he was forced to retreat and needed their high stone walls. He shook his head as he considered finding fording points on the banks. There would be no retreat.

'Continue the line of march to the far side,' he ordered Domitius over the wind's howl. 'I want a solid camp in the foothills there.'

Julius watched as the extraordinarii streamed around him, freed at last from the need to guard the flanks. The enemy were all behind and Julius heard his riders whoop as they kicked their mounts into a gallop, drawn to speed by the openness of the land. He too felt the lift in spirits and tightened his hands on the reins.

'We will stop them *here*,' he shouted to Octavian and those who heard him grinned savagely. They knew Caesar had no other enemies after Pompey. Once the old man had been broken, they would be able to retire at last. Those who had grown old in Julius' service felt the change in the air and marched a little taller, despite their tiredness. Aching bones were ignored and any man who looked around him saw the irresistible confidence of those who had brought Gaul to her knees.

Only the new Fourth legion under Octavian remained grim and silent as they crossed the plain. Once more, they had to prove the right to walk in Caesar's steps.

CHAPTER TWENTY

The light of dawn spilled over Pharsalus, cloud shapes racing across its surface. The armies of Rome had woken long before, while it was still dark. By the light of torches, they had prepared themselves for the coming of day. Kit had been stowed with routine care; leather tents folded and bound in silence. They had eaten a steaming stew mopped up with fresh bread from clay ovens. It would give them strength for what lay ahead. The camp followers and tradesmen stood with their heads respectfully bowed. Even the whores were silent, clustering together as they watched the legions move out onto the plain. Horns wailed at either end of Pharsalus and the tramp of feet sounded like a heartbeat.

The veterans of Gaul found themselves eager for the fight. They pushed forward like the finest horses and the lines had to be dressed and orders shouted to keep the pace steady. Despite the best efforts of optios and centurions, cheerful jibes and insults were exchanged by men who had fought together for too many years to count. As Pompey's army grew before them, the calls and banter lessened until they were grimly silent, each man making ready for what was to come.

The patterns of men and cavalry changed constantly as the armies closed. At first, Julius placed his Tenth at the centre of his fighting line, but then sent them to the right flank, bolstering the strength there. Pompey saw the movement and his own ranks shifted like shining liquid, manoeuvring for the slightest advantage. It was a game of bluff and counterbluff as the two commanders altered formations like pieces on a latrunculi board.

Pompey had known both fear and exultation when he saw Caesar's legions would turn at bay and face him at last. It was an act of colossal confidence for Julius to choose the open plain. Another man might have tried for broken ground: something more suited to stratagem and skill. Caesar's message was clear to Pompey's soldiers. He feared them not at all. Perhaps it was that which made Pompey deploy his legions in three wide lines, each ten ranks deep, stretching for more than a mile across Pharsalus. With the river protecting his right flank, he could use his left as a hammer.

When Julius saw the heavy formation, he felt a surge of new confidence. If a commander thought his men could break, he might shelter them in such ponderous blocks, supporting and trapping them among friends and officers. Julius knew the Greek legions would feel Pompey's lack of faith and it would drag their morale even lower. He planned accordingly, sending a string of new orders to his generals. The armies drew closer.

Julius rode at walking pace on his best Spanish mount. He had surrounded himself with scouts to take his orders, but on such a wide line the command structure was dangerously slow. He was forced to trust in the initiative of his generals. He had known them long enough, he thought. He knew their strengths and weaknesses as well as his own. Pompey could not have that advantage, at least.

Julius saw that Pompey had concentrated his horsemen on the left flank as he faced them. The sheer numbers were intimidating and Julius sent quick orders to detach a thousand men to form a mobile fourth line. If he allowed his veterans to be flanked by so many, there would be no saving them. He positioned himself on the right with his Tenth, so that he and Pompey would face each other. He touched the pommel of his sword and scanned his lines again and again, looking for flaws. He had been in enough battles to know that the illusion of time to spare would vanish as quickly as dawn mist in summer. He had seen even experienced commanders leave it too late to move their men to the best position. He would not make that mistake and chose to send them early, letting Pompey react.

The wind had lessened and the dust spirals were trampled down unnoticed as the two armies marched inexorably towards each other. Julius squinted at the formation Pompey had created. With just another thousand extraordinarii, he might have threatened the far edge of Pompey's army and forced him to split his cavalry. As it was, Pompey was free to muster them in one great mass. Behind them the ground was black with archers, protecting Pompey's own position. It would begin there.

'Send to General Octavian and have his Fourth move back towards the centre,' Julius told the closest scout. 'When it begins, he must push forward with all speed.' He looked around him and selected another, little older than a boy. 'The extraordinarii are not to advance past the flank. They must hold the position.'

As the man scurried away, Julius fretted, sweating despite the wind. Had he thought of everything? His scorpion bows and heavy engines were being pulled into position by oxen and shouting men, all along the marching mile. Pompey too had assembled his massive weapons and Julius shuddered at the thought of what they could do. Pompey had many more than he had been able to bring to the field. No doubt they would play a part in deciding the battle.

At two thousand feet, both Julius and Pompey ceased looking for an advantage from their formations. The battle lines were set and what followed would be a test of courage and skill that neither man had experienced before. For all the skirmishes and minor battles between them, they had not faced the best of Roman legions on good, dry land. The outcome could not be known.

Julius continued to give orders, as he knew Pompey must be doing. Part of him was almost hypnotised by the ritual moves of the dance as the armies neared each other. It was formal and terrifying and Julius wondered if Pompey would close to the exact distance specified in the manuals before beginning the final charge. His memory flickered back to the dry voices of his tutors telling him that six hundred feet was perfect on good ground. Any more and the men would be flagging before they reached a charging enemy in the middle. Any less and they risked losing the advantage of a crashing first strike. Julius reached up and pulled down the full-face helmet that hid his features. As it clicked shut, the wind became a dull thrumming and sweat trickled down from his hair.

The vast lines were a thousand feet apart and Julius felt the tension in his legions as he walked his horse forward with them. The animal snorted and fought the tight rein he held on it, bowing its head almost back to the neck. His horses and men had been fed and waterboys marched with them. The grindstones had been busy all night to put an edge on their swords. He had done everything he could think of to weaken the host he faced.

He did not know if it was enough and he felt the old signs of fear from every battle of his youth. His bladder tightened, though he had emptied it into the piss trench before mounting. His mouth was dry with the grit that swirled in the cold air. His vision became sharper as every sense drank in the land and men around him. He knew he could die on the plain and he scorned the thought. He had been consul twice and had taken Gaul and Britain. He had taken Rome herself. He had written his legacy into the laws of his city and he would not easily be forgotten.

He searched for silver armour somewhere amongst the enemy. Brutus would be there and Julius knew him well enough to imagine his thoughts, his expression as the armies neared. The pain of the betrayal was constant in him, with the need to see Brutus one more time, even if it was over a sword's length.

He looked across the ranks at Octavian. He wished he had left sons to carry on his line, but the blood would survive even if he did not. Had he told Octavian how proud he was of him? He thought he had.

'Let him live, if I fall,' Julius whispered against the clasp of his helmet. 'By Mars, let them *both* live.'

Pompey looked at the legions coming against him and he could not feel the gods. Memories of Caesar's victories in Gaul slipped like tongues into his mind. The man had beaten the hordes of the Helvetii. Pompey's sickness throbbed at his waist, draining his confidence.

There were men in Rome and Greece who said Caesar was the greatest general of an age; and now Pompey would try to kill him. He wished he could summon the reckless courage of his youth, but it was not there for this enemy. He was cold and uncomfortable on the saddle, at times so angry with the pain that he could barely see. Sweat poured under his armour and chilled so that he felt the cloth of his tunic chafe wetly against his neck.

Pompey glanced to his left, where Labienus sat on his horse, stiff with anger. The general had argued against the order to place the men in such deep ranks, but Pompey knew them better than he. He had watched them closely and seen the reluctance that was the death of fighting spirit. They feared the legions of Gaul. It would not matter once they saw his cavalry crush the flank, but until the battle began, Pompey did not dare trust them.

Even as the veteran legions neared, he could see signs of distress in his ranks. They took their positions as he had ordered, but his experienced eye saw flaws and hesitation.

'Have General Labienus approach me,' Pompey told his messengers.

They cantered along the shifting lines and returned with him.

'General, at six hundred feet, we will stop and await their charge,' Pompey said.

For a moment, Labienus was too shocked to speak. 'Sir?' he said.

Pompey beckoned him closer.

'They will break at the first charge unless we *make* them stand, General. I have deep lines and now I will use them. Have the men ready to halt. Their spears will be thrown accurately, at least.' He paused for a moment, his eyes glittering. 'If my extraordinarii break the flank as quickly as I think they will, the legions may not even have the chance to throw!'

'Sir, you must not force . . .'

Pompey turned abruptly away from him. 'You have orders. Follow them.'

Instinct made Labienus salute before he rode back to his legions, sending the new command up and down the lines. Pompey felt the gaze of his soldiers as they turned to him in puzzlement, but he stared stonily ahead. If they had shown a better spirit, he would have let them charge against the veterans. Instead, they would be his wall against the charge.

As the armies crossed a thousand feet, the noise of so many marching men could be heard as dim thunder, felt by all of them through the soles of their sandals. Hundreds of standards flew on each side and the bronze eagles were held proudly up to catch the sun. At eight hundred feet, both armies readied their spears. The front lines were punctuated with the heavy weapons and those who marched opposite them felt the first silken touch of terror.

At six hundred feet, Pompey saw Caesar's entire front line twitch as they expected his men to begin the charge. Instead, Pompey raised his sword and brought it down, halting fifty thousand men in three paces. Orders echoed up and down the lines and Pompey began to breathe faster in anticipation as teams winched back the machines. He could see the faces of the enemy as the gap narrowed all along the mile.

The scorpion bows hammered into their rests on both sides, sending bolts as long as a man out so fast they could be seen only as a dark blur. They punched their way through the ranks, scattering men in tangles of limbs.

As Pompey's cavalry began to accelerate on the wing, Caesar sent in the charge at less than two hundred feet, his men pounding across the dry earth. Twenty thousand spears went up on both sides, sending a writhing shadow over the ribbon of ground between them.

If there were screams, they were swallowed by thunder as they met.

Across a mile of land, thousands of armoured men crashed into the shields and swords of their enemies. There was no thought of brotherhood. They killed with a manic ferocity that gave no quarter and expected none in that bloody slash across Pharsalus. The fighting mile was solid as they gave their lives.

Pompey's extraordinarii galloped along the edge, riding at the smaller force of cavalry they had come to destroy. Pompey wiped slippery sweat from his eyes and craned to see. As his horsemen began to push back the flank, he found himself shaking. He could not tear his eyes from their progress, knowing the battle depended on it. They hammered into Caesar's cavalry, shattering their ranks with sheer numbers, so that every one was faced by two or three of Pompey's riders.

'Break, you bastards. Break! Give him to me,' he shouted into the wind.

Then the Tenth counterattacked. They widened their line to include the cavalry on the wing and Pompey saw them gutting his precious horses and riders as they slowed in the mass. Pompey cried out as he saw them press towards him. He flickered a glance at the centuries guarding his position and was reassured. As well as the best of his guards, he had kept archers back to wreak carnage on any force that threatened him. He was safe enough.

Even the blades of the Tenth could not stop Pompey's cavalry as they went round them. They were too fast and mobile to be caught for long and Pompey saw the line of battle blister out to the east as Caesar's riders struggled hopelessly to halt the advance.

Pompey could see Julius on his horse over the heads of thousands. The slight figure was gesturing calmly, sending orders over the field. Pompey looked along his own lines to check that they were holding. He stared back at the cavalry charge and with a rush of joy saw Caesar's riders break at last, turning their backs on the enemy and galloping away. Pompey's pain was forgotten as he raised both hands.

Men and horses lay dying on ground made slippery with blood. Pompey saw his officers detach two hundred riders from the furthest edge and send them after the fleeing enemy. He nodded sharply, his face savage. It had happened as he had hoped it would and he thanked the gods. His messengers looked to him for new orders, but there was no need.

The noise was appalling and the dust had risen above the ranks in such heavy clouds that riders and men appeared out of it like shadows. Pompey saw his cavalry break away to re-form and knew once they struck at full gallop, they would carve their way to the very heart of the veterans. Even the Tenth could not hold them while they fought on two sides. The reputation Caesar had built around himself would be destroyed.

Four cohorts of the Tenth turned neatly to face the charge they knew was coming and Pompey swore at the concealing dust. These were the core of Caesar's legend and he wanted to see them humbled as much as their commander. Julius himself was somewhere in the mass, but it was getting harder and harder to see.

'Come on, come *on*. Cut into them,' he said, his voice breaking. 'Make the charge.'

In the centre of the battle line, Brutus shoved a dying man backwards and raised his shield to stop a blow. His horse was dead and he had barely cleared the saddle before it collapsed. He did not know if it was deliberate that Julius had sent his old legion against him. Perhaps they had expected it would weaken his arm. It had not. Though he had trained the men he faced, though he knew them as brothers, he killed them without a thought.

As he had known it would, his armour drew them to him, distorting the fighting ranks as they caught sight of the silver and struggled to bring him down.

'Are you afraid of your old teacher?' he called to them, laughing wildly. 'Is there not one of you good enough to face me now? Try me, boys. Come here and try me.'

They heard and the response was so savage that Brutus was shoved back, his sword trapped against his body by the press of men. Something heavy thumped into his helmet and broke the strap at his chin. He swore as he hit the ground and felt the helmet come loose, but he rose up with a jerk and killed two men before they could recover.

More came at him then and his shield was torn from his hand as he raised it, ripping flesh from his fingers. He cried out in pain and ducked a sword, ramming his own into a man's groin from below. His foot slipped as his sandal studs raked the face of a corpse. He saw it was Seneca, his open eyes coated in dust.

Brutus fought without reason for a long time, cutting anything that came into range and bellowing weary defiance at the lines of men. He caught a glimpse of silver armour in a set that matched his own and yelled a challenge, seeing Octavian jerk his head around as he heard. Brutus waited for him. He could not make a space to breathe as they pressed him and he was growing tired. The endless energy of youth had somehow slipped away without him noticing. At his back, he heard Labienus calling for the Fourth to advance and the shout seemed to galvanise his old legion. They roared again and fought like berserkers, ignoring wounds. Octavian was straining to reach him and Brutus beckoned him on wearily.

Blood spattered him as he struggled, panting. He wanted to see Julius, but he could not find him.

His sword blade turned uselessly against a shield. He did not see the blow that brought him to his knees, or the second that left him on his back.

'Where are you?' he called for his old friend, looking up at the sky. A crushing weight squeezed the air from his lungs and he heard his right arm snap. Then he knew nothing more.

Two hundred of Pompey's horsemen galloped across the plain, leaving the noise and blood and death behind until all they could hear were the pounding rhythm of hooves and the snorting breath of their mounts. They were fierce with exhilaration as they chased the beaten enemy. They held their long spatha swords high over their heads and yelled with the pleasure of it. Casitas had risen to the post of decurion without seeing battle in the slow years of his Greece posting. He had not known it would be so exciting and he laughed aloud as he shot across Pharsalus, feeling as if he were flying.

Ahead of them, the extraordinarii of Caesar responded to a single horn and the wild rout changed. The ranks pulled together with the precision of a parade ground and the flying column slowed to wheel as one, turning back towards the battle.

Casitas could not believe what he was seeing. In dawning fear, he realised that the best part of two thousand crack cavalry were coming back in perfect riding order. He looked over his shoulder and considered trying to prevent them rejoining Caesar's army. One glance at the dark line of enemy horses was enough to know it was a pointless gesture.

'Get back to the lines. We'll gut them there,' he shouted, heaving his horse around and leading them. He saw his men look nervously over their shoulders as they rode and tried to resist the temptation himself. It was going to be close. Casitas could hear them coming.

The bulk of Pompey's cavalry seemed to leap from distant figures to a mass of men and horses, churning amidst a cloud of dark dust. Casitas shouted uselessly into the wind to warn them, but his voice went unheard.

Julius bellowed orders to men he could barely see in the dust that cloaked them. His Tenth were fighting in perfect order, closing the holes in their ranks as they were cut out. It was agony to see them so hard-pressed, but Julius could not bring their whole strength to bear on the soldiers around Pompey. Out on the edges, he could see the mass of riders forming up for a charge. He could hear the whinnying of horses through the dust and every nerve and muscle was tight with strain. If they smashed his lines from behind, he knew the battle would be lost and he searched for anything he could use to blunt the attack when it came.

There was nothing. He looked over the lines and saw more of the Tenth die, fighting to the last as he would have expected. The dust would blind the horses, he realised. Even a solid shield wall would be broken as they smashed into them. He shook his head, shivering. The Tenth could not lock shields and defend the main line at the same time. They would be destroyed.

'Sir! To the east!' one of his scouts shouted.

The man had been taken from the extraordinarii and perhaps it was that allegiance that made him look for them. Julius turned in the saddle and his heart leapt. He saw Pompey's chasers returning to the battle. Behind them came his extraordinarii, at full gallop.

Julius watched dry-mouthed as the fleeing riders tried to enter their own lines. There was no time for them to slow and the result was instant chaos. The attempt to form a charge was sent reeling and then Caesar's extraordinarii struck them from behind.

Pompey's riders were ruined by them. Their own men opened

the holes in the ranks that the extraordinarii battered through, scattering them apart. Julius saw horses rear in terror before the choking dust swallowed them. It swelled to a thick cloud over the killing and out of it came Pompey's riders, broken and bloody. Some were dying and fell from their saddles. Others were pulling uselessly at the reins of their bolting mounts.

The Tenth rushed forward as Pompey's cavalry were smashed. Julius shouted and kicked his own horse into the chaos, his eyes fixed on the desolate figure of Pompey in the distance. The dust cloud swirled across him and he swore, pushing forward with his men.

Pompey's flank buckled as if a great pressure had been removed and they almost fell towards the archers surrounding the Dictator. Julius was about to order shields raised when they too broke and the Tenth slaughtered those who dared to show their backs.

As the dust blew on, Julius saw Pompey's cavalry were clear of the field and still going. His extraordinarii were not chasing them, he saw, almost delirious with the change in fortunes. He watched his riders cut along the rear of Pompey's lines, selecting their points of entry to begin carving them in slices.

Julius searched again for Pompey, but he was not there. His horse rode over the broken bodies of archers, stabbed by every rank that passed. The hooves threw up clots of blood and earth that hit his legs and slid away, leaving cold smears he did not feel.

Somewhere in the distance horns blew and Julius snapped around in the saddle. It was the tone for surrender and he had a sudden terror that his veterans had failed while he had been busy on the right flank. He heard a crash of arms as men threw down their weapons and in the press he still did not know if he had won or lost.

Octavian rode along the lines towards him, breathing heavily. His greave hung from a single strap and his armour and skin were torn, bruised and scraped in equal measure. One eye had swollen completely shut, but it didn't matter. He had survived and Julius' heart leapt to see him.

'They have surrendered, sir,' he said. 'As soon as Pompey left the field. It is over.' He saluted and Julius saw he was trembling with reaction.

Julius sagged in his saddle, leaning forward with his head bowed. After a long moment, he drew himself straight and looked north. He could not let Pompey escape, but the fighting could erupt again at the slightest provocation unless he stayed with his legions. His duty was to remain on the plain and bring order, not to chase a beaten man. He knew it, but he hungered to call his extraordinarii back and ride Pompey down. He shook his head clear of the warring emotions.

'Disarm them all and begin taking the wounded back to Pompey's camp,' he said. 'Bring the generals to me and treat them with courtesy. They did well to surrender, but it will be hurting them. Make sure the men understand there will be no mistreatment. They are not enemies. They will be given every courtesy.'

'Yes, sir,' Octavian said. His voice shook slightly and Julius looked at him, smiling wryly at the worship in the younger man's bloodshot eyes.

'I will accept a new oath of loyalty from them, as consul of Rome. Tell them the war is over.'

He could hardly believe it himself and he knew the reality would not sink in for hours or days. He had been fighting for as long as he could remember and it had all brought him to the plain of Pharsalus in the middle of Greece. It was enough.

'Sir, I saw Brutus fall,' Octavian said.

Julius broke out of his reverie. 'Where?' he snapped, ready to move.

'In the centre, sir. He fought with Labienus.'

'Take me there,' Julius replied, urging his horse into a trot. A sick dread settled on him then. His hands shook slightly as

251

he rode, though whether in reaction or fear, he could not have said.

The two riders passed through the lines of men already involved in the routines they knew so well. Piles of captured swords were being formed and water passed to those who had not drunk for hours. When the legions saw their general, cheering began and swelled until they were all shouting in relief and triumph.

Julius barely heard them, his eyes on a limp figure in silver armour being pulled from a pile of corpses. He felt tears sting his eyes as he dismounted. He could not speak. The men of the New Fourth legion stood back respectfully to give him room and he went down on one knee to look into the face of his oldest friend.

There was blood everywhere and Brutus' skin was marble white against the stain. Julius took a cloth from his belt and reached out with it, gently wiping away the caked filth.

Brutus opened his eyes. With consciousness came pain and he groaned in agony. His cheek and mouth were swollen and deformed and blood trickled from his ear. His gaze seemed vacant as it swivelled towards Julius, then slowly a dim awareness returned. Brutus tried to lift himself, but the broken arm was useless. He fell back, crying out weakly. His lips moved over bloody teeth and Julius bent closer to hear him speak.

'Will you kill me now?' Brutus whispered.

'I won't,' Julius said.

Brutus let out a long shuddering breath. 'Am I dying then?' he said.

Julius looked him over. 'Perhaps. You deserve to.'

'Pompey?'

'He ran. I'll find him,' Julius replied.

Brutus tried to smile, a cough wracking him with agony. Julius watched, his dark eyes colder than death.

'So we lost then,' Brutus said weakly, trying to spit blood onto

252

the ground. He didn't have the strength. 'I was worried when I couldn't see you, before,' he said. 'I thought I was finished.'

Julius shook his head in slow sadness.

'What am I to do with you?' he murmured. 'Did you think I didn't value you? Did you think I wouldn't miss having you in Rome? I didn't believe your mother when she told me. I told her you wouldn't betray me, not *you*. You hurt me then. You hurt me still.'

Tears came into Brutus' eyes, screwed out by pain and misery. 'Sometimes I just wanted to do something without the thought that the great Julius can do it better. Even when we were young I wanted that.' He stopped to let a spasm run its course, clenching his jaw. 'Everything I am, I've made. I've struggled through things that would have broken weak bastards. While I flogged myself, you made everything seem easy. It *was* easy for you. You are the only man ever to make me feel I've had a wasted life.'

Julius looked at the broken figure of the man he had known for too many years to remember. His voice broke as he spoke. 'Why couldn't you have been happy for me?' he said. 'Why betray me?'

'I wanted to be an equal,' Brutus said, showing red teeth. Fresh pain made him gasp as he shifted. 'I didn't expect Pompey to be such a fool.' He looked up into Julius' cold gaze and knew his life, his fate was being decided while he lay helpless. 'Can you forgive me this?' Brutus murmured, raising his head. 'Can I ask you for this last thing?'

Julius did not reply for so long that Brutus fell back, his eyes closing.

'If you live,' Julius said at last, 'I will let the past rest. Do you understand me? I will need you, Brutus.'

He did not know if he had been heard. Brutus' battered face had paled even further and only the flutter of a vein in his throat showed he still lived. With great gentleness, Julius wiped his friend's mouth free of blood and pressed the cloth into the limp hand before standing.

He faced Octavian and saw the younger man's blank shock at what he had heard.

'Look after this one, Octavian. He is badly hurt.'

Octavian closed his mouth slowly. 'Sir, please . . .' he began.

'Let it go, lad. We've come too far together for anything else.'

After a long moment, Octavian bowed his head.

'Yes, sir,' he said.

CHAPTER TWENTY-ONE

Pompey's camp crested a hill that overlooked the plain. Bare grey rock showed through green lichen like bones and the only sound came from the wind. At such a height, the gale was free to moan and howl around them as Julius made his way to the gates. He saw Pompey's camp workers had lit great torches, and streamers of black smoke reached over the plain below.

Julius paused to look down on Pharsalus. His generals were creating order on the battlefield, but from his vantage point Julius could see the line of bodies that marked where the armies had clashed. They lay where they had fallen. From so far away, it looked like a meandering scar on the land, a feature of the plain rather than a place of death. He pulled his cloak tightly around his shoulders and refastened the clasp that held it to him.

Pompey had chosen the site well for his stronghold. The path to the flat crest was narrow and overgrown in places as if even wild goats shunned the steepest trails. His horse picked its way carefully and Julius did not press the pace. He was still stunned at the new reality and his usual swift thought seemed to have been buried beneath a crushing weight of memory. All his life he had fought against enemies. He had defined himself in their shadow, saying that he was not Sulla, not Cato, not Pompey. It was a new world without them and there was fear in the freedom.

He wished he could have brought Cabera up to the fort on

the hill. The old man would have understood how he could not exult in the moment. Perhaps it was just the wind and great height, but it was easy to imagine the ghosts of those who had fallen. There was no sense in death. Men like Renius and Tubruk filled graves as long and wide as Cato or Sulla. In the end, all that was flesh would be ash.

Later, he would make offerings to the gods and give thanks, but as he made his way up he felt numb. Only hours before, he had faced a vast army and victory was still too fresh and raw to be real.

The great fort Pompey had built loomed over him as he grew closer. To know that every piece of it had been brought up from the lowlands was a testament to Roman ingenuity and strength. Julius had thought he would have it burnt, but as he reached the flat ground of the crest, he knew it should be left as a memorial to those who had died. It was fitting to leave them something on that bare landscape where even bloody dust soon vanished in the scouring wind. In a few days, when the legions had been sent away, the fort would be shelter for wild animals until age and decay made it slump and fall.

The gates stood open as Julius rode towards them. A thousand of his Tenth had made the climb with him and he could hear them panting as he passed through the walls and looked over the neat order of Pompey's last camp.

Cooking pits and tents lay untended for as far as he could see. It was a lonely place and Julius shuddered to think how many of the men who had left it at dawn were now cold on the plain. Perhaps they had known they would surrender to him even then, but duty had held them until Pompey fled the field.

The old Senate of Rome formed silent lines on the main road through the camp, their heads bowed. Julius did not look at them, his eyes on the praetorium tent where Pompey had woken that morning. He dismounted in front of it and paused to untie the thongs that kept out the wind. His Tenth came forward to help him and two of them threw back the heavy leather, tying it securely as he strode into the gloom.

Julius looked around him, unnerved by the dark chamber and feeling as if he were an intruder. He waited as his men lit the lamps and braziers and flickering gold illuminated the interior. It was bitterly cold, and he shivered.

'Wait outside,' he told them and in a moment he was alone. He brushed past a partition and saw Pompey's bed had been neatly made for his return. There was a sense of order to the place, no doubt the work of slaves after the army had gone. Julius picked up a clay bowl crusted with white paste from a table and sniffed at it. He opened a chest and looked quickly through the contents. He felt nervous, as if at any moment Pompey would come through the door and demand to know what he was doing.

Julius continued his examination of the Dictator's private belongings, finally shaking his head. He had hoped against reason that the seal ring of the Senate might have been left behind, but there was no sign of it and no reason for him to stay.

As he walked across the packed earth, his gaze fell on Pompey's desk and a packet of his private papers. On impulse, he reached out for the red silk that tied them and his fingers picked at the knot as he thought. He knew he should read them. The journal and letters would complete the picture of the man he had fought across Greece. They would reveal his mistakes as well as Julius' own, his most private thoughts. Somewhere in the neat packet would be word of Brutus, the details Julius craved to know.

The crackle of flames from a brazier broke into his thoughts and he acted before his wandering mind could begin its arguments, lifting the package and dropping it whole onto the flames. Almost immediately he reached to pull it back, but then he mastered himself and stood watching as the red band charred and curled, browning slowly until flames leapt along the edges.

The smoke was not thick, but still it seemed to sting Julius' eyes as he walked back into the weak sunlight. He saw the thousand soldiers of the Tenth had formed up outside and he took pride in their bearing. They would expect him to lead them back to Dyrrhachium, to negotiate with Pompey's Senate in a city rather than a battlefield. Part of him knew he should complete that work. There were a thousand things to do. The legions had to be paid, and with a start he realised he had assumed responsibility for the legions Pompey had led. They too would expect their silver on time, as well as food, equipment and shelter. Pyres for the dead would have to be built.

Julius walked back to the edge of the hill crest and looked into the far distance. Pompey was broken and there was no need to chase him further. It was true he carried a Senate ring, but from Rome Julius could send ships and letters denying his authority. The Dictator would be forced to take his straggling riders away from Roman lands and disappear.

Julius blew out a long breath into the wind. His legions had fought for years for this moment. They wanted to retire to the farms he had promised them, with silver and gold to build fine houses in the colonies. He had given them part of what they had earned in Gaul, but they deserved a thousand times more. They had given everything.

Julius saw Octavian walking his horse up the winding track. The younger man looked weary, though he tried to hide it under Julius' scrutiny. He arrived at the top with a new sheen of sweat on his face, smearing the dust of Pharsalus.

'Orders, sir?' Octavian said as he saluted.

Julius looked towards the horizon. He could see for miles and Greece had never seemed so vast and empty as from that height.

'I will stay for the funerals of the dead tonight, Octavian.' He took a deep breath, feeling his own exhaustion in his bones. 'Tomorrow I will go after Pompey. I'll need the extraordinarii, the

Tenth and the Fourth. I'll speak to the others and send them home.'

Octavian followed his commander's gaze before replying. 'They won't want to go back, sir,' he said at last.

Julius turned to him. 'I'll write letters to Mark Antony. They will be paid and those that want it can have the land I promised them. I'll make good my oath to all of them.'

'No, sir, it's not that. They won't want to be sent back while you go on. I've heard them. Ciro even came to me to put in a word for him. They want to see it to the end.'

Julius thought of the promise he had made to his daughter. Would she hate him if he killed Pompey? For an instant he imagined taking the Senate ring from Pompey's dead hand. Perhaps it would be enough to bring him peace. He did not know, but until he was able to stand before the Dictator it would never be over. Sulla had left Mithridates alive in this same land and Roman blood had been the price.

Julius rubbed his face roughly. He needed a bath and fresh clothes and something to eat. The body was always weak.

'I will speak to the men. Their loyalty . . .' He paused, unable to find words. 'Rome must be kept safe and we stripped her bare to come here. I will take the Fourth and Tenth and the extra-ordinarii, no more. Tell Ciro to commission his senior tribune in his place. I'll take him with me. I suppose it is fitting that those who were on the Rubicon should see this out.'

Julius smiled at the thought, but he saw Octavian's expression had hardened at his words.

'Brutus too, sir? What would you have me do with him?'

Julius' smile faded. 'Bring him. Put him in one of the carts for provisions. He can heal on the way.'

'Sir,' Octavian began. He fell silent under Julius' eyes.

'He's been with me since the very beginning,' Julius said softly, his words almost lost in the wind. 'Let him come.'

*   *   *

Brutus lay in darkness and pain. Under a full moon, the plain was a ghostly place of white shadow that barely reached the wounded in their tents. Brutus closed his eyes, wishing sleep would take him once more. His arm had been set and splinted and his ribs bound where they had cracked under the weight of dead men. The pain was worse when he tried to move and the last time his swollen bladder forced him to sit up, the effort made him grind his teeth against screaming. The pot brimmed under his cot, growing dark and foetid. His mind still swam from the blows he had received and he had only a vague memory of speaking to Julius in the blood and filth after the battle. It burned worse than his wounds to think of it.

Someone nearby cried out in their sleep, making him jump. He wished he had the strength to stagger out of the stinking tent into the night air. He sweated constantly and when his thoughts were clear he knew he was running a fever. He croaked for water, but it did not come. At last, he slid away into blacker depths and peace.

He surfaced from unconsciousness with a moan, tugged from deathlike sleep by a rough hand on his arm. Fear made his heart race as he saw men standing around him. He knew them. Each one had been with him in Spain and Gaul. They had been brothers once, but now their expressions were cruel.

One of them reached down and pressed a small blade into his left hand.

'If you have any honour left, you should cut your throat with this,' the man said, spitting the words.

Brutus passed out for a time, but when he woke again they were still there and the knife was tucked between his arm and his bandaged chest. Had it only been moments? It had seemed like hours, but none of the men had moved.

'If he won't do it, we should,' one of the soldiers said in a hoarse growl.

Another nodded and reached for the knife. Brutus swore and tried to writhe away from the probing fingers. He was too weak. Fear of dying in the stinking tent filled him and he tried to cry out, but his throat was too swollen and dry. He felt the knife pulled clear and winced in anticipation.

'Put it in his hand,' he heard and felt his lifeless fingers opened.

A new voice broke through his terror in the dark. 'What are you men doing in here?'

He didn't recognise it, but they scattered and the newcomer shouted angrily as they shoved their way past him in the gloom. Brutus panted as he lay on his back, the little knife clutched unfelt in his hand. He heard footsteps approach and looked into the face of a centurion as he bent over him.

'I need a guard,' Brutus whispered.

'I can't spare one for you,' the centurion replied coldly.

Outside on the plain a rush of flame from the funeral pyres lit the night. The darkness of the tent lessened slightly and the centurion's gaze fell on a bowl of soup on a wooden stool. He picked it up and grimaced at the shining clots of phlegm that floated there.

'I'll get you some clean food and a clean pot to piss in,' he said, in disgust. 'I can do that much for you.'

'Thank you,' Brutus said, closing his eyes against the pain.

'*Don't* thank me. I don't want anything from you,' the man snapped.

Brutus could hear the outrage in his voice. He raised the knife without looking. 'They left this,' he said. He heard the centurion snort.

'You keep it. I heard what they were saying to you. Maybe they were right. Not by their hands, though, not on my watch. But maybe you should think about doing it yourself. It would be clean.'

With a huge effort, Brutus threw the knife away from him, hearing it thump into the earth somewhere near. The centurion did not speak again and after a time he left.

The crackle of the pyres went on for hours and Brutus listened to the prayers before he slid into sleep once again.

As dawn came, the cries of the wounded men in the tent grew louder. The legion healers bathed and stitched and splinted as best they could. Infection and sickness would come later for most of them.

Brutus slept lightly, but it was the sudden silence that woke him. He raised his head and saw Julius had come into the tent. The men would not let the consul see their pain and those who moaned in sleep were shaken awake.

With a struggle, Brutus raised himself up as best he could. The men lying nearby stared openly at him. He could feel their dislike and resolved not to reveal his own pain, clenching his jaw against the sharp stabs from his broken arm.

Brutus watched as Julius spoke to each of the men, exchanging a few words and leaving them sitting proudly in his wake, their agony suppressed. Whether it was his imagination, Brutus did not know, but he felt the tension increase as Julius neared him until at last the consul of Rome pulled up a stool at his side and sat heavily on it.

Julius' eyes were red-rimmed from smoke. His armour had been polished and, compared to the men in the ward, he seemed cool and rested.

'Are they looking after you?' Julius asked, glancing over the splints and bandages that tied his battered frame.

'Flowers and grapes every morning,' Brutus replied.

He opened his mouth again to speak the words he wanted to say, but could not begin them. There was no guile in the dark eyes that looked so steadily into his. He had not been able to believe it at first, but somehow he had been forgiven. He felt his heart race in his chest until sparks fired on the edges of his vision.

He knew the fever was still in him and he wanted to lie back into the darkness. He could not face Julius and he looked away.

'Why didn't you kill me?' he whispered.

'Because you are my oldest friend,' Julius replied, leaning closer. 'How many times have you saved my life over the years? Do you think I could take yours? I can't.'

Brutus shook his head, unable to comprehend. In the night, he had thought the shame would kill him and there had been moments when he had wanted the knife he had thrown away.

'The men think you should,' he said, thinking of the dark figures and the tainted food.

'They don't understand,' Julius said and Brutus hated him for his mercy. Every citizen of Rome would hear how Julius had spared the friend who had betrayed him. Brutus could imagine the heart-wrenching verses the poets would write until it was all he could do not to spit.

He showed Julius nothing of his thoughts as he looked up at him. This was a new world after Pharsalus and he had been reborn. Perhaps a new beginning was possible for him. He had imagined casting off the dead skin of the past and finding his place as Julius' friend once more. But not his equal. That had been denied for ever by the sickening nobility of his pardon. His life had been given by Julius' hand and he did not know if he could bear to go on.

Despite himself, he clenched his teeth and groaned, overwhelmed by pounding emotions. As if from a distance, he felt Julius' hand rest on his forehead.

'Steady there, you're still weak,' he heard Julius say.

Tears shone in Brutus' eyes as he wrestled with despair. He wanted desperately to have the last two years back, or to be able to accept what had happened. He could not bear it. He could not.

He closed his eyes tightly against the sight of the man sitting by his side. When he opened them after an interval, Julius had gone and he was left with the accusing glares of the wounded soldiers. Their fascination prevented him sobbing out his hatred and his love.

CHAPTER TWENTY-TWO

The legions of the Tenth and Fourth were tired and gaunt after many days of marching. The carts had been stripped of provisions and the spring grain was still little more than dark green shoots. Their water had soured and they were always hungry. Even the horses of the extraordinarii showed their ribs under a coat of dark dust, but they did not falter. Whenever Julius thought they had reached the end of endurance, another village gave news of Pompey's riders and drew them ever further into the east. They knew they were closing on Pompey as he raced to reach the sea.

Julius rubbed weary eyes as he stood on the docks and looked out over the grey waves. There were six galleys there, slim and deadly as birds of prey. They guarded the strait between Greece and Asia Minor and they waited for him.

Pompey had reached the coast just the night before and Julius had hoped he would be trapped, forced to face his pursuers. Instead, the Dictator's ships had been ready to take him off. Pompey had hardly paused in his flight and the plains of Greece had been left behind.

'To come this far . . .' Julius said aloud.

He felt his men look up all around him. If the way had been clear, Julius would not have hesitated. The east coast of Greece was busy with merchant vessels and he could have crossed. He narrowed his eyes as he watched Pompey's ships manoeuvre over the deep water, their prows white with spray. They could not be well-manned, with most able soldiers taken out of them, but that was no comfort. In the open sea, they could tear merchant shipping apart. Even a night crossing was impossible, now that his legions had been seen. He could not hope to surprise the enemy galleys and the response would be brutal.

Despairing, he wondered how many more lay up and down the rocky coast out of sight. They made a wall of wood and iron that he could not break.

On the docks, his men waited patiently. Though Pompey had stripped the port of almost everything, there was water enough to wash the dust from their faces and fill the skins and barrels. They sat in quiet groups of eight or ten across the docks, gambling and sharing what little food they had been able to find. The problem of the crossing was not theirs, after all. They had done their part.

Julius clenched his fist, tapping it on the heavy wooden column he leaned against. He could not turn back and let Pompey go after such a chase. He had come too far. His gaze fell on a fishing boat, its owners busy with ropes and sails.

'Stop those men,' he ordered, watching as three soldiers of the Tenth grabbed hold of the little boat before the fishermen could pull away. The sail flapped noisily in the breeze as Julius strode over to the stone quay.

'You will take me to those ships,' he told the fishermen in halting Greek. They looked blankly at him and he called for Adàn.

'Tell them I will pay for passage out to the galleys,' he said, as the Spaniard approached.

Adàn produced two silver coins and tossed them to the men. In elaborate mime, he pointed to the ships and Julius until the fishermen's frowns disappeared.

Julius looked at his interpreter in disbelief. 'I thought you said you were learning Greek?' he said.

'It is a difficult language,' Adàn replied, embarrassed.

Octavian walked to the edge and looked into the tiny boat. 'Sir, you can't be thinking of going alone,' he said. 'They'll kill you.'

'What choice do I have? If I go out in force, the galleys will attack. They may listen to me.'

Julius watched as Octavian handed his sword to a soldier and began to remove his armour.

'What are you doing?' Julius asked.

'I'm coming with you, but I can't swim in this if they sink us.' He looked meaningfully at his general's breastplate, but Julius ignored him.

'Go on then,' Julius said, gesturing to the frail craft. 'One more will make no difference.'

He watched carefully to see how Octavian found a place on the slippery nets, wincing at the smell of fish. Julius followed him, making the boat rock dangerously before he was settled.

'Up sail,' Julius said to the fishermen.

He sighed at their expressions before pointing to it and raising his hands. In a few moments, the boat was easing away from the quayside. Julius looked back to see the worried expressions of his soldiers and he grinned, enjoying the motion.

'Are you ever seasick, Octavian?' he asked.

'Never. Stomach like iron,' Octavian lied cheerfully.

The galleys loomed and still both men felt an inexplicable rise in spirits. The fishing boat passed out of the sheltering bay and Julius breathed deeply, enjoying the pitch and roll of the sea.

'They've seen us,' he said. 'Here they come.'

Two galleys were backing oars and swinging round to face the boat that dared the deep water. As they grew closer, Julius heard the lookouts call. Perhaps a fishing crew would have been ignored, but the sight of soldiers on board was enough to bring them heeling swiftly round. Julius watched flags go up to the highest point of the masts, and in the distance more of the deadly craft began to turn.

His lightness of mood vanished as quickly as it had arrived. He sat stiff-backed as the galley sculled towards him and the fishermen dropped the sail. Without the hiss of speed, the only noise came from Roman throats calling orders and he felt a pang of nostalgia for his own days on the swift ships on a different coast.

As they drew closer, Julius looked up at the soldiers lining the sides, wishing he could stand. He felt fear, but the decision was made and he was determined to see it through. He could not have escaped them then, even if he had wanted to. The galleys could outrace the little boat under oars alone. With an effort, he swallowed his nervousness.

The galley's side was green and slick, showing they had been at sea for months while Julius struggled against Pompey. The oars were raised and Julius shivered as cold water dripped onto his upturned face as the boat passed under them. He saw the uniform of a centurion appear amongst the soldiers.

'Who are you?' the man asked.

'Consul Gaius Julius Caesar,' Julius replied. 'Throw me a rope.'

The motion of the two vessels made it impossible for him to hold the centurion's gaze, though Julius tried. He appreciated the man's difficulty. No doubt Pompey had given strict orders to sink and burn those who followed.

Julius did not smile as a long rope ladder came clattering down the side of the galley, its weighted ends disappearing beneath the surface of the sea. With difficulty, he reached for it, ignoring the warning shouts of the fishermen as their boat threatened to spill.

He climbed carefully. It did not help his composure to be watched by the crew of more than three galleys close by, nor the thought that his armour would drown him if he fell. His breathing was heavy by the time he reached the railing and accepted the captain's arm to help him over it. The ropes creaked as Octavian followed him up.

'And your name, Captain?' Julius said as soon as he stood on the deck.

The officer did not reply and stood frowning, tapping one hand on the other.

'Then I will tell you mine once more. I am Julius Caesar. I am a consul of Rome and the only elected authority you are sworn to serve. All orders given by Pompey are revoked. You are under my command as of this moment.'

The captain opened his mouth but Julius went on, unwilling to lose the momentary advantage. He spoke as if there was not the slightest chance of being disobeyed.

'You will pass the word to the other galleys to summon their captains here to be given orders. I have six thousand men and horses waiting to be picked up on the docks. You are my transport to Asia Minor, Captain.'

Deliberately, Julius turned away to help Octavian over the railing. When he faced the captain once more, he showed the first sign of anger.

'Did you not understand the orders I gave you, Captain? As consul, I am the Senate in transit. The orders I give take precedence over any others you may have received. Acknowledge now, or I will have you relieved.'

The captain struggled to reply. It was an impossible position. He was being asked to choose between two commanders and the conflict slowly brought a flush to his cheeks.

'Acknowledge!' Julius roared, standing closer.

The captain blinked in desperation. 'Yes, sir. The orders are acknowledged. You have authority. I will send the signals to the other galleys.'

He was sweating as Julius nodded at last and the crew ran to raise the flags that would bring the other captains in.

Julius felt Octavian staring at him and did not dare risk a smile.

'Return to the docks and get the men ready to leave, General,' he said. 'We go on.'

Brutus stood on the stone dock, scratching a scab under his sling as he watched the galleys. His arm and ribs were healing at last, though he'd thought being carried in a jolting cart would drive him mad at first. It had been a clean break, but he had seen enough injuries to know it would take as long to build back the muscle as it did to heal the bones. He still wore the sword he had carried at Pharsalus, but he could draw it only with his left hand and felt as clumsy as a child. He *hated* to be weak. The soldiers of the Tenth and Fourth had grown bold with their sneers and insults, perhaps because he had too much pride to complain. They would not have dared when he was well. Though it burned him, Brutus could do nothing but wait, his fury well hidden.

With him stood Domitius, Octavian, Regulus and Ciro, their nervousness showing as they strained their eyes on the darkening sea. Octavian had returned with the news and they had all watched as the galley captains rowed across to meet Pompey's enemy. No word had come since the last of them had climbed onto the deck and the tension mounted by the hour.

'What if they're holding him?' Domitius said suddenly. 'We'd never know.'

'What can we do if they are?' Octavian replied. 'Take those fat merchant ships out to do battle? They'd sink us before we could get close and you know it.' He spoke without his eyes ever leaving the sleek shapes of the galleys as they rocked in the swell outside the port. 'He chose the risk.'

Ciro glanced at the setting sun, frowning to himself. 'If he's not back by dark, we could slip out. If we packed onto a single ship, we'd have enough to storm one of the galleys. Take one and you can take another.'

Brutus looked at him in surprise. The years had subtly altered the men he thought he knew. Ciro had become accustomed to command and his confidence had grown. Brutus replied without thinking.

'If they hold him, they'll expect us to try that. They'll anchor as far out as they can get and spend the night in close formation. That's if they don't head straight for Asia Minor with Julius, to give him to Pompey.'

Octavian stiffened as he spoke. 'Shut your mouth,' he said flatly. 'You hold no command. You are here only because my general did not see fit to execute you. You have nothing to say to us.'

Brutus glared back at him, but dropped his gaze under the combined stares of the men he had known. It did not matter, he told himself, though he was surprised how much they could still hurt him. He noted how they looked to Octavian in Julius' absence. Perhaps it was something in the blood. He took a deep, angry breath and his right hand twitched in the sling before he gained control.

'I don't think . . .' he began.

Octavian rounded on him. 'If it were my choice, I would nail you to a cross on these docks. Do you think the men would object?'

Brutus did not have to consider it. He knew the answer very well indeed.

'No, they'd love a chance at me. But you won't let them, will you, boy? You'll follow his orders even if it means everything you value is destroyed.'

'You can still try to justify what you did?' Octavian demanded. 'There aren't words enough. I don't understand why he brought you here, but I will tell you this. If Julius expects you back as one of us, I won't do it. The first time you ever try to give me an order, I'll cut your throat.'

Brutus narrowed his eyes, leaning forward. 'You're brave now, boy, but bones heal. When they do . . .'

'I'll do it now!' Octavian said, raging.

He surged at Brutus, and Regulus and Ciro grabbed hold of his arm as it came up with a blade. Brutus staggered back out of range.

'I wonder how you would explain killing me to Julius,' he said. His eyes were full of malice as the younger man struggled to reach him. 'He can be cruel as well, Octavian. Perhaps that's why he let me live.'

Octavian subsided as Ciro prised the knife from his hand.

'You think you'll heal, Brutus?' he said. 'What if I had the men take you somewhere quiet and smash your arm properly? They could shatter your hand so badly you'd never use a sword again.'

Octavian smiled as he saw a trace of fear in Brutus' eyes.

'That would hurt you, wouldn't it? You'd never ride a horse, or write your name, even. That would break the arrogance out of you at last.'

'Ah, you're a *noble* man, Octavian,' Brutus said. 'I wish I had your principles.'

Octavian went on, his hatred barely in check. 'One more word out of you and I'll do it. No one will stop me, not to save you. They know you deserve it. Go *on*, General. One more *word.*'

Brutus stared at him for a long time, then shook his head in disgust before turning and walking away from the group. Octavian nodded sharply, shaking with reaction. He hardly felt Domitius' grip on his shoulder, steadying him.

'You shouldn't let it show,' Domitius said softly, looking after the broken man he had once revered.

Octavian snorted. 'I can't help it. After all he's done, he stands with us as if he has a right. I don't know what Julius was thinking, bringing him here.'

'Neither do I,' Domitius replied. 'It's between them, though.'

Regulus hissed in a breath, making them all turn back to the sea.

As the sun sank in the west, the galleys were moving, their great oars sweeping them in towards the dock.

Octavian looked at the others. 'Until we know he is safe, I want the men in formation to repel an attack. Get spears ready. Domitius, have the extraordinarii stand back as foot reserves. They're no good to us here.'

Caesar's generals moved away quickly to give the orders, not thinking to question his right to command them. Octavian was left alone to watch the galleys sweep in.

The little port could not take all six of the ships that clustered around the bay. Two of them came in together and Octavian watched as one bank of oars withdrew, leaving the other to scull the final gap to the dock. In the gloom, he could hardly make out the details of the great corvus bridges that were sent crashing down. Crewmen carrying ropes thumped across them and then Octavian saw Julius on the wooden slope. He sagged in relief.

Julius raised an arm in formal greeting. 'Are the men ready to board, General?' he called.

'They are, sir,' Octavian replied, smiling. Julius could still astonish him, he realised with amusement.

'Then get them on. There is no time to waste. The galleys carried his horses only two days ago – we have almost closed the gap.' He paused, feeling again the thrill of the hunt. 'Tell them there are good stocks of food on board and they'll move a little faster.'

Octavian saluted and walked over to the men he commanded. Julius would have noted the formations and ready spears, though he could hardly mention it with the galley crews in earshot. Octavian could not help but grin as he relayed the order to the centurions of the Fourth legion. Though there would be harder days of marching ahead, he felt a growing confidence. Pompey would not escape them.

* * *

The slow dawn brought the coast of Asia Minor into view, with sharp, grey-green mountains plunging into the sea. Geese called overhead, and pelicans floated high above the galleys, watching for silver shoals beneath the surface. The first touches of spring were in the air and the morning seemed full of promise.

It was a new land for all of them, further east from Rome than Britain lay to the west. Asia Minor supplied the cedar that built galleys for Rome. Its figs, apricots and nuts would pack the holds of merchant ships heading for home markets. It was a golden land, an ancient one, and somewhere in the north were the ruins of Troy. Julius remembered how he had bothered his tutors to be told the stories of that place. Alexander had been there and offered sacrifice at the tomb of Achilles. Julius ached to stand where the Greek king had stood.

He shivered in the spray from the bows as the oar slaves propelled them towards a tiny port.

'When I return to Rome after all this,' he said to Domitius, 'I will have seen the ends of Roman land, both east and west. It makes me proud to be so far from home and still hear the speech of my city. To find *our* soldiers here; our laws and ships. Is it not wonderful?'

Domitius smiled at Julius' enthusiasm, feeling it himself. Though the pursuit across Greece had been hard, a different mood was stealing through the legions. Perhaps it was the aftermath of Pharsalus, as they realised they had come to the end of their years of battle. The sight of Julius commanding the enemy galleys had made it a reality. They were no longer at war. Their task was merely to stamp out the last embers of Pompey's rule. Those who had been with Julius from Spain and Gaul felt it most strongly of all. They clustered at the rails of the six galleys, laughing and talking with unaccustomed lightness.

Domitius glanced up to where Adàn had climbed the mast.

Even so far above their heads, the Spaniard's voice could be heard as he sang some ballad from his youth.

The quaestor of the tiny coastal port spoke excellent Latin, though he had grown up in sight of the local barracks. He was a short, dark man who bowed as Julius entered the dock buildings and did not rise until permission came.

'Consul,' he said. 'You are welcome here.'

'How long since Pompey's riders left this place?' Julius asked impatiently.

The little man did not hesitate and Julius realised Pompey had left no orders to stop the pursuit. He had not expected them to cross against his galleys. It gave Julius hope that Pompey might have slowed his pace.

'The Dictator left last night, Consul. Is your business urgent? I can have messengers sent south if you wish.'

Julius blinked in surprise. 'No. I am hunting the man. I do not want him warned.'

The quaestor looked confused. In two days, he had seen more foreign soldiers than at any other point in his life. It would be a story for his children that he had spoken with not one but two of the masters of Rome.

'Then I wish you luck in the hunt, Consul,' he said.

CHAPTER TWENTY-THREE

They sighted Pompey's riders after four days of hard marching. They had made good time heading south and when at last the scouts rode in with the news, Julius' men let out a great cheer. It had been a long chase, but when the horns sounded and they formed ranks for an attack, they were ready to crush the enemy for the last time.

Pompey's men heard the horns and Julius could only imagine the fear and consternation in their ranks. These were the same extraordinarii who had run at Pharsalus. To find themselves hunted in another country would be a terrible blow. They had been beaten once and Julius did not doubt his men could do it again. It gave him pleasure to outnumber Pompey's small force, as he had been at Pharsalus. Let them know what it felt like to face so many warriors bent on their destruction.

In the distance, Julius saw the ranks of Roman horsemen wheel, turning to face the threat. It was a hopeless gesture, but he admired their courage. Perhaps they wished to wipe the slate clean for the rout they had suffered before. He saw them kick their mounts into a steady trot back towards the Tenth and he showed his teeth in anticipation, looking for Pompey's red cloak amongst them.

Along the ranks of the Tenth and Fourth, the legionaries readied spears. As the thunder of hooves came to them, they lifted their heads, swept up in savagery that was a little like joy.

'Go, sir, please! Let us hold them here,' the decurion, Casitas, shouted to Pompey.

The Dictator sat as if stunned. He had not spoken since the first appalling moment when Roman war horns had sounded behind. It was not a sound he had ever expected to hear again.

As he watched the legions from Pharsalus, Pompey mopped at a dark stain on his lips and considered riding with the last of his armies. It would be a grand gesture perhaps. The poets of Rome would write it into their ballads when they spoke of his life.

His vision blurred as his pain writhed inside him. He wore armour no longer, having none that could contain the swelling. It grew daily, pressing up into his lungs until it was hard to breathe. There were times when he would have given anything just to slip into the peaceful dark. He dreamed of an end to the agony and as he patted his horse's neck he yearned to kick his mount into a last gallop.

'Sir! You can get clear. The coast is only a few miles further south,' Casitas bellowed, trying to break through the stupor that held his commanding general.

Pompey blinked slowly, then Caesar's legions seemed to sharpen in his vision and his wits returned. He looked across at the decurion. The man was desperate for Pompey to ride and his eyes pleaded.

'Do what you can,' Pompey said at last and somehow, over the noise of the horses, Casitas heard and nodded in relief. He called quick orders to those around him.

'Fall out, Quintus! Take Lucius and go with the consul. We will hold them as long as we can.'

The named riders pulled out of the formation to Pompey's side. Pompey looked around him at the men who had come so far from home. The vagueness that had smothered his mind as the sickness worsened seemed to have lifted for a few precious moments.

'I have been well served by you all,' he called to them.

He turned his back and as he rode away he heard the order given to begin the advance that would end in a desperate blow against Caesar's soldiers.

The sea was not too far away and there would be ships there to take him clear of Roman lands at last. He would lose himself where Rome had no authority and Julius could search for years without finding him.

Pompey patted the leather bag that was strapped to his saddle, taking comfort from the gold within. He would not be poor when he reached the ports of Egypt. They had healers there who would take away the pain at last.

The Tenth and Fourth launched their spears less than thirty feet from the charging line. The heavy shafts destroyed the first horses and hampered those behind as they found the way blocked. The veteran legions moved quickly forward, darting in to gut the milling horses and pull men down from saddles. They had fought cavalry in Gaul and had no fear of the stamping, rearing beasts.

Pompey's riders did not give their lives easily and Julius was staggered at their recklessness. Even when it was hopeless, they fought on with grim despair. He could hardly believe they were the same soldiers he had seen fleeing the plain of Pharsalus.

The field was filled with guttural shouts and the hacking sound of metal cutting flesh. Julius' own riders had moved to flank the single charge and began to batter them on all sides. They trampled purple flowers under the feet of their mounts, spattering the ground with strips of blood until they were numb with killing.

When Pompey's men were reduced to less than a thousand,

Julius signalled the cornicens to sound the disengage. His legions stepped back from piles of broken flesh, and in the lull he offered an end to it.

'What does it profit you to fight to the last?' he shouted to them.

One man in the armour of a decurion rode up and saluted, his face grim.

'It is not such a great thing, to die here,' Casitas said. 'Our honour is restored.'

'I grant you all honour, Decurion. Accept my pardon and tell your men to stand down.'

Casitas smiled and shook his head. 'It is not yours to offer,' he said, turning his horse away.

Julius gave him time to reach his companions before he sent the legions in once more. It took a long time to kill them all. When there were no more than a few weary men standing on the red field, he tried for peace a final time and was refused. The last man alive had lost his horse and still raised his sword as he was smashed from his feet.

The legionaries did not cheer the victory. They stood, bloody and panting, like dogs in the sun. The silence stretched across the field and there were many in the ranks who whispered prayers for the men they had faced.

Julius shook his head in awe at what he had witnessed. He barely noticed as the search began for the body of Pompey. When it was not found, Julius looked south, his face thoughtful.

'He did not deserve such loyalty,' he said. 'Find me a clear spot to make a camp and rest. We will move on tomorrow when we have honoured our Roman dead. Make no distinction between them. They were men of the same city.'

In three merchant ships, only the two thousand survivors of Julius' beloved Tenth made the final crossing to Alexandria. His extraordinarii had been left behind with the Fourth to wait for transport. He did not know if he could find Pompey there. The land had never been conquered by Rome and all he knew of the customs were memories taught to him as a child. It was Alexander's city, named for him. Though Egypt was another world to Julius, Alexandria was the resting place of the Greek king he had idolised all his life.

The mark he had left on the world had endured for centuries and even the Egyptian kings were descended from one of Alexander's generals, Ptolemy. If Pompey had not fled across the sea to escape him, Julius knew he might well have travelled there just to see the glories he had heard described as a boy. He remembered standing once at a broken statue of the Greek king and wondering if his own life could be used so well. Now he would step onto the soil of Egypt as ruler of the greatest empire in the world. He need not bow his head to any man, or any man's memory.

The thought brought a wave of homesickness as he realised spring would have come in the forum in Rome. The orators would be addressing the crowds, teaching points of philosophy and law for small coins. Julius had spent only a few months in his birthplace in almost twenty years and grown old in her service. He had left his youth on foreign lands and lost more than Rome had ever given him.

What had he gained in comparison to the lives of men he called friends? It was strange to think that he had spent the years so freely. He had earned the right to be first in his city, but he could take no joy in it. Perhaps the path had changed him, but he had expected more.

The main entrance to the port of Alexandria was through a deep-water passage between enclosing arms of rock that made the experienced men frown. The gap through which they sailed was narrow enough to be easily blocked and Julius could not escape the feeling that the harbour was a natural trap.

As the ships glided under sail towards the docks, the heat seemed to increase and Julius wiped sweat from his brow. The soldiers on deck gestured in amazement at a vast square column of white marble built at the edge of the port. It stood higher than any building in Rome and Julius was touched by nostalgia for the days when he had nothing more to fear than a whipping from his tutors. The Pharos lighthouse had seemed impossibly distant then. He had never expected to pass so close and he craned his neck with the others, lost in wonder. Somewhere in the city lay the greatest library in the world, containing all the works of philosophy and mathematics that had ever been written. It was somehow obscene to bring his killers into such a place of wealth and learning, but soon his vengeance would be over and he would be free to see the lands of gold.

The water was busy with hundreds of other craft carrying the trade of nations. Julius' merchant captains had to work to avoid collision as they approached the spit of land reaching out into the perfect anchorage that had once attracted Alexander.

Julius turned his gaze at last to the city, frowning as distant figures resolved into armed warriors, waiting on the docks. He saw bows and spears held upright. The front ranks carried oval shields, though they wore no armour and only a breechcloth and sandals, leaving their chests bare. It was clear enough that they were not Roman. They could not have been.

At their head stood a tall man in bulky robes that glittered in the sun. The man's gaze could be felt even at a distance and Julius swallowed dryly. Were they there to welcome him or prevent a landing? Julius felt the first prickle of alarm as he saw that the closest soldiers carried drawn swords of bronze, gleaming like gold.

'Let me go first, sir,' Octavian murmured at his shoulder. The legionaries of the Tenth had fallen silent as they caught sight of the army on the docks and they were listening.

'No,' Julius replied without turning round. He would not show fear in the face of these strange people. The consul of Rome walked where he chose.

The corvus bridge was lowered with ropes and Julius walked over it. He heard the clatter of iron studs as his men followed and he sensed Octavian close at his side. With deliberate dignity, Julius strode to the man who waited for him.

'My name is Porphiris, courtier to King Ptolemy, thirteenth of that name,' the man began, his voice oddly sibilant. 'He who is King of lower and upper Egypt, who displays the regalia and propitiates the gods. He who is beloved . . .'

'I am looking for a man of Rome,' Julius interrupted, pitching his voice to carry. He ignored the shock and anger in Porphiris' eyes. 'I know he came here and I want him brought to me.'

Porphiris bowed his head, concealing his dislike. 'We have received word from the merchants of your search, Consul. Know that Egypt is a friend of Rome. My king was distressed to think of your armies clashing in our fragile cities and prepared a gift to you.'

Julius narrowed his eyes as the ranks of armed men parted and a muscular slave walked forward with a measured tread. He carried a clay vessel in his outstretched arms. Julius saw figures of great beauty worked into the surface.

As it was placed at his feet, the slave stood back and knelt on the docks. Julius met the gaze of the king's representative and did not move. His question had not been answered and he felt his temper fray. He did not know what they expected of him.

'Where is Pompey?' he demanded. 'I . . .'

'Please. Open the jar,' the man replied.

With an impatient jerk, Julius removed the lid. He cried out in horror then and the lid slipped from his fingers to shatter on the stones.

Pompey's sightless eyes looked up from under fragrant oil. Julius could see the gleam of his Senate ring resting against his pale cheek. He reached slowly down and broke the surface, touching the cold flesh as he drew out the gold band.

He had met Pompey first in the old senate house, when Julius had been little more than a boy. He recalled the sense of awe he had felt in the presence of legends like Marius, Cicero, Sulla and a young general named Gnaeus Pompey. It had been Pompey who cleared the Mare Internum of pirates in forty days. It had been he who broke the rebellion under Spartacus. For all he had become an enemy, Julius had bound his family and his fate with Pompey in a triumvirate to rule.

There were too many names on the scrolls of the dead, too many who had fallen. Pompey had been a proud man. He deserved better than to be murdered by the hands of strangers, far from home.

In front of them all, Julius wept.

PART TWO

CHAPTER TWENTY-FOUR

As the chamber doors swung silently open, Julius caught his breath at what he saw within. He had expected his audience to take the form of a private meeting, but the vast hall was filled with hundreds of royal subjects, leaving only the central aisle free right up to the throne. They turned to see him and he was astonished at the range of colours that swirled and mingled. This was the court of the king, painted and bejewelled in opulence.

Lamps on heavy chains swung in unseen currents above his head as he crossed the threshold, trying not to show his awe. It was not an easy task. Everywhere he looked, there were black basalt statues of Egyptian gods looming over the courtiers. Among them, he recognised the figures of Greek deities and he could only shake his head in amazement when he saw the features of Alexander himself. The Greek legacy was everywhere, from the architecture to the customs of dress, subtly blended with the Egyptian until there was nowhere else like Alexandria.

The scent of pungent incense was strong enough to make Julius feel drowsy and he had to concentrate to keep his wits about him. He wore his best armour and cloak, but against the finery of the courtiers he felt shabby and unprepared. He raised his head in irritation as he felt the pressure of hundreds of eyes on him. He had seen the edges of the world. He would not be cowed by gold and granite.

The throne of kings lay at the far end of the hall and Julius strode towards its occupant. His footsteps clicked loudly and, like gaudy insects, the courtiers ceased all movement as he approached. Julius glanced to his side and saw that Porphiris was keeping pace without a sound. Julius had heard rumours of eunuchs serving the kingdoms of the east and wondered if Porphiris was one of that strange breed.

The long walk towards the throne seemed to take forever, and Julius found to his annoyance that it was raised on a stone dais so that he must look up as a petitioner to the king. He halted as two of Ptolemy's personal guard stepped across his path, blocking it with ornate staffs of gold. Julius frowned, refusing to be impressed. He thought Ptolemy regarded him with interest, though it was hard to be certain. The king wore a gold headdress and mask that obscured all but his eyes. His robes too had threads of that metal woven into them, so that he gleamed. Even with slaves to fan him, Julius could only guess at the heat of wearing such a thing in the stifling chamber. Porphiris stepped forward.

'I present Gaius Julius Caesar,' Porphiris said, his voice echoing, 'consul of Roman lands, of Italy, Greece, of Cyprus and Crete, Sardinia and Sicily, of Gaul, of Spain and of the African provinces.'

'You are welcome here,' Ptolemy replied and Julius hid his surprise at the soft, high-pitched tone. The voice of a young boy was hard to reconcile with the wealth and power he had seen, or with a queen renowned for her beauty and intelligence. Julius found himself hesitating. Fumes of myrrh hung in his throat, making him want to cough.

'I am grateful for the quarters provided to me, great king,' Julius said after a moment.

Another man stood to one side of the golden figure and leaned down to whisper into his ear before drawing himself up. Julius glanced at him, noting the vulpine features of a true Egyptian.

His eyelids were stained with some dark sheen that gave him an eerie, almost feminine beauty. There was no Greek blood in this one, Julius thought.

'I speak with Ptolemy's voice,' the man said, staring into Julius' eyes. 'We honour great Rome that has brought trade here for generations. We have watched her rise from simple herdsmen into the glorious strength she has today.'

Julius found himself growing irritated again. He did not know whether it would be a breach of manners to address the man directly, or whether he should reply to Ptolemy himself. The king's eyes were bright with interest, but gave no clue.

'If you would speak to me, tell me your name,' Julius snapped at the courtier.

A ripple of shock went around the hall and Ptolemy leaned a little closer in his seat, his interest obvious. The Egyptian was unflustered.

'My name is Panek, Consul. I speak with the voice of the king.'

'Be silent then, Panek. I am not here to speak with you,' Julius said. A babble of noise came from behind him and he heard Porphiris take a sharp breath. Julius ignored him, facing Ptolemy.

'My people are indeed a young nation, as Alexander's was when he came here,' Julius began. To his astonishment, every single head in the chamber bowed briefly at the mention of the name.

Panek spoke again before Julius could continue, 'We honour the god who began this great city. His mortal flesh lies here as mark of our love for him.'

Julius let the silence stretch as he glared at Panek. The man returned his gaze with placid blankness, as if he had no memory of Julius' command. Julius shook his head to clear it of the fumes of incense. He could not seem to summon the words he had intended to say. Alexander a god?

'A Roman consul came before me,' he said. 'By what right was his life taken?'

There was silence then and the gold figure of the king was as still as his statues. Panek's gaze seemed to sharpen and Julius thought he had irritated him at last.

'The petty troubles of Rome are not to be brought to Alexandria. This is the word of the king,' Panek said, his voice booming around the hall. 'Your armies and your wars have no place here. You have the head of your enemy as Ptolemy's gift.'

Julius stared hard at Ptolemy and saw the king blink. Was he nervous? It was difficult to judge behind the heavy gold. After a moment, Julius let his anger show. 'You dare to call the head of a consul of Rome a gift, Panek? Will you answer me, Majesty, or let this painted thing speak for you?'

The king shifted uncomfortably and Julius saw Panek's hand drop to Ptolemy's shoulder, as if in warning. Now all trace of calm had vanished from the oiled face. Panek spoke as if the words burned his mouth.

'The hospitality you have been offered extends for only seven days, Consul. After that, you will board your ships and leave Alexandria.'

Julius ignored Panek, his eyes firmly on the gold mask. Ptolemy did not move again and after a time Julius looked away in fury. He could feel the anger of the guards around him and cared nothing for it.

'Then we have nothing more to say. Your Majesty, it has been an honour.'

Julius turned away abruptly, surprising Porphiris so that he had to hurry to catch him before the far doors.

As they closed behind him, Porphiris deliberately blocked his path. 'Consul, you have a talent for making enemies,' he said.

Julius did not speak and after a moment Porphiris sagged under his stare.

'If the king considers you have insulted him, your men will not be allowed to live,' Porphiris said. 'The people will tear you apart.'

Julius looked into the man's dark eyes. 'Are you a eunuch, Porphiris? I have been wondering.'

Porphiris moved his hands in agitation. 'What? Did you not hear what I said to you?'

'I heard you, as I have heard the threats of a dozen kings in my life. What is one more, to me?'

Porphiris gaped in amazement. 'King Ptolemy is a god, Consul. If he speaks your death, there is nothing in the world that will save you.'

Julius seemed to consider this. 'I will think on it. Now take me back to my men in that fine palace your god provided. The incense is too strong for me in there.'

Porphiris bowed over his confusion.

'Yes, Consul,' he said, leading the way down.

As night came, Julius paced up and down the marble floor of his quarters, brooding. The palace he had been given was larger and more spacious than any building he had ever owned in Rome and the room where he had eaten was but one of many dozens available. Porphiris had provided slaves for his comfort, but Julius had dismissed them on his return from the king's court. He preferred the company of his own Tenth to spies and potential assassins.

He paused at an open window, looking out at the port of Alexandria and letting the breeze cool his indignation. As well as the eternal flame on Pharos, he could see thousands of lights in homes, shops and warehouses. The docks were busy with ships and cargo and darkness had changed nothing. In another mood, he might have enjoyed the scene, but he tightened his grip on the stone sill, oblivious to its craftsmanship. He had been awed at first at the level of ornamentation in the city. His quarters were no exception and the walls around him were lined with some blue ceramic, overlaid in gold leaf. It had palled after only a short time.

Perhaps because he had been so long in the field, or because his roots lay in a simpler Rome, but Julius no longer walked as if his steps could break the delicate statuary on every side. He didn't care if they fell into dust at his tread.

'I was all but dismissed, Octavian!' he said, clenching his hands behind his back. 'You cannot imagine the arrogance of those courtiers in their paints and oils. A flock of pretty birds without enough wits to fill a good Roman head between them.'

'What did their king say about Pompey?' Octavian asked.

He had taken a seat on a cushioned bench carved from what looked to be a single piece of black granite. He too had experienced the Egyptian welcome, with half-naked guards preventing his men from exploring the city. Domitius had managed to evade them for an hour, then been brought back like an errant child, with the guards shaking their heads in disapproval.

'The king might as well have been a mute, for all I had from him,' Julius said. 'From the few words I heard, I'd say he was only a boy. I never even saw his famous queen. More insults! His courtiers are the real power in this city and they have dismissed us like unwelcome tradesmen. It is insufferable! To think that this is Alexander's city and I have a chance to see it. I could have spent days in the great library alone and perhaps gone further inland to see the Nile. Rome would have waited a little longer for me to return.'

'You have what you came for, Julius. Pompey's head and ring . . .'

'Yes! I have that grisly remnant of a great man. His life was not theirs to take, Octavian. By the gods, it makes me furious to think of those golden-skinned eunuchs killing him.'

He thought of his promise to his daughter, that he would refrain from taking Pompey's life. How would she react when she heard the news? Pompey had not died at his hand, but perhaps the manner of his passing was worse, so far from his home and people. He clenched his jaw in anger.

'They made it sound as if we would have sacked the city in our search for him, Octavian. As if we were barbarians to be placated and sent on our way with a few beads and pots! He was my enemy, but he deserved better than to be killed at the hands of those men. A consul of Rome, no less. Shall I let it pass without revenge?'

'I think you must,' Octavian said, frowning to himself.

He knew Julius was capable of declaring war on the city over Pompey's death. Though the courtiers and king could not know it, almost four thousand men and horses could arrive at the port at any time. If Julius sent word back to Greece, he could order a dozen legions to march. One spark and Octavian knew he would not see Rome again for years.

'They believed they were doing your will when they gave you Pompey's head,' Octavian said. 'By their standards, they have treated us with courtesy. Is it an insult to be given a palace?'

He decided not to mention the humiliations the Tenth had endured from the palace guards. Julius was more protective of his beloved legion than his own life. If he heard they had been ill-treated, he would be blowing the war-horns before the sun rose.

Julius had paused to listen and in the silence Octavian could hear the tap-tap of his fingers behind his back.

'Seven days, though!' Julius snapped. 'Shall I turn tail and meekly follow the orders of the gold-faced boy? That's if they were his orders at all and not just the whim of one of his controlling clique. Alexander would be appalled if he could see this city treat me in such a fashion. Did I say they revere him as a god?'

'You mentioned it,' Octavian replied, though Julius did not seem to hear him. He stared in wonder as he considered the idea.

'His statue adorns the temples of their gods here, with incense and offerings. It is astonishing. Porphiris said that Ptolemy himself is divine. These are a strange people, Octavian. And why would you cut the testicles from a man? Does it make him stronger, or better able to concentrate? What benefit is there in such a practice?

There were some with the king who could have been men or women, I couldn't tell. Perhaps they had been gelded. I have seen some strange things over the years – do you remember the skulls of the Suebi? Incredible.'

Octavian watched Julius closely, suspecting that the tirade was finally coming to an end. He had not dared leave Julius alone in the grip of such a temper, but he could not help yawning as the night slipped by. Surely dawn could not be far off.

Domitius entered through tall bronze doors. Octavian rose as soon as he saw his friend's expression.

'Julius,' Domitius said, 'you should see this.'

'What is it?' Julius replied.

'I'm not sure if I know,' Domitius said with a grin. 'There's a man the size of Ciro at the gate. He's carrying a carpet.'

Julius looked blankly at him. 'Is he selling it?'

'No, sir, he says it's a gift from the queen of Egypt.'

Julius exchanged a glance with Octavian.

'Perhaps they want to make amends,' Octavian said, shrugging.

'Send him up,' Julius said.

Domitius vanished, returning with a man who loomed over the three Romans. Julius and Octavian heard his heavy step before he came through the doors and they saw Domitius had not exaggerated. The man was tall and bearded, with powerful arms wrapped around a tube of gold cloth.

'Greetings and honour to you, Consul,' the man said in flawless Latin. 'I bear the gift of Cleopatra, daughter of Isis, queen of Egypt, honoured wife to Ptolemy.'

As he spoke, the man lowered his burden to the floor with immense care. Something moved within it and Octavian whipped his sword from its sheath.

The stranger spun at the sound, his palms held up. 'Please, there is no danger to you,' he said.

Octavian stepped forward with his blade and the man knelt quickly, unrolling the carpet with a jerk.

A young woman tumbled out, landing catlike on her hands and knees. Julius' jaw dropped as she came to rest. A scanty patch of yellow silk covered her breasts and another wound around her waist, revealing long legs down to bare feet. Her skin was dark gold and her hair wild from her time in the carpet. Tendrils of it fell forward to cover a face flushed with heat and embarrassment. It may have been Julius' imagination, but he thought he could hear her swearing softly under her breath.

As the Romans watched in astonishment, she put her lower lip half over the other and blew a tendril of hair out of her vision. Her gaze fixed on Julius as she arranged herself in a more dignified position and rose slowly.

'I am Cleopatra,' she said. 'I would speak with you alone, Caesar.'

Julius was entranced. She had the body of a dancer with heavy-lidded eyes and a full mouth that suggested a rare sensuality. Gold earrings gleamed and a red garnet like a drop of blood hung around her throat. She was as beautiful as he had heard.

'Leave us,' Julius said, without looking at the others.

Octavian hesitated for a moment until Julius met his eyes, then he left with Domitius and the bearded servant.

Julius crossed to a table and filled a silver cup with red wine, using the action to give him time to think. She came with him and accepted the cup in both hands.

'Why did you have yourself delivered in such a fashion?' Julius asked.

She drank deeply before replying and he wondered what it had been like to be trapped in the stifling cloth of the carpet for so long.

'If I had come openly, the courtiers would have imprisoned me. I am not welcome in Alexandria, not any more.'

Her eyes never left his as she spoke and Julius found her

directness uncomfortable. He gestured to a bench and she followed him to it, drawing her legs up slowly under her.

'How can the queen be unwelcome?' Julius asked.

'Because I am at war, Caesar. My loyal warriors are at the borders of Syria, unable to enter Egypt. My life would have been worth nothing if I had come by day.'

'I don't understand,' Julius said.

She leaned closer to him and he could smell a rich perfume coming from her bare skin like smoke. He found himself becoming aroused by the near-naked girl and struggled not to show it.

'My brother Ptolemy is thirteen years old,' she said. 'Under Panek he has no say in the rule of my lands.'

'Your brother?' Julius said.

She nodded. 'My brother and my husband, in one.' She saw his expression and laughed, a low chuckle that he enjoyed.

'It is a formal thing, Roman, to keep the bloodline pure. We were king and queen together, as my father married his own sister. When Ptolemy was of an age, I would have borne his children to rule after us.'

Julius felt lost amidst these revelations. He struggled to find something to break the silence that had sprung up between them.

'You speak my language beautifully,' he ventured.

She laughed again, delighting him. 'My father taught it, though I am the first of his line to speak Egyptian. Would you prefer to converse in Greek? It was the language of my childhood.'

'It makes me glad to hear you say it,' he said earnestly. 'I have admired Alexander all my life. To be here with the descendant of his general is intoxicating.'

'Egypt claims me now, Caesar; runs like fire in me,' she said.

Her skin was smooth copper-gold, oiled every day of her life. He knew she would be extraordinary to touch.

'But you cannot take your throne, for fear,' he said softly.

Cleopatra snorted. 'Not of my people. They are loyal to the goddess in me.'

Julius frowned at the statement from such a youthful girl. 'I do not believe such things.'

She looked at him with interest and he felt his pulses throb. 'The flesh you see is nothing, Caesar. My Ka is divine within me, held until my death. You could not see it.'

'Your Ka?'

'My . . . spirit. My soul. Like a flame in a shuttered lamp, if you wish.'

Julius shook his head. Her perfume seemed to fill every breath he took, so close was he sitting to her. He had not seen her move, but the distance between them seemed to have shrunk and the room felt hot.

'You have not said why you came to me,' he said.

'Is it not obvious? I have heard of you, Caesar. I have prayed to Isis to be delivered from my exile and you were sent to me. You have an army to tip the balance in the very heart of Alexandria.' Her eyes pleaded.

'What of your own soldiers?' he asked.

'They are too few and spies crawl like flies around their camp. I risked death to reach you, Caesar, and I am only one.' She reached out to him and touched his face with a cool hand. 'I need a man of honour, Caesar. I need him desperately. You may claim not to believe, but the gods led you here for this.'

Julius shook his head. 'I followed Gnaeus Pompey, murdered on your own docks.'

She did not look away. 'And what made him come to Alexander's city? There are many ports. If you cannot believe, then give me my revenge as you take yours! The order for Pompey's death bore the name of my family, in dishonour. Panek uses the royal seal as if it were his own. Will you help me, Roman?'

Julius rose clumsily from the couch, overwhelmed by her. The

297

idea of bringing the arrogant courtiers to their knees appealed to him. He thought of the extraordinarii and soldiers coming over from Asia Minor and wondered if they would arrive before his seven days were up.

'How many men do they have?' he said.

She smiled, unfolding her legs until her toes touched the bare marble floor.

Domitius and Octavian watched as Julius paced with new energy. He had not slept or taken time to shave, though the sun had risen over the city and the noise of trade and life came in through the high windows.

'This is not our struggle, Julius,' Octavian said, worried and upset. He could see the prospect of returning to Rome dwindling before him and had conceived an instant dislike for the woman who had brought the change.

'It is, if I make it so,' Julius replied. 'My word alone is reason enough.' He paused, wanting the younger man to understand. 'If we intervene here, then perhaps one day this city will be part of our empire – and all of Egypt beyond it. Imagine that! Cities older than Greece and a pathway to the east.' His eyes were shining with the vision and Octavian knew there would be no turning him home.

'I assume her beauty has not affected your judgement,' Octavian said.

Julius set his jaw in anger, then shrugged. 'I am not immune, but this is a chance to set the precedent of Roman interest. I could not have asked for a better chance than to cut the knots of their tangled politics. If the gods are on our side, they are Roman gods! It cries out to me, Octavian.'

'And Rome cries out for your return!' Octavian snapped, surprising them both. 'You have won all your battles. It is time to return to the rewards, surely? The men are expecting your word on it.'

Julius rubbed his chin with his hand, looking suddenly weary.

'If I go back, I may never leave Rome again. I've grown too old to be planning new campaigns. But not old enough to fear one more for the right cause. How can I claim to bring the light of our civilisation and then turn away from this? If we only look inward to our own affairs, the influence we have gained will be wasted.' He paused in front of Octavian, gripping him by the shoulder. 'I intend to use the influence those years of battle have won for me. I would have you join me willingly, but if you cannot, you may return.'

'Without you?' Octavian said, knowing the answer. Julius nodded and Octavian sighed. 'My place is at your right hand. If you say we must go on, I will be there, as I always have been.'

'You are a good man, Octavian. If there are no sons to follow me, I would be proud to see you in my place.' He chuckled. 'Where else would you find an education like this one! I can teach you more politics here than you would find in a decade of Senate meetings. Think of the future, Octavian. Think of what you will accomplish when I am gone. This is Alexander's city and it could be a prize for Rome. Who better than we to take his mantle?'

Octavian nodded slowly, and Julius clapped him on the arm.

'How many are we facing, exactly?' Domitius said, interrupting. Both men seemed to break free of some private communication.

'Too many for the Tenth alone,' Julius said. 'We must wait for the Fourth to arrive. Even then, we might need Cleopatra's army before we are done. Though they are so ringed about with informers that the courtiers will know if they begin to move. We need to wrench an advantage from the first moment, while they still think we are going to leave in peace. We have surprise. With the Fourth here in strength, we'll strike where they don't expect it.'

He grinned and Octavian responded, feeling the excitement despite his misgivings.

'What do you have in mind?' Octavian asked.

'It is like a game of latrunculi,' Julius said. 'We must capture the king.'

CHAPTER TWENTY-FIVE

In gloom, the legions waited, crammed into every corner of the Roman quarters. Julius himself had gone down to the docks to greet the soldiers of the Fourth as they sailed in. They had come expecting to pursue Pompey across a new continent, but instead found themselves part of a plot to kidnap a boy king. It may have been the return of warm nights, or simply the fact that Pompey was dead and they were free at last, but a rare mood of juvenile excitement had stolen amongst them. They nudged each other and smiled in the darkness. Caesar had triumphed over his enemies, and they had been there to see it happen.

Julius waited by the heavy doors, peering out at the moon. He heard a snort from a Roman mount and glanced at the source, watching shadows move. The horses had been well fed on grain, better than they had seen in weeks. The palace too was filled with stores, the first choice of cargoes from Cyprus, Greece, even Sicily. Roman gold had weight on the docks of Alexandria.

Despite the tension, Julius could not hide the fact that he was enjoying himself. Ciro, Brutus and Regulus had come across to Egypt. He had his generals around him once more and he felt gloriously alive.

At Julius' side, Brutus could not share the lightness of the others. His broken arm had healed in the weeks of pursuit, but the muscles were still too weak to risk on such a venture. He yearned to go with them, for things to be as they had once been. There were times when he could forget everything that had happened and imagine they were back in Gaul or Spain, with trust and friendship binding them together. He could not miss the glances of dislike from the men to remind him of his new status. They did not allow him the luxury of any doubt on the subject. He sensed Octavian was watching him and stared at nothing until the feeling faded. It would change when his strength returned. He would make it change. Until then, he accepted that he would stay and barricade the palace ready for their return.

Facing the night, Julius did not see Cleopatra at first. She came silently into the packed entrance hall without announcement, weaving her way in and out of startled soldiers. Julius turned in time to see her smile as one of the men let out a low whistle and a ripple of laughter went through them. He was at a loss to say how she had done it, but she had found a new costume only slightly less revealing than the one she had worn on their first meeting. Her lithe movement was girlish, though her eyes were older. Her hair was held back by a bar of gold and her legs and bare stomach drew sidelong glances as she walked amongst them.

Julius found himself blushing as she approached him, knowing his soldiers were happily drawing their own conclusions for his sudden interest in Egypt. His generals had met her before, but they still stood rooted as she spun in place to face the men.

'I have heard of Roman courage,' she said, her voice soft. 'And I have seen your honour in coming to my aid in this. You will learn the gratitude of a queen when I have my throne again.'

She bowed to the rough killers of Rome and in that moment they would have gone anywhere for her. They knew better than to cheer the beauty who came so humbly amongst them, but a low murmur of approval went through the palace, almost a growl.

'It's time,' Julius said, looking strangely at the queen.

Her skin gleamed in the shadows and her eyes were bright with the moon as she turned to him. Before he could react, she took a step and kissed him lightly on the lips. He knew he was blushing again with embarrassment. She was less than half his age and he could practically feel the grins of the men as they exchanged glances.

He cleared his throat, trying to summon his dignity. 'You have your orders, gentlemen. Remember that you must not engage the enemy unless you have to. We find the king and get straight back here before they can muster enough of a force to slow us. You'll hear the retreat horn blown when Ptolemy is captured and when you do, get out as fast as you can. If you are separated, come here. Understood?'

A chorus of assenting murmurs answered him and he nodded, heaving open the door to the moonlit garden.

'Then follow me, gentlemen,' he said, responding at last to their bright eyes and smothered laughter with a grin. 'Follow me.'

They drew their swords and rose to their feet, moving out into the darkness. It took a long time for the last of them to pass through from the furthest reaches of the palace. Only one cohort remained behind as Brutus closed the doors, plunging them all into a deeper dark. He turned to them and hesitated in the presence of the queen who stood like a scented statue, watching him.

'Block the windows and entrances,' he ordered, his voice sounding harsh after the echoing silence. 'Use grain sacks and anything else you can lift – the heavier the better.'

The single cohort moved quickly into action, its six centurions snapping out orders until the last of them had work. The entrance hall emptied, leaving Brutus standing uncomfortably with the Egyptian queen.

Her voice came from the shadows. 'The general in silver armour . . .'

His eyes adjusted to see the moon outline her bare shoulders in a faint glimmer. He shivered. 'I am, mistress. Or should I call you goddess?' He could feel her gaze like a weight.

'August Majesty is one title, though I carry the goddess in me. Does the idea offend you, Roman?'

Brutus shrugged. 'I have seen a lot of foreign lands. I've seen people who paint their skins blue. There isn't much that can surprise me now.'

'You must have been with Caesar for many years,' she said.

He looked away, suddenly unnerved. Would Julius have spoken of him? 'More than I care to tell you,' he said.

'How were you injured? In his service?'

He snorted to himself then, growing irritated with the stream of questions. 'I was injured in battle, Majesty. I think you may have already heard the details.'

He raised his splinted arm, as if to have it inspected. In response, she came closer. She reached out and, despite himself, he shivered again at her cool touch. She wore a heavy ring of gold with a carved ruby. In the gloom it was as black as the night sky.

'You are the one who betrayed him,' she said in fascination. 'Tell me, why did he let you live?'

He blinked at her bluntness. Here was a woman used to every question being answered, every whim met. She seemed unaware of the pain she was causing him. 'He could not find a better general. I am a perfect scourge in the field, though not as you see me now.'

He spoke with sardonic amusement, but when she did not respond, he could not hold the expression. His features slowly drooped into blankness. 'We were young together,' he said. 'I made a mistake and he forgave me.' He was surprised at his own honesty. It was less painful to spin a tale.

'I would have killed you,' she muttered, biting her lower lip.

Brutus could only look at her, sensing she spoke the truth. He reminded himself that the queen had known absolute power from her youngest years. She was every bit as deadly as the black snakes of the Nile.

'I could never forgive a betrayal, General. Your Caesar is either a great man or a fool. Which do you think it is?'

'I think you and he have much in common. I do not answer to you, however, nor will I explain myself to you any longer.'

'He has gone tonight to kidnap my husband, my brother and my king. He has seen only the edges of the army Egypt can field. Caesar may die in the striving, or my brother fall and be pierced with arrows. This is the great game, General. These are the stakes involved. Listen to the words when I say this to you. He let you live because he is blind to you. He does not know what goes on in your heart.'

She touched his neck with the palm of her hand, pressing. He thought she must bathe in lotus oil to have such an effect. He felt a tiny scratch, as if from a thorn. He might have jerked away, but his senses pressed in on him and he longed for a breath of cold air. He heard her speak through layers and layers of winding cloth, muffled.

'I know you, General. I know every small sin, and every great one. I know your heart as Caesar never can. I know hatred. I know jealousy. I know you.'

Her hand dropped away and he staggered, still able to feel where her nails had pressed.

'Be loyal now, General, or measure your life in beats. His fate is tied up in Egypt, in me. And my arm is long. I will not suffer another betrayal, nor even the shadow of one.'

He gaped at her intensity, stunned and bewildered. 'Egyptian bitch, what have you done to me?' he said, groggily.

'I have saved your life, Roman,' she said.

Her lips formed a smile then, but the eyes were cold and watchful. Without another word, she left him alone in the entrance

305

hall, slumped against a pillar and shaking his head like a wounded animal.

The Canopic Way cut through the heart of Alexandria. The two legions with Julius jogged east along its length, their clattering sandals shattering the peace of the night. In the darkness, the main artery of the city was an eerie place. Temples to strange gods loomed over them and statues seemed ready to leap into life on every side. The flickering of night lamps cast shadows on the grim men who ran with drawn swords towards the palace quarter.

Julius kept pace with them, measuring his breaths as his legs and chest began to loosen. The feeling of excitement had not lessened. If anything, he had wound himself to an even tighter pitch of tension and he felt young as he counted the roads they passed. At the fifth, he gestured left and the snake of legionaries turned into the outskirts of the palace, following the same route he had taken with Porphiris three days before.

The royal palace was not a single building but a complex of many structures, set in sculpted gardens. The first gates were manned by nervous guards, long alerted by the crash of pounding feet. Soldiers of the Tenth stepped forward with heavy hammers and brought the barrier down in a few swift blows. The first blood of the evening was shed as the guards raised their weapons and were left to be trampled as the legions went on into the dark grounds.

The main building where Julius had met the boy king was lit at all points and gleamed in the night. Julius had no need to direct the men towards it. There were more guards there and they died bravely, but the Tenth had spread out into their fighting line and only an army could have held them.

Panic was spreading through the palace quarters and the resistance they met was sporadic and badly organised. Julius had the impression that a direct assault had never even been considered. The outer gates had been designed for artifice and beauty rather than solid defence and the defenders seemed to be in chaos, shouting and screaming at each other.

Armed soldiers began to spill from an unseen barracks, trying desperately to form before the Tenth reached them. They were slaughtered like cattle and lambs, their blood spilling down the steps to the main entrance. The doors of bronze that had been open for Julius' first visit were now closed, and as he reached them he could hear bars thumping into place. He thanked his gods for Cleopatra's knowledge and leapt over a stone wall at the side of the steps, calling for hammers as he ran to a lesser entrance.

The ringing blows sounded far in the dark. As if to answer them, an alarm bell began to ring somewhere near and Julius despatched a century to silence it.

The side door was solidly made and Julius was forced to control his impatience. He checked the edge of his sword, though he had yet to blood it. Then the tone of the impacts changed and the door fell. His Tenth roared into the breach and Julius heard screaming inside. He stayed close to the front, shouting orders and directing them as best he could. The palace looked very different from his previous visit by day, and it took a few moments to get his bearings.

'Tenth with me!' he shouted, racing through a hall.

He heard Octavian and Domitius panting at his back and allowed his pace to slow a little. It would do no good for him to run straight onto the swords of defenders around the king and the two generals were better able to clear the way.

Even as he had the thought, the black corridor seemed to fill with men and Julius saw Octavian and Domitius dart in with their swords swinging. The only light was from a lamp much further down and the combat was brief and terrifying, bodies struggling in shadows. The Roman armour held against the bronze blades of the palace guard and in only a few moments the first of the Tenth were stepping over the dead and rushing on.

'Which way?' Octavian said, spitting blood from a broken lip.

Julius wished for more light, but he could make out the white gleam of marble stairs he had ascended a lifetime before.

'Up there!' he said, pointing.

His breath was coming harshly and his sword had lost its shine with the stain of an unknown guard, but he ran with the others as they pounded up the steps. Cleopatra had told him where her brother slept and Julius took a turning away from the meeting hall into a corridor that was better lit than the rest of the labyrinth. Once more, he saw Octavian and Domitius take positions ahead and suddenly he was shouting for them to stop.

They had passed a door that seemed to be made of solid gold. Julius looked around for the men who carried hammers.

'Here! He's in here,' Julius called. 'Hammers to me!' He threw his weight against the door, but felt no give in it.

'If you'd stand back, sir,' a burly soldier of the Tenth said at his shoulder.

Julius stepped clear as the man raised the iron head and began a pounding rhythm, quickly joined by two more. The corridor became the focus for the Roman force, with defensive stations taken up around it while the last obstacles were broken.

The gold was heavy but it dented under each blow and it was not long before one of the great oblong barriers sagged away on a broken hinge.

An arrow flew through the gap, ricocheting off the head of a hammer and slicing into a soldier's cheek. With an oath, he yanked at it and three of the Tenth held him down while the arrow was snapped and the head removed with brutal efficiency. Shields were raised as the second door fell and two more of the whining shafts struck uselessly against them as the Tenth surged into the room.

The lamps were lit in the royal chambers and Julius was

astonished to see two naked girls with bows inside. They cried out in terror as they tried to pull back one more shaft. Almost with contempt, the legionaries stepped forward and slapped the weapons out of their hands. The women struggled wildly as they were shoved away from the doorway they guarded.

The king's bedroom was dark and Julius knew the first ones through would be silhouetted against the light. His soldiers hardly hesitated, trusting to speed to keep them safe. They leapt into the shadows, rolling and coming up ready to kill.

'He's here,' one shouted back. 'The king alone.'

As Julius crossed the outer chamber, he saw the wall was marked in lighter patches where the bows had been torn from their wires. Other weapons were held against the polished marble and Julius wondered if the boy Ptolemy collected them. The women were concubines rather than guards, Julius guessed, glancing at them. The king could clearly have his pick of the beauties of Alexandria.

Ptolemy's bed was a huge construction that dominated the private rooms. The boy himself stood part dressed by its side and only the rumpled sheets showed where he had been sleeping. It was strange to see his face in the dim light after their first meeting and Julius was impressed at the courage of the slight figure standing with his bare chest heaving and a knife held too tightly in his fist.

'Put that away,' Julius said. 'You will not be harmed.'

The boy recognised him then and took in a hiss of breath. The soldiers of the Tenth moved closer to the king and with a jerk he raised the blade to his own throat, glaring at Julius.

A legionary snapped out an arm and gripped the king's wrist, making him cry out in pain and astonishment. The knife was thrown down with a clatter. Ptolemy began to shout for help and the man who held his wrist took careful aim and hit him on the point of his chin, heaving him onto his shoulder as the boy went limp.

'Sound the signal horns. We have the king,' Julius said, already turning away.

'There'll be more of them by now, waiting for us,' Domitius said, gazing at the limp body of Ptolemy. The king's head lolled as he was carried back down the corridor, his arms swinging.

The fighting began again with even greater ferocity as the legions tried to retrace their steps back to the gardens. The sight of the unconscious king stung the roaring Egyptians into greater efforts and three of the Fourth were wounded, slowing the retreat. Even so, the ceremonial guards were no match for the hardened soldiers of Rome and they fought their way through to the gardens, leaving a trail of dead behind.

The night met them with a cool breeze that dried their sweat as they ran. Julius heard more voices calling out words he did not know, and as they reached the broken gates to the streets a flight of spears came from somewhere near, one of them knocking down a panting optio. He was dragged to his feet by two of his men and he screamed as they hacked through the shaft, leaving only a blood-wet stump of wood sticking out of his back. They carried him onto the streets with the king.

The disturbance at the palace had roused the people of Alexandria and crowds were gathering. Julius urged his men to hurry. If they saw their king being carried like a sack of wheat, they could be shocked into an attack and Julius felt every moment pass, increasing his anxiety.

The legions pounded along the Canopic Way at their best speed, spittle turning to thick soup in their mouths as the breath burned out of them. In full armour, the mile of road seemed to stretch further than it had on the way in, but the crowds parted before them and they did not falter.

It seemed hours before Julius saw the gates of his quarters open and ran through them, gasping in relief. The palace began to fill with his men once again and this time there were no restrictions on their noise. They whooped and shouted at the victory, even as the wounded were passed overhead to where healers waited with sutures and clean cloths. Not a man had been killed, though the optio who had stopped a spear was not likely to walk again. Julius spent a moment with him before he was borne away, passing on a few words of comfort as best he could.

When the last of them were in, the doors were closed and barred. Every lamp Brutus could find had been lit and Julius could see the windows were blocked with heavy sacks and stones. The palace had become a fortress and he anticipated the dawn with enormous pleasure.

'Let them wail and bluster now,' he said to the men around him. 'We have their *king*.'

They cheered and Julius sent an order to open the kitchens below to prepare a meal. His centurions set the first watches against a counterattack and he finally had a moment to himself.

'Where is Cleopatra?' he asked.

Brutus was close by, watching him. 'She has taken rooms on the floor above,' he replied, his expression strange. 'She waits there for you.'

Julius smiled at him, still flushed with the victory. 'I will tell you about it when I've seen her. Find a secure place for our new guest and set guards.' He paused to take a deep breath, steadying himself. 'It was easy, Brutus.'

'They will strike back,' Brutus said, wanting to puncture the pride he saw. 'She said we have seen only the edges of their army.'

His head ached terribly as if he were recovering from drunkenness. He remembered the queen speaking to him, though the details were dim and wavering in his mind. Julius didn't see his distress.

'How will they attack us while their king is in my hands?' Julius replied. 'I will humble the men who controlled him, Brutus, when they come.' He laughed at the thought and walked away to see Cleopatra, leaving Brutus behind.

* * *

311

The suite of rooms Cleopatra had taken had not been touched by the soldiers. All the others Julius passed were stripped bare of anything that could be used in the barricades, but her chambers were warm and comfortable with rugs and hangings. Flames crackled in tall braziers at either end, though Julius hardly saw them. His eyes were drawn to the slender figure of the queen as her shadow moved behind gauze hangings on a bed to match Ptolemy's own. He could make out the outline that had aroused him on their first meeting and wondered why she did not speak.

His heart beating strongly, Julius closed the doors behind him and crossed the room, his footsteps loud in the silence. He could smell her scent in the air as well as wisps of steam and warm dampness that came from another room off the main one. She had been bathing, he realised, finding the thought fascinating. Without her slaves to heat and carry water, he did not doubt that his own men had been willing.

He reached the bed and still she did not speak as he ran his callused palms down the gauze, the noise like a whisper.

'We have him, Cleopatra,' he said softly, feeling her stir at his voice. As he spoke, his hands moved the gauze aside.

She lay on her back, naked, as he had somehow known she would be, with only shadows to cover her. Her skin shone gold as she looked up at him and her eyes were dark. 'He is not hurt?' she said.

Julius shook his head, unable to reply. His gaze travelled down the length of her body and he found it difficult to take a breath.

In an instant, she had risen and fastened her mouth on his. He could taste the sweetness of honey and cloves and her perfume washed over him like a drug. Her fingers pulled at the fastenings on his armour and he had to help her. His chestplate fell away with a clang of metal that made them both jump. Her hands were cool where they touched his skin and then he was naked. Her hands reached to his hips and pulled him gently towards her mouth. He cried out at the warmth, shuddering as he closed his eyes.

His hands strayed down to her breasts and he pulled away from her, climbing onto the bed and letting the gauze fall back behind him.

'Is this my reward?' he said, his voice hoarse.

She smiled slowly, her hands roaming him, touching old scars. Holding his gaze, she turned lithely onto her stomach, raising herself and reaching behind to hold his hot flesh in her hands as he rose over her.

'It is just the beginning,' she said.

CHAPTER TWENTY-SIX

With dawn yet to break, Julius strode through the lower corridors, nodding to the guards as they stood to attention. The king of Egypt was locked in a room that had once held jars of oil. It had no windows to tempt a rescue and the door was solid.

'Has he been quiet?' Julius asked.

Before his legionary could reply, a high voice yelled a stream of oaths and curses inside, barely muffled by the heavy wood.

'He's been doing that for hours, sir,' the soldier said.

'Open the door,' Julius replied, pursing his lips. 'I'll speak to him.'

As he entered, he saw that Brutus had stripped this room as bare as any of the others. No bed had been provided and a small bench and bucket were the only furniture. A single lamp burned steadily on the wall and in its glow Julius could see white smears of dust on the boy's skin. The king of Egypt had clearly spent the night on the cold floor.

Ptolemy stood with stiff dignity, facing his captor with his arms folded over his narrow chest. Julius could see the outline of his ribs and the dust had smeared on his cheeks as if he had tried to hide his crying.

'Good morning,' Julius said, seating himself on the bench. 'I will have some clothes found for you when the men bring breakfast. There is no need for you to be uncomfortable while you are here.'

Ptolemy glared at him without speaking. He was smaller than Julius had realised the night before and his face was pale and delicate, as if it had never seen the sun. His features lent themselves easily to expressions of sullen anger. The dark eyes and long lashes were twinned in Cleopatra and Julius repressed a shudder of dislike at the thought of their relationship.

Julius let the silence stretch for a little longer, then stood. 'If there is nothing else, I will go back to my work,' he said.

He turned to leave and Ptolemy snapped words at his back. 'You will release me immediately!' he said. His Latin was faultless.

Julius faced him and this time could not prevent a smile. 'No, I will not, Your Majesty. I need you, you see.'

'What do you want? Gold?' The boy's lips twisted into a sneer.

'I want to see Cleopatra restored as queen,' Julius replied, watching the boy closely. As he spoke, he wondered if that was truly what he desired. Before meeting Cleopatra the night before, his aims had been clear. Now, the thought of restoring her to the incestuous arms of her brother did not seem as attractive.

'I knew she would be behind this!' Ptolemy burst out. 'I knew it! You think I want her back? She treated me as a child.'

'You *are* a child,' Julius snapped, instantly regretting it. Sighing, he seated himself once more. 'Your courtiers honoured your every wish, I suppose?' he said.

Ptolemy hesitated. 'When I acted with honour and with the traditions, they did. They respected the office and the blood, despite my youth.' His eyes would not meet Julius' as he spoke, but then he stiffened in fresh anger. 'Your men struck me, invaded my private rooms. You will be burnt and torn when . . .'

'From what I saw, Panek barely listened to you,' Julius murmured.

Ptolemy's eyes flashed. 'You know nothing of my life, Roman! I am a child and I am a king. I carry the god flame within me. Panek is . . .'

He hesitated again and Julius spoke quickly, wanting to probe

315

the weakness. 'Panek is the power behind the throne, I think. Are you expecting him to stand back when you are older? It would never happen. There would be an accident – a tragic fall, or an illness – and Panek would have another decade to rule while the next child grows. I have known the compulsion of power, lad. Take that warning from me, if nothing else.'

He watched while the boy considered his words, quietly surprised at Ptolemy's composure. Julius had half expected him to be in tears when he entered, but instead he had found himself addressed as an equal or a servant. The king may have been a child, but he had a sharp mind and Julius could see him thinking and planning.

'Panek will be furious when he hears I have been taken,' Ptolemy said thoughtfully.

Julius could see the idea amused the boy and he waited for more.

'You will have to show him I am unharmed, or he will raze this place to the ground.'

'I can do that,' Julius said. 'If you wish it.' Ptolemy glanced quizzically at him and Julius went on. 'You might not want to be returned to him. Have you thought of that? I could demand that your courtiers are banished and you could rule with Cleopatra once more without their influence.'

The boy's eyes were dark and unfathomable. Julius did not know him well enough to see if he had reached him.

'Why are you doing this?' Ptolemy said at last. 'Are you lusting after my sister? Or is it my younger flesh you desire?'

Julius controlled his temper. 'If you were a son of mine, I would have you beaten for speaking to me in that way,' he said. 'I may still.'

'You would *not* dare,' Ptolemy replied, with such confidence that Julius was taken aback. He considered calling for a switch, but settled himself, resting his hands on his knees.

'You were very rude to Panek,' Ptolemy said, clearly enjoying the memory. 'He had to lie down afterwards, with cool drinks and slaves to massage away his anger. You are a rude people, I think.'

'He is an irritating vulture,' Julius replied.

Some of the tension eased out of Ptolemy and Julius suspected he had struck a chord at last.

'May I see your sword?' Ptolemy asked suddenly.

Without a word, Julius drew the short gladius and handed it over. The boy seemed astonished as he took it from Julius' hand and immediately pointed it at the seated consul.

'Are you not afraid I will kill you with it?' he asked.

Julius shook his head slowly, watching for the slightest move. 'I am not. The blade is nothing without the man to hold it. You could not strike before I had taken it from you.'

Ptolemy looked into his eyes and saw nothing but honesty. He turned away and tried to swing the short blade, his wrist bending under the weight.

'Would you like to learn its use?' Julius said.

For a moment, he saw Ptolemy's face light up, then clouds of suspicion dimmed his interest. He turned it round awkwardly and handed it back hilt-first.

'Do not pretend to be my friend, Roman. I am nothing more than a bargaining piece to you, yes? Something to be used for whatever it is you really want. You are my enemy and I will not forget it.' He paused and clenched one of his fists. 'When I am a man, I will make you remember how you kept me prisoner, Roman. I will come for you with an army like locusts. I will see your joints smashed with hammers and your skin burnt. You will know me then!'

Julius stared at the ferocious expression on the boy. 'You have some growing to do, first,' he said, rising to his feet.

For a moment, he thought Ptolemy might attack him, before the

317

boy turned his back in impotent fury. Julius left him alone in the little room, walking out to the day with a light step.

Panek arrived with a delegation of courtiers at the first light of dawn. They approached the guards Julius had placed in the gardens and suffered a rough inspection for weapons before the three most senior were allowed inside.

Julius stood as they were brought into his presence, feeling again the wave of dislike from Panek's cold eyes. It did not matter, now that he had the king.

Julius gestured to a stone block and sat down on a padded couch facing them, enjoying their discomfort. Five soldiers of the Tenth stood nearby and Octavian took position directly behind the courtiers, making them nervous. Panek's face and neck shone with oil or sweat, Julius could not tell. His eyes were unpainted and he looked a little more human in the morning light without that decoration. The omission spoke volumes.

'You cannot hope to survive this crime,' Panek said, wrenching out the words as if the barest trace of civility was painful. 'If the citizens learn that you are holding the king, I will not be able to restrain them. Do you understand me? You have only hours before the rumours spread and then they will come to burn you out of this nest.'

'I do not fear untrained men,' Julius said, casually. He signalled to a guard to bring him wine and sipped at it.

Panek raised his eyes in exasperation. 'What do you want then, for the boy's return? I'm sure you have a *price*.'

Julius reflected that Panek was not the best man to have sent. His anger was too obvious and if it had merely been a matter of gold, he would have asked for more after such a sneering tone.

'We will start with the free run of the city, obviously,' Julius said. 'No more of this seven days you mentioned. I want to see the library and Alexander's tomb. Perhaps you can arrange guides for my officers.'

Panek blinked in confusion. 'You would be torn apart by the mob, Consul, the first moment you set foot outside these walls.'

'That is unfortunate,' Julius said, frowning. 'My second demand is for the court to leave Egypt. I have ships to take you to Cyprus or Sardinia, far away from the difficulties of your lives here. I imagine it will be a peaceful retirement and I'm sure I can arrange for a little gold to make it comfortable for you.'

The three Egyptians went very still and Panek's eyes glittered dangerously.

'You mock me in my own city, Consul. Do you think I will not respond? The army has been summoned. The city is filling with soldiers crying out in rage at what you have dared. If you do not return the king, they will sweep your small force away in the flood. Understand that I do not lie.'

'The boy will not survive an attack on this place,' Julius told them. 'You will be killing him if I see a single sword drawn in anger. I suggest you do your best to keep the peace.'

'You cannot hold him here for ever,' Panek replied. 'How long do you think your food will last? Your water?'

'We have enough,' Julius said, shrugging. 'Perhaps you are right. We should not be threatening each other. Instead, you can begin by telling me how much you value his life. What can you offer me for your king?'

The three men conferred in their own language for a few moments and then Panek spoke again, his anger rigidly controlled.

'Trade deals could be arranged between Roman ports and the Egyptian interior. I can arrange to have your merchants given first access to our goods.'

'Excellent,' Julius said, signalling that wine should be brought for the men. 'I believe the negotiations have begun.'

It took thirty days of argument and discussion to reach a final agreement. Neither Julius nor Panek attended every hour of the meetings, instead sending subordinates to make offers and counter-offers. It could not have worked without Cleopatra's influence, but she seemed to know exactly how far the delegation of courtiers could be pushed in each area.

She did not attend the negotiations herself, instead spending her days with her younger brother, who had been given the run of the palace. It was strange to see the pair of them walking the halls, deep in discussion, and stranger still for Julius to consider their relationship. She was his elder sister and a mature wife used to the intrigues of the court. He listened to her as no one else and his angry outbursts had not been repeated.

At night, she told Julius how much her brother had hated the stifling life of court. It seemed his smallest request would have to be approved by Panek, and Ptolemy had admitted his hatred for the man. In a sense, he had been confined far more thoroughly before Julius stole him away. Panek spoke with the voice of the king and the army would obey his every order.

'But your brother *is* the king, by the gods!' Julius had exclaimed, when she told him. 'Why couldn't he just have Panek taken out and beaten?'

'He is a boy and he has known no other life. Panek frightened him,' she said. 'He does not frighten me, but even I missed the lust for power in him.' She paused and clenched her fists in the sheets. 'A year ago, he brought orders from the king to have me banished. I knew they could not have come from my brother, but I was not allowed to plead my case. Those loyal to me marched into exile and the women tore their hair and rubbed ashes on their breasts. Believe me, Panek is too clever for a sheltered boy to resist.'

On the thirtieth day, Julius had contracts drawn up and Ptolemy was brought to fix his signature to them. Cleopatra came with him and Panek staggered to his feet as he saw her.

'My queen,' he stammered, falling to his knees and lowering his head to the floor.

The other courtiers followed suit and she smiled.

'Get up and finish what you have begun here, Panek. You have bound us in gold to Rome as I wished and with your king's approval.'

Panek's eyes flickered to where Ptolemy sat watching them. Slowly, Ptolemy nodded.

'We have reached an agreement, my brother and I,' Cleopatra purred. 'Your influence is over, Panek. We will take our places on the thrones of the upper and lower kingdoms once more. We will rule, Panek, though you will not go unrewarded for your work.'

Panek watched as Ptolemy handed a quill to his sister and she scribbled the words 'Let it be so', as she signed all official documents. The papyrus sheets marked trade agreements that would hurt the growth of Alexandria, not to mention the heavy tithe of gold to be sent to Rome for ten years. Against them, Julius had made the astonishing offer of returning Cyprus to Egypt, as she had been owned centuries before. The Roman's apparent generosity had troubled Panek deeply, not knowing that the suggestion had come from Cleopatra. Cyprus had been lost since Alexander's death and its return would have almost been worth the weeks of torment and the insults to the king. Panek realised the queen had been the silent voice behind the negotiations, the reason that his bluffs were revealed and his strategies undone. He stood like a broken man and bowed stiffly to the first family of Egypt.

'I will await your return, Majesty,' he said to Ptolemy.

'You will have him tomorrow at dawn,' Julius said, interrupting the intense gaze between the two of them.

Panek gathered his copies and writing materials and left, his slaves and colleagues going with him. The room seemed empty without the tension he had brought and Cleopatra turned to her brother to embrace him.

'Now you will truly be king, Ptolemy, as our father would have wished. I will have Panek killed and my army will protect you from his spite.'

The boy accepted the embrace, looking over her shoulder at Caesar. 'You are a strange man, Roman,' he said. 'My sister trusts you. I wonder if that is enough.'

'You have nothing to fear from me,' Julius replied.

Ptolemy nodded. 'I will go out to them at dawn, for the people to see me safe. There will be a new order then, in Egypt. I will not have my wife taken from me again.'

His eyes were intense and Julius wondered how much Ptolemy had guessed about their relationship. The marriage was too ludicrous for him to think he had come between husband and wife and he was not even sure if he had. Despite their intimacy, Cleopatra was still a mystery to him. It was possible that she would simply rearrange her court and resume her role as queen, politely dismissing the Roman who had made it possible.

'I have a gift for you,' Julius said, signalling the armourer of the Tenth who waited nearby.

The burly man stepped forward with a bundle of cloth and Julius unwrapped it to reveal a gladius reduced in size for the king. Ptolemy's eyes widened with pleasure as he took it. He had tried the simple forms of attack and defence with Domitius at Julius' request, but the heavy swords had been too much for his arms. Julius could see the smaller blade was exactly right and the king's boyish smile was mirrored in his own face.

'It is magnificent,' Ptolemy said, rubbing his thumb along the bronze wire and leather of the grip.

Julius nodded. 'I hope you will have time to continue your lessons,' he replied.

'I will try. Thank you for the gift, Roman.'

Julius chuckled at the wry tone, remembering the furious little boy he had met on the first morning a month before.

'Until tomorrow then,' he said.

As dawn came, the army of the house of Ptolemy gathered on the streets of Alexandria, waiting to welcome the return of their king. Julius looked out through a hole in the barricaded windows and whistled softly to himself. There were many thousands waiting there, a show of strength.

The citizens themselves had come out to catch the first sight of Ptolemy. There had been no mobs to threaten the palace after Julius had spoken to Panek and he wondered if it had been a bluff, or whether his influence reached further than even Cleopatra knew.

Ptolemy's footsteps were loud on the marble as he approached the great doors and looked up at Julius. He carried himself well and Julius was pleased to see the small sword on his hip.

Julius eased the door open a little further, so that Ptolemy could see the army gathered in his honour.

'Are you ready?' he asked the boy king.

Ptolemy did not reply and when Julius looked at him, he was astonished to see there were tears in his eyes.

'I do not trust Panek,' Ptolemy whispered aloud, his gaze on the warriors in the distance.

'We have to send you out,' Julius said. 'Your army must see you alive. As proof of our good faith, you must be released. Panek is not a fool. He knows you have been united with your sister. He would not dare hold you. I would see him dead and he knows it.'

Gently, he put a hand on Ptolemy's shoulder and began moving him towards the doorway. The young king reached up with a jerk and grabbed Julius' hand in his own.

'He cannot be trusted! The agreements will mean nothing to him, I know it. If you send me out, I will be powerless once more. Let me remain and we will find another way.'

Gently, Julius removed the boy's hands. 'We are running out of food, Ptolemy, and I gave my word that you would be released. The negotiations are over.' His voice became harder. 'Now do your part and I will see you on your throne later today. First you must be given back to your people.'

Tears streamed down Ptolemy's face and he held Julius' arm with desperation. 'You don't understand! Out there, I will be the king once more. I am *afraid*!'

Julius looked away, embarrassed for the sobbing boy. Where was Cleopatra? She had a way with her young brother that calmed his spirits. Julius was on the point of calling for her when Ptolemy wiped angrily at his tears and let his grip loosen.

'I will go out to them,' he said.

Julius saw terror in his eyes and could not understand it. No matter what Panek intended, Ptolemy would be safe for the few hours it took to return him to his palace and then bring Cleopatra out with the legions.

'Courage, lad,' Julius said softly, giving Ptolemy the slightest push.

The king took in a great heave of breath and squared his shoulders, his hand dropping to touch the hilt of his sword as he had seen the Romans do. He nodded once and walked out into the sun.

The army cheered as they saw his slight figure at the top of the steps. They raised their arms in perfect unison and Julius wondered if these were indeed better soldiers than the ones he had faced on palace duty. Even from the elevation of the doorway, he could not estimate their full number.

Brutus came to stand by his side with Octavian, each man carefully ignoring the presence of the other. With Julius, they watched Ptolemy descend the steps and make his way to the first ranks of men. Panek was there, waiting for him with his head bowed.

Horns blew in a crash of sound as Ptolemy reached them and Julius and the others watched in fascination as the lines of men parted.

'What's happening?' Octavian asked.

Julius shook his head in answer.

Before their eyes, the cloth of gold Ptolemy had worn at his first meeting was brought forward and draped around his shoulders. The Romans squinted as the rising sun seemed to intensify around him, making Ptolemy shine. Panek lifted the headdress and his voice could be heard crying out a chant to the gods.

Ptolemy stood looking up into the mask as it was lowered onto him. For a long time he did not move, then slowly he turned to face the watching Roman soldiers at every window and door. The mask hid his youth and had a malevolence that made Julius frown. Time seemed to slow and an oven heat blew across the gardens.

'He wouldn't . . .' Brutus said in disbelief, but the golden figure raised his hand and brought it down in a sharp gesture. The army roared its battle rage and came surging into the gardens.

Julius jerked back in horrified disbelief. There was no time to consider the implications. 'Bar the doors and be ready!' he cried. 'I want men on the roof with spears and bows. They are coming!'

CHAPTER TWENTY-SEVEN

The Egyptian army killed the horses of the extraordinarii. Inside the palace, the Romans could hear their mounts screaming.

High above their heads, more than a hundred of the Fourth legion had climbed onto the tiles to send a withering fire down into the horde that crashed against the palace. They could hardly miss against such a mass of besieging warriors.

In the chaos of the first few minutes, grapnels and ropes were sent spinning upwards for any purchase. Some were cut before the men below could begin to climb, but the Egyptians had archers of their own and legionaries fell as they hacked at them. The attack was loud and violent, but the palace was not an easy place to storm. Only the highest windows had been left open and everything below that was solid with barricades. Even the warriors who clung to ledges could not find a way in. As they scrabbled at the windows, swords came through the gaps to send them screaming onto the heads of their own men.

A dull booming was heard as Ptolemy's army thumped a wooden beam against the main doors. Arrows rained down on them, but as fast as they died, more rushed forward. Inside, Julius had Cleopatra's rooms stripped and the contents piled against the door for when it broke. He had not had time to consider a strategy against the army. He knew he could not stay there for ever and regretted telling the boy king how little food they had left. Even on half-rations, they would be starving inside a week.

Ptolemy himself stayed out of range of spears, though Julius sent Ciro up to the roof to try for a long shot. The sudden change in manner was beyond comprehension to the Romans. Cleopatra at least had seemed to understand when Julius described the gold headdress being placed on the boy. He remembered Ptolemy's warning that outside, he would be the king.

The first attack came to nothing and those who battered at the doors were driven back at last by a storm of heavy tiles from the roof. Though they had retreated, Julius was sure they would return with more to hold shields over their heads. It was what he would have done.

Over the noise outside, Julius called to his generals: 'Brutus! Go to Cleopatra and tell her I need a way out of here. We cannot stay in this place and let them smash it. If they burn us out, we'll have to rush them.'

Cleopatra had come to the entrance hall as he spoke. 'They would not dare to set fires while I am here,' she said.

Julius wanted to believe it, but he couldn't take the risk. 'They have us surrounded. Are there no tunnels, no secret routes?' he demanded, wincing as the battering ram struck again. No doubt the men were better protected this time.

Cleopatra shook her head. 'I would have used one by now if there were,' she snapped.

Julius swore under his breath, turning away to peer through the cracks of daylight at the warriors beyond. The palace felt claustrophobic and he hated to play such a passive role. Apart from the men on the roof, he had no way of attacking his enemies unless he sent the legions out in a direct assault that could very well have been suicide.

'Do they have heavy weapons, catapults and the like?' he shouted

327

over the noise. The palace could be reduced to rubble by such things and he had a sudden terror of them.

'Not close,' Cleopatra replied. She ran her tongue over her lips, tasting the dust in the air and frowning. 'Follow me to the roof and I'll show you.'

Julius hesitated, unwilling to leave his men. Brutus stepped forward a fraction before Domitius and Octavian.

'Go, sir,' he said. 'We'll hold them here for a while.'

Julius nodded in relief and raced after the queen, taking flights of stairs to the highest floors without slowing down. He was panting by the time he reached the top and climbed a ladder into the sunlight.

Summer had come to Alexandria and he felt the heat like a blow. The tiles stretched away in all directions, though his gaze was immediately drawn to the line of efficient killers he had sent to the edge of the roof. Ciro was with them and as Julius watched he took careful aim and sent a spear down at a difficult angle. The big man smiled at the result and the others clapped him on his shoulders. Then a rush of arrows sent them all leaping backwards. They saluted as they recognised Julius and he waved them back to their task.

Julius took a sharp breath at the view of the city and sea the height gave him. The port was laid out in miniature below and the horizon was split between the deep ocean and the brown blur of the Egyptian heartlands.

Cleopatra stood beside him, her hair whipped into curls by the wind.

'There are barracks at Canopus, two days to the east, along the coast,' she said, pointing into the dim distance. 'They have catapults there and ships to carry them.'

Julius studied the mouth of the port. He could see the tiny galleys of the port watch on patrol. Merchants sailed or rowed across the harbour and dozens more sat at anchor, protected from storms. Alexander had chosen well when he built his city.

'I must get men out tonight,' Julius said. 'I can block the entrances to the port with ships sunk in the entrance. Where will the army go then, to reach us?'

Cleopatra shrugged. 'The coast is rocky and dangerous anywhere else. You will delay them for days, wherever they try to land.'

'Can they still pass with the heavy weapons, though?' Julius asked.

'Eventually. We are an ingenious people, Julius.'

He studied the coast, his gaze darting from place to place as he thought.

'I could lower men from ropes tethered up here,' he said at last.

He strode to the far edge and looked down, swallowing painfully as he saw how far his men would have to descend. An arrow hummed past him, its force almost spent. He ignored it.

Cleopatra had come with him and stood looking down the sheer walls at her brother's army.

'Just one man could carry a message to my own forces,' she said. 'My slave, Ahmose, can take the news. They will tip the balance and give you the chance to break free of the siege.'

'It's not enough,' Julius replied. 'Send him if you wish, but I cannot stay here without knowing whether he reached them or was killed. We don't have food for more than a few days.'

Julius walked along the edge, looking down at the minor buildings surrounding the palace. He reached the rear and had to edge around a sloping section, thankful the old tiles were dry and steady underfoot. Behind the palace, there were smaller structures used by slaves and servants. As Julius saw them, he smiled.

'Can you see this?' he said.

Cleopatra peered over the edge with him.

Below, a sloping line of tiles seemed to come close to the main wall. Julius knelt, then lay on his stomach. The other roof looked near enough to jump to, or climb over on ropes. From there, he could see a mismatched trail of homes and temples leading across the city.

'That's the place,' he said. 'If I can get men down to that first roof, they can cross above the heads of Ptolemy's soldiers. They'll never know we are there. Can you see a window at the same level?'

Cleopatra lay flat to crane her head over the rim. She nodded and both of them became aware of their closeness at the same time. Julius knew his men would be watching, but he was still captivated by her. He shook himself.

'I must go down and find the room that looks out onto those roofs.'

'Isis has favoured you, Julius, in showing you the way,' Cleopatra said.

He frowned. 'My own eyes had something to do with it.'

She laughed at that, coming quickly to her feet with all the easy grace of youth. Beside her, he felt old, but then she kissed him, her tongue grazing his with the taste of marble dust.

Ciro and Domitius eased their heads a fraction out of the rear window, looking down before jerking back. The Egyptian archers were good and they did not want to risk even a long shot.

'Twenty feet down and about six across,' Domitius said. 'We can make it, if they don't see us coming. After that I don't know. I couldn't see how far the roofs reach before we'd have to come down. It may not be far enough.'

'There's no other way,' Julius replied. They could all hear the hammering below while the army milled in the grounds. 'As soon as they bring catapults, we're finished, unless our food and water run out first. We need to draw some of them away at the very least.'

'Let me have this one, sir,' Domitius said. 'With a cohort of the youngest men to try for the ships.'

Julius looked at him. 'Very well. Ciro, you go with him. Pick your men ready for sunset.'

Brutus had come to see what delayed his commander and he seemed nervous. 'I would like to go as well,' he said.

Julius frowned. 'Your arm is barely healed. How would you climb down twenty feet of rope?'

Brutus looked relieved not to have had a straight refusal. 'After the rope is anchored, the rest will slide down. I can do that.' He raised his right arm and opened and closed his fist.

Julius shook his head. 'Not this time, Brutus. The gods alone know how difficult it will be to cross those roofs. Worse, if your arm gave way and you fell, they would know we were trying to get out.'

Brutus took a deep breath. 'As you order, sir,' he said, disappointment clear on his face.

'We could tie his wrists to the rope we'll use to slide, sir,' Domitius said suddenly. 'Even if his arm goes, he won't fall then.'

Brutus turned in astonishment to Domitius, and Julius saw how much his old friend needed to be back in the fight.

'If you sink the ships, you could have to swim. There's a good chance you won't be coming back. Do you understand that?'

Brutus nodded, a touch of his old wildness showing. 'Let me go. Please,' he said.

'All right, but if your arm snaps, you stay on the first roof until it is over.'

'Yes, sir,' Brutus replied, his face strained with tension. He clapped his hand on Domitius' shoulder as Julius turned away and Domitius accepted it with a nod.

Below their feet, the hammering went on.

Though the sun had set, the grounds of the palace were lit with bonfires at all points and arrows soared sporadically up to the roof and against the windows. The army had either settled in to starve them out, or were waiting for catapults to arrive. Julius watched from a high window, well hidden from the sight of their archers. He hated to be trapped and hardly dared reveal how much his hopes were pinned on the men clambering across to lower roofs at the back.

The time would come when he was forced to send the legions out against the army that faced them, he knew. When the moment was perfect, he would try for a shattering blow, but against such numbers he feared he would be leading them straight to destruction. Cleopatra had been invaluable with her knowledge of their tactics and strengths, but the Tenth and Fourth were vastly outnumbered even so. In his most private of thoughts, there were times when he wished he had simply left the city when his time was up. Then he would grow angry in reaction. He would not run from a rabble of foreign soldiers. If he had to, he would find supplies and send for reinforcements from Greece and Spain. The Egyptians would learn what it meant to threaten the life of the man who ruled Rome.

Behind the palace, Domitius was at the window with Brutus, tying his wrists securely to the piece of waxed cloth that would send him sliding into the arms of the waiting legionaries. Moving five hundred soldiers in strained silence was difficult, but there had been no cries of alarm and the plan was moving without a fault.

As Domitius tugged the knot, he felt Brutus looking at him in the dark.

'We were friends once,' Brutus said.

Domitius snorted to himself. 'We could be again, old son. The men will accept you in time, though Octavian . . . well, he might not.'

'I am glad you spoke up for me,' Brutus replied.

Domitius gripped him by the shoulder. 'You risked all our lives for your pride and temper. There have been times when I would rather have put a knife in you.'

'If I could change it, I would,' Brutus said truthfully.

Domitius nodded, helping his legs over the edge. 'I stood on the white cliffs of Britain with you,' he said. 'You killed that big blue bastard with the hatchet when I was flat on my back. That counts for something.' He spoke slowly, his voice low and serious. 'I can't call you a brother, after what you did. Perhaps we can get by without spitting in each other's bread.'

Brutus nodded slowly, without looking round.

'I'm glad of it,' Domitius said, heaving him off the ledge.

Brutus gasped as the rope sagged and his initial rush was jerked into a slow descent. Halfway down, when there was nothing but yawning darkness beneath him, he spun and the cloth twisted, halting him. His weakened muscles protested as he swung his legs frantically. With an effort, he managed to turn himself back round and the slide began once more. His arm ached worse than he cared to admit, but he gritted his teeth against the pain and then found himself being held by the men on the roof below. They untied his wrists in silence and handed him his sword, which he strapped to his waist. Like him, they wore no armour, and carried no shields. Their faces were black with soot and only the whiteness of their teeth and eyes in the moonlight showed their positions, spread over the roofs like mould. The hulking figure of Cleopatra's slave, Ahmose, was there with them, unsmiling and silent as he crouched on the tiles.

Before Brutus could step clear, Domitius thumped into his back and sent him sprawling.

'No more to come,' he heard Domitius whisper as he guided Brutus through the men to the front.

The tiles creaked under their feet and they could only hope their progress wasn't being followed from below, with archers ready to catch them as they came down. The first roof blended into the next without a gap, but the third was too far away to step across.

'I need a man to jump this,' Domitius said.

In the moonlight, the alleyway seemed larger than it had any right to. A young soldier of the Fourth stepped forward and removed his sword. With barely a nod to his officers, he took two quick steps and launched himself over. The clatter as he landed made them all freeze, but already the palace seemed far behind and no one came. The rope was thrown to him, and one by one they used it to cross. Brutus went first this time, trusting his arm to hold his weight. The muscles were sending shooting pains, but the bones held and he reached the other side, sweating but exhilarated.

Four more roofs were passed in the same way before they came to a space too great to bridge. The street below seemed empty as the front rank lay on their stomachs and looked down. At the crouch, they came back and reported that the way was clear, then sent ropes skipping down to the stones below.

Brutus lost skin on his palms as he opted to slide, not trusting his arm to take his full weight yet again. With some misgiving, he realised there would be no retreat that way, not for him. Ahmose landed behind him without a sound. With a smile, he raised a hand to the Romans and strode away into the darkness. Brutus wished him luck in bringing Cleopatra's army. Even if they managed to block the harbour entrance, Julius needed an edge.

The cohort jogged through the streets in almost complete silence. For better grip on the roofs, they had tied cloths around their sandals and no challenges were shouted as they made their way to the docks.

The harbour of Alexandria was well lit and busy. Domitius halted the men in the last shadows of the road, passing the word for them to be ready. They would be seen at any moment, and after that it would be a rush to block the port before the army could respond.

A voice began to yell and Domitius saw two men pointing

in their direction. 'That's it, then. We go,' he said, running out into the light.

There were never fewer than a dozen merchant vessels working their cargoes on or off the quayside. The cohort of five hundred Roman legionaries raced towards them, ignoring the shouts of panic as word spread. As they reached the docks, they split into four groups and ran up the loading planks of the nearest ships to them.

The crews were terrified at the sudden attack and three of them surrendered without hesitation. In the fourth, two sailors reacted more from instinct than sense, trying to stab the first men to board them. They were cut down and their bodies heaved over the side into the dirty water. The rest did not resist and moved down the loading planks as they were told until the Romans had the ships to themselves.

The sails went up with only a little confusion and the mooring ropes were cast free or cut. All four of the vessels began to ease away from the docks, leaving their shouting crews behind them.

Brutus could see men racing off into the dark streets to alert Ptolemy's army. By the time their night's work was over, the docks would be crowded with soldiers. At least it would give Julius a respite, he hoped. He could not regret having come, and for the first time in months he felt alive enough to cheer as the sails fluttered and the ships began their crisscrossing courses to the mouth of the port.

'Get two men up top, as lookouts,' he ordered, smiling as he remembered a time in his youth when he had climbed to that position himself. He did not imagine he could reach it now, but it gave him pleasure to recall the journey across Greece with Renius, when the world lay before them. The legionary who had been first over the roofs was climbing even before Brutus had finished giving the order. Brutus thought he should learn the man's name and was embarrassed that he did not know it. He had been apart from the workings of the legions for too long. Even if he did not survive

335

the night, it felt right to be back in command. He had missed it more than he knew.

Away from the lights of the port, the moon followed their movement on the still, black water. The same barriers that prevented storms from wrecking Alexandria allowed only the smallest of breezes and progress was painfully slow. It did not suit the mood of the men on board. They all turned to see the great fire on the lighthouse of Pharos, its gleam warning ships for miles. The glow of its flames lit their faces as they passed and they cast long shadows on the decks.

'Port watch coming!' a voice called from above.

Brutus could see them clearly, silhouetted against the glow of the lighthouse. Three galleys had altered course to intercept them, with oars working easily against the wind. Brutus wondered how well they were manned. He welcomed their presence, fully aware that he would have to try and swim home otherwise.

The spits of rock that formed the outermost gates of the port came slowly into view, marked for shipping with smaller lights that were never allowed to go out. Brutus had his men steer steadily for them, seeing that two of the other ships would reach the point first. Movement was still gentle over the waters and he could see their pursuers were gaining. It would be close, he realised. Brutus shook his head as he watched the galleys sweep closer. Julius had said axes or fire, but cutting through the lower holds would take too long. It would have to be fire.

'Find me a lamp, or a flint and iron,' he said.

A shuttered lamp was found and lit without delay and Brutus nursed the flame, extending the wick. The merchant vessels were built of old timber and would burn to rival the lighthouse.

Two of the stolen ships were in position and Brutus could see men lashing them together. He was thankful for the limp sails and weak breeze then. Such delicate manoeuvring would have been difficult in anything stronger.

As he came alongside, ropes were thrown and his own ship creaked and groaned as the lines tautened, finally resting to rock in the waves from the deeper waters. As the anchors were sent splashing over the side, Brutus could see the galleys of the port watch were almost on them.

He wished he had a corvus bridge to be lowered onto the enemy ships as they came alongside and acted on the idea, calling his men to lash planking together into a rough substitute.

'Light them up!' Brutus bellowed, hoping his voice could be heard on the other ships. He spilled the oil of his lamp across a pile of broken wood and watched flames rush along tar-covered ropes. The speed of it was appalling and Brutus hoped he had not acted too soon.

As the fire spread, he could hear angry shouts on the galleys and then his ship shuddered as they were rammed. Brutus laughed aloud at the thought of the hull being broken down below. The port watch were doing their work for them.

As the ship began to list, Brutus had his men heave the great section of planking over their heads, letting it fall onto the railing of the ramming galley. It was not solid and it shifted with the rocking motion, threatening to fall. The galley oars were already backing to pull them free. Despite the danger, the legionaries leapt onto their bridge and charged the other deck, facing the terrified crew.

It was carnage. As Brutus had hoped, the galleys were manned with only a few dozen above deck and the chained slaves below were unable to join the fight. In a few heartbeats, a slick of blood stained the dark wood and the legionaries had transferred across, letting their makeshift bridge fall back into the sea.

Behind them, the flames were roaring, making an inferno of the tilting ship. It went down fast and for a moment Brutus feared the vessel would sink so deep that the harbour would still be passable. As he watched with a pounding heart, the vessel stuck with a full third out of water. Cleopatra had been right. The harbour had not been dredged in generations and even shallow-hulled ships were sometimes caught there on a low tide.

Brutus turned back to his work, his face alive with pleasure. The other galleys were holding off after the fate of the first. He did not hesitate, seeing flames spring up on all four of the blocking ships. He sent his men down below to order the slaves to take oars once more and grinned as the galley turned into the wind. They would not have to swim.

As the ships burned, the breeze freshened, carrying hot sparks upwards. By the time Brutus had filled his galley with the last of the cohort, the heat was like a furnace and many of the men had suffered burns as they waited to be picked up. Fat cinders sizzled in the sea, while more caught in the rigging of anchored ships. Brutus laughed as he saw them burn. His own men were busy with buckets of seawater for their own safety.

In the far distance, some of the glowing ashes reached the dry roofs of buildings around the docks. They licked and flickered there, spreading.

Julius watched as the voices and order in Ptolemy's army changed subtly. He saw runners come in from the direction of the port and guessed his men were causing chaos. Angry faces were turned towards the palace and, unseen, he smiled down at them.

In the light of their own torches, Julius saw Panek arrive from wherever he had been sleeping, pointing towards the harbour and giving orders in a frenzy. Hundreds of men began to form up and march to the east and Julius knew he would never have a better chance. Dawn was almost on them.

'Get the men ready to move,' he shouted down to Regulus and Octavian. 'We're going out.'

CHAPTER TWENTY-EIGHT

The warriors of Alexandria wore no armour or helmets. Against the fury of the Egyptian sun, metal became too hot to bear against the skin and marching any distance would be impossible.

Julius had chosen the coolest moment of the day to attack. The sun was barely a glimmer on the horizon and the Roman legions could use their advantage. The doors to the palace were pulled open and the Tenth and Fourth came out at full speed, shields held high.

They surged through the gardens and those who had been in the extraordinarii roared in anger at the piled corpses of their mounts, already dark with flies. To see the best bloodlines of the legion lying sprawled with blackened tongues was enough to make them wild with hatred and disgust.

The centurions and optios were hard-pressed to hold their men from racing forward. The front ranks threw spears with grunts of effort, smashing the Egyptians as they tried to meet the sudden threat. Then the shield wall reached the enemy and the killing ranks slammed into them, fighting on all sides.

The Roman armour was crucial to the impetus. Where Ptolemy's army struck, they were met with a ring of metal. The veteran legionaries used their helmets to butt, their greaves to break shins, their swords to cut limbs from the enemy. They had been confined while Ptolemy's men jeered and sent their missiles. Now the chance had come to repay every insult.

'Regulus! Open the line!' Julius shouted to his general.

He saw the Fourth legion slow their headlong advance into the midst of the Egyptians and the attack widened, bringing more and more swords to bear. Julius looked back at the palace and saw they were still coming out. He marched forward as his men cleared the way and when Ptolemy's forces tried to counter-attack, Julius brought his shield up against arrows and stalked on, intent on the progress of his legions.

Near Regulus, a man went down with an arrow in the thigh and staggered back to his feet. He tried to go on, but the wound was gushing and Julius saw the man's optio grab him and send him back through the lines.

As the sun rose, its heat seemed to seek out the Roman armour and they sweated and began to gasp. The palace grounds were behind and the Roman line was hampered by the narrow streets. Still they cut and killed and walked over the dead.

To Julius' astonishment, he saw the citizens too had come out with daylight. Thousands of Egyptians shouted and wailed, filling the roads around the struggling armies. Many of them carried weapons and Julius began to consider a retreat back to the palace. His Tenth and Fourth were smashing Ptolemy's warriors, but the odds were still overwhelming.

On the right, towards the docks, Julius heard warning horns sounding. One of his extraordinarii scouts ran over, so spattered with blood that his eyes and teeth seemed unnaturally white.

'The harbour cohort is back, sir.'

Julius wiped stinging sweat from his eyes. 'Any sign of those sent after them?'

'No, sir.'

Julius wondered what had become of the men Ptolemy had sent to kill the Roman cohort at the docks. If the king had understood who led them, perhaps he would have ordered many more to the harbour.

'If you can reach them, tell Brutus to hit the flank,' Julius ordered. 'If they see Ptolemy, they are to kill him.'

The scout saluted and vanished back into the press.

Julius found himself panting. How long had it been since they had come out and hammered into the waiting army? The sun had cleared the horizon, but he could not tell for certain. Step by step, his legions moved forward and among the bronze bodies of the Egyptians were men he knew and had fought with for years. He gritted his teeth and moved on.

Brutus cursed his weak right arm as his smoke-blackened cohort came racing along the street. He could hear the sound of battle and for the first time in his life he did not welcome it or feel the excitement that usually drew him in. The ambush they had set for the Egyptians at the harbour had shown him his weakness. Still, the Roman veterans had crushed the enemy force as if it was an exercise. In a dark, narrow street off the docks, they had fallen on the Egyptians like wolves on lambs, cutting them to pieces.

Brutus held his sword awkwardly, feeling the weight of the heavy gladius pull at his weak shoulder. Domitius glanced at him as the tumult of heaving lines came into view. He saw the frustration in Brutus' face and understood.

'Take this,' Domitius shouted, tossing a dagger.

Brutus caught it in his left hand. He would rather have had a shield, or his silver armour, but at least he would be able to strike. His first blow in the ambush had turned in his hand, achieving nothing more than a scratch down a bare chest. He should have been killed then, but Ciro had hacked the man's wrist and Brutus had been saved.

As they neared the king's army, they formed into a rank six across, with Ciro in the centre. Ptolemy's flank men turned to face them and all six picked their targets, calling their choices to each other.

They hit the Egyptian soldiers at almost full speed against raised shields. Ciro's bulk knocked his man flat, but the edges held and the charge faltered. It was Ciro who broke the hole for them to follow, swinging his gladius like an iron bar and using his free fist to club men down. Whether he hit with the flat or the edge, the man's strength was enormous and he towered over the enemy. Brutus followed him into the press, stabbing his dagger and using his gladius only to block. Even then, the shock of blows seemed to bite at him and he wondered if his bones would stand it for long.

Brutus stumbled over a fallen shield and, with a pang of regret, threw down the sword he had won in Rome to pick it up. He moved to Ciro's right side, protecting him. Domitius appeared on his own right with another shield and the Roman line moved further into the claustrophobic heart of the battle.

It was a far cry from the open plain of Pharsalus. Brutus could see men climb gates and statues, still hacking with their swords at those who pressed them. Arrows flew without being aimed and against the screaming the Egyptians chanted in their alien language, their voices low and frightening.

It did not help them. Without armour, they were being hammered and the return of the port cohort sent a shudder through their ranks. The chanting changed into a low moan of fear that wailed and echoed through the swelling crowds at their backs. Brutus saw two of the extraordinarii defending well, before both were downed by clubs and daggers from the people of Alexandria. He ducked under a thrown spear, knocking it aside with his shield.

Somewhere nearby, Brutus could hear the tramp of feet and

he groaned. He had seen enough of the Roman lines to know that Julius had committed them all.

'Enemy reinforcements coming,' he shouted to Domitius.

Strange horns blared to confirm his suspicions and Brutus took a numbing impact against the shield that made him cry out. His mind flashed back to the final moments of Pharsalus and he stabbed his dagger in a wild frenzy, cleansing his rage with every death.

'There's the boy,' Domitius roared, pointing.

They all saw the slight figure of Ptolemy, shining in the risen sun as he sat a horse, surrounded by his courtiers. The royal party watched the battle with an aloofness that enraged the Romans. The men with Brutus forgot their weariness to push forward once more, struggling to reach the one they had seen betray them. There was hardly a man who had not exchanged a few words with the boy king in his month of imprisonment. To have him turn on them, on Caesar, after the first bonds of friendship was enough to draw the Roman killers like moths.

Ptolemy's gold mask turned jerkily as he watched the deaths of his followers. Panek stood by him, giving orders without a sign of fear. Brutus saw messengers bow to the courtier and run to where the horns had sounded. If the reinforcements were large, he knew there was a chance none of them would survive the morning.

Ciro searched the ground as they struggled forward, then dipped to come up with a Roman spear, its length crusted in blood and dust. He took a sight on Ptolemy and cast it with a growl, sending it high. Brutus did not see it land, though when the ranks parted again, the king remained. Panek was gone from his side and Brutus did not know if he still lived. Another blow crashed against his shield arm and he yelled in pain. It felt too heavy to raise in his defence and three times Domitius saved him from a bronze blade.

Ciro cast again and again as he found spears to throw, and then Brutus saw Ptolemy's courtiers scuttling out of range. He heard a howl of frustration from the legion lines ahead of them and, without warning, his weary cohort reached the armoured Roman flank. They had cut their way through and now both forces seemed to gain fresh strength from the contact. The Fourth were off on the wing, holding the new arrivals, but the Tenth were free to push for the king.

Missiles began to come from the crowd in greater and greater numbers. Curds of cattle dung were harmless enough, but the stones and tiles were a constant danger and distracted more than one legionary long enough to be killed.

Brutus strode through the fighting square of the Tenth to Julius, panting in reaction. They let him pass with little more than a glance.

Julius saw him and smiled at his battered appearance. 'They can't hold us,' he shouted above the crash of battle. 'I think the king's down.'

'What about the reinforcements?' Brutus answered, yelling into Julius' ear.

As he spoke, they both felt a shift in the movement of men and Julius turned to see the Fourth legion being pushed back. They did not run. Every man there had been saved by the honour of the Tenth against Pompey and they would not give way. For the lines to buckle, Julius knew the reinforcements must be large.

'Tenth! Cohorts one to four! Saw into the Fourth! Move to support! One to Four!'

Julius kept roaring the orders until the cohorts heard him and began to move. The whole left wing was being compressed and Julius shook his head.

'I could use a horse, if the bastards hadn't slaughtered them,' he said, bitterly. 'I can't see what's happening.'

As he turned to face Brutus, he caught sight of something out of the corner of his eye and froze. 'What are you *doing*?' Julius whispered.

Brutus jerked around to see. Cleopatra had walked out behind the legions and both men watched in amazement as she climbed onto the base of a statue to Isis, swinging herself up with neat agility until she stood at the feet of the goddess, looking down on the armies.

'Get her off there before the archers see her!' Julius shouted, pointing.

She had a horn in her hand, and before he could wonder what she intended she raised it to her lips and blew.

The note was deep and low, going on and on until she had no more breath. By the end of it, heads were turning in her direction and Julius was terrified she would be torn from her perch by a cloud of shafts.

'You will stop!' she cried. 'In the name of Cleopatra, your queen. I am returned to you and you will stand back!'

Julius saw Roman hands reaching up, imploring her to come down. She ignored them, calling again. Her voice reached the lines of Egyptian soldiers and the reaction was like a shock of cold water. They pointed to her and their eyes went wide with awe. They had not known of her return to the city. Julius saw their swords begin to lower and the Tenth immediately launched themselves forward, killing indiscriminately.

'Sound the halt,' Julius snapped to his cornicens. 'Quickly!'

Roman horns wailed their echo to Cleopatra and an eerie silence fell over the bloody streets.

'I am returned to you, my people. These men are my allies. You will stop the killing *now*.'

Her voice seemed louder than it had before, without the clash of arms to drown it. Ptolemy's army seemed dazed by her appearance and Julius wondered if she had chosen the statue of Isis deliberately, or whether it was simply the closest. He was surrounded by gasping, bloody men and his mind was blank.

'I wonder what she . . .' Julius began, then the people of Alexandria lost their stunned expressions and dropped to their knees.

Julius looked around in astonishment as Ptolemy's soldiers knelt with them, pressing their heads to the ground. The Roman legionaries stood stunned, looking to Julius for orders.

'Tenth and Fourth, kneel!' Julius bellowed instinctively.

His men glanced at each other, but they did as they were ordered, though their swords were ready. Ciro, Regulus and Domitius went down onto one knee. Brutus followed as Julius' eyes fell on him and then only Julius and Octavian were still on their feet.

'Don't ask me,' Octavian said softly.

Julius looked him in the eye and waited. Octavian grimaced and knelt.

Against the foreground of thousands of bowed heads, one other group still stood on the far side of the battleground. The courtiers of the king held their heads high, watching the development in sick horror. Julius saw one of them kick out at a soldier, clearly demanding the fight go on. The man flinched, but did not rise. To Julius' eye, they looked like a pack of painted vultures. He relished the fear he saw in their gleaming faces.

'Where is my brother, Ptolemy? Where is my king?' Cleopatra called to them.

Julius saw her leap lightly down and stride long-legged through the gashed flesh and kneeling men. She walked proudly and as she passed Julius she beckoned to him.

'Where is my brother?' she demanded again.

Her voice struck at the courtiers like a blow and they seemed to wilt as she approached, as if her presence was more than they could bear. They parted as Cleopatra walked into their midst.

346

Julius followed closely, his glare daring them to raise a hand against her.

Ptolemy lay pale and bloodless on a cloak of dusty gold cloth. His limbs had been placed with dignity, his right hand high on his chest where it almost covered a gaping wound. His mask had been smashed and lay in the dirt at his feet. Julius looked at the childish features as Cleopatra reached down to touch her brother and felt a pang of regret at the sight of the small gladius at his waist. As he watched, Cleopatra leaned forward to kiss her brother's lips, before sitting back. Her eyes were wide with pain, but there were no tears.

As Cleopatra sat in silence, Julius looked around for Panek, knowing he would not be far away. He narrowed his eyes as he saw dark robes he knew. Panek was sitting in the dust, his breathing slow and loud. Julius took two quick steps as his anger rekindled, but the eyes that turned at the sound were dull and the chest was ragged. Panek was dying and Julius had no more words for him.

At his back, Cleopatra rose to her feet. Not a sound came from the crowd and the breeze could be heard.

'The king is dead,' she said, her voice echoing across them. 'Carry my brother to his palace, my people. Know that you lay hands on a god when you do.'

Her voice cracked then and she hesitated. Julius touched her lightly on the shoulder, but she did not seem to feel it.

'I who am Isis, am returned to you. My own blood has been shed this day, a death caused not by the men of Rome, but by the betrayal of my court. Rise and mourn, my people. Tear your clothes and rub ash into your skin. Honour your god with grief and tears.'

The small body of Ptolemy was lifted into the air, his cloak hanging beneath him.

For a long time, Cleopatra could not drag her eyes from the body of her brother. Then she turned to face the courtiers.

'Was it not your task to keep my brother alive?' she murmured, reaching up to the throat of the nearest. He struggled not to flinch from the touch of her painted nails and it was somehow obscene as she caressed the length of his jaw.

'Caesar, I would have you bind these men for punishment. They will serve my brother in his tomb.'

The courtiers prostrated themselves at last, stunned with fear and misery. Julius signalled to Domitius to bring ropes. A tenuous drift of smoke reached them as the courtiers were trussed. Cleopatra's head snapped up as she smelled the hot and heavy air. She rounded on Julius in sudden fury.

'What have you done to my city?' she asked.

It was Brutus who answered. 'You know we fired ships in the port. The flames may have reached the dock buildings.'

'And you let them burn?' she snapped, facing him.

Brutus looked back calmly. 'We were under attack,' he said, with a shrug.

Cleopatra was speechless for a moment. She turned cold eyes on Julius. 'Your men must stop it before it spreads.'

Julius frowned at her tone and she seemed to sense the irritation that was building in him.

'Please, Julius,' she said, more gently.

He nodded and signalled to his generals to attend him. 'I will do what I can,' he said, troubled by her flashing changes of mood. She had lost a brother and regained her throne, he thought. Much could be forgiven on such a day.

Cleopatra did not leave until royal guards had brought a shaded platform for her, lifting it onto their shoulders as she lay back. Their faces were proud, Julius saw, as they bore their queen to her palace.

'Have trenches dug for the dead, Octavian,' Julius ordered, watching her departure. 'Before they spoil in the heat. The Fourth had better make their way to the docks to see to this fire.'

As he spoke, a cold cinder floated above his head, riding the breeze. He watched as it settled, still dazed by events. The boy king who had clung to his arm was dead. The battle was won.

He did not know if they would have achieved victory without the queen's intervention. The veteran legions were growing old and could not have fought on for long against the rising sun. Perhaps Cleopatra's slave would have brought reinforcements, or perhaps Julius would have bled his life out on Egyptian sand.

In her absence, he felt an ache start in him. He could smell her scent over the bitter taste of burnt air. He had known her as a woman. To see her as a queen had disturbed and enthralled him, from the moment the crowd and soldiers had knelt in the dirt at her word. He looked after the procession heading for the palace and wondered how the citizens of Rome would react if he brought her home.

'We are free to leave,' Octavian said. 'To Rome, Julius.'

Julius looked at him and he smiled. He could not imagine leaving Cleopatra behind. 'I have fought for more years than I can remember,' he said. 'Rome will wait a little longer, for me.'

CHAPTER TWENTY-NINE

The great library of Alexandria burned as the sun rose, thousands of scrolls making a furnace so hot that the soldiers of Rome could not come close to it. Marble columns raised by Alexander split and shattered in the furnace of a million thoughts and words. The men of the Fourth legion formed bucket chains to the docks, struggling against the sun and exhaustion until they were numb and their blistered skin was red and black with cinders. The closest buildings had been stripped and their walls and roofs saturated, but the library could not be saved.

Julius stood with Brutus, watching as the vast skeleton of roof timbers sagged and then collapsed over the work of generations. Both men were exhausted, their faces smeared with soot. They could hear the shouted orders as fire teams ran to stamp out new flames again and again, accompanied by chanting lines of bucket carriers.

'This is an evil thing to see,' Julius murmured.

He seemed stunned by the destruction and Brutus glanced at him, wondering if blame would fall on his shoulders. The ships carrying catapults from Canopus had been denied entry to the port, but it was galling to know the battle had been won before they could have added their strength to the siege.

'Some of the scrolls were brought here by Alexander himself,' Julius said, wiping a hand across his forehead. 'Plato, Aristotle,

Socrates, hundreds of others. Scholars came thousands of miles to read the works. It was said to be the greatest collection in the world.'

'And we *burned* it,' Brutus thought wryly to himself, not quite daring to say the words aloud. 'Their work must survive in other places,' he managed.

Julius shook his head. 'Nothing like this. Nothing complete.'

Brutus looked at him, unable to understand his mood. For his own part, he was quietly in awe of the sheer scale of the destruction. He was fascinated by it and had spent part of the morning simply watching as the fire raged. He cared nothing for the stunned faces of the crowds.

'There's nothing more you can do here,' he said.

With a grimace, Julius nodded and walked away through the silent throng that had come to see the devastation. They were eerily silent and it was strange for the men responsible to pass through them, unrecognised.

The tomb of Alexander was a temple of white stone pillars in the centre of the city, dedicated to the founding god. The sight of stern Roman legionaries kept the curious public away as Julius stood on the threshold. He found his heart racing as he looked up at the coffin of glass and gold. It was raised above head height, with white steps on all sides for worshippers to ascend. Even from the edges, Julius could see the figure resting within it. Julius swallowed spit, uncomfortably. As a boy he had drawn the tomb from a Greek tutor's description. He had kissed Servilia at the foot of Alexander's statue in Spain. He had read accounts of every battle and idolised the man.

He climbed the steps to the stone plinth, breathing shallowly of the incense that hung in the air. It seemed appropriate there, in surroundings of cool death without decay. Julius placed his

351

hands on the glass, marvelling at the artisan's skill that had produced the panes and the bronze web to hold them. When he was ready, he looked down and held his breath.

Alexander's skin and armour had been layered in gold leaf. As Julius watched, clouds moved above and sunlight poured in from an opening. Only Julius' shadow remained dark and he wondered in awe at the glory of it.

'My image is on you, Alexander,' he whispered, committing every aspect of the moment to memory. The eyes were sunken and the nose little more than a hole, but Julius could see the bones and gold flesh like stone, and guess at how the Greek must have looked in life. It was not an old face.

At first he had thought it wrong to have Alexander treated as one of the gods of Egypt. There, in that temple, it seemed an appropriate honour. Julius glanced around him, but the entrances were blocked by the solid backs of his soldiers. He was alone.

'I wonder what you would say to me,' he murmured in Greek. 'I wonder whether you would approve of a brash Roman standing in your city.'

He thought of Alexander's children and the fact that none of them had survived to adulthood. The Greek king's first-born son had been strangled at fourteen. Julius shook his head, looking into the distances of mortality. It was impossible not to contemplate his own death in such a place. Would another man stand over him a hundred years after he was dead? Better to be ashes. Without sons, everything he had achieved would slip away. His daughter could not command the respect of the Senate and, like Alexander's, her son might never be allowed to survive. Julius frowned in irritation. He had named Octavian as his heir, but he could not be certain the younger man had the skill to navigate the treacheries of Rome. In truth, he could not believe anyone else had the gift to build on his achievement. He had come so far, but unless he lived to begin a male line, it would not be enough.

In the distance, he could hear the din of the city. In the silence of the temple, his age bore down heavily on him.

Ptolemy's body lay in state in a room lined with gold. Images of Horus and Osiris were everywhere as he began the death path. His cold flesh had been washed and purified and then his left side had been split open and his organs removed. There was no judgement waiting for royalty. When the rituals ended, Ptolemy would take his place with the gods, as an equal.

When Julius was brought to see the boy king, he found the air heavy and hot. Curls of sweet smoke lifted lazily from the red hearts of enormous braziers. Ptolemy's body had been packed with salt natron to dry the flesh, and the bitter tang mingled with the fumes and made Julius dizzy. Alexander's tomb had been cold in comparison, but better suited to the realities of death.

Cleopatra knelt before the body of her brother and prayed. Julius stood watching, knowing he could not bring himself to honour an enemy who had caused the death of some of his most loyal men. The boy's eyes were sewn shut and his skin gleamed with sticky oils. Julius wanted to gag at the sight of the four jars around him, knowing what they contained. He could not understand the process, or the reverence that Cleopatra displayed. She too had been threatened by her brother's army, but she honoured him in death with rituals that would last almost two months before he was finally interred in his tomb.

In a rhythmic chant, Cleopatra prayed aloud in the language of her people and Julius saw her eyes were clear and calm. He had not seen her weep since the day Ptolemy died and he knew he still could not understand her. Her army had returned from Syria to take their places around the royal palace and there had already been incidents between the Romans and the desert-hardened warriors. Julius had been forced to have three of his men whipped for starting a drunken fracas in the city, leaving two men dead in their wake. Two more awaited punishment for using loaded dice with Cleopatra's soldiers, relieving them of their weapons as well as all the silver in their pouches.

The waiting chafed on him, as the death rites wound through to their conclusion. Julius had thought the boy would be quickly in the ground, knowing what the summer's heat could do, even to royal flesh. Instead, the days crept by with narcotic slowness and he was growing as restless as his men.

Octavian had made his feelings clear. He wanted to return to Rome and to the rewards they had all earned. Julius too could feel the city beckoning him over sea and land. He wanted to ride under the gates and into the forum once more. He had achieved every dream he had ever had as a boy. His enemies were dust and ashes, but still he waited.

He watched as Cleopatra began a new ritual, lighting clay pots of incense from a taper. Death was too close to life, in Alexandria. The people seemed to prepare for it all their lives and lived with the certainty of another existence. It made them fatalistic, but with a confidence that was as alien in its way as anything he had seen. Julius could not share it.

Cleopatra rose and bowed her head to the shrunken figure of Ptolemy. She took two steps backwards and knelt once more before rising.

'You are a patient man, Julius. I understand your people move faster than we over such things.'

'There is a dignity to death here,' he replied, searching for the right words.

She raised an eyebrow, suddenly amused. 'And a tactful man,' she said. 'Will you walk through the gardens with me? The smoke is like a drug after so long and I want to breathe.'

Relieved, Julius took her arm and they made their way out into the sun. She did not seem to notice as slaves prostrated themselves as she passed, not daring to look on the queen who mourned her brother.

The warm air outside helped to clear Julius' thoughts and he took deep breaths of it, feeling his spirits rise. Seeing the body of the boy king had been disquieting. He felt as if a weight had lifted as he breathed the scent of living gardens. Even that pleasure was tainted as he remembered running through the same paths and arbours to capture Ptolemy in his bed. It had seemed an adventure then, without consequence. The results of it lay in the king's tomb, and in ashes on the docks.

'Your men have told me a great deal about you,' Cleopatra said.

Julius shot a sharp glance at her.

'You have been blessed to survive the battles they described,' she continued.

Julius did not reply, instead pausing on a path of glassy stone to touch a red bloom, leaning out from green leaves.

'They say you are a god of war, did you know that?' she said.

'I've heard it said,' Julius replied uncomfortably. 'They boast on my behalf.'

'Then you did not defeat a million men in Gaul?'

Julius looked at her as she reached out to the same flower and caressed its petals. 'I did, though it took ten years of my life,' he replied.

She used her nails to nip through the stalk, grazing the flower over her lips as she breathed its scent. Again, he wondered how Rome would react if he brought her there. The citizens would probably adore Cleopatra, but the Senate would reject her claims to divinity. Rome had enough gods. They would not dare to object to a foreign mistress, but taking her as a wife would raise hackles right across the great houses. In addition, he was not sure if she would even want to come back with him.

'You pardoned your general, Brutus, when he had betrayed you,' she said, walking on. 'That is a strange act for a ruler of men. Yet

355

they still respect you. More, they revere you, did you know it? They would follow you anywhere and not because of your birth, but because of who you are.'

Julius tapped the fingers of one hand on the wrist of the other behind his back, unsure how to respond. 'Whoever you have been speaking to has let his mouth run away with him,' he said after a pause.

She laughed, tossing the flower onto the path behind them. 'You are a strange man, Julius. I have seen you with them, remember? You can be as arrogant as a king, as arrogant as I am myself. We are well suited to one another, though I think you would not like the slow pace of existence here. My country has seen five thousand years of life and death. We have grown old and tired under this sun and your men are young in comparison. They have the energy of youth and think nothing of running through lands like a summer storm. It is a frightening thing to see, in comparison to my sleepy Alexandria, yet I love it.'

She turned to face him, her nearness intoxicating. Without thinking, he reached out and held her by her slim waist.

'My advisers warn me daily that you are too dangerous to remain in Egypt,' she said. 'They see the lust and the strength and nothing else in your men. They remind me that you burned my beautiful library and your soldiers laughed and played dice in the ashes.'

'They are fighting men,' Julius replied. 'You cannot expect . . .'

Her laughter silenced him and a slow blush appeared on his cheeks and neck.

'You are so quick to defend them!' she said. She reached up and kissed the underside of his jaw and laid her head against his chest.

'My advisers do not rule here,' she said, 'and they have no answer when I tell them you returned Cyprus to us. That was not the act of a destroyer. It gained you great good will amongst my people.

356

They saw it as a sign that the old glories are on the rise again. They watch us and wait to see what we will accomplish together.'

Julius did not want to spoil the mood, but he had to speak. 'There will come a time when I have to return to my city,' he said. 'I will wait until the funeral is finished for your brother, but I must go back.'

She lifted her head and looked into his eyes with a troubled gaze. He could feel her distance herself from him. 'This is what you want?' she said, her voice revealing nothing of her thoughts.

Julius shook his head. 'No. I want to stay here and forget the years of battle. I want you at my side.'

The tension vanished from her as if it had not been there. She reached up and brought his head down to her scented mouth.

When they broke apart, her face was as flushed as his and her eyes were bright.

'It is not so much longer until I am free,' she said. 'If you will stay with me then, I will show you the great Nile. I will have grapes and fruit lowered into your mouth by the most beautiful girls in Egypt. Musicians will play for us each evening as we slip through the waters. I will be yours for every night, for every hour. Will you stay for that?'

'I do not need the most beautiful girls in Egypt,' he replied. 'And your music makes my ears ache. But if you are there and mine alone, I will leave Rome to fend for herself for a while. She has survived without me this long, after all.'

Even as he said it, he knew it was true, but still it astonished him. He had always dreamed of returning in triumph to the city of his birth, to all the honours and rewards he had won over the years. Yet with a word from her, none of it mattered. Perhaps, just for a little while, he could be free of the care and worry that seemed the core of his life. Perhaps he could throw it all off and feel the sun on his face with a beautiful, enrapturing girl who was queen of Egypt.

'I am too old for you,' he said softly, wanting her to deny it.

Cleopatra laughed and kissed him again. 'You have shown me you are not!' she said, dropping her hand to his thigh and letting it rest there. He could feel the heat of her hand on his bare skin and as always, it aroused him unmercifully.

'If we had a child,' she said, 'he would inherit Egypt and Rome together. He would be another Alexander.'

Julius looked off into the distance, his mind bright with dreams. 'I would give *anything* to see that. I have no other sons,' he said, smiling.

Her hand moved slightly on his thigh, making him catch his breath. 'Then pray to your gods that the one I carry is a boy,' she said, seriously. He reached for her, but she slipped from his grasp. 'When the mourning is finished, I will show you the mysteries of Egypt, in me,' she called over her shoulder.

Julius watched her go in frustration, overwhelmed by her words. He could hardly take in what he had learned and he would have called after her, but she vanished back into the palace with light steps.

The noise of celebration in Alexandria was enough to leave the ears of the Romans ringing and numb. Cymbals and horns crashed and moaned on every street and the voices of the people were raised in a great shout of joy to send Ptolemy into the arms of the gods. Julius shuddered at the memory of the final rites he had witnessed.

The boy king's flesh had been dried like old leather when the chanting priests came for him for the last time. Cleopatra had not insisted Julius be there, but he had been drawn to the last ritual, knowing he would never again have the chance to see the secrets of Egyptian death.

He had watched as the priests took a chisel formed of meteoric iron and broke open Ptolemy's lips with a rocking motion across the mouth. Without the translator Cleopatra had sent to him, Julius would have been lost and appalled at the apparent desecration of the body. The man's sibilant whisper into his ear still gave him chills in memory.

'Osiris the king, awake!' the priest had said. 'I split open your mouth for you with iron of the gods. Live again, rejuvenated every day, while the gods protect you as their own.'

The fumes of incense had swirled around the tiny figure of the boy king and when the last rites were complete, the priests had moved outside into the air, to give the news to the city. The tomb had been sealed behind them with bronze, gold and brass.

The horns had begun then, sounding in their thousands. The noise had built and built and every lamp and brazier was lit, making Alexandria shine under the heavens. The gods would see the light and know one of their own was ready to come to them.

Julius watched the festival of death from the high windows of the royal palace, Brutus at his side. Octavian had gone down into the city to lose himself in drink and women with many of the other officers. On the night of a king's death, there were no taboos and Julius hoped his men would survive the feasting and debauchery without causing riots. It was probably a vain hope, but the responsibility would be on another's shoulders for a while. Cleopatra's barge rocked in the swell of the port, waiting to take him along the coast. They would have to survive without him until he returned. The news Cleopatra had brought overshadowed anything else.

As if he shared the thought, Brutus spoke, looking out over a city lit as brightly as day. He could sense the strange mood of excitement in Julius, though he could not guess at the reason.

'When will you return, do you know?'

'Before the year ends,' Julius replied. 'The legions have their quarters here. They have earned a rest. I have sent letters to Mark

Antony in Rome. In a month or so the back pay will come. Let them take houses here, Brutus, while they wait for me. Let them grow fat and sleepy.'

'You know them better than that,' Brutus replied. 'We've had to punish two more for looting the temples already. I'll have to take them out into the desert after the first weeks, or anything that can be lifted will vanish from Alexandria. As it is, the markets in Rome will be glutted with artefacts when we return.'

Julius chuckled, and Brutus smiled. The darkest moments of the past seemed to have been forgotten between them, and his strength was returning. By the time the sun rose each day, Brutus had completed an hour of heavy sword practice with Domitius. He had lost some of the speed that had won tournaments, but he was no longer weak. He had not told Julius of a centurion who had sneered at him the day before. Brutus had taken him out to the training yard and beaten the man almost to death.

Perhaps Julius knew, Brutus thought, looking at him.

'Octavian is furious with my return to rank,' Brutus said. 'Or because of your pleasure cruise on the Nile. It is difficult to be sure which has annoyed him more.'

Julius shook his head, exasperated. 'He wants me to spend my final years in sleepy Senate debates.' He snorted. 'I suppose we seem ancient to the younger ones, fit for nothing more than patting each other on the back for past glories.'

Brutus glanced at the alert, trim figure of his general, burnt a dark brown. If anything, Julius had been invigorated by the months in Egypt, no small part of it due to the prospect of peace at last. He and Brutus had suffered decades of war and privation. Perhaps the prize was simply an end to striving. Brutus could not imagine him contemplating cruises if Pompey still lived or Sulla threatened his city.

Brutus could not love the man who had pardoned him at Pharsalus, though when Julius had given him command in Alexandria, he felt a brief, uncluttered joy.

He sighed inwardly. Rome seemed far away, but he knew he should think of the future. There were years ahead to forget the shame of his defection to Pompey. Julius had trusted him with authority and the message would not be lost on the legions. It was time to rebuild a career that should have ended at Pharsalus. After all, Rome had been built by men who had survived defeat.

Brutus looked steadily at Julius, missing the old friendship. There were precious moments when he thought they shared an understanding impossible to voice. Yet without warning, he could feel an old jealousy and a destructive pride. With time, perhaps that too would ease.

'This is an old land,' Julius said suddenly, interrupting Brutus' thoughts. 'It could be a second Rome, a twin capital of an empire. I'm not too old to dream of that. I know there is work ahead, but for a little while I want to forget it all and see the Nile with my queen.'

Brutus dropped his head an inch, wondering at the choice of words. 'Will you take her back with you?' he asked.

'I think I will,' Julius replied, smiling slowly at the thought. 'She brings new life to my bones. With her at my side, I could make an empire to rival Alexander's own. It would be fitting to make his city the second heart of it.'

Brutus felt himself growing cold. 'So you will be a king? Like Ptolemy?'

Julius turned to him, his dark eyes seeming to bore into his oldest friend.

'What else would you have me call myself? I am the first in Rome. Rome is first in the world.'

'What of my mother, Servilia? Will you cast her off as you did Pompeia? Or your wife, Calpurnia? Will you divorce her as well?'

Julius hesitated, blind to Brutus' growing anger. 'It is too early to plan such things. When I am home, I will do what is necessary. Calpurnia will not resist, I know.'

361

'The Senate *will* resist your ambition,' Brutus said softly.

Julius laughed. 'They would not dare to, my friend. They will honour me and they will honour the queen I bring home. Rome was built on kings. It will be reborn from my line.'

'From your daughter?' Brutus asked.

Julius' eyes were bright as he looked across the city. He gripped the stone windowsill like its owner. 'I cannot hold the news, Brutus. It is too much for me. From my *son*, who will be born. The queen is pregnant, and her omen-takers say it will be a boy. A son to rule two empires.' He laughed aloud in wonder. It had to be a boy, he thought. The gods would not be so cruel.

Brutus took a step away from him, his calm shattering. What friendship could survive such a relentless ambition? Brutus saw that Julius had not sated his appetite in Egypt. He would return to Rome with greater dreams than any one of those they had destroyed. Not Sulla, not Cato, not even Pompey had reached so far.

'The Republic . . .' Brutus began, shocked into stammering.

Julius shook his head. '. . . was a glorious experiment. I honour it, but it has served its purpose. When I return to Rome, we will begin an empire.'

CHAPTER THIRTY

The Nile bore them south through lands made lush by its waters. Birds soared and shrieked in their thousands, rising into the air with the passing of the royal barge. White egrets stalked amongst cattle as they made their way down to the shallows in the evenings. In such a setting, Julius allowed the cares of years to fall from him. He had not suffered a fit for many months and he felt strong. Rome was far away and he lost himself in Cleopatra.

They made love as the whim took them, by day or night. He had found it difficult at first to ignore the slaves on the barge, with no more than a canopy of fine silk to protect the queen from their gaze. She who had been attended from birth had laughed at his embarrassment, prodding at his dignity until he had slipped the robe from her shoulders and kissed her skin, turning her laughter into a deeper rhythm of breath.

There were eight oars on either side of the barge to ease them through the waters. The blades had been dipped in silver and shone like sunken coins as they sliced beneath the surface. The Nile wound through valleys and vast flats and plains as if it had no end and there were times when Julius could imagine the journey continuing for ever.

In the evenings, he talked for hours with her astrologer, Sosigenes, who had predicted the birth of a son. The man had hesitated to speak to the Roman leader at first, but as the weeks slid by Julius fell naturally into conversation with him. He was hungry for confirmation of the omens Sosigenes had cast and though at first he doubted the power of augury, his hope turned slowly to belief. The Greek had a sharp mind and Julius spent many hours discussing the course of planets, the seasons and even the calendar with him. Sosigenes had struggled not to show his contempt for the Roman system and said even the Egyptian years were flawed. By his calculations, three hundred and sixty-five days was almost correct, needing only another day in every fourth spring to be perfect. Julius demanded proof of his assertions and the man rose to the challenge, covering the deck with sheets of papyrus marked in charcoal until Julius was dizzy with the flights of planets and stars. In Rome, the high priest took or added days each year, but Sosigenes' love of simplicity and order was appealing. Julius wondered how the Senate would react if he imposed such a system on the citizens of Rome.

As Cleopatra's pregnancy progressed, she felt the heat more fiercely and spent the afternoons in sleep behind the awnings. Julius was left to stare for hours at the sinister shapes of crocodiles amongst the bulrushes, waiting patiently for an ibis or calf to come too close. Seeing them snatch at prey was the only touch of fire to interrupt the long dream of the Nile. The silver oars rose and fell, only still when the breeze filled the purple sail above their heads. Julius had Sosigenes tell him stories when the sun was too hot to bear. He let the legends wash over him until he felt he was a part of the drifting landscape, part of its future.

In the cool of the pre-dawn, Cleopatra's slaves bathed and dressed her, painting her eyes in black kohl that lifted up at the edges. Julius was naked and lay on one elbow, watching the ritual. He was no longer uncomfortable with the slave girls, though he had refused Cleopatra's offer for them to entertain him more intimately. He did not think they were unwilling. In fact, the girl dressing her queen had made her interest evident as she bathed him with cloths on the deck. More of the cool water had drifted across her full breasts than down his body and she had laughed at his reaction, teasing him. Perhaps it was the heat, or the semi-naked presence of the slaves, but he felt erotically charged by the days on the Nile, refreshed by swimming where the water was clear, rubbed down with oil by skilful hands, fed as well as a breeding bull. He ran a hand lightly down his stomach, feeling the muscle there. The dreaming life was like water to a dry soul after so long at war. Yet even there, with the sun rising, he knew he could not rest for ever. The itch to act was always at the back of his mind, growing daily. Rome waited for him and it took a greater and greater effort to ignore the call.

He could see the swelling of the child she would bear. He lay entranced until it was hidden from view by a cloth so thin he could see the line of her legs through it. When she came to look down on him, she raised her eyebrows at the smile that played on his face.

'Will you be walking naked amongst the people then?' she asked sweetly.

Julius chuckled. 'I was watching you and thinking that I am going to wake up suddenly and be in some tent somewhere, with the battle horns blowing and my officers roaring for one last charge.'

She did not smile at his words. She had heard him call out too many times in his sleep and woken to see his face twisted in pain and anger. He did not remember his dreams, or at least they did not seem to trouble him in the day. Her eyes travelled over the scars on his body and she shook her head.

'Dress, Caesar, and see something new,' she said.

He opened his mouth to ask the question, but she put a hand down to his lips and then left him alone to be dressed by her bright-eyed slaves. With a sigh, he rose and beckoned for them to bring his lightest robe.

When he came on deck he found the barge was edging towards the shore. A town like many others reached to the water's edge, with a small wooden dock extending out into the brown waters. Red geese flew honking overhead as he saw the planking had been laid with fresh rushes in a path leading away from the river. Hundreds of people lined the shore in a blaze of coloured robes and every eye seemed to be on him. Julius stared back uncomfortably as the crew worked the steering oars to bring them in to dock. A platform wide enough for a rank of legionaries was brought up and attached to the side, resting in the clean path.

Cleopatra walked to it and the crowd knelt in the mud, pressing their heads down as she stepped onto the land. Drums sounded on the edges and when she looked back at Julius he saw the cold features that had dominated the army in Alexandria. He had fallen out of the habit of wearing a sword on the river, and his fingers twitched at empty air. He followed her, his sandals crunching on the rushes. When he reached her side, she turned to him and smiled.

'I wanted you to see this,' she said.

Her bodyguard of ten clattered onto the rickety dock behind them, taking up positions. She walked through the crowd with Julius and he saw that the line of kneeling men and women extended right through the town.

'How did they know you were coming?' he murmured.

'It is the anniversary of the day I became queen,' she said. 'They know when it is time.'

The town was clean and well kept, though it seemed deserted, with every man, woman and child kneeling on the road. Cleopatra reached down to touch them at intervals, and in her wake he saw tears of gratitude.

The path of rushes ended at the entrance of a tiny square, swept meticulously clean of dust. Her guards moved ahead to search a temple of red marble that gleamed in the morning sun. The silence was eerie and Julius was reminded of a deserted village in Spain where he had once ridden with Servilia. He had seen a statue of Alexander there and it was unnerving to have the experience echoed in the very lands of the king.

He found his thoughts drifting, mourning all that had been lost since that other time and place. The last vestiges of innocence had been ground out of him in Gaul and Greece. Perhaps that was why he had shed tears at the sight of Pompey's dead face. Julius remembered the young boy he had once been, but it was all too far away to know him well. His father, Marius, Tubruk; they were all shadows. There had been too many tragedies, too many memories closed and barred away, somewhere deep. He had dug a wolf trap for Suetonius and let him live. If this Egyptian morning had given him the chance again, he would have killed him without a second thought.

Perhaps it was age that brought the hardness, or the brutal choices of a campaign. He had pulled men back, knowing it would mean the death of other loyal soldiers. He had saved the many at the expense of the few. He had directed surgeons to those who had a chance to survive. He had even sent good men to Pompey's camp, knowing they could not deliver his message and live. He thought such cold decisions seeped into the bone after a while, numbing the joy of life. Even the sun of Egypt could not reach him, though Cleopatra could. He found his eyes were stinging, inexplicably.

The guards returned and Julius and Cleopatra walked slowly into the gloom, their steps echoing under a domed roof, high above them. It was clearly a place of worship and Julius wondered why she had brought him there. The walls were decorated with reliefs of star patterns in yellow agate, darker lines running through the stone like veins of blood. To his astonishment, he thought he could hear the mewing of cats and as he looked for the source of the sound he saw a dozen of them padding out towards Cleopatra.

Murmuring words in Egyptian, she reached down and let them rub themselves against her hands. 'Are they not beautiful?' she said, kneeling in their midst.

Julius could only nod, wondering which unfortunate had the task of cleaning the marble floors after them. She saw his expression and her laughter echoed in the space.

'They are the guardians of the temple, Julius. Can you see their claws? Who would dare to enter here against such hunters?'

As she spoke, the cats preened and purred around her, content. She stood gently and they followed her, their tails waving lazily upright.

In the far end of the temple was a statue that filled a concave wall. Julius glanced up at it and missed his step in confusion. It towered above them both, so that Cleopatra's head came up to the knee of the white stone.

Julius could only stare from one to the other. In creamy marble, he saw the features of the queen staring down at him. The statue held a boy child in her arms and looked outwards in pride. It was an expression he knew well.

Cleopatra saw his upwards gaze and smiled. 'This is Isis, Caesar, mother of Horus, whom she holds.'

'With your face,' Julius said, wonderingly.

'The temple is a thousand years old, before Alexander came here. Yet she lives in me.'

He looked at her as the cats rubbed themselves against her legs.

'My son will be a god, Julius; your son. Do you understand now?'

He did not say that the face of the statue was fractionally different as he studied it. The woman in stone was a little older than Cleopatra, and as the first shock faded he could see the line of the jaw was different. The eyes were wider spaced and yet . . . it was astonishing. She nodded, pleased with his reaction.

'Will you pray to her, with me?' she said.

Julius frowned. 'If she is in you, how can you pray?' he asked.

Her teeth showed as she grinned. 'So very blunt, Roman. I should have expected it. It is a mystery, is it not? I carry the flame hidden in flesh, yet she is still there. When I travel the dead path, it will be a return, not a beginning. Understand that and you understand me. It would please me to have you pray to her. She will bless our son and keep him safe.'

Julius could not refuse as she gazed at him. He knelt and bowed his head, pleased there were no other eyes to see him do it.

The scribes' quarter of the royal palace at Alexandria was almost a town in itself, with thousands of scholars working within its walls. After the destruction of the great library, the lamps were lit all night and day as the written works of masters were brought in from all over Egypt and Greece and copied with painstaking care.

One wing of the sprawling annexe had been taken over by the Roman administration and Brutus had claimed the best rooms for himself. At his order, legion craftsmen had stripped out the statuary and gold, crating and packing it where possible to be shipped home. In its place, they lined the walls in light, carved oak, building a Roman sanctuary. New barracks had been built for the Tenth and Fourth, after one too many incidents of trophy-taking in the city. Brutus had let them run a little wild at first, but it was clear that discipline was suffering after only a few weeks and he had been forced to impose the harsh order they knew best. There had been some who complained and even a petition signed by idiots who ended the day of its delivery marching out to desert postings. The city was quiet and, in the absence of Julius, Brutus was thoroughly enjoying his freedom.

Those men who had taken advantage of his weakness after Pharsalus found themselves shovelling excrement in the hot sun until they collapsed. He had taken care to remember every face and took enormous satisfaction from giving them the dirtiest tasks he could find. More than one had suffered from cuts and scratches that quickly became infected. Brutus had made a point of visiting them in the sickrooms, as any other conscientious officer would. Good Roman sewers would run under Alexandria by the time Julius returned.

In the meeting room, Brutus watched Octavian carefully, enjoying his struggle.

'. . . and I am passing the problem on to you, General,' Brutus continued. 'Julius has summoned these new legions to Egypt and they must be fed, paid and found barracks. If you are incapable of carrying out your duty, I will . . .'

'He said nothing to me about them,' Octavian interrupted, making Brutus frown.

The tension between them had not lessened since Julius' departure. At first, Brutus had thought Octavian would refuse the authority Julius had placed in him. He still remembered the younger man's threats on a Greek dock and part of Brutus wanted Octavian to dare them again now that he had his strength. The confrontation had not come, though the effort of will had been perfectly visible to the other senior officers. Octavian seemed content to walk a fine line between duty and insolence and Brutus was willing to play the game for as long as Octavian could bear it. It was always easier to press down than to push up.

'In my experience,' Brutus said airily, 'Julius is not in the habit of consulting his juniors on every decision. His letters have brought a garrison from Greece to Egypt. Whether they are an escort home or a force of occupation, I really do not care. Until his return, they are your responsibility.'

Malice glinted in Octavian's face and Brutus sat up in his chair, anticipating the first crack in the calm. Nothing would give him more pleasure than to have Octavian sent home in disgrace.

Regardless of circumstances, the Senate would be harsh with any man who disobeyed an order from his appointed commander. If Octavian drew his sword or raised a fist, he would be finished.

Octavian saw the eagerness and at first controlled his dislike. He was on the point of saluting when his anger surfaced uncontrollably.

'Is it that you don't want to see the faces of men you fought with as a traitor?' he snapped. 'Is that why you won't go out to see them?'

Brutus smiled slowly in triumph. 'Now, is that any way to speak to your superior, boy? Is it? I think you have gone a little too far today. I suppose I should demand an apology, in case Julius asks me about it afterwards.'

Octavian was not a fool. Brutus watched him weigh the difference in their ages and positions. The younger man made a decision and became calm.

'You are not fit for your rank,' Octavian said. 'He should have known better than to trust you again.'

With infinite satisfaction, Brutus rose. It had been an enjoyable month of goading the younger man, but he had known the moment would come.

'I can have Domitius come in here and do this formally, or you and I can go out to find a quiet place and I'll teach you manners. What's it to be?'

Octavian had come too far to back down from any threat. He tapped his fingers on his sword hilt in answer. Brutus grinned, delighted with the morning's work.

'I will enter it in the staff record as a training session,' he said. He gestured to the door. 'You go first, boy. I'll be behind you all the way.'

Legion guards saluted automatically as the two men strode past them. Brutus followed Octavian down a flight of stairs and a corridor that still bore the marks of Roman treasure hunting. Brutus rolled his shoulders as he walked, loosening the muscles.

The training yard was busy with men, as it was every morning. Dressed in only loincloths and sandals, the sun-darkened Romans used heavy leather balls and iron weights to keep themselves trim. Others fought in pairs with the lead-weighted practice swords, the clack and clatter loud after the silence of the halls.

'Return to your duties, gentlemen,' Brutus said without taking his eyes from Octavian. He waited patiently as the soldiers put away their equipment and left them alone. He could feel their curiosity, but an audience would shape the manner of the lesson he intended to give. He did not want to feel restrained.

When the last man had left, Octavian turned and drew his sword in a smooth motion, stalking across the sandy ground to one of the fighting circles. Brutus watched him for weakness, reminded that he too had won silver armour in Julius' tournament. He was fast and young, but Brutus drew his own gladius as if it were a part of his arm. He had searched for it amongst Egyptian dead, before the scavengers could bear it away. He had trained through pain to recover the skill for exactly this moment.

Brutus took position opposite Octavian and raised his sword into first position.

'I remember you threatening to have my arm rebroken,' he murmured, beginning to circle. 'Would you like to try it now?'

Octavian ignored him, reversing step so quickly that it almost caught Brutus by surprise. The first blow was a test of his strength, with Octavian's weight behind it. Brutus took it easily, with a clang of metal.

'You mustn't tense your hip like that, boy. It restricts your movement,' Brutus said.

For a few moments, they fought in silence as Octavian tried a combination of cuts that ended with a lunge at his knee. Brutus batted the blade aside.

'Better,' he said. 'Though I see Domitius has been working with you. He loves that little lunge.'

372

He saw that Octavian was circling too closely and darted at him. His sword was countered, but Brutus managed to hammer a punch into Octavian's cheek before they broke apart. Octavian touched his face and held up the palm to show there was no blood.

'Are you thinking this is just to the first cut, boy?' Brutus said. 'You're as naive as Julius. Perhaps that's why he likes you.'

As he spoke, he began a series of strikes that built in speed. Both men crashed together, and Octavian used his elbow to knock Brutus' head back.

'You're getting old,' Octavian said as they circled once more.

Brutus glared at him, feeling the truth of the words. He had lost the blinding speed of his youth, but he had experience enough to humble one more young dog, he was sure of it. 'I wonder if Julius shared his plans with you for when he returns?' he said. Both men were sweating by then. Brutus saw Octavian's eyes narrow and he went on, watching for an attack. 'This city is to become the second capital of his empire, did he tell you that? I doubt he bothered. You were always first in line to kiss his feet. What does it matter if you kneel to a general or an emperor?'

The response was fast and the clash of swords went on and on until the breath came hard from Brutus' lungs. There was no weakness in his defence and Octavian could batter all day before he found a way through. The younger man sensed his confidence and backed to the edge of the circle.

'You're a bag of old wind,' Octavian said. 'A liar, a traitor, a *coward*.'

His eyes glittered as he waited for the attack, but Brutus only laughed, confusing him.

'Ask him when he returns, then, boy. Ask him what he thinks about your beloved Republic. He told me . . .' They met again and Brutus cut a stripe down Octavian's leg. The blood ran like water and he continued cheerfully, knowing weakness would follow. 'He told me the Senate's day was over, but perhaps he will lie to you, to spare your tender pride.'

They circled more slowly and Brutus did not force the pace.

'What did you think, that we were fighting for the Republic?' Brutus asked, mockingly. 'Maybe once, when we were all young, but he has a queen now and she carries his son.'

'You liar!' Octavian roared, leaping in.

His leg felt like it was on fire, but even through the pain he knew that Brutus was letting him tire himself. A poor stroke let Brutus gash his left hand before he could jerk it back. He clenched the fist in reflex and blood dripped between his knuckles.

'I wonder if I wasn't on the right side at Pharsalus, after all,' Brutus said, switching gaits and leaving Octavian to stumble. He looked dazed, though whether it was the words or the wounds, Brutus did not know.

'Don't pretend to be dying, boy. I've seen that trick a few times before,' he jeered.

Octavian straightened subtly and his sword lashed out in a perfect lunge that Brutus missed. It jolted against his shoulder plate, snapping the leather ties. Brutus swore, before yanking it loose with his free hand and tossing it away.

'That beautiful girl is carrying a son. Now why would that make you angry?' Brutus paused, breaking the rhythm. 'It can't be that you expected to inherit? Mind you, why not? He's bald and ancient compared to you. Why would you not look forward to sitting in his place one day? Gods, it must *eat* at you to know it won't happen. When his son is born, how much time do you think he'll find for a distant relative?'

His laughter was cruel, and against the cry of his instinct Octavian was stung again into an attack. Brutus swayed out of its path and crashed another blow into the same cheek, splitting it.

'You look a proper butcher's shop, did you know?' Brutus said. 'You're getting slower every moment.'

They were both panting by then and yet as they met they struck to kill. Brutus kneed upwards into Octavian's groin as they came together, but a lucky blow opened a gash on his leg, making him cry out.

'Hurts, does it?' Octavian snarled at him.

'Stings a little, yes,' Brutus replied, coming in fast.

The swords blurred as they cracked and rang against each other, both men straining with all their strength. Blows landed and cut without being felt in the heat of the struggle. The silver armour dented and then Octavian grunted as Brutus' sword punctured through the metal into his side. He raised a hand to it, gasping. The light in the yard seemed too bright and his legs were wet with blood. He slipped to his knees, expecting the bite of a sword at his throat.

Brutus kicked his gladius away onto the sand and stood looking down at him.

'Nothing that can't be stitched, boy,' he said, resting his hands on his knees. 'I wonder if I should break your arm?'

The oval gash in his thigh ached terribly, but he ignored it. He'd lived through worse.

Octavian looked up. 'If he wants an empire, I'll give it to him,' he said.

Brutus sighed as he brought back his fist and knocked him onto his back, unconscious. 'You really *are* a fool,' he told the prone figure.

CHAPTER THIRTY-ONE

Horns blew across Alexandria as the royal barge was sighted in the last days of summer. Brutus sent a dozen trim Roman galleys to meet them and food enough for banquets was given out from the dock stores. The purple sail could be seen from a great distance and hundreds of boats joined the exodus through the mouth of the port, gathering around the queen's ship like a flight of brightly coloured birds.

Though the shorter days were on them, the air was still heavy with heat. Cleopatra's slaves fanned her as she stood on deck and watched the fleet come out. Her advancing pregnancy had brought an end to the peaceful days on the Nile and she could no longer find comfort in any position for long. Julius had learned to tread carefully as her temper frayed, and at the sight of Roman galleys her eyes narrowed in a flash of anger.

'You have brought your army here?' she said, looking at him.

'A tiny part of it,' he replied. 'You would not have me leave Alexandria undefended when you come to Rome.'

'My warriors have seen to our defence over the years,' she replied, indignantly.

Julius chose his words with care. 'I would not take even a small risk with Egypt,' he murmured. 'The galleys protect our son's inheritance. Trust me in this. I have given you my oath.'

She felt the child move within her and she shuddered as she

listened. Had she lost her throne to the Roman? Egypt had grown tired over five thousand years and she knew her enemies watched for weakness. The young strength of Rome would keep the wolves away from her lands, like a flaming torch thrust into their faces. Julius could fire her blood when he talked of twin capitals, but the sight of his legionaries swarming on her docks made her fear. He could be kind as a man, as a lover, but as a general he was a destroying storm and her city had come to his notice.

Julius saw her shiver and took a shawl from one of her slave girls. He placed it about Cleopatra's shoulders and his tenderness brought tears to her eyes.

'You must believe me,' he said softly. 'This is a beginning.'

Legion centuries stood in perfect order on the docks as the queen's crew moored the barge. As Julius and Cleopatra stepped down, the Romans cheered the return of the consul and victor of Rome. A litter was brought for Cleopatra, removing her from the vulgar gaze behind a canopy raised on the shoulders of slaves. Julius stood on her right side, taking in the changes that had occurred in his absence.

The busy port had a sense of order that had been missing before. In the distance, he could see legionaries on patrol. New custom houses had been built or commandeered to control the wealth of trade that came through Alexandria. Brutus had clearly been busy.

As the procession made its way through the city towards the royal palace, the presence of legions became even more obvious. Soldiers stood to attention on every corner, saluting as Julius came into sight. The citizens of Alexandria who might have clustered around their queen were held back by solid barriers at every street mouth, leaving the main path clear.

Julius winced to himself at how the casual efficiency must look to Cleopatra. He had sent his orders to Greece before leaving, but the reality of seeing twenty thousand more of his countrymen descend on the city was strangely disturbing. Alexandria had been an alien place when he arrived. His men were busy turning it into an outpost of Rome.

At the palace, Cleopatra's slaves gathered around her in a flurry of excitement. Her feet hurt and she was weary, but as she stood again on the steps, she turned to Julius before entering the cooler rooms within.

'How can I trust you?' she said.

'You carry my son, Cleopatra. Even if you did not, you are more valuable to me than anything else. Let me protect you.'

She opened her mouth to speak, then thought better of it, compressing her lips into a thin line of disapproval.

Julius sighed. Thousands of his soldiers were in view. 'Very well, my queen. Let me show my men, at least.'

Without another word, he knelt on the steps before her.

The tension slid away from Cleopatra as she looked down on his flushed face. A smile tugged at the corners of her lips. 'I have never known a man to kneel with such pride,' she murmured into his ear, making him laugh.

Julius summoned his Gaul generals to him after he had eaten and bathed. The new officers from Greece would have to wait a little longer for an audience. He chose the room Brutus had been using in the scribes' quarter and looked around him in interest at the changes as he waited for them to arrive.

Brutus and Domitius entered first, saluting and taking the chairs he offered. Regulus came behind them, his usual grim manner made lighter by Julius' return. Octavian and Ciro took their seats as Domitius poured wine for the rest.

Julius watched them all as they accepted the goblets and raised them in his direction before drinking. They looked fit and dark from the sun, Ciro in particular. He might have passed for one of the native Egyptians. Octavian had a new scar on his cheek that stood out against his skin. Of all of them, his manner was the most reserved and Julius missed the relaxed camaraderie of their years together. He had been away for almost six months and felt uncomfortable at the distance that had grown between them.

'Should I ask for a formal report, gentlemen?' he said. 'Or shall we drink and talk until the sun goes down?'

Regulus smiled, but the others were oddly wary. It was Octavian who broke the silence.

'I'm glad to see you back, sir,' he said.

Brutus was staring at the younger man in what could have been polite interest and Julius wondered what had gone on between them. He did not want to hear of squabbling and bad feeling. His time on the Nile made such things seem trivial.

'The city is quiet, Julius,' Brutus said, 'as you might expect with the best part of thirty thousand soldiers here. We've had a few incidents of looting and some of the men are in desert barracks on punishment drills. Nothing that couldn't be handled. We've given them a decent sewage system and brought a little order to the docks. Apart from that, it's been a pleasant rest for some of us. How is the queen?'

Julius nodded to Brutus, pleased at the lack of fuss. 'The birth is due in a few weeks, or even less,' he said, his eyes softening at the thought.

'A son and heir,' Brutus said. Julius did not see him glance at Octavian. 'You'll have to make peace with Calpurnia when you return.'

Julius nodded, sipping at his wine. The thought of his latest wife weeping on his shoulder was not a pleasant one. 'I could not have known this would happen when I married her,' he said, musing. 'So much has changed since I set out for Greece.'

'Are we going home then, when the child is born?' Octavian said suddenly.

Julius looked at him, seeing a tension he did not understand. 'We are. I will leave two legions here to keep the peace. I'll write to Mark Antony and have him set up the galley routes for pay and orders. By the gods, it will be *good* to see him again. I've missed the old place. Just to speak about it here makes me long to see Rome.'

He seemed to collect himself as he looked around at their earnest faces.

'We will take Pompey's remains back to be buried in the city, and I'll raise a statue to him, perhaps in his own theatre. Even now the manner of his death sits poorly with me. I have written to my daughter to tell her, and I will honour him in death, for her sake at least.'

He paused, staring off into space. It was a year since Pharsalus and the memory of crossing the Rubicon seemed impossibly distant. The hiatus in his life that had come on the slow Nile had changed him, he realised. The other men in the room still had the look of lean wolves, hardened by years of conflict. He did not feel quite in step with them.

'It will be a strange thing to have the Republic restored after so many years of conflict,' Octavian murmured, looking into his wine. 'The city will welcome you back as a saviour of the old ways.' It took an effort for him to look up into Julius' eyes as his general regarded him thoughtfully.

'Perhaps they will,' Julius said. 'I will have to see how things stand when I'm back.' He missed the glimmer of hope in Octavian's eyes as he refilled his cup from a silver jug. 'Things change, though,' he went on. 'I've had time to think on that slow river. I have been granted the chance to raise Rome higher than any other city. I should not waste it.'

He felt Octavian's stare and raised his cup in salute.

'Alexander's dreams have fallen into my hands here. In this place, I can see further. We could bring the light of Rome to the world.'

He smiled, oblivious to Octavian's distress. 'Like the Pharos light-house,' he said. 'We could make an empire.'

'Does this come from the queen?' Octavian said softly.

Julius glanced at him in puzzlement. 'My blood is joined in her. Egypt and I are already one. Rome will come with me.' He gestured towards the window with his cup, feeling the wine heat his thoughts. 'The years ahead are golden, Octavian. I have seen them.'

'Welcome *back*, sir,' Brutus said.

Julius paced up and down the hall of the palace, wincing at every cry from Cleopatra's lips. His son was coming into the world and he could hardly remember being more nervous. Her courtiers had come to wake him in his quarters and he had dressed hurriedly in a toga and sandals, calling for Brutus to attend him.

The two men had come barrelling into the meeting hall only to be told that the queen's privacy was not to be interrupted. To Julius' irritation, the door to her chambers was guarded by her own men and he had been left to pace and fret, his empty stomach growling hungrily as the hours wore on. Messengers came and went at the run, carrying steaming pails of water and piles of white linen. Julius could hear the voices of women inside and at intervals Cleopatra cried out in pain. He clenched his fists in frustration and barely noticed the warm tisane that Brutus pressed into his hands.

At dawn, Sosigenes came out, snapping orders for more cloths to a waiting slave. The astrologer was flushed and busy, but a glance at Julius' face brought him up short.

'Your son is coming, Caesar. It is a great omen that he is to be born in the first light of day,' Sosigenes said.

Julius gripped his arm. 'Is she well? The birth, is it all right?'

Sosigenes smiled and nodded his head. 'You should rest, Consul. You will be called in soon enough. My queen is young and strong, as her mother was. Rest.'

He returned the grip on his arm with a brief pressure of his hand, then he walked past the guards. A long scream could be heard then, which made Julius groan.

'By the gods, I can't bear it,' he said.

'Were you like this when Julia was born?' Brutus asked him.

Julius shook his head. 'I don't remember. No, I wasn't, I think. But I am older now. If the child dies, how many other chances will I have?'

'What will he be called then, this son of yours?' Brutus asked, in part to take Julius' mind off the chanting they could hear within. He had no idea what strange rituals were being enacted and it showed the depth of Julius' agitation that he had hardly noticed them.

The question seemed to calm Julius a little. 'His name will be Ptolemy Caesarion,' he said, with pride. 'Two houses joined.'

'You will show him in the forum,' Brutus prompted.

Julius' face lit up. 'I will. As soon as he can be moved, I will take him home. The king of Syria has invited me to visit him and I will take Cleopatra there. Then Crete, perhaps, or Cyprus, Greece and home at last. We will stand in the forum in a Roman summer and I'll hold the boy up to the crowd for them to see.'

'There will be a struggle ahead, if you still intend a dynasty, an empire,' Brutus murmured.

Julius shook his head. 'Not now, Brutus. Can't you see it? The legions are loyal to me and the Senate will be hand-picked. Whether they realise it or not, the empire is already begun. Who is left to resist my claim, after all? Pompey was the last of them.'

Brutus nodded, his eyes dark with thought.

An hour later, Sosigenes came bustling out to them, surprising the guards. The man was beaming as if personally responsible for the events of the night.

'You have your son, Caesar, as I said you would. Will you come in?'

Julius clapped a hand on his shoulder, making him wince. 'Show me,' he said.

Brutus did not follow and was left alone to spread the happy news to the legions that had gathered outside in the dawn.

Cleopatra lay on her bed with the hangings tied back to give her air. She looked exhausted and dazed, with shadows under her eyes. Her skin was pale and as Julius rushed over to her a slave girl dried the perspiration from her skin, dabbing gently with a cloth.

There were many others in the room, though Julius didn't notice them. Cleopatra's breasts were bared and against one was the baby he had hoped for, the tiny face lost as it pressed against the yielding flesh.

Julius sat on the bed and leaned over them, ignoring the slave girl as she moved away. Cleopatra opened her eyes.

'My beautiful queen,' Julius murmured, smiling. 'Sosigenes said it was a boy.'

'The old fool is very proud of himself,' Cleopatra said, wincing as the baby clenched her nipple in its gums. 'You have a son, Julius.'

Gently, he reached up and smoothed a tendril of hair from her forehead.

'I have waited all my life for you,' he said to her.

Tears filled her eyes and she laughed at her own reaction. 'I seem to cry at the slightest thing,' she said, then grimaced as the baby shifted once more. For an instant, her nipple was revealed before the hungry mouth found it and clamped on, sucking busily. 'He is strong,' she said.

Julius looked at the tiny figure half-concealed by cloths. Fresh from the womb, the baby was wrinkled, his skin a shade of blue that faded even as Julius watched. A smear of blood lay on his head, mingled with hair as black as his mother's.

'He'll have to be if he stays that ugly,' Julius said, laughing as Cleopatra swatted at him with a free hand.

'He is beautiful,' she said, 'and he is ours. He will be a great king, Sosigenes has sworn it. Greater than you or I, Julius.'

He kissed her gently and she sagged back into the pillows, her eyes closing. Julius felt a presence at his shoulder and turned to look into the stern gaze of one of the royal midwives.

'Yes?' he said.

Cleopatra sighed without opening her eyes. 'She does not speak Latin, Julius.'

The woman gestured to Julius and the door, muttering under her breath.

'I understand,' he said. 'I will return when you have had a chance to rest.'

He took her hand and squeezed it, before standing. He looked down on his family and thanked his gods for having lived long enough to see it.

PART THREE

CHAPTER THIRTY-TWO

The city of Rome was awake. Galloping messengers had brought the news that Caesar had landed at the coast and he was coming home. Mark Antony had not been idle in the weeks of waiting and the preparations were all in place. Almost a million citizens had lit lamps on the great walls, prepared banquets, cleaned and scrubbed the streets until Rome seemed almost new. Corn, bread and meat had been given to every citizen and a public holiday announced. The city gleamed and temple chests were filled with coins offered in thanks for Caesar's safety. Many were tired from their labours, but they sat up with their children and listened for the horns that would announce his arrival.

Brutus rode slowly at Julius' side, looking at the city in the distance. The sheer size of it made Alexandria seem a provincial town. The citizens had made it glow under the heavens for Caesar. Would they have done more to welcome a king? Brutus found he could hardly bear the look of awe on Octavian's face at the jewel of Rome on the horizon. It was an expression all those in the column seemed to share, from the soldiers of the Tenth to Julius himself. They came as victors and walked with pride they had earned. Brutus could not feel a part of their hope and their glory.

What joy could *he* find within those walls? He would be the man Julius forgave for a betrayal, whispered about and pointed at as he strode through his city. He would see his mother again, he thought. Perhaps when she saw Cleopatra she would understand what had driven him away from Julius. His eyes prickled and he took a deep breath, ashamed of himself. He had entered many cities. What was Rome but one more, to him? He would survive it. He would endure.

He felt as if he had been riding for years in a procession of the legions. Julius had been welcomed as a brother king in Syria, given slaves and gifts of gems and weapons. Cleopatra had rejoiced in his shadow, perhaps understanding at last how a small king would see Julius. She could not hide her delight at showing Ptolemy Caesarion, red and tiny as he was. The ruler of Syria had many children, but he had honoured the couple by bringing his first-born, Herod, into their presence, and having him bow to the leader of Rome. The little prince had been shaking with nerves, Brutus remembered.

He glanced behind him to where the queen lay hidden from sight in a carriage that was more like a comfortable room drawn by oxen. Her son was with her and the child's irritable screams pierced the night.

In its way, the return to Rome had been like a Triumph on a grand scale. The praetor of Crete had kissed Julius' hand and given over his own home for their stay. The soldiers ate and drank their way through the praetor's private stores, but there was no fighting or lack of discipline. They seemed to understand the dignity of their position as escort for Caesar and his son. Their reverence made Brutus want to be ill.

It had shocked him at first, to see powerful men kneeling as Julius approached them. Brutus had seen his friend swear and spit and bicker with Cabera or Renius like an irritable old woman. He had known him as a boy, and the obsequious fawning of officials seemed obscene. They did not know Caesar. They saw only the cloak and the soldiers. They had read the reports and heard of his victories, creating a mask for the lesser man within. Brutus had seen Julius' pleasure at their treatment of him and it ate at him like a worm.

It had been worst in Greece, where Brutus was known. Perhaps he had been shielded from the reality of his position during the year in Alexandria. He had forgotten how painful it would be to have old friends turn their backs and others sneer as they saw him at Julius' side. Labienus had been there, his dark eyes full of private amusement at seeing Brutus back at the heel of his general.

If Pompey had won, Brutus knew he would have been rewarded. He would perhaps have stood for consul himself and the fickle citizens would have voted for a man who had put Rome before friendship, one who had saved them from a tyrant. With just one battle, at Pharsalus, he could have turned his life onto a new path. That was what hurt the most, he told himself. Not to be forgiven, but to have come so close to having it all. There were times when he was almost convinced of it.

The road into Rome was not empty. Mark Antony had sent out the city legion under Ahenobarbus to line the stones as far west as they had numbers. As Julius reached each pair of soldiers, they held a stiff salute. They too had done their work, Brutus admitted grudgingly. Rome had been safe while Julius was away. It would have been some sort of justice had the city been attacked while Julius was ignoring his duty on the Nile, but, no, the gods had granted peace to Rome, as if they too were willing to rest until Caesar took up the reins once more.

The Greeks had tried another rebellion, choosing their moment with the worst of all timing, so that the fighting began as Julius arrived. Brutus could almost feel sorry for the men who had risen against their Roman masters. Labienus could have ended it on his own, but Julius had intervened. The men said it showed he understood his responsibilities as first in Rome, that all lands were his to order and control. Brutus rather suspected it was to show Cleopatra what his legions could do.

The battle had been tiny compared to some they had known. Julius had ridden with his generals and his queen to where the Greek army had risen. Brutus could still shudder at the sight of shouting warriors rushing up a hill towards the Roman positions. Of *course* they were tired by the time they had reached the crest. The rebellion had been ended in only four hours, more littered flesh in the Roman wake.

The fleet made final landfall at Ostia, west of the city. Julius had knelt to kiss the ground. The legions had cheered him then and the first taste of the excitement that gripped Rome came from the villages and towns to the west. They bustled and pushed to catch a glimpse of him. They wore their best clothes and the women had braided their hair with as much attention as for the festival of Bona Dea. Children were held up as he would hold his own son high to the forum.

The horses sensed the excitement around them and tossed their heads, snorting. The cheering became louder as the legions approached Rome and saw that the heavy gates of the west stood open for them. The walls were lined with waving citizens and yet the legions did not break discipline to return the gestures. They smiled as their legs lost their weariness and gazed at the torches and walls as if they had never seen the city before.

Brutus could see the white togas of senators inside the gate. He wondered how they would feel about Julius' plans for the future. Had they any idea of the force they were welcoming back so trustingly? If they expected age to have banked the fires in Julius, they were going to be disappointed. He was rejuvenated, as if Cleopatra and his son were new magic in his life. Rome should be trembling, Brutus thought, but Cicero was not a fool. No matter what the senator might fear, there was no one in the world who could have raised a warning voice at that moment. Sometimes it is better just to let the wave crash over you and pick up the pieces after it has passed.

Horns sounded, first at the gate, then spreading all over the city as every old bronze piece was lifted to lips and blown. Julius kicked in his heels to move slightly ahead of the first rank of his Tenth. He did not duck his head as he rode under the arch and raised his hand to acknowledge the people pressing in on all sides. He was home.

Julius stood on the steps of the senate house in front of a packed forum. He lifted his arms for silence, but it would not come. He signalled two of his men to blow the legion horns above the tumult and even then the crowd were slow to become still. He looked across at Mark Antony and the two men shared a grin.

When at last they were quiet, Julius was content merely to stand and enjoy the sight of Rome around him, drinking it in. The steps were packed with faces of men he had known for years. The temples and buildings around the forum shone in the light of late summer.

'Nowhere else in the world is home as this city is home,' he said at last. His voice echoed across the crowds as they watched with faces raised up to him. 'I have seen Gaul. I have seen Asia Minor. I have seen Greece and Spain and Britain. I have walked in Alexander's cities and seen jewels and strange gods. I have found Roman voices in all those lands, cutting the soil, trading and making a life for themselves. I have seen our laws and our honour in countries so distant as to seem like dreams. This city nourishes the world.'

He bowed his head as they cheered, and when it seemed that they would not stop, he had his soldiers crash the butts of their spears on the stones of the forum.

'It gives me grief to bring Pompey's remains home with me. He did not die by my hand and his passing is a black day for Rome. Those who killed him have been punished and the gods will not let them forget the price of a consul. Let them weep for ever for laying a hand on a man of Rome. In the years to come, they will remember the answer we gave them! Those of you who travel and trade will carry that protection of this city with you. If you are taken by enemies, tell them you are a Roman citizen and let them fear the storm that will answer a single drop of your blood. The storm *will* come in your defence. This I pledge to you all.'

He raised his hands before they could cheer again, impatient to tell them more. In his mind, he could see the reality he could make with Cleopatra, so bright and perfect as to make words base in comparison.

'I grant an amnesty to all those who raised arms against me in this civil war. As I pardoned the men of Corfinium and Greece, I pardon all others who have followed their duty and their honour as they saw it. We are brothers and sisters of the same blood. We will begin afresh from this day, and let the past go. I am not another Sulla to be seeking enemies behind every door. I have other dreams for Rome.'

He paused, aware of the senators who strained to hear every word.

'The gods have blessed my line with a son, of the blood of royal Egypt. I have brought him home for you to welcome him, as you have welcomed me.'

One of Cleopatra's midwives stepped forward with the child and Julius took his son in his arms. The boy began to scream with astonishing ferocity, the sound echoing back and forth across the forum. It tore at the heart of Calpurnia as she watched the pride of the man she adored. She had lost him, and she turned away.

The citizens of Rome roared their approval as Julius turned in place to show them all. Their emotions had always been his to command and he knew they loved a show above all things. Julius laughed aloud with delight at their response, before passing his son back to the disapproving nurse. The crowd's reaction had frightened the child and there was no comforting him as she bustled away.

'I have dreams of a world where Roman courts judge the laws from the furthest edges of Africa to the frozen lands of the north. You will tell your children that you were here when Caesar returned. You will tell them the new world began on that day. We will *make* it new, and greater than that which has gone before.'

He quietened them once more, patting empty air with his hands. 'These things do not come without a cost, or without labour. Good Roman sweat and even blood will be shed before we can make an age of gold for our children and theirs. I do not fear the price. I do not fear the work. I do not fear these things because I *am* a Roman citizen, of the greatest city in the world.'

He turned away from the crash of their cheers, almost glowing with pleasure. The senators at his back had lost the smiles of reflected glory. Their eyes had hardened and grown cold as the words spilled out over the forum, lighting flames in the hearts of the mob. More than one of the older men wondered whether he could be controlled at all.

After the applause and grandiloquent speeches, the senate house seemed to be filled with echoing ghosts as evening came. The celebrations would continue for days, and as Cicero stood alone in shadows he could hear muted laughter and old songs in the forum. There would be little time for peace or contemplation in the days ahead, at least until the wine had run dry. He wondered how many children would be conceived across the city and how many of them would be named for the man Rome honoured.

He sighed to himself. An amphora of good red lay at his feet, unopened. He had intended to be among the first to toast Caesar, but somehow he had forgotten it as he witnessed the new breeze blowing through the city. The Republic had died at last, and the tragedy was that no one seemed to have noticed. What men like Pompey or Sulla could not achieve with fear and force of arms, Caesar had with indifference, shattering the traditions of centuries.

Cicero had known hope at first, when Julius stood to address the members of the nobilitas. Pompey's death had not stained him and Cicero thought the old compact with the citizens could still be remade.

That thin faith had lasted only moments. The laws of Rome were there to limit power and prestige, so that no man could rise too far above his fellows. Even in the dying days, there was strength enough to rein in Marius or Sulla. Somehow, Caesar had dragged himself above the rest, away from Rome. He had addressed the Senate as if they were supplicants, while the mob chanted his name outside.

Cicero could not find it in himself to love the people of his city. In the abstract, he took pride in the earnest voting that was the foundation of the Republic. The powers of the Senate had always been granted rather than taken. Yet in the end, those same citizens had found themselves a champion. There was no holding Caesar now, if there ever had been.

Cicero shook his head as he remembered how Julius had accepted the trite speeches of senators. He had let them talk, but when he rose the Republic fell away from him like an old skin. The scribes had been aching by the time he had finished and the senators who had welcomed him could only sit in stunned awareness.

Cicero rose slowly to his feet, wincing as his knees cracked. The noise of the city seemed to surround the senate house and he shuddered at the thought of going out through the drunken crowd. Would it have been different if they could have heard Caesar speak? He had promised to remake Rome: a new forum, great temples and roads, coins minted fresh from the gold of Gaul. His supporters would all have places in the Senate, his legions would be given the best lands and made wealthy. He planned four Triumphs over the months to come, more than any general of Rome had ever had. Gods, there was no end to it! In the midst of all the promises, Cicero had been desperate to hear some sign that Julius needed the Senate. Just a word to salve their dignity would have been enough, but it did not come. He told them the future and it never occurred to him that every word he spoke went further to cut himself free of them.

It was not how they had planned it, Cicero remembered. When Mark Antony had read the letters Julius sent from Egypt, they had discussed how they might honour the greatest general under Rome. In private, they had wondered whether he would accept the Senate at all. Cicero had voted with the others to bestow a Dictatorship of ten years, unheard of in history. The balanced scales of the Republic had been thrown down. It was all they could do.

Julius had nodded at the news as if it was no more than he had expected, and Cicero had known despair. He had not missed the significance of Julius holding his son up to the voracious mob. The man had no true peers to lay a hand on his shoulder and force him to caution. Cicero wondered if Caesar's Triumphs would include the boy to ride with him and whisper, 'Remember, you are mortal' into his ear.

The bronze doors creaked and Cicero jerked around to see who dared to breach the privacy of the Senate. Surely there were guards outside? He would not have been surprised to hear they had succumbed to drink and the hysterical crowd were stumbling in to vomit in the halls of their masters.

'Who is there?' he called, ashamed to hear the quaver in his voice. It was the nervous tone of an old man, he thought bitterly.

'Suetonius,' came a reply. 'I tried your home, but Terentia said you had not come back. She is worried about you.'

Cicero sighed aloud in a mixture of relief and irritation. 'Can a man not find a little quiet in this city?' he demanded.

'You should not be sitting in the dark,' Suetonius replied, walking out of the gloom. He could not meet Cicero's eyes at first and the air of defeat hung heavily around him. He too had been there to hear Caesar speak.

Outside, someone began an ancient song of lost love and the crowd in the forum joined the single voice. The harmonies were rough, but beautiful nonetheless. Cicero was tempted to go out and add his broken wind to theirs, just to be part of it before the day brought back its hard realities.

Suetonius tilted his head to listen. 'They don't know him,' he whispered.

Cicero glanced up, shaken from his thoughts. In the semi-darkness, Suetonius' eyes were shadows.

'Are we to be his servants, then?' he asked. 'Is that all we have achieved?'

Cicero shook his head, more for himself than for his companion. 'You must practise patience in this city, Senator. It will remain long after we are all dead.'

Suetonius snorted in disgust. 'What do I care for that? You heard his plans, Cicero. You nodded your head with all the others who would not dare speak up.'

'You did not speak,' Cicero reminded him.

'Alone, I could not,' Suetonius snapped.

'Perhaps we all felt alone, even as you did.'

'He needs us, to rule,' Suetonius said. 'Does he think our dominions will run themselves? Did you hear one word of thanks for the work we have done in his absence? I did not.'

Cicero found himself growing angry at the whining tone that reminded him of his children. 'He does *not* need us,' he snapped. 'Can't you understand? He has armies loyal only to him and he has taken the mantle of power. We are the last embers of the old Rome, fanning ourselves alive with our own breath. The great men are all dead now.'

In the forum, he heard the song reach its final poignant lines before a wave of cheering broke out.

'What do we do then?' Suetonius asked.

His voice was plaintive and Cicero winced to hear it. He did not answer for a long time.

'We find some way to bind him to us,' he said at last. 'The people love him today and tomorrow, but after that? They will have spent the money he gives them and they will need more than dreams to fill their stomachs, more than golden promises. Perhaps they will even need us again.'

He rubbed his sandal on the polished floor as he thought. The weakness of the younger man had stung him into anger and his thoughts came faster.

'Who else can pass the laws he wants, or grant him honours? They do not come simply because he shouts it in the forum. It is a weight of centuries that he has pushed aside. It may yet swing back with even greater force.'

'So that is how you respond?' Suetonius asked. Cicero could hear the sneering tone and it infuriated him. 'We shall resist him by passing every law? By honouring him further?'

With an effort, Cicero controlled his temper. He had so few allies now. Even a man of this calibre could not be scorned.

'If we baulk his will, we will be swept away. This senate house will fill again in hours with men more willing to bow their heads. Where is the gain in such a course?' He paused to wipe sweat from his face. 'We must *never* let him see he can walk alone. He suspects it already, but he does not know it in his stomach, where it matters. If you told him he could disband the Senate on a whim, he would be appalled. It is a dangerous line to walk, but while we stand as a body, there is hope. If we force his hand, there is none.'

'You are frightened of him,' Suetonius said.

'So should you be,' Cicero replied.

CHAPTER THIRTY-THREE

In gardens that had once belonged to Marius, Julius sat by a fountain, rubbing his thumb over a thick gold coin. Brutus munched on a chicken leg, enjoying the peace. The daily Senate meeting would already have resumed, but neither man felt any urgency. Unseasonable heat had come to Rome, long after the summer had ended. With the new spring only a month away, the short days should have been wet and cold, but instead the Tiber had shrunk and the city suffered in thick air and heat. While Rome baked, Julius and Brutus had eaten and slept. The cool of evening would dispel the pleasant lethargy, but for the moment they were content to lounge in the sun, each lost in his own thoughts.

Brutus saw the small movement of Julius' fingers and reached out for the coin, grunting as Julius passed it over.

'It makes you look a little thinner than you really are,' he said, holding the aureus up to the sun. 'And I notice you have more hair.'

Julius touched his head self-consciously and Brutus flipped the coin back to him.

'It still amazes me sometimes,' Julius said. 'This coin will travel for thousands of miles, through the hands of strangers. Perhaps long after me, someone will hand a copy of my face over in exchange for a saddle or a plough.'

Brutus raised an eyebrow. 'The face, of course, will give it value, not the gold,' he said.

Julius smiled. 'All right, but it's still strange to think of men and women I will never meet – who will never see Rome even – but who will carry my face in their purses. I hope they do give it a glance before they exchange it.'

'You expect too much of people. You always did,' Brutus said seriously. 'They'll take the land and coin you give them and next year they'll be back to clamour for more.'

Julius raised a hand, shutting weary eyes. 'Is this the colonies again? I've heard the speeches from Suetonius. He called it corruption to give the poor of Rome their dignity. You tell me how it damages a man to give him a little land and coin to get the first crop in the ground? With my own funds I gave eighty thousand a new chance in life, and the only protests came from the pampered men of my own Senate.' He snorted in indignation. 'It's been a year, Brutus, have the exiles come back yet? Have they turned up as beggars in the forum? I haven't seen them.' He frowned fiercely, waiting to be contradicted.

Brutus shrugged, tossing the chicken bone over his shoulder to land in the fountain. 'For myself, I have never worried whether some peasant farmer will live or die. Some will starve or gamble away what you gave them. Others will be robbed. Perhaps a thousand will survive the first year working a trade they don't understand. Rome has fewer beggars, though, which is pleasant. I can't argue with you there.'

'Suetonius described it as both "courageous and flawed", as if it were a child's idea.'

'They did not try to stop you,' Brutus said.

'They wouldn't dare to try!' Julius snapped. 'I could count the useful minds in the Senate on one hand. The rest are fawning idiots who can't see further than their own vanity.'

Brutus looked sharply at the man he had known for so many

years. 'Can they be anything else? They are the Senate you wanted. They raise statues to you over Rome and invent new honours just for a nod of approval from you. Were you expecting passionate debate when just a word could have them dragged out by your guards? You've made them what they are, Julius.' He reached over to take the coin again, reading from it. 'They have made you "Dictator Perpetuus", and now they are struggling to find more pretty words to gild your name. How it must sicken you.'

Julius sighed and closed his eyes for a moment. 'I have earned anything they can think of,' he said softly.

When his eyes opened, Brutus could not meet the cold gaze.

'Well, have I not?' Julius demanded. 'Tell me where I have over-reached myself, since my return. Have my promises not been made good? Ask the Tenth, or the Fourth you once commanded. They would not see any harm in my appointments.'

Brutus sensed the rising temper and cooled his own. Julius allowed him a greater freedom than anyone else, more even than Mark Antony, but he was not an equal.

'You have done what you said you would,' he replied, neutrally.

Julius narrowed his eyes as he looked for some hidden meaning, then his face cleared and Brutus felt sweat break out on his skin in relief.

'It has been a good year,' Julius said, nodding to himself. 'My son grows and in time I think the people will accept Cleopatra.'

Brutus forced his mouth shut, knowing the subject was tender. The citizens had welcomed the new temple to Venus. On the day of its consecration, they had come in great numbers to admire the work and leave offerings. Inside, they found the goddess had the face of the Egyptian queen. To Julius' fury, someone had defaced the statue by painting golden nipples on it. A permanent guard had to be posted and a reward offered for the names of those responsible. As yet, it had gone unclaimed.

Brutus did not dare look at Julius in case his glowering

expression made him laugh. He could only be pushed so far and Brutus was adept at finding the limit whenever his bitterness needed some outlet. Pricking at Julius' vanity was a dangerous pleasure, indulged only when he could no longer bear the constant stream of festivals and Triumphs.

Unnoticed, Brutus wound his fingers into a knot. He wondered if the citizens ever hungered for the honest tedium of normal life. The city had no routine when the Dictator could announce another great games or suddenly decide his latest Triumph would last another week. The citizens would always cheer and drink what they were given, but Brutus imagined a strained edge to their voices that matched his own dissatisfaction.

He had enjoyed the Triumph scenes of Gaul, with a lice-ridden Vercingetorix dragged in chains to a public execution. Brutus had been given the best seats to witness the death of wolves and boar. Even the Tiber had been dammed to fill a circus with water stained red by fighting ships on its surface. Wonder had followed wonder and the Senate had responded in a desperate frenzy, calling Julius 'Imperator' and Dictator for Life. His latest statue had a simple plaque to the 'Unconquered God', and when Brutus had seen it, he had drunk himself unconscious and lost two days.

There were times when he thought he should just take a horse and leave Rome. Julius had showered him with enough wealth to buy a house and live in comfort. When he was sick of it all, he dreamed of taking ship somewhere too far for Julius to reach and finding his own kind of peace there. He did not know if such a place existed any longer. He returned to Julius like a child to a festering scab, plumbing new depths of misery with a horrified fascination.

'Are you going to the senate house?' Brutus asked just to break the silence.

Julius blew air through his lips. 'Back to the talking shop, where I can buy a thousand words for a bronze coin? No, I have letters

401

to write to the kings of Parthia. I have not forgotten those who caused the death of Crassus and his son. It is an old debt, but I will answer it for those who can't speak.'

'I thought you were still drunk on the pleasures of Rome,' Brutus said, softly. 'Are you sniffing the spring wind again?'

Julius smiled at the image. 'Perhaps. I may be an old warhorse, my friend, but an empire does not build itself from a comfortable seat in the Senate. I must be seen.'

'The Tenth are old men now,' Brutus replied. 'I would never have believed it, but they went to the farms and houses you gave them without looking back.'

Julius snorted. 'There are new men to blood, Brutus. New legions that have never heard the battle horns or marched to exhaustion as we have. What would you have me do when my last Triumph has ended, sit and smile until my son is grown? I am not a man for the quiet times. I never have been.' He smiled. 'But there is still the Egyptian Triumph to come. A host of scribes and architects arrive in just a few hours to plan it.' Julius stared off into space as he contemplated bringing Rome to a standstill once more. 'It will be the greatest in the city's history, Brutus, I guarantee it.'

'How can it be, after the last one? They're still talking about the sea battle in the Campus,' Brutus said, remembering to hide his distaste.

The vast stone bowl had been shallow enough to see the dead clustered like dark coral on the bottom. In tiny galleys, captured warriors had struggled against criminals and men condemned to death. The pale waters had become a broth and when it was drained back into the Tiber, the river itself had run red. The scent of rotting flesh crept through Rome for days afterwards.

Julius clapped him on the shoulder, rising to his feet and stretching. 'I have something new in mind for my last Triumph.' He seemed on the verge of revealing his plans, then he chuckled.

'I will make sure you have a seat in the forum for the climax. You should bring this new wife of yours.'

Brutus nodded, knowing he wouldn't. He wondered if his mother would be interested in seeing Julius parade his queen and swollen ego one more time.

'I'm looking forward to it,' he said.

When the Senate meeting ended, Mark Antony made his way up from the forum to Julius' home. He walked with six armed lictors at his back, though he hardly noticed them, nor how the crowds parted before his tread.

In Julius' absence, he had expected a livelier debate than usual in the Senate. He should have known better. The empty seat had more menace than the presence of the man. They all knew the meeting would be reported in full detail. Julius' scribes recorded the most inane of conversations and even those like Cicero were made nervous by their incessant scribbling.

There had been times when the subject under discussion brought back some of the old honesty and fire Mark Antony remembered. Julius had abolished the tax system of Roman domin-ions, devolving the right to collect coins to local men in a dozen countries. The Greeks knew better than to let revenues fall after their last failed rebellion, but the praetor of Spain had made the trip to Rome to complain of new levels of corruption. It was the sort of thing that had been meat and drink to the Senate before the civil war. Some of the subtle restraint had slipped away as they wrangled and argued over details and proposals.

Mark Antony could still see the moment when Cassius had implied the problem was with the system itself, his glance straying to the scribe who faithfully recorded his words. The senator's thin face had paled slightly and his fingers had begun to tap nervously on the lectern. After that, the debate had foundered and the praetor of Spain had been sent home with no new resolution to his problems.

It was not how Mark Antony had dreamed it would be, when Julius gave him command of Italy years before. While the civil war wound through to a conclusion, Rome had been peaceful. It was true that he had made no great changes, but the city had been stable and she prospered. Men who applied for trading rights knew that they would be considered on their merits. The Senate passed difficult points of law on to the courts and accepted the decisions made, whether they approved or not. Mark Antony had worked harder than at any other time in his life and had taken a quiet satisfaction from the order in the city.

That had changed when Julius returned. The courts still functioned, but no one was foolish enough to bring a charge against a favourite of Caesar. The rule of law had lost its foundation and Mark Antony found himself sickened by the new attitude of caution. He and Cicero had spent many evenings in discussion, though even then they had been forced to send their servants away. Julius had spies all over Rome and it was rare to find a man who cared so little for his life that he was willing to speak out against the Dictator, even in private.

It had been a long year, Mark Antony thought to himself as he walked up the hill. Longer than any other in Roman history. The new calendar had set the city in an uproar of misunderstandings and chaos. Julius had declared that it would last for four hundred and forty-five days, before his new months could begin. The freak summer that had hit so late seemed just a symptom of the confusion, as if the seasons themselves had been upset. With a smile, Mark Antony remembered Cicero's complaint that even the planets and stars had to run to Caesar's order.

In older days, the city would have employed astronomers from all over the world to test the notions Julius had brought back from Egypt. Instead, the Senate had vied with each other to acclaim the new system and have their names reach Caesar's ears.

Mark Antony sighed as he reached the street gate to the old Marius property. The general he had known in Gaul would have scorned the attitude that had infected the august Senate. He would have allowed them their dignity, to honour the traditions if for no other reason.

Mark Antony took a deep breath and gripped the bridge of his nose in hard fingers. The man he had known would resurface, he hoped. Of course Julius had gone a little wild on his return. He had been drunk with the success of a civil war and a new son. He had been plunged from a life of struggle into a great city that hailed him as a god. It had turned his head, but Mark Antony remembered Julius when Gaul was a cauldron of war, and he still looked for a sign that the worst was over.

Julius was waiting for him inside, as Mark Antony passed through the gardens. He left his lictors on the street rather than bring armed men into the presence of the Dictator of Rome.

Julius embraced him and ordered iced drinks and food to be brought over his protests. Mark Antony saw that Julius seemed unusually nervous and his hand shook slightly as he held out a cup of wine.

'My last Triumph is almost ready,' Julius said, after both men had made themselves comfortable. 'I have a favour to ask of you.'

Brutus lay on his stomach and groaned at the stiff fingers that worked themselves into old scars and muscles. The evening was cool and quiet and his mother's house still employed the very best of girls. It was his habit to come and go as he pleased and his moods were well known to the women Servilia employed. The girl who used her elbows to work at a knot of muscle had not said a word since he stripped naked and lay down on the long bench, his dangling arms grazing the floor. Brutus had felt the unspoken invitation as she let her oiled hands linger, but he had not responded. His mind was too filled with despair and anger to find release in her practised embrace.

He opened his eyes as he heard light footsteps tap across the floor of the room. Servilia was there, wearing a sardonic expression as she viewed the naked flesh of her son.

'Thank you, Talia, you may leave us,' she said.

Brutus frowned at the interruption. Without embarrassment, he pushed himself up and sat on the bench as the girl scurried out. His mother did not speak until the door had closed and Brutus raised an eyebrow in interest. She too knew his moods and allowed him privacy when he came to the house. To have broken the routine meant something else was in the wind.

Her hair was a cloud grey, almost white now that she had abandoned her dyes and colours. It no longer hung loose, but was tied back with pinned severity. She still stood with the erect posture that had drawn men's eyes in her youth, but age had melted the flesh from her, so that she was lean and hard. Brutus supposed he loved her, for her dignity and refusal to be broken in the life of Rome.

She had been there in the forum when Julius held up his son, but when Brutus had come to the house that first evening, she had shown him a cool reserve that demanded respect. He might have believed it, if there had not been moments when fire flashed in her eyes at the mention of Julius' name. Then she would raise her hand to touch the great pearl that was always around her neck and look into distances too far for Brutus to follow.

'You should dress yourself, my son. You have visitors waiting for you,' she said. The toga he had worn lay folded and Servilia brought it to him as he stood. 'You go naked under this?' she asked, before he could speak.

Brutus shrugged. 'When it is hot. What visitors do you mean? No one knows I am here.'

'No names, Brutus, not yet,' she said as she draped the long cloth around his shoulders. 'I asked them here.'

Brutus regarded his mother in irritation. His gaze flickered to his dagger where it lay on a stool. 'I do not share my movements with the city, Servilia. Are the men armed?'

She tucked and tweaked at the robe until it was ready to be clasped. 'They are no danger to you. I told them you would listen to what they have to say. Then they will leave and Talia can finish her work, or you can join me for a meal in my rooms.'

'What are you doing, Mother?' Brutus asked, his voice growing hard. 'I don't like games or mysteries, or secrets.'

'See these men. Listen to them,' she said, as if he had not spoken. 'That is all.' She watched in silence as he tucked his dagger away and then she stood back to look at him. 'You look strong, Brutus. Age has given you more than scars. I will send them in.'

She left and moments later the door swung open to admit two men of the Senate. Brutus knew them instantly and he narrowed his eyes in suspicion. Suetonius and Cassius were stiff with tension as they closed the door behind them and approached.

'What is so important that you must come to my mother's house?' Brutus said. He crossed his arms carefully, leaving his right hand near the hilt of his dagger under the cloth.

Cassius spoke first. 'Where else is private, in Rome?' he said.

Brutus could see the sinews standing out in the man's neck and he wondered if his mother had been foolish enough to invite assassins into her home. The senator was clearly under an enormous strain and Brutus disliked being so close to him.

'I will hear what you have to say,' Brutus said, slowly.

He gestured to the bench and watched closely as both men sat down. He did not join them, preferring to remain able to move quickly if the need arose. Every instinct warned him to caution, but he showed them nothing. The hilt of his knife was comforting under his fingers.

'We will have no names, here,' Cassius said. 'It is dark outside and we have not been seen. We have never met, in fact.' His taut features stretched into an unpleasant smile.

'Go on,' Brutus said, sharply, anger surfacing. 'My mother has bought you a few moments. If you can say nothing of use, then leave.'

The two men exchanged glances and Cassius swallowed nervously.

Suetonius cleared his throat. 'There are some in the city who have not forgotten the Republic,' he said. 'There are some who do not enjoy the Senate being treated as servants.'

Brutus took in a sharp breath as he began to understand. 'Go on,' he said.

'Those who love Rome may be dissatisfied with too much power in one man's hands,' Suetonius continued. A fat bead of sweat worked its way down his cheek from his hairline. 'They do not want a line of kings built on a corruption of foreign blood.'

The words hung in the air between them and Brutus stared, his thoughts whirling. How much had his mother guessed of their intentions? All their lives were in danger if even a single one of her girls listened at the walls.

'Wait here,' he said, striding to the door.

The sudden movement brought Cassius and Suetonius almost to panic. Brutus flung open the door and saw his mother seated down the corridor. She rose to her feet and walked to him.

'Are you part of this?' he said, his voice low.

Her eyes glittered. 'I have brought you together. The rest is up to you.'

Brutus looked at his mother and saw her coldness was a mask.

'Listen to them,' she said again, as he hesitated.

'Are we alone?' he asked.

She nodded. 'No one knows they are here, or that they are meeting you. This is my house and I know.'

Brutus grimaced. 'You could get us all killed,' he said.

Her smile mocked him. 'Just listen to them, and be quick,' she said.

He closed the door then and turned to face the two senators. He knew what they wanted, but it was too much to take in at once. 'Go on,' he said again to Suetonius.

'I speak for the good of Rome,' Suetonius replied in the old formula. 'We want you to join us in this.'

'In what?' Brutus demanded. 'Say the words or get out.'

Suetonius took a slow breath. 'We want you for a death. We want you to help us bring back the power of the Senate. There are weak men there who will vote in a new king if they are not restrained.'

Brutus felt cold with an unnatural fear. He could not demand they speak the name. He did not know if he could bear to hear it.

'How many are with you?' he said.

Suetonius and Cassius exchanged another glance of warning.

'Perhaps it is better for you not to know at this time,' Cassius said. 'We have not heard your answer.'

Brutus did not speak and Cassius' face hardened subtly.

'You *must* answer. We have gone too far to let it rest now.'

Brutus looked at the two men and knew they could not let him live if he refused. There would be archers outside to cut him down as he left. It was how he would have planned it.

It did not matter. He had known from the beginning what he would say.

'I am the right man,' he said in a whisper. The tension began to ease from the pair. 'There must be some trust in this, but I do not want my mother involved again,' Brutus went on. 'I will rent another house for us to meet.'

'I had thought . . .' Suetonius began.

Brutus silenced him with a wave of his hand. 'No. I am the right man to *lead* you in this. I will not risk my life on fools and secrets. If this is to be done, let it be done well.' He paused, taking a deep breath. 'If we are to risk our lives for the good of Rome, it must be before spring. He plans a campaign in Parthia that will take him away, perhaps for years.'

Cassius smiled in triumph. He stood and held out his hand.

'The Republic is worth a life,' he said as Brutus gripped his thin fingers.

CHAPTER THIRTY-FOUR

From the highest rooftops, the petals of red roses filled the air by the million, drifting down on the Dictator's procession. The citizens of Rome reached up to them like children, entranced. For weeks, they had walked to the city from their farms and homes, drawn by the lure of glory and spectacle. The price of a bed had soared, but Julius had given every family a bag of silver, a jug of sweet oil and corn to make bread. The city had been rich with the smell of baking as they rose at dawn to watch Julius sacrifice a white bull at the temple of Jupiter. The omens had been good, as he had known they would be.

He had employed hundreds in the arrangements for the Triumph, from the ex-legion adventurers charged with capturing animals in Africa, to the stonemasons given the task of recreating Alexandria in Rome. Statues of Egyptian gods lined the route through the city and by noon many were draped with climbing children, laughing and calling to one another.

The ancient streets had a festive air, with every junction festooned in bright banners fluttering gaily over the city. By nightfall, there would be many girls with Julius to thank for a wedding dress from the material. Until then, Rome was a riot of colour and noise.

The column that wound its way through the main streets at noon was more than a mile long and lined at every step by cheering citizens. Soldiers of the Tenth and Fourth had been recalled from retirement to lead Julius through the city. They walked like heroes and those who knew their history showed appreciation at the sight of the men who had taken Gaul and beaten Pompey at Pharsalus.

The gladiators of Rome marched wearing heads of falcons and jackals, while chained leopards spat and struggled to the delight of the crowd.

In the heart of the procession was its centrepiece, a huge carriage more than twenty feet high, with sphinxes to the fore and rear. Eighty white horses heaved against the traces, tossing their heads. Julius and Cleopatra sat together on a balustraded platform, flushed with the success of the spectacle. She wore cloth of blood red that showed her stomach had regained its lines from before the birth. Her eyes were painted darkly and her hair was bound in gold. For this formal occasion, she wore rubies that shone on her ears and throat. Rose petals fluttered about them both and Julius was in his element, pointing out the wonders of Rome to her as they inched through the city. His aureus coins had been thrown like rain onto outstretched hands below and free wine and food would fill every stomach in Rome to bursting.

Cleopatra herself had sent for the best temple dancers in Egypt, not trusting Julius' agents to judge their quality. A thousand pretty girls whirled and leapt to the strange music of her home and the sight of their flashing bare legs drew smiles of appreciation from the crowds. They carried sticks of incense in their hands and their movements were followed by thin smoke trails that filled the streets in lingering pungency. It was sensuous and wild and Cleopatra laughed aloud with the pleasure of it. She had made the right choice, in Caesar. His people were noisy in their appreciation, and she found herself exhilarated by the life of the city. There was so much energy in them! These were the ones who built galleys and bridges and laid pipes for hundreds of miles. The waving crowd thought nothing of crossing chasms and oceans and the world to bring trade. From their wombs came soldiers like men of brass to carry on the work.

Her son would be safe in the care of such a people, she was certain. Egypt would be safe.

It took hours to make their way through Rome, but the crowds did not grow tired of the sights and sounds of another continent. Teams of hunters had trapped a huge male gorilla that Cleopatra knew had never seen the Nile. The beast bellowed at the citizens as they gazed in awe, pulling back in fear and laughing as it hammered its great arms against solid bars. Julius planned to have the monster fight a team of swordsmen in the circus and there could have been no better advertisement than its rage. His people loved new things and Julius had brought the strangest animals of Africa for their enjoyment.

When the forum came into sight once more, Cleopatra had retired behind the screens of the carriage, a room of silk and gold that jolted along in restful motion. Her slaves were there to bring her cool drinks and food, though her son was safely asleep in the old house of Marius. With a few quick movements, she shrugged out of her dress to stand naked, holding her arms out for a costume even richer than the last. The rubies went into a chest and great emeralds on silver clasps were fastened at her wrists and ankles. Tiny bells chimed as her slaves dressed her and touched fresh kohl to her eyes. Let them stare at the queen Julius had found, she thought. Let them envy.

As the music of her people swelled from below, Cleopatra danced a few steps of a sequence she had learned as a girl, pressing down on the wooden floor with small, firm feet. She heard Julius laugh as he saw her, and she twirled in place to please him.

'I will toast you in the best wine of Rome when I am finished here,' he said, his eyes tender. 'Let them see you now, while I go down to them.'

Cleopatra bowed her head. 'Your will, master.'

He smiled at her mock humility, stepping back into public view. The horses had been halted and the proud men of the Tenth had made a path for him to a raised platform with a single chair. Julius lingered at the top of the steps, enjoying the sight of the packed forum from such a vantage point.

Cleopatra came out and the crowd exclaimed at her new apparel, whistling and calling. Julius cast a glance up at her and wondered how many of the matrons of Rome would be sending new orders to seamstresses and tailors the following day.

As he touched the ground, the Tenth began to sing a mournful legion ballad he had not heard in years. The strings of the Egyptian musicians fell silent and the deep voices soared, recalling old battles and his youth. Julius had not planned this part of the Triumph and he found his eyes were stinging as he walked between the upright spears of men who knew him better than anyone.

As he strode over the stones, the line closed behind him and the crowd moved forward, with those who knew the words joining in. Even the cheering was drowned by the throats of thousands of old soldiers and Julius was deeply moved.

Mark Antony was already on the platform and Julius grew tense as he approached the final steps up to where he would speak. With an effort of will, he turned at the top and smiled at the people of Rome who had come to show their appreciation of his life.

The song died away with the final line repeated three times and the silence that followed was shattered by a great roar.

Julius glanced at Mark Antony, knowing it was time. He raised his hands as if to quiet them, while Mark Antony stepped forward. Julius stood very still, his heart racing fast enough to make him light-headed.

Mark Antony held a crown in his hands, a simple band of gold. Julius looked out over the crowd as it was placed on his head, listening, listening for a change in the voices of Rome.

The applause began to fail as they saw what had happened.

Julius waited as long as he could, painfully sensitive to the drop in volume. With a bitter smile, he forced himself to remove the crown before the cheering failed completely. Pale with tension, he handed it back.

The change was instant as the crowd responded, waves of sound that were almost a physical force. Julius could barely think at the heart of their bellowing, though a slow fury began to kindle in his breast.

On the steps of the senate house, a group of young men exchanged guarded glances as they witnessed the event. Suetonius frowned in suspicion and Cassius gripped the arm of another. They did not applaud and yell with the rest. They were a blot of silence in the noisy forum, with eyes that were cold and hard.

Mark Antony did not seem to have understood the reaction of the crowd, and he stepped forward again, pressing the crown onto Julius' brow. Julius raised a hand to touch the soft metal and knew they wanted him to refuse it once more. His hopes were dashed, but the play had to continue.

He pressed it back into Mark Antony's hands.

'No more,' he muttered through closed teeth, though his voice was lost in ten thousand others.

Mark Antony did not hear the warning. He had feared the worst when Julius had asked to be crowned in the forum. Now that he saw it was to be a demonstration of Republican honour, he was almost hysterical with excitement, buoyed up on the spirits of the citizens. Laughing, he raised the crown for a third time, and Julius lost his temper.

'Touch that thing to my head one more time and you'll never see Rome again,' he snapped, making Mark Antony fall back in confusion.

Julius' face was stained with rage. The gods alone knew what he would say to them now. The speech he had prepared had depended on their acceptance of the crown. He could not see

415

where he had failed, but he knew it was impossible to take the gold band again. They would think it a great game. He glanced up to where Cleopatra stood above the mob and shared a gaze of disappointment with her. She had known his hopes and to have them crushed before her eyes was more than he could stand.

Blind and ignorant to the reality before them, the crowd had quieted at last, waiting for him to speak. Julius stood as if dazed while he struggled to find something to say.

'There will come a day when Rome accepts a king once more,' he said at last, 'but it will not be today.'

They battered him with noise and he hid his anger and disappointment. It was all he could trust himself to say. He stepped down without waiting for his Tenth to form a path, but the people gave way in awe and dignity after what they had seen.

As he walked stiffly through them, he burned in humiliation. The Triumph had not finished yet. The horses and cages, dancers and carriages would make their way to his new forum and end at the temple of Venus. He vowed silently to himself that if the crowd failed to show proper appreciation there, blood would be shed before the day ended.

As the crowd moved on, a figure in silver armour turned towards the senate house steps, seeing the white togas of wolves he knew. Brutus understood far better than they what Julius had tried to do and the knowledge helped to firm his resolution and his strength. Rome would be washed clean and he would find his path without the shadow of Caesar to torment him.

The new spring would take Julius away from the capital. It would have to be soon.

Servilia lay awake in darkness, unable to sleep. The days had turned cold at last and Julius' calendar had begun as Februarius ended, bringing rain to a parched city. She could hear it pounding on the tiles overhead and sluicing through the gutters, carrying away the dust.

Her house was quiet, the final patrons having set out for their own homes hours before. Sleep should have come easily, but instead her aching joints could not rest as her thoughts raced and writhed in the dark.

She did not want to think of him, but memories stole through her, their brightness the sole consolation of weakening age. Even in the sun, she would find her thoughts drifting back to other times, but at night there was nothing to hold the flood of recollection that slid into troubled dreams.

She had loved him at the feet of Alexander and he had been hers, in flesh and spirit. She had been his. He had burned for her then, before the cruelty of experience had hardened him.

She sighed to herself, clutching blankets around her thin legs. There was no hope for rest, not on this night. Perhaps it was only right that she spend it in memory of him.

She could still see his face as he held up the son he had always wanted. If he had noticed her in the crowd, he had not recognised the white-haired old woman she had become. At the moment of his greatest joy, she had hated him with a passion her bones had almost forgotten. Brutus had known the shallowness of his love. She tasted bitterness in her throat at the thought of how she had once pleaded with her son. His betrayal had frightened her then, when Pompey had ruled Rome with iron. She had not listened to his warning that Julius would never need her as she had needed him.

She did not care about the pompous arguments of men like Suetonius and Cassius. She saw their jealousy for what it was, despite the honour they claimed. They were too small to love the Republic, or even to understand what it had once meant. Better by far to stand and say that they hated him because he did not notice them. Vanity and pride would be the strength that drove their knives. She knew it, as she had always known the hearts of men. They would play their games of passwords and whispers as they met in the shadows, but the truth did not frighten her as it did them. Her hatred was a clean thing.

She raised a hand to her face, surprised to find tears on her wrinkled skin. That was the reality of the years that stole, she thought. They took the joys and left only bitter pain and tears that came from emptiness.

How many wives had he taken to press his seed into life? Not once had he asked the whore he kept. Not once, even when there was life in her womb and her flesh was firm and strong. He had used her knowledge a hundred times against his enemies. She had kept him safe and now she had been forgotten. Her hands were claws in the cloth as she thought of his pride in his son. There was always a price to pay.

The rain increased in power as it swept across the city, and Servilia wept again. Rome would be clean by the dawn of the Ides of March. The past would no longer trouble her sleep.

CHAPTER THIRTY-FIVE

Julius walked alone through a waking city to the senate house. His son had disturbed his sleep with crying and he was red-eyed, rising as the market stalls and traders were still setting up for the business of the day.

He preferred Rome at these moments after rain, when the air smelled fresh and clean and the day stretched far ahead with promise. It was true that the wind was cold, but he wore a heavy tunic under his toga and the touch of frozen air was pleasant as he breathed deeply.

No guards were there to disturb the peace of the morning. He needed no lictors to frown at his people as they passed with their eyes downcast. They may not have accepted the crown Mark Antony had offered, but the man himself was untouchable. He did not fear them as men like Sulla and Pompey had feared. They had treated the citizens as violent children, terrified of the same force that had brought them to power. He needed no such protection. Julius sighed to himself as he strolled along the stone walkway, lost in thought.

Without Cleopatra, he might well have left Rome months before. When he was far away, he could love his city as an abstract. He could talk of his home in the same breath as Alexandria, Carthage and Athens, the centres of empires gone and still rising. The distance somehow lent a romance to the heaving ant-heap of reality. When Rome was thousands of miles to the west, he could see the glory of her scholarship, her inventions and trade. It was difficult to remember those things existed when he was suffocated amongst the petty rivalries and vanity of the Senate. There was such a chasm between the two. When he despaired, he saw only the worst face of the city of his birth. Life teemed there in filthy alleys and a few coins would have bought a woman, a man or a child. When it was hot, the city stank like an open drain and when there was frost, thousands starved and froze on a knife edge of survival. Those were the times when he could barely catch his breath. His inner vision crumbled against the hard truths and he ached to ride clear and leave it all behind.

To have the power to make changes had been intoxicating at first. Whatever he had the wit to imagine could be made, created new. It was a temporary joy, like so much else. He hungered for something he could never quite name and when fresh-faced generals had come with news of unrest in Parthia, he had not sent them away. Mark Antony would rule Rome again, or Octavian perhaps. He had earned the right to leave his mark on the city and until Julius' son became a man, the boy would need strong protectors. It would be Octavian, Julius decided, already imagining the expression on his face when he heard the news.

Outside the city, there were legions of young men gathering to march against the Parthians. His unease vanished in the presence of so much youthful hope. They had not been made cynical. They carried more than a sword and shield for Rome, he thought, groping for the idea. When they left, they carried a distilled form of the city with them, the purest part. It took them through pain and exhaustion. It kept their discipline when they saw death coming and suddenly knew it would *not* pass them by. By pledging their strength, each one of them gave a value to what they left behind.

They were saying 'This is worth my life.' And they made it so. There could be no value in a city without those young men to stand in the Campus.

Julius remembered what Brutus had said about the spring air raising his head and he smiled as he walked. It was true that the thought of another campaign had stirred his blood. His time in Rome had been everything he had wanted it to be. His Triumphs would be remembered for generations and the Senate had honoured him as no one else in history. Scipio would have given his right arm for the titles they had bestowed. Marius would have loved every moment.

Before Julius reached the bottom of the hill, he saw a lone figure in a toga so white it looked like winter frost. He frowned as the man began to walk in his direction. Could they do nothing until he had arrived? What new problem was so vexing and difficult that they must interrupt his thoughts before the day had even begun? He recognised Cassius as the man drew closer and bowed his head.

'Caesar, the Senate are meeting in Pompey's theatre this morning. I have stayed to let you know.'

'Why, what has happened?' Julius said, his calm evaporating.

'The Ides of March fall on the anniversary of Pompey being made consul, sir,' Cassius replied. 'It was decided to honour his family in this way. The resolution was passed in your absence. I was worried it might not have reached you, and . . .'

'All right, enough,' Julius snapped. 'I do not have time to read every line of the speeches.'

Cassius bowed his head again and Julius repressed his irritation at the intrusion. They fell into step together as they crossed the road on stepping stones and took a right turn that would take them over the Capitoline hill.

Without warning, Julius stopped suddenly.

'Sir?' Cassius asked.

'No, it's nothing. I was just thinking of an old man I knew, a long time ago.'

'I see, sir,' Cassius replied automatically.

'You are sweating, Cassius,' Julius observed. 'You should walk more often, for fitness.'

'It is a chill, sir, nothing more,' Cassius replied, staring ahead.

Pompey's theatre had been used as a second senate house many times since its completion. It could accommodate even the swollen numbers of new senators Julius had introduced since his return to the city. There was a certain pleasure in debating with the senators of Rome at the foot of Pompey's statue. It loomed over them all, a matchless casting that captured the stern features of the man in his prime.

As the sun rose, Julius was surprised to find only a few senators clustered around the main doors. They saw his arrival and two broke away to walk inside. Julius frowned at the thought of the work ahead. When he had been young, he had watched their discussions in something approaching awe. He had seen great men stand and dominate their fellows, changing Rome with the force of their thoughts and words. Julius had responded to the power of their oratory, been inspired by it.

It was the tragedy of experience that heroes lost the shine they had once had. Perhaps the new men he had brought into the ranks of the nobilitas still walked with soft steps as the laws were passed. He did not know if they did, or whether it was just that the great issues of the age had been decided. Perhaps he had seen the last of the grand figures to stride through Rome. He had known the men with strength enough to challenge the restrictions of the Republic. He had learned from them, but those battles were over, whether he wore a crown or not.

He passed through the entrance with barely a nod to those who stood around in the grey light, taking his place on a bench close to the central stage. He would speak today. Perhaps he would try once more to make them understand the need to expand the lands under Rome. He would speak even though they seemed deaf to the words he used; blind to the ideas. Rome could never rest on what had been brought to her feet. How many times had he seen small rebellions take fire throughout a country, the strength of the Senate tested from outside? From the Mytilene fort to Syria, he had been witness to the hawks that waited for Rome to nod in sleep, just once.

There were a thousand small kings in the world who bent their knee and still watched for a moment of weakness. Only a fool would give it to them. If Roman generals ever reached a line and said, 'This is far enough', that would be the end of a million lives given to reach that point. That would be the crack that would break the glass.

Julius was so deep in his inner thoughts that he did not notice Tillius Cimber approach him, striding along the curved line of benches. Julius assumed the younger man had stumbled when he felt a hand grip the cloth of his toga, yanking it aside.

In an instant, rage spiked in him as the man held on. Cimber's face was rigid with effort and Julius gripped his fingers with both hands, twisting at them.

'What are you doing?' Julius shouted at his attacker, struggling to stand.

He saw faces turn towards him from the corners of his eyes and more men rush to his aid. Through his fury, he knew he had only to wait for Cimber to be dragged away. The punishment for daring to lay a hand on him was death, and he would not be merciful.

Cimber was young and strong, but Julius had weathered like an oak on a thousand miles of march. His arms shook with the strain, yet he could not break the deathless fingers that writhed against his neck.

423

More men clustered around on the benches, crying out as they came closer. Julius saw Suetonius draw a dagger, his face flushed with vicious excitement. The shock strained at his heart as he understood at last what was happening. Cimber smiled as he saw the realisation come to the Dictator and he renewed his grip, holding Julius in place for Suetonius to strike.

Julius looked desperately around for anyone he could call. Where was Ciro? Brutus? Where was Octavian or Mark Antony? He bellowed as Suetonius gashed at him, the knife scoring a line of blood on his shoulder. Cimber's hold was broken by others who swarmed in to kill and Julius struck out blindly, yelling for help. He grunted as a knife sank into his side and was withdrawn to strike again.

A man fell across him, hindering the others. Julius was able to stand for a moment and raised his arm against a dagger slashing towards his neck. It sliced his hand and he cried out in agony, shoved back in his seat by the press of snarling men.

There was blood everywhere, staining their white togas and spattering their faces. Julius thought of his son and was terrified for what they would do to him. In his agony, he shoved one of his attackers backwards with fading strength. More knives punched into his legs as he kicked out in spasm.

He did not stop calling for help, knowing he could survive even the worst of the wounds. If Octavian could be summoned, he would strike fear into the animals that screamed and yelped around him in a frenzy.

Two of them held him by shoulders slippery with blood. Hot liquid bubbled from the corner of his mouth as his strength vanished. He could only look up in despair as they panted into his face, close enough to smell their breath.

'Wait,' he heard a voice say, somewhere close.

The bloody hands shoved Julius against the back of his seat and he turned in an agony of hope to see who had stopped them.

Brutus walked across the central floor of the theatre, his hands clasped behind his back. Even as Julius felt relief, he saw his old friend too carried a blade in his hand and he slumped brokenly. Blood poured from his wounds and his vision seemed to sharpen as every sense screamed to live. He felt the hands of his enemies fall away, but he could not move or fight them any longer.

'You too, Brutus?' he said.

Brutus stepped into the line of benches and raised his knife up to Julius' face. His eyes held a great sadness and a triumph Julius could not bear to witness.

'Yes,' Brutus replied softly.

'Then kill me quickly. I cannot live and know this,' Julius said, his voice a whisper.

The other men stood back in awe, seeing the blood they had released. Julius did not look at them. Slowly, without dropping his gaze from Brutus, he reached to the twisted folds of his toga and drew it slowly upwards.

Brutus watched in silence as Julius showed his contempt for them all. He bowed his head under the toga, folding his shaking hands into the cloth. Then he sat perfectly still and waited for death.

Brutus showed his teeth for an instant, then shoved his knife through the cloth, finding the heart. The tableau broke as the others joined him, stabbing and stabbing at the small figure until it slumped to the side and the last of life was gone.

The susurration of panting breath was the only sound in the world as Brutus looked around the men in the echoing theatre. Every eye was on the body that lay between the benches, limp and slick with blood. The dark liquid stained their faces and arms and rested in tiny droplets in their hair.

'He's dead at last,' Suetonius murmured, shaking as the draining frenzy left him weak and dazed. 'What happens now?'

The men who had come so far looked to Brutus for an answer.

'Now we walk out,' Brutus said. His voice shook. 'We *walk*. We go to the senate house and we tell them what we have done. We have cut the tyrant out of Rome and we will not go in shame.'

He saw Suetonius begin to wipe his knife clean and Brutus reached out a hand, stopping him.

'We will not hide the marks. Let the blood show the honour of those with courage to stand against a tyrant. This is how we have saved the Republic. Let it show. Now he is gone, Rome can begin to heal.'

His eyes glittered as he looked down at the figure of the man he had known and loved.

'We will honour him in death,' he said, almost too quietly to hear.

Those closest to the doors began to walk away and Brutus went with them. The rest followed, glancing back at the scene, as if to reassure themselves of its reality.

They walked red-handed on the ancient streets of Rome and they walked with pride.

HISTORICAL NOTE

Gaius Julius Caesar is remembered for much more than being an extraordinary general. It is true that there are few military leaders who could have equalled his strategic skill, or charismatic leadership, but that is only a part of the tale. Republican Rome may have eased into empire without Julius Caesar, but it could also have torn itself apart. In one of the hardest schools in history, Caesar rose to pre-eminence, finally crushing Pompey at Pharsalus. His life was the bridge between two eras of history; the catalyst for empire.

Throughout his career, he showed a fine understanding of politics, power and manipulation. I will not say he invented propaganda, but he must surely be one of its greatest and earliest exponents. Undermining Pompey through public displays of clemency was a deliberate policy. As Julius wrote in a letter, 'Let this be a new way of gaining victory; let us secure ourselves through mercy and magnanimity!'

Pompey never understood the technique, though Cicero clearly saw through at least part of it. He referred to the policy as 'insidious clemency' and said that 'Whatever evil he refrains from, arouses the same gratitude as if he had prevented another from inflicting it.'

Pompey was outmatched from the start of the civil war, when he demanded the Gaul general return to Rome without the support of his legions. Caesar spent a night of soul-searching on the river Rubicon where he debated whether the loss of life resulting from a civil war would be worth his own. With characteristic self-belief, he decided it would be and launched a lightning strike south, at such a speed that Pompey was caught completely by surprise. He could not defend the city and even forgot to empty the treasury in his haste to leave. Not that it was needed. The vast sums of gold Caesar brought back from Gaul devalued the Roman aureus by an astonishing *thirty* per cent.

The incident on the feast of Bona Dea was as I have described it, including the fact that Publius dressed as a woman to escape detection. Publius was actually found innocent of adultery by a court, but Caesar divorced his wife anyway, saying that 'Caesar's wife must be above suspicion.' Having an heir was no doubt increasingly important to him and he would have understood the need for a son's legitimacy to be beyond question.

For reasons of plot and length, I have omitted battles in Spain and Africa as Julius and his generals crushed legions loyal to Pompey. When the time came for him to seek Pompey in Greece, he gave control of Italy to Mark Antony and, as a result, Marcus Brutus betrayed him for the first time, joining Pompey against his old friend. Julius gave orders for him to be spared if possible in what, for me, is one of the most poignant scenes in the history. Forgiving Brutus after such a betrayal shows Caesar's greatness as nothing else.

Julius landed in Oricum on the west coast of Greece. I have not included the fact that he had to return to Italy in a small boat to fetch more men. The boat hit a storm and Caesar is reported to have told the boatmen not to fear, saying that they carried 'Caesar and his fortune.' He was a great believer in his own luck and this seems to have been borne out through the events of his life.

He did manage to take Dyrrhachium from Pompey's control, after an exhausting night march.

Though the centurion Decimus is fictional, one of Caesar's officers did take his own life when captured, saying that he was used to dispensing mercy rather than receiving it. The disdain this shows can only be imagined. Another small change is that Cicero's wife Terentia was in fact in Rome during the civil war. She did not travel to Greece.

Pompey's failure may have been in part due to an illness, for which there is some evidence, or simply the fact that he was facing a Roman enemy with the most astonishing record of any general alive. It may have been that having the Senate with him was a greater handicap than we can know. Either way, Pompey had twice as many men and at least four times the cavalry. He should not have needed to build fortifications and fight a defensive war.

At one point, Pompey had victory for the taking. The disastrous pincer attack on Pompey's forces is a real event. One of the sides was held up and Caesar's cohorts were routed. Caesar grabbed the standard and tried to rally the fleeing men, but they went around him, leaving him alone. Pompey was convinced it was an ambush and did not pursue the fleeing forces, leading Julius to comment, 'Today, victory would have gone to our opponents if they had someone who knew how to win.' He lost nine hundred and sixty soldiers in the rout. Those who were captured were executed by Labienus. Pompey had lost the best chance he would ever have. The senators with Pompey were contemptuous of his unwillingness to close with the enemy. They demanded that he wage a more aggressive war and eventually he agreed.

At Pharsalus, Pompey commanded troops from Spain and Syria, Gaul, Germany and Macedonia as well as Roman legionaries. Caesar gives the numbers of Pompeian cavalry as 7,000, though it seems likely to have been an exaggeration.

The interesting incident of Pompey holding back his front line is well attested, though different reasons are suggested in various sources. My own feeling, based on Pompey's ten deep lines, is that morale was appalling amongst his men and he saw nervousness in the ranks as Caesar's army approached. Needless to say, it is a uniquely poor decision from the general who destroyed Spartacus and cleared the Mediterranean of pirates. The true state of Pompey's mind can never now be known. His private papers were left behind after Pharsalus and Julius had them burnt without looking at them.

I have followed the main events of Pharsalus as far as they are known. Pompey used his cavalry to rout Caesar's on the right wing. It took time for Pompey's riders to re-form and turn and in that period Caesar's smaller force came back and attacked them from behind, driving their own men into their lines. Caesar's extraordinarii pushed on to destroy the archers and broke through to hit the flank and rear of Pompey's lines. A full rout followed quickly after that.

The inescapable conclusion regarding Pharsalus is that Caesar should not have been able to win. Pompey had every advantage, but still his men folded before the veterans. Julius, it should be remembered, was a lawfully elected consul with a record of extraordinary, unprecedented shows of mercy. Corfinium is only one example in the civil war where he pardoned men who fought against him. His policy was intended to undermine Pompey in the field and it seems to have worked. I believe Pharsalus is as much a triumph of propaganda and perception as it is a military victory.

Caesar was indeed given a jar containing Pompey's head on the docks of Alexandria. The Egyptians did not want a Roman war in their lands, though this attempt to avert one was to prove futile. Julius is recorded as having wept at the death of Pompey, though we can only guess at his reasons.

The Alexandria that Caesar would have seen is lost to the

modern world. As well as the Pharos lighthouse, one of the seven ancient wonders that no longer exists, most of the streets and buildings in this book are now underwater. Modern excavations are still finding statues of Cleopatra and the son she had with Caesar, Ptolemy Caesarion.

Perhaps it is not surprising that a Roman consul who had been at war for most of his adult life should suddenly give it all up on meeting the twenty-one-year-old Cleopatra. The story of her being delivered to Caesar by her Greek attendant is well attested, though some sources say it was a long bag rather than a rolled carpet.

Cleopatra was indeed a descendant of Ptolemy, one of Alexander's generals. She spoke five languages and was the first of her line to speak Egyptian. In her time, Alexandria was a real blend of cultures, with Greek colonnaded buildings and Egyptian statues in streets such as the Canopic Way.

The eunuch who played such a part in controlling the young Ptolemy was in fact named Pothinus, though I changed it so as not to have too similar a name to Porphiris, which I liked. Panek, in fact, means 'snake', which seemed appropriate. Caesar did give Cyprus back to the Egyptians as part of the negotiations after capturing the boy king. The scene where the young Ptolemy cried and refused to leave the barricaded palace is true. It is also true that on reaching his army and being dressed once again as the king, the thirteen-year-old ordered an immediate attack. He did not survive the struggle for power in Alexandria.

The body of Alexander the Great is also lost, though it rested in Alexandria in Caesar's time, in a coffin of glass, as I have described. The body was covered in gold leaf and, given his status as a pharaoh and god, had presumably been embalmed.

I have only skated over Caesar's marriage to Calpurnia, in 59 BC. Cleopatra too was married to another younger brother by the time she came to Rome. There was clearly a vast difference between formal alliances and real feeling.

Julius Caesar did indeed meet the son of the king of Syria on his grand tour before returning to Rome. Herod would grow to be the man who ordered the death of every first-born son in an attempt to break a prophecy predicting the birth of Christ.

The famous line 'Veni, Vidi, Vici', 'I came, I saw, I conquered', comes from the four-hour battle against the son of Mithridates in Greece. If not for that line, it would be one of the forgotten moments of history.

Mark Antony tried three times to crown Julius on the feast of Lupercalia in February rather than the Egyptian Triumph. Julius is recorded as having lost his temper on the third try, perhaps because the crowd did not applaud the sight of a crown on his head.

Despite the lack of a crown, the Senate showered Caesar with unprecedented honours. As well as 'Dictator Perpetuus', 'Imperator' and 'Father of His Country', Julius was accorded the right to divine worship. A statue was raised to him with the words 'To the Unconquerable God'. He was given the right to wear the regalia of the old kings.

We cannot know the full reasons for these honours now. Perhaps it was an attempt by men like Cicero to have Julius reach too far and alienate the citizens that loved him. Alternatively, such accolades could have been the only way the Senate were able to remain valuable to Caesar. Cassius is said to have brought Brutus into the conspiracy with the warning that the Senate would make Julius a king. It may even have been true.

The death of Caesar happened on the Ides (the 15th day) of March in 44 BC. The Senate were indeed meeting in Pompey's theatre, though how many witnessed the murder is unknown. After a lot of thought, I did not include the fact that Caesar was handed a scroll warning him of the conspiracy. The man who passed it into his hands had once been employed by Brutus and the suspicion will always be there that Brutus himself was behind the warning, as complex a man as Caesar himself. It was never read and I felt this was an unnecessary complication.

Tillius Cimber held Caesar for the first blow by Casca – the first of twenty-three wounds. Only one was directly fatal, which shows the chaos of the murder. Caesar struggled until he saw Brutus was part of it, then pulled his toga over his head and sat like stone until they had completed their task. The courage of such an act defies description.

The night before, Caesar is said to have expressed a preference for a quick end rather than the agony of disease or weakness. His epilepsy may have troubled him, but a man does not welcome death and plan a campaign in Parthia at the same time. Nor does he give up the struggle for life when he has, *at last*, a son to follow his line. Suetonius said he was fifty-five years old, though the figure cannot be certain, as his birth date is unknown.

Julius Caesar named Octavian his heir in his will and it is one of the great tragedies that Octavian did not allow Ptolemy Caesarion to reach manhood. Though Cleopatra fled back to Egypt after the murder, it did not save her, or her young son. Perhaps it is true that those who have power do not allow future enemies to grow, but it does seem a particularly pitiless act.

History is littered with the stories of men who rose through fire and battle to positions of power – only to have their empires shattered on their deaths. Caesar achieved a position in Rome that no one else had ever managed on such a scale. He used the power to introduce a new calendar, give citizenship to all doctors and teachers, and move 80,000 of the poorest to new starts in colonies. He gave every Roman 300 sesterces, grain and oil. His legions were made rich to a man, with the centurions alone receiving 10,000 silver coins each. His Triumphs were unparalleled, including using the Tiber to flood a great basin on the Campus Martius for a violent 'sea battle'. Tens of thousands attended his banquets. Yet perhaps his greatest good fortune was to be followed by Octavian, who took the name Gaius Julius Caesar to honour him and was only later known as Augustus. It was his steady hand that birthed the longest empire the world has ever known. Augustus was the first emperor, but Julius Caesar prepared his seat.

I have never been able to believe that Brutus took part in the murder of Julius Caesar out of a desire to restore the Republic. That was certainly the reason he gave and he had coins made that actually celebrate the events of the Ides of March. I think the complex relationship with Servilia played a part, brought to a head by the fact that Julius had at last fathered an heir. As Servilia survived Julius, she also survived her son and was brought his ashes after the battle of Philippi.

One change that I have made in these pages also has a bearing on Brutus' motives. Caesar's daughter Julia was originally promised to Brutus, a union that would have helped his rise through the echelons of Roman society. Always the pragmatist, Julius broke off the engagement to give her to Pompey instead. These are more human reasons for hatred, but the strongest may be the subtleties of envy and frustration in their own relationship. The final damage may simply have been that Julius publicly forgave the betrayal at Pharsalus. For Brutus, I suspect that would have been unbearable.

On a final note, I called this series 'Emperor' as I intended to show how the era of men such as Marius, Cato, Sulla and Julius created the empire that followed. The title 'Imperator' was given to any successful general. Julius may not have been crowned, but in everything but name, he was the one who brought the empire into the world.

In years to come, I may have to write the story of the aftermath of the assassination. Not a single man who stood with bloody hands in Pompey's theatre died a natural death. In its way, it is a tale as great as any other, but it will have to wait for another day.

Conn Iggulden

COMING SOON

The final book in the masterful EMPEROR series . . .

Julius Caesar has been assassinated.
A nation is in mourning. Revenge will be bloody.

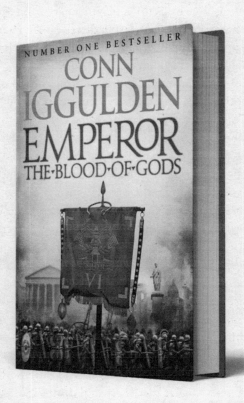

'Iggulden is in a class of his own when
it comes to epic, historical fiction'
Daily Mirror